PROPHECY

By

Robert Burson

Prologue

"Do you have it?

Lifting a small amber bottle to show the old man he said simply, "Yes."

"Good. We will need it."

"How is he?" The young monk whispered.

Struggling to hear over the howling wind, the abbot responded. "Sadly, the bishop is worse again today. But he continues to work on his manuscript, a man possessed."

"It is so hard to believe. Fifty-four is old but he was so robust, so strong, and so full of life. Wasn't it just a week ago that he met with the Benedictine who had traveled from Rome?"

"Yes."

"Do you know why he came?"

"No."

"But surely you must know something about this parchment. He must have confided in your."

"On this matter he has kept his own counsel."

The young man, knowing that asking more questions would be fruitless, waited shivering to be told what to do next. The first early storm of the season had pushed in from the North Atlantic two days ago and enveloped the French coast; bringing pelting rain, biting wind and wintery temperatures, more like their guests home in County Armagh than France.

"Come, it is time."

The two men re-wrapped themselves in their robes in a futile effort to stay warm and headed down the corridor to the bishop's room.

The elder man rapped on the heavy oak door and waited to be invited in. They waited in silence. Finally, after hearing nothing, the abbot opened it and stepped in followed by the young monk. The room was the largest of its kind in the monastery but was still very small. A fire burned fitfully in the corner fireplace giving off little warmth or light. Next to it, in the shadows, Malachy, Bishop of Armagh sat slumped in a chair. The table where he had been working was several feet away and at an odd angle. It appeared to have been pushed away as the illuminated manuscripts and quills he had been using were scattered about on the floor. "Is he asleep?" The young man asked his superior, who didn't respond.

The air in the room was stale with a hint of something sour. Both men walked slowly towards their guest from Ireland both unconsciously crossing themselves. The bishop failed to stir as they drew near. The abbot held out his hand and the young man stopped. "Stay here while I draw closer."

The older man continued on until he stood directly in front of the Bishop. He stared; searching, hoping to find some signs of life. The Bishop didn't move. Finally the abbot moistened his hand, crouched and moved it under the Bishop's nose. He held it there and waited, hoping, yes there was something very faint but the Bishop still had life. The abbot then knelt, eased his guest from the chair in which he had been sitting and gathered the Bishop in his arms and waited, a wait he knew would be brief. This great man, this seer shouldn't be allowed to die without human contact; Christ would not have wanted such a thing. Within a minute there was a brief shudder and the abbot knew then end had come. The abbot gently eased the bishop from his arms and while doing so

3

trying not to draw attention to himself, he looked down; the manuscript he had expected to see was not there. Quickly glancing towards the nearby table he didn't see the document lying there either. He straightened himself while standing; he took a deep breath to calm his nerves and said quietly, "There is no need for your elixir. The bishop is dead."

"It's God's message of love that this holy man should pass on All Souls Day," The young priest said and immediately fell to his knees and began to pray. This good and holy man, some had even called him a saint was dead.

The abbot knew what he had to do. He needed time. He turned to the young man who was still on his knees. "Get up, go to my cell and get my stole and holy water. We must give the bishop the Last Rites." The abbot's room was not far, probably not far enough but he could think of no other excuse to be alone. Hopefully, there would be enough time, time to find Malachy's manuscript.

-1-

Where to begin? I think the story began on the day of my annual physical. I have always had a bad case of "white coat" syndrome, but as I have aged, as with so many things, it has gotten worse. When I was younger I solved the problem as most young people, by simply not going to the doctor. In that way I didn't have to listen to all the things that could go wrong with me or what I should do to keep those human maladies at bay. However, I've finally reached the point, where I've decided it's a good idea to an annual medical thing. Of course, the constant nagging from my wife and her semi-veiled threats about our sex life, along with the fact the Bureau highly recommends it hadn't hurt my decision-making process either.

But, the truth be told, none of those things were enough to actually drive me into a doctor's office. What had done it was my partner, now ex-partner, Andy Young. He hadn't been feeling well for several months. "How are you feeling?" I would ask him every morning.

"I feel like shit," would be his usual response.

"I'll bet you are just tired or ate something that didn't agree with you."

"I suppose." Andy would typically answer.

As a good male partner I continued to re-assure him that he was basically okay and he would start feeling his usual self shortly. "No need to go to the doctor."

"I suppose."

However he started sounding more poorly than usual and began looking even worse. "I think you should see a doctor.

"I suppose."

Finally he did make an appointment. He must have felt really bad, because Andy is a bigger procrastinator than I.

During the usual blood work-up, the doctor had found that his blood chemistry was, in layman's terms, all screwed up.

Thankfully, it wasn't something that was soon to be fatal, but, if left untreated, it could have definitely made Andy an invitee to the last roundup. He had immediately gone on administrative leave for treatments. That was about six months ago and now I am in the doctor's office. You can see how fast I jump on things when I make up my mind.

As I sat in the waiting room—an appropriately named room, I might add—my thoughts wandered to my own demise and what lay beyond. I'm Irish and, by extension, Catholic. It is true that not all Irish are Catholic; just ask those living in Ulster. But most Irishmen in America came from what would become the Irish Republic at the time of the Great Hunger. My family was no exception.

As a regular churchgoing Catholic, I shouldn't have had any questions about eternity and what lay beyond. Every Sunday I got my weekly dose on the certainty of the afterlife. But since no one I knew ever came back and said, "Sean, it's okay, there is a heaven, and I saw your name on the waiting list," I still had my nagging doubts.

I consider myself a lucky man: I have a wonderful wife, who cares more for me than I deserve. We have three healthy children—two boys, Sean Jr. and Thomas, and a girl, Kelly. My boys are suffering from that common male malady I've

affectionately called "male brain-shrivel syndrome." I'm sure you are familiar with the disease. Its most common manifestation is when you ask a male why he did something particularly stupid, and the best he can come up with is the openmouthed stare and

those comforting words "I don't know." My daughter, on the other

hand, is still my friend, although I can't say the same for her relationship with my wife, Maureen.

As I sat waiting to be called, I checked my watch for the umpteenth time. I made my appointment more than two months ago for 9:30 a.m. It was now ten minutes after eleven. Over the years I have reconciled myself to the fact that there is no such

thing as an appointment in a doctor's office; the time given is only a suggestion. Today my boss called a mandatory meeting for 1:30 p.m. Mandatory with my boss means mandatory. The only acceptable excuse is death, and that one only works sometimes.

I was beginning to think I would to have to make another

appointment, something I truly hated doing. Once I've finally

worked up the nerve to come in, I want to get it over with. I know

it's no big deal, but it is to me. As I waited I decided that a

postponement might be better. I can only assume my blood pressure had increased proportionally with my growing concern over missing my meeting. I killed time and I thought about the exchange I would never have with the nurse.

"My, Mr. Murphy, your blood pressure seems to be up. Are

you exercising and eating properly?"

"Yes, I am, to both. Do you suppose my pressure has

increased because I have been wasting the greater part of an hour and forty-five minutes sitting here doing nothing because the cell reception is so poor and that I might have other things to do today?" At that point I'm sure I would get the blank stare I'm used to from my sons.

But I digress. My daughter attends a Catholic high school, specifically Bishop O'Connell High School in Arlington. She came to me to talk about a homework assignment. She had to do a paper on the history of the popes. As part of her assignment, she was asked to include a final page on the future of the papacy. Her question was whether or not I thought there would ever be an American pope. "I don't think so, but one never knew what the future might hold," I answered.

"I was thinking there would be, it seems it is our turn."

"I have to run but we can talk about it later if you like." That answer seemed to help.

Having completed the mental family checklist, I let my mind wander back to the topic of work. I couldn't help pondering what was so urgent about the upcoming meeting, when, finally, I heard, "Mr. Murphy, the doctor will see you now.

- 2 -

"Your Eminence, please slow down!" Monsignor Giovanni Bartolo breathlessly called out to Francesco Cardinal Camperelle as he crossed the vastness that made up Vatican Square.

Though the monsignor was at least fifteen years younger than Cardinal Camperelle, the cardinal was a robust man with a substantial head start. Camperelle did not slow until Bartolo shouted to him again, "Please wait!" The older man waited until Monsignor Bartolo caught up.

"Has he arrived?" the cardinal asked as he turned to walk again.

"Not yet; he has been delayed."

"Is anything wrong?" Camperelle asked, with a worried look.

"Apparently, the plane had mechanical problems. But he should arrive before 7 p.m.," Bartolo answered.

Checking his watch, Camperelle looked at his assistant. "I want you to personally accompany the driver to the airport."

"That was my plan."

Apparently not listening, Camperelle continued. "Be sure to call me as soon as you leave the airport."

Bartolo nodded.

"And then bring the Patriarch directly to the papal apartments. I will meet you there."

"Is there anything you want me to tell the Patriarch?"

"Yes, to pray for His Holiness."

Bartolo noted a look of concern had crossed Camperelle's face.

The pair continued on across the piazza in silence holding their own thoughts.

Finally, Bartolo spoke. "How is His Holiness?"

"He is worse but we are still hopeful," the cardinal said flatly.

"I thought he had improved and things were looking up."

"They were but then, unexpectedly, he started to worsen. No one seems to know why."

"Then I should go, Eminence, to check on the other

arrangements."

"Yes, agreed."

Bartolo remained where he had stopped as Cardinal Camperelle continued toward his Vatican offices, located beyond the great basilica designed by Michelangelo.

Monsignor Bartolo continued to watch his boss, Cardinal Francesco Camperelle, Secretary of State of Vatican City, the second most powerful man in the Catholic Church behind the Pope himself, disappear around the corner of the cathedral near the Sistine Chapel. Bartolo wondered what God had planned. The state of the world seemed worse than ever. Now, at such a time, His Holiness, the man who had reigned as Pope longer than any other, would soon see God face-to-face. Bartolo could only speculate as to what was so special about the traveler he was soon to pick up at Rome's Leonardo da Vinci Airport. The Church's Prime Minister Cardinal Camperelle had not taken him into his confidence on this matter. All he could do was pray. Even though as a priest of the Catholic Church he lived a life of prayer, it seemed he was praying now more than ever.

-3-

Monsignor Bartolo headed for the barracks of the Swiss Guard, where his driver would be waiting. He checked his watch and immediately picked up his pace as he feared he would be late. Under normal conditions, if there was such a thing in Rome, he would make it on time. But now he knew it would take longer than the usual forty-five minutes to Rome's main airport. The normally chaotic Italian roads, always crowded, were even more so now that it was construction season. To make matters worse, newly imposed security measures made parking a nightmare.

Several months earlier there had been a new, yet more violent round of terrorist bombings. A number of the capitals of Europe had been affected. This was the first time such a coordinated attack had occurred within the European community.

Bartolo had been surprised at the politicians' collective reaction.

Didn't they think it could happen here? There had been coordinated strikes both in Asia and the United States. How could they have thought that Europe was somehow immune to such sectarian violence? He supposed it was simply arrogance, the belief they were somehow immune from the spreading Middle Eastern violence. The carnage had stripped away any such delusions.

In the old days the driver would have simply parked outside Arrivals and waited until his passenger arrived. There was nothing the police could or would do about it; couldn't because of the Vatican's diplomatic status and wouldn't because Italy was still a very Catholic country. Today all that was different. True, there was a special parking place for officials, but it was a good distance from the terminal. He remained unsure as to how he was going to get his guest from Customs to the car. It would be unseemly to have the Latin Patriarch of Jerusalem, Archbishop Salim Ateek, schlepping his bags through Leonardo da Vinci Airport.

- 4 -

The reason for the urgency was the pontiff's recent health problems. However, there was something more. Bartolo sensed it, from both what his boss had said and what he hadn't. There was also lack of precedent. Since the restoration of the Patriarchate of Jerusalem in 1847, the archbishop had come to Rome only once, and that was to attend the Second Vatican Council. Furthermore from Bartolo's experience he knew it usually took a prolonged period of negotiation before any meeting could be scheduled between high ranking bishops, let alone one between any of the patriarchs of the Church. But this had not happened, not this time.

Bartolo usually could put these kinds' questions out of his

mind. The whys and wherefores were the providence of his superior, Cardinal Camperelle and he had been the cardinal's assistant since before Camperelle's appointment by the Pope to the office of Vatican Prime Minister. But now he couldn't as much as he had tried. During their association, he had never known the cardinal to be agitated, upset, or even impatient. However, in the past several days, it appeared to Bartolo that all these characteristics had been present. Perhaps he could learn something from his future passenger, Salim Ateek. But he doubted it. Men like him seldom spoke out of turn.

As he approached the barracks he saw a young man coming toward him. "Are you my driver?"

"Yes monsignor."

"Do you have a friend who can come as well? I will need some help with the Patriarch's luggage."

"Yes monsignor."

"Good get him and please hurry. We can't have the Archbishop standing around the airport waiting for his ride to show up."

"It will only take a minute. Why don't you wait in the car while I get him?"

"Good, thanks I will."

The addition of the second member of the Swiss Guard relieved him of his concern about getting the archbishop back to the Vatican with dignity. Relieved, Bartolo sat back in the Mercedes limo and focused his thoughts on the man he was about to meet.

Salim Ateek was young. Age forty-eight if he recalled properly, young to be the archbishop and Latin Patriarch of

Jerusalem. Not only that, he was Palestinian, having converted to Catholicism as a teenager. He was also highly educated. He had received two doctorates, one in philosophy and another in theology, both from the University of Notre Dame. Bartolo knew the Patriarch was fluent in at least five languages and could understand several more. The man was charismatic as well: the Latin Christian population had grown for the first time in years.

Although the church wasn't large in number, running a Latin Christian church in the Holy Land took both diplomatic and administrative skills. By all appearances Ateek possessed both in abundance. Monsignor Bartolo was both excited and intimidated by the man he was about to meet.

- 5 -

Actually, the doctor didn't see me right away. I did, however, reach what appeared to be the inner sanctum of the medical office. The nurse or physician's assistant, I'm not sure which, escorted me from my original holding cell to another waiting room.

"Mr. Murphy, have you completed your medical history form?"

I wondered how I couldn't have. The form was only four pages long and I had had over an hour and half to work on it. No one could be that slow could they? "Yes, here it is."

"Thank you. The next step in our checkup process is to weigh you and take your vitals."

"Okay." Then will I see the doctor? I had my vitals taken and was given one of those demeaning open-back smocks to wear. That is, of course, where I draw the line. I preserve, or at least I think I preserve, my individuality by continuing to wear boxer shorts. After another half hour my doctor finally arrives and gives me the good news that I'm alive, but he'll say nothing more definitive until I have had the usual blood, urine, and—my particular favorite—stool sample tests. I always think of the plight of the postal workers as they sort my package to the lab, knowing full well what lies inside.

"Mr. Murphy"

"Call me Sean."

"Sean, I'm going to check your heart, lungs and skeletal structure." Good we are now getting somewhere. It took about five minutes for him to check me out. I would have thought it would have taken longer.

"Sean, to complete the exam I will do a prostate and testicular cancer check." Well you know what comes next so I don't really need to describe it to you, other than to say it is, as I recall, a ton of fun.

"Sean, everything seems okay. Of course we won't know for sure until we get the other scheduled test results."

"Thanks." At least there was some good news.

"The nurse will be back in a few minutes with the additional forms you will need." Oh goody more forms.

The doctor leaves and the nurse returns; "Here you go Mr. Murphy." She hands me the additional necessary paperwork.

"Thanks." At that moment, I have a desire to simply toss it all into the trash and run screaming out of the exam room. However, in my mind's eye I can still see Andy Young's face when he told me about his test results and how lucky he had been to catch the problem in time.

- 6 -

Much to my relief, and I'm certain a lowering of my blood pressure, I made it back to the office in time for my mandatory engagement, not however having time to make my next appointment so "we" could go over my test results or having time to pick up lunch, a true disaster. The meeting had been called by my boss and the head of a new counterterrorism unit, Alan Mitchell. Prior to this posting, my assignments had been in banking and international commerce. I like to think that my transfer was due to ability. I had developed an expertise in computers, and this, combined with my accounting background, had me tracking down bank fraud and illegal currency transactions. Because terrorists need money to function, and because you can never go wrong tracing the money, I had been transferred to Counterterrorism. It might have also had something to do with the fact my previous boss wanted me out of his department. He considered me to be a bit of a rebel and a nonconformist and, to my irritation, had so noted in my fitness evaluation. I considered him to be a tight ass. We were, therefore, both happy with my change of departments.

It hardly seems possible to me, but I've been with the Bureau for twenty-two years, my first and only job out of college. As I sit waiting for the meeting to begin, I look around at strangers' faces. Odd, I'd have thought I would have known at least a few people in my unit. But no such luck. Everyone was new to me. I was soon to learn that everyone else was in the same position. The members of this particular group had been drawn from all the various branches of the FBI. If they were anything like me, then this was a band of misfits. I didn't have time to contemplate it, though, as Alan Mitchell entered the room and called the meeting to order.

Alan Mitchell, Special Agent in Charge of the Religious Counterterrorism Unit (SACRCTU), was average-looking. He was everyman. He also happened to be a legend in the Bureau. Inside that average-looking head was an extraordinary mind. His name was spoken in reverential terms. He was known as a fair man but with an extraordinary temper when it came to dealing with screw-ups. I made a mental note to stay out of that club. It was common knowledge that over his thirty-five years with the Bureau, he had foiled at least four presidential assassinations. Two of which the public never knew of. Impressive as it was, his reputation was sealed when he discovered a Middle Eastern group trying to smuggle a nuclear device through the harbor in Baltimore.

"Fellow agents, welcome. I'm sure you are all wondering why you are here. Sometimes I ask myself why any of us are here." Mitchell paused and got the expected courtesy laugh. "As you looked around the room waiting for me, I know you are surprised you don't recognize anyone." A number of heads were bobbing up and down in acknowledgment. "The reason you are strangers and the reason you are here is the same reason. The director instructed me, at the request of the President and the Attorney General, to form a new special purpose counterterrorism unit. The mission of this unit requires a group of strangers to come together as a new team and to look at old data and information in a new way." I straightened my posture as I listened. It felt good to be special, even if, later, being special would probably be the major pain in the ass I was sure it would be.

"Each of you has been selected for this unit for a variety of reasons, from your technical expertise to certain personal backgrounds and traits." A bit of a murmur went up but was quickly stifled. "I want to introduce my assistant. She is not a member of the Bureau, but make no mistake about it, she is second in command." With that, a rather short, nondescript woman entered the room from a side door. She had a dark complexion and walked with a noticeable limp.

I did a double take. This person reminded me of my fifth-grade teacher at Saint Mark's Elementary School. Well, my teacher wasn't really a person; she was a nun. Nuns were a separate classification of life, their very own phylum or order or whatever. That might have been part of the problem I had with Sister Mary Clarence. She was into science and discipline, and I was, to say the least, not. My horizon at the time was sports, almost any kind of sports. I wasn't old enough yet for girls, but it seems I wasn't too old for the ruler brigade. She was a firm believer in not sparing the rod, and she didn't spare it on me.

We did have one thing in common, and I believe that was the only reason I survived to make it to the sixth grade. She loved baseball. The Red Sox were her favorite team. In those days the Sox weren't very good, and anyone with a lick of sense knew nobody ever beat the Yankees anyway.

But she believed in them and would say next year the Bo Sox would be winners. I often wanted to say, "Never in your lifetime." Sadly, this turned out to be true, as she died when I was in the seventh grade.

- 7 -

"Agents, I would like to introduce myself and give you my background, at least as much as you need to know." A nervous chuckle went up from the group. "My name is Amanda Chehwan. I was born in Lebanon into the Maronite Christian community. In case you don't know what a Maronite is, we are Eastern Rite Catholics. I was, for a time, a nun living in Beirut." As she spoke I wondered if Amanda was really her name. Amanda didn't seem like a Lebanese name. My next thought, if she wasn't being honest about her name, what else wasn't she telling us? My cynical side was creeping out.

Pushing my negative thoughts aside, I continued to listen. "You might have noticed that I walk with a limp. It came from blows I received from a Syrian Army sergeant. He took offense at my actions." She paused to take a sip of water. "You see, I was tending to a man who had been wounded in the endless fighting that had occurred in Beirut. He was either a Christian or a Jew. I never found out. But the only thing that mattered to the Syrian soldier was that the man was not an Arab. In horror I watched the sergeant kill the man I had been aiding. This was to be my last day as a nun. I was so horrified that I knew I could no longer keep my vows. I needed to be proactive, and my religious order's rules were passive.

"Through an interesting turn of events, I came to America and today I work for the CIA. Because of my background, the deputy director of Intelligence believed I could be an asset to Homeland Security, and that is how I came to be here today."

Her accent intrigued me. It was soft and enchanting, most likely a combination of French and Arabic. I was sure that was the only soft thing about her. She was no doubt a woman of steel. I also wondered what made up the interesting chain of events that had brought her to our doorstep. I was certain I would never find out. What I found amazing was the fact that she, a CIA outworlder, admittedly one so high up the food chain that DDI knew she existed, had an unheard of level of authority in a Bureau operation.

There was silence in the room. Chehwan neither spoke nor left the podium. She then began again; this time her tone was quieter but more intense. "You are wondering what is so special about me that I could be involved to any degree with a Bureau task force. The answer is simple and sad. I bring a life experience that I wish none of you ever have to live through.

"The country of my birth was part of the Ottoman Empire. After World War One the League of Nations gave it to France as a protectorate. Lebanon became independent of France in 1943, and Beirut was made its capital. Before our sixteen-year civil war, Beirut was a beautiful city, an island of civility and tranquility in a sea of violence. It became the banking center for the entire region. The civil war that raged from 1975 to 1991 destroyed all that. Peace or, more precisely, its poor imitation, occurred only after the Syrian Army occupied my country and declared martial law.

"Agents, Lebanon, my homeland, was destroyed by religious hatred. While ninety-five percent of the population is Arab, only about sixty percent is Muslim. Christian denominations make up almost all the rest. However, these groupings are not monolithic. The major Muslim groups consist of Sunnis, Shi'ites, and Druze. The Christian denominations are even more varied. There are Maronite, Greek Orthodox, Greek Catholic, Armenian Orthodox, Armenian Catholic, as well as a minority of Protestant faiths. None of whom could get along."

Listening to the agent made for a semi-interesting history lesson, but I didn't see the relevance.

"You in America take for granted your religious freedom. You shouldn't. In historical terms religious tolerance is something rare. Europeans killed themselves by the thousands over the correct brand of worship. People are dying in Africa every day over the same issue. Think about your country in global terms. Since your independence, America has evolved from a strict Protestant country to one of diversified beliefs. At the same time it has grown materially wealthy and less rigorous in its approach to organized religion and its associated tenants. In many eyes it has become less religious. However, in my opinion, being less religious has been a blessing, though a strange one."

"Up until the past twenty or so years, Americans simply didn't care enough about religion or God to get worked up. The era of nonchalance appears to be ending. Fundamentalist groups of all religious persuasion are on the rise. Many exert a disproportionate influence. People are beginning to care about God and religion in a way not seen before in this country. Religious leaders and their groups are pushing political agendas. This is the very same thing that happened in Lebanon before 1975. The signs are unmistakable. Tragically, I fear you will find your country is not immune from religious hatred and all the evil it can bring."

With that, Amanda Chehwan stepped back from the podium as we sat in stunned silence.

- 8 -

I don't know what everyone else was thinking, but two thoughts kept running through my brain. The first was a complete rejection of what I had just heard. There was simply no way this country was going to fall into a period of sectarian violence. The second was, even if she were right, what could I or, for that matter, the FBI do about it? As I mulled these two thoughts, Alan Mitchell stepped back to the microphone.

"Thank you, Agent Chehwan. Agents, I suspect most of you have a couple of thoughts on what you just heard. I know I did. They probably go something like this: *no way and what can be done about it anyway?"*

I looked around the room and saw almost all heads nod. It was nice to know I wasn't alone.

"Normally, I would agree with both assessments," said Mitchell, "but today things are different. Worldwide terrorism has singled out the United States as its main enemy and has sworn to bring pain and suffering to us here at home. Rhetorically speaking, what better way to do this than to attack our most fundamental beliefs?"

He was correct, of course, but I remained skeptical.

"The Bureau has received preliminary yet credible evidence from Central Intelligence and other sources that a variety of terrorist organizations have banded together to create the chaos that Agent Chehwan described." Mitchell paused and took a drink of water, no doubt to let what he had said soak in. "Our job is to confirm or refute this working hypothesis. If we determine the threat is real, we will be required to propose a course of action. Agent Chehwan will be giving you a number of handouts presenting all we know at the present time." Mitchell nodded in Chehwan's direction, and she began to distribute the material. "Please review the information. We meet back here first thing Monday morning, where you'll be given your specific assignments and be broken into working groups."

Several got up to leave. I was about to do the same when Alan Mitchell shot a withering look around the room. Thank God I'd been slow to move.

"Agents, I haven't dismissed you. There is one more thing I need to say. Do not, I repeat, do not tell anyone about your assignment. You'll be provided a working cover story Monday. Also, remember the collective memory in this country can be measured in weeks. In many ways that is a good thing. For one, it keeps us from carrying grudges; for another, it allows us to focus on the future and not the past. These traits are not exhibited in other parts of the world. Arabs in the Middle East are still bitter about the Crusades and talk about them as if they were yesterday.

Finally, money is the mother's milk of terrorism. With enough money provided to the right groups, even here at home we could easily be prone to the violence we associate with other parts of the world. Thank you and have a relaxing weekend. It may be the last one you have in a while."

- 9 -

I was about to get up when Mitchell said, "Murphy, would you please stick around a few minutes?" I loved the way this request was phrased as a question. I wanted to respond, "Well, no, Alan, I can't. Since its Friday, I wanted to get home early. How about before our Monday meeting? It works for me, how about you?" Instead, I said, "Sure, Mr. Mitchell, no problem at all." I felt like a conflicted suck-up as I remained seated until everyone but Agents Chehwan and Mitchell had cleared the room.

"Sean, may I call you Sean?"

Again, my split brain wanted to respond with something like, "Sure, no problem, if I can call you Alan." But I simply said, "Certainly, Chief."

Mitchell remained standing, while Agent Chehwan took a seat next to me. I hoped that meant this one-on-one—well, two-on-

one—session would be short.

"Sean, I've seen your reports. That's why you are here."

"Thank you, sir." I assumed he was referring to my last assignment of which I was still mighty proud and not my latest evaluation. The assignment was my first without my partner Andy Young.

"Sean, I have also talked to some of your former supervisors. They say you are creative and resourceful. We need those traits if we are going to beat the sons of bitches who want to destroy our way of life."

"I try to think out of the box, Chief."

"Sean, they also tell me you can be a nonconformist pain in the ass."

I remained silent; what could I say? I could be a pain in the ass.

"Tell me about your last job."

This was clearly an assignment interview. Working for Mitchell would definitely help my career, but I didn't know if I wanted that kind of help. "I had been loaned to the Richmond office. I was told at the time it was because they needed someone with my background."

"What background was that?"

"I had reluctantly majored in accounting in college. And over the years with the Bureau, I had actually used my degree."

"Why reluctantly?"

"I liked history and political science much better. Of course, one can't do crap with a history major; at least that was what my parents told me on more than one occasion."

"Well, your parents were right."

I knew they were but I didn't need to hear Mitchell tell me this again after all these years. Swallowing hard, I answered, "Yes, sir, they were. To my surprise I was good at accounting, though, to this day I don't know why."

"Sean, why didn't you go into public accounting?"

"Because I had absolutely no desire to do so. When I was about to graduate, the FBI was looking for accounting majors, so I applied and got a job with the Bureau."

"Were your parents happy?"

I wondered what difference it made. They were both dead now. "Yes, my parents were happy because I had found a good job with health insurance and a retirement plan. I was happy because they were off my ass."

"Any other reason?"

"Yes sir, I had always wanted to make a difference, and I believed and still believe that I can do that in federal law enforcement."

"Sean, we have digressed. Tell me more about Richmond."

We didn't digress, Mitchell did. I just answered his questions. "Well, sir, in earlier years the area just south of Washington, D.C. had experienced rapid growth. Historic preservationists had repeatedly lost to developers. There had been a particularly nasty fight over the Manassas Battlefield site. The developer wanted to put up a mini-mall where the first battle of the Civil War had been fought. The only concession to history had been a proposed marker in the parking lot. This time the preservationists managed to stop the mall but only after some rather suspicious fires had taken place at other properties being built by the development company."

"That was when the Bureau was called in?"

"Not yet, even though the fires had occurred in Maryland, as well as Virginia. Anyway, growth continued to move south toward Richmond. Had McClellan been as successful getting to the Confederate Capital, the Civil War would have been over by 1862."

"Still the historian?"

"It doesn't pay as a profession, but I still find it interesting. Anyway, over time the antigrowth battles became more and more rancorous. Violence became common."

"And that was when the Bureau was called in?"

"Exactly, A new phrase was coined to describe the tactics being used."

"Eco-terrorism?"

"Yes. I was assigned to see if I could find a money trail."

"I am curious, what got your attention in the first place?"

"Well, Mr. Mitchell." I was still waiting for him to say, "Call me Alan," but he remained silent, so I continued. "The commute from my home in Alexandria to the Richmond office was lengthy and boring. Over the weeks I had tried everything to distract myself: thinking about the case, not thinking about the case, listening to music or books on tape. It struck me during one of my trips that something was going on that didn't fit the usual pattern."

"What do you mean?"

"Preservationists and developers were generic terms applied to differing groups on both sides of the issue. There were two things that struck me as odd. One was the large number of new Save Our Battlefield groups. From experience I knew there are generally only two or three players representing the preservationist group. However, this time there were at least nine or ten, with new ones popping up each time there was an incident. The second thing was that one development company seemed to be attacked more than others and by a substantial margin. I decided to see if there was any sort of connection."

"The developer was the American subsidiary of a French construction company. It turned out the parent company was in deep financial distress. It seemed to be living off its American entity. The problem was that interest rates were rising and development was slowing down. Neither the American sub nor the French parent would survive under such conditions. I thought their solution was ingenious."

"Tell me."

"The French company formed a number of new subsidiaries. The new companies proceeded to go out and acquire land to develop."

"I thought it was broke?"

"The companies tied up the land by buying the option to buy. This was much cheaper, particularly when there was no intent to build in the first place. Each of these companies then contracted with the American developer to build the most obnoxious development possible for the area in question."

"Okay, then what?"

26

"There would be a fire or some other kind of incident. Each time there was a claim of responsibility."

"Why would anyone claim it?"

"I wondered the same thing. Not only that, but the group mentioned was always a large, well-known conservationist group. For example, a number of town homes were destroyed near Fredericksburg. The group claiming responsibility was the Sierra Club of Virginia. The developer promptly sued the Sierra Club and its own insurance company, as well as the Sierra Club's insurance company."

"Odd; what eventually happened?"

"The developer got rich on insurance claims and lawsuit settlements for several years before I traced the cash flows back to good old' Paree."

Chehwan, who had remained silent during Mitchell's and my conversation, commented, "Very interesting story but let me change the subject, Sean, how would you find these suspected cash flows to religious groups in the US?"

"Assuming they are real?" I asked.

"Assuming they are real," was her reply.

- 10 -

I wasn't prepared for the question. "Can you give me a minute to think about it?"

"Just off the top of your head, when we meet again you can be more specific."

I hated this pop quiz approach. It was the latest fad making its way around government. I think it was supposed to tell how well someone reacted to stress. This wasn't the first time I had heard this type of question. I was thinking of providing a stock answer to see how the interviewer would react to my stress. Something like "I would nuke the hell out of Luxemburg" or maybe "I would hack into the IRS database." I was afraid, though, if I gave that last response, someone would pat me on the shoulder and say, "You are the kind of guy we have been looking for," and the next thing I knew, I would be at NSA headquarters with some guy named Igor reading the president's tax return. I looked at Mitchell and Chehwan and said, "I would begin by pulling the not-for-profit organization data available from the IRS to see what religious-based organizations had the most dramatic change in donations. I would then compare this list to those that had become most active on the Internet."

Both Mitchell and Chehwan did not immediately say anything, but their body language indicated they approved of my answer. Agent Mitchell said "Sounds like a good starting point."

He looked at Chehwan and then turned back to me. "I want you to work directly with Amanda on this. You can start by taking your own advice on searching the databases you mentioned. Get with her—and only her—as soon as you find anything."

I looked at the CIA agent and back at Mitchell. "Yes sir." I didn't want to show it, but I was more than a little glad to hear this. Frankly, I had gotten to the point where I was willing to admit to myself that some of the more physical things about the job were getting tough. This approach sounded safer and more sedentary.

- 11 -

Finally I was in my car heading for home. The traffic had cleared out, which was about the only good thing about having my meeting with spy mistress Chehwan and SAC Alan Mitchell run so late. It was Friday night, and I was thinking that all I wanted to do was to settle into my Lazy Boy with a glass of wine when my cell rang.

"Sean hi, how was your day?"

"Long, Mo."

"Did everything go okay at the doctor's office?"

"Sure he rotated the tires, looked under the hood and said I was good to go for at least another fifty thousand more miles."

"He didn't say that."

"Of course not, he only mumbled something about the usual tests and that I was in okay shape for someone my age and that "we" would meet again to go over the results of those tests."

"Anything else?"

"Just work stuff. I'm on new task force, an anti-terrorism unit."

"Is this good or bad?"

"Can't say for sure but it is different and right now different is better."

"Why because of your on-going midlife crises?"

I didn't want to go down that road with Mo as it was a certain loser. "You know what was weird though was that one of the team leaders looked exactly like my fifth grade teacher."

"You mean Sister Mary Clarence."

"The very same."

"Wasn't she the one you tried to schmooze by claiming you were a Red Sox fan?"

"That's the one."

"I recall that you were only partially successful at hoodwinking her. Maybe you'll do a better job with your new boss."

"I did a fine job. I was just overly exuberant."

"You mean you were the class clown."

"I was funny."

"Yea to your pre-adolescent friends"

"Mo, I was a cute kid at the time."

"Well that's something you've outgrown."

"Why did you call?"

"I wanted to remind you of your meeting tonight."

"Thanks." I said without a great deal of enthusiasm. I had forgotten. And the last thing in the world I wanted to do was to go to a meeting with our pastor, the Reverend Lukas Schafer.

About six months ago, I found I had been volunteered to serve as the chairman of our parish's Education Outreach Committee. I don't quite know how this happened, though I suspected my wife thought it would be good for me and hence I volunteered. However, I was certain I was probably the most unlikely person to hold this type position, being somewhat non-traditional or orthodox in my beliefs. My job clearly had something to do with this evaluation. Because of my work I might have been a little jaded; you know, spending my entire working life hunting down what I affectionately called the "scum of the earth." But it could have had something to do with how I fundamentally thought of the world when I couldn't sleep in the middle of the night.

I was, for the want of a better term, a Catholic deist. I know that term is an oxymoron at best. Deism originated in England in the early 17th century and began as a rejection of orthodox Christianity. Deists asserted that reason could find evidence of God in nature and that God had created the world and then left it to operate under the natural laws he had devised. It didn't surprise me to learn that our first three U.S. presidents were deists. In my opinion, the reason America was America was that Washington, Adams and Jefferson had decided to walk away from power when any one of them could have invoked a higher authority as a reason for staying on either in the form of a king or a dictator.

In my line of work it was easy to accept that once God had created the world, he left it to man to screw up, which we have done in spades. If one believed it was mankind who screwed things up, then you didn't have to go through serious mental contortions to explain why a Benevolent Higher Being would allow something evil to happen. Assuming that humankind could follow the golden rule, even natural disasters would be less costly both in terms of human life and money. Consider the possibility of rather than billions spent on the military the same money went to disaster prevention.

Maureen knew my general feelings regarding religion, but rather than cause a problem at home I acquiesced and accepted the committee position. My role was essentially that of coordinator between the various Bible study groups in our parish and our ecumenical group. I met with Father Schafer on Saturday afternoons, but this week he had a previously scheduled meeting and asked if I could make it Friday night. I said yes and then promptly forgot; that is, until I was so conveniently reminded by my wife.

I liked our relatively new pastor. Lukas Schafer had taken over two years ago when Monsignor Flannery died. Flannery had been pastor for no less than thirty-five years. Schafer was everything Flannery was not: outgoing, friendly and funny - in a word, charismatic. Nonetheless, I was tired and as I pulled into the parking lot outside the community center of Saint Charles Borromeo Parish, I hoped tonight's meeting would be brief.

- 12 -

I could tell Father Schafer had been waiting for me. "Father, I'm sorry if I've kept you waiting."

"Oh, nothing to apologize for, Sean, waiting allows me to pray and work on my patience. Sadly I could use more of both."

I smiled at the priest's frank comments.

"Father, you look tired. Did you have a long week?"

"Yes, it was a long week with a lengthy meeting at the end."

"Want to talk about it? Without me prying into the details of course." I was prying but it was a by-product of the job.

"You're right; I need to talk about it."

We both sat down and Father Schafer began. "Priests from all over the country were here at the community center last night. Our meeting started at eight pm with Mass."

"So it started late?"

32

"Yes. The pizzas didn't even get here until after ten pm."

I shook my head. I was glad I hadn't been waiting until that hour to eat pizza for dinner. "Wow, was there something clandestine about the meeting?"

"No, not really. The meeting wasn't a secret though each priest present preferred to have his individual bishop not know about it, at least not for a while. We've been planning the meeting for months. I suppose because of the high level of confidentiality and the time to put it all together everyone wanted to have his input."

"A long session of thoughts and topics flowing back forth," I remarked.

"Exactly."

"What did you talk about?"

"The usual pressing topics."

I could guess what they were but I wanted to hear Father Schafer's version so I remained silent.

"We talked about marriage for priests and the ordination of women. Divorce, child welfare and various other social justice issues also came up."

"So why the confidential meeting? What's wrong with a free exchange of ideas?" I asked.

"The local Bishop of Arlington is somewhat conservative."

"And your group was made up of progressives?"

"Sean if his Eminence had listened in on our get-together he would have chosen the term *neo-heretics* as a more appropriate description."

"Why was the meeting here?"

"I was chosen to lead it."

"Was this an honor or a booby prize?"

"A little of both. I'm conservative enough to question the group's most wild ideas and open-minded enough to press for a new and fresh approach to the age old dream of spreading the message of Jesus Christ. I seem to have the yin and yang of a man in the middle."

"Hard on the soul," I remarked.

"Indeed, it is hard but that's nothing. There is no doubt in my mind that the Catholic Church has to change. If it doesn't do it soon, it will be in even deeper trouble than it is now. It'll survive, of course. It always has, but it will not be the institution it needs to be. It will become a hollow anachronistic religion. Certainly not something what Christ would want. I've come to believe the bishops are too set in their ways to change, too stuck in the system. I've prayed for a change and I believe God has answered my prayers. It is up to our group and other friends to begin the process, to renew the Church from the bottom up."

I knew that Father Schafer was considered a progressive. I liked that because I thought that any organization as old as the Catholic Church needed a bit of shaking up now and then. The depth of the man's passion shouldn't have surprised me either but it did. Probably because I wasn't in touch with the daily goings-on at the parish.

"Sounds like you have quite the task in front of you."

Schafer didn't say anything for a moment. Then he spoke. It was almost like he had come out of a trance

"Sean, I didn't mean to unburden myself on you. That wasn't fair. I apologize."

"Hey, no problem Father, you can confess to me anytime." We both smiled.

"We should get back to the reason for meeting." Father Schafer said, "I'm sure you are eager to get home."

"Yes, I am. Anyway as you know, I'm in the group of parishioners who have been having quarterly meetings with a group from the synagogue. Our next get together is in three weeks. And at our last meeting, I was delegated to invite members of a local mosque to join us. But I've been unsuccessful at making any contact. I can't figure it out. Father, I just can't seem to get to the decision maker. I have sent letters and emails with no luck."

"What do you mean?"

"I haven't heard anything."

"Not a rejection?"

"Nothing, I was just hoping you knew someone. I would hate to go back and tell the group I failed. It just seems odd to me, that's all."

"People who believe they are being persecuted do not act in the way one would normally anticipate."

"Good point, Father." I was thinking about what had been said at work and wanted to hear what Schafer might say, even at the risk of lengthening our meeting. "Maybe Islam can't function in a democratic pluralistic society?"

The priest said nothing for some time. I was getting ready to change the subject when he finally spoke.

"Is any religion suited for democracy?"

I said nothing.

"Whether it's Islam, Judaism or Christianity, I have found fundamental believers do not probably cannot, differentiate between societal and religious beliefs. For the true believer they are one in the same."

"I see."

"Take a look at different social issues, for example Prohibition or abortion. Prohibition came from strong religious belief about the evils of drinking alcohol. The problem was that a vast portion of the population disagreed with the entire concept and didn't see it as a religious issue at all."

"Yes, Father, it was a classic case of unintended consequences. But isn't abortion different?"

"Many Christians believe abortion to be evil and would make it illegal in this country. Clearly large segments of the public disagree. However, these Christians wouldn't have a problem imposing their anti-abortion beliefs on society as a whole."

"So, Father, you seem to be saying that democracy is better served by those who are not true believers?"

"Oh, Sean, you know you won't get me to answer that. But just think back to when John Kennedy ran for President. Didn't he have to pledge to the public that if elected he would not listen to the Pope when it came to resolving moral issues in America?"

"Yes, as I recall, he did." Usually when I talked to Lukas Schafer I felt uplifted, and on the whole better for having had our conversation. Unfortunately, this time everything he said confirmed, if not in fact at least in the general tenor what had been said earlier in the day by CIA Agent Chehwan. My long day had just gotten longer. I was ready for a drink and grateful that Prohibition was no longer the law of the land.

I must have looked as tired as Father Schafer because his response was, "Let's call it a night."

"Thanks, Padre."

As I got up to leave, Father Schafer added, "On the matter of contacting a local Imam, I may be able to help."

- 13 -

I slowly opened my eyes and waited for them to focus enough for me to read the clock on my nightstand. To my surprise, I had slept in. Now you have to remember that sleeping in means different things to different generations. In my case, it meant just past 7:30 am. My children would have hardly classified this as sleeping late. It's funny how work and responsibility changes one's view of time.

I had only one important task this Saturday: A promise to Kelly that I would help with her paper. Once that was done, I intended to devote the rest of the day to puttering and lounging around. This wouldn't have been the case if my wife were home. Undoubtedly she would have several heretofore unknown problems that needed fixing. She was gone for the weekend visiting her mother, a situation that worked for both of us, my mother-in-law and me. Mo just accepted the fact that her husband and her mother were closer when apart.

With my short-lived freedom, I even considered going to

the driving range. It had been months since I had swung a club, and I felt I needed to be ready for the season. Golf was a funny activity. I'm not sure it can be called a game. I readily admitted I wasn't very good at it, but I enjoyed it nonetheless. From observing others on the course, I knew I wasn't alone in the state of either my talents or feelings. It isn't often that people enjoy things they're not good at. I would put sex in that category, although of course no one would admit to not being good at that.

I headed downstairs to fix a cup of coffee. No doubt I would have at least a couple of hours before my daughter would be up, so I would have plenty of time to get ready for a day of relaxing. To my surprise, my daughter was seated at the kitchen table. "Hey, my darling, what are you doing up so early?"

"I couldn't sleep. My paper is due Monday and I can't seem to finish it."

Did I mention my daughter takes after my wife a lot more than she takes after me, though my daughter can be a procrastinator like her father? Both of the ladies in my life are champion worriers. In the case of my Maureen, I've delegated all the family worrying to her. I figure why not? She is good at it, and it saves me the time of duplicating her efforts. Kelly wants to get into a *good* college, meaning Ivy League, so she treats every paper and test as a make or break occurrence. I am proud of her. This was something new for me. My boys, now both away at state college, were and still are academically average. As students they both have the unstated but very obvious policy of following the path of least resistance.

"Let me fix a cup of coffee and some breakfast and then we can go over your paper."

"Thanks Daddy." She got up and gave me a big hug. There

38

were times when she could still be my little girl.

- 14 -

I looked at my daughter and just to make sure asked, "This is the one about the popes, right?"

"Yes, Daddy." The words were nice but the look was classic. *Boy, you sure can be a dunce when you like. Do you have Alzheimer's or something?* Actually it is CRS disease, can't remember shit.

Not to be deterred I said, "Let's see what you have." I reached out and Kelly handed me her paper. I quickly scanned what she had written. "Problem with the conclusion, huh?" I said as I returned the pages to her.

"Gee, Dad, you're quick." She waved her nearly blank conclusion page in my face.

I shook my head - quality sarcasm at such a young age. Not to let such small things get in the way of our bonding, I asked, "What's hanging you up?"

"The paper is supposed to be on the history of the papacy. That was easy. All I had to do was to regurgitate history."

"So what's the big deal?"

"The extra credit part of the paper, the AP portion, is to make a prediction about the future of the Holy See and then give reasons why."

"Kelly, there are only two words on the conclusion page," I pointed out.

"Daddy, I know. I just can't seem to finish this paper. I

don't know why."

I could tell she was frustrated. I knew her feeling well, being the master of putting things off and its associated frustration. Because of that I knew any additional anxiety wasn't going to get the job done. "So what have you been thinking about instead?"

Kelly looked at me. She wasn't sure whether I was trying to help or was just being a pain-in-the-butt parent. Thankfully she decided I wanted to help.

"I don't know why but I have been thinking about the weekends we used to have with your partner and his family."

"You mean Andy."

"Yes, of course," she said looking strangely at me.

I had seen that identical look before from my sons. It was as if she was thinking I was a simpleton. But since she still hadn't gone completely over to the dark side she kept the look somewhat neutral. I looked at her and nodded. "I think about those times too. Maybe it was because our families had such fun together. Remembering any one thing in particular?"

"My first real kiss."

As a father I must have blotted out the fact that Andy had a son a couple of years older than Kelly. As I now recall they had hit it off well obviously too well. "Isn't this something you and your mother should discuss?"

"Oh Daddy you can be so stupid."

It was time to get Kelly back on task. I picked up her paper and asked, "What does *Malachy Prophecy* mean?"

"You see, there was this Irish bishop, Saint Malachy, born

a long time ago in 1094. It is said that he predicted all the popes from Celestine II in 1143 to the end of time."

I looked at my daughter and smiled with my, you-are-young-and-impressionable-and-I-have-been-around smile. "I've never heard of Saint Malachy. But these stories are probably just like the ones that get attributed to Nostradamus."

"I don't think so."

"Why?"

"Well, two reasons. He also predicted that Ireland would be persecuted by England and he died mysteriously."

"How's that?"

"At the time of his death, Malachy was Bishop of Armagh in Northern Ireland and he was in excellent health until a week before he died."

"How old was he?"

"Fifty-four, when he died in 1148. Not only that but he predicted the date of his death on November 2nd."

"That was very old for those days."

"Doesn't matter. An unknown Benedictine priest came from Rome to speak to him and in a week he was dead. The story goes that he was working on a manuscript that disappeared when he died."

"The one listing the popes?"

"Possibly or what happens after the last pope dies. That's the guess, though no one knows for certain. Anyway, the manuscript was lost until it was published in 1595 by guess who?"

"A Benedictine."

"You got it."

"And the manuscript predicted the remaining popes?"

"Yep, all one hundred and twelve of them."

"And?"

"And John Paul II was number one hundred eleven."

"I see your difficulty predicting the future when there isn't going to be one. Kelly, just for argument's sake, are they sure John Paul II was number one hundred eleven? What about John Paul I, for example. Did he count?"

"That's a good point. Some argue that John Paul I didn't count because he was only Pope for a few weeks."

"Okay, then just for purposes of your discussion, tell me what's supposed to happen, I mean according to Saint Malachy."

"He didn't or the paper that was attributed to him didn't actually list the popes by name, rather they were given symbolic titles, a Latin clue if you would. The mottos given by Malachy usually referred to the coat of arms of the pontiff, or to his birthplace, or even sometimes his physical actions, and sometimes to major events that occurred during the Pope's reign."

"Isn't it easy enough to match up pope and prophetic clue after the fact?'

"Yes."

"I suppose that helps complicate your assignment?"

"It doesn't help."

"So what was the symbol for JP I supposed to be?"

"The sign for the one hundred tenth Pope was *Of the Half Moon.*"

I had to stifle a laugh. I loved the way these things went. Some obscure meaning that could pertain to anything. I mean, why couldn't the prophecy simply say the one hundred tenth Pope is Albino Luciani and then list his date and place of birth followed by when and where he died? "I suppose the term could have referred to the fact that the man used an outhouse in his lifetime."

"He was born October 17, 1912, in Forno di Canale, Italy and died September 28, 1978 in Rome," in case you were wondering. Kelly ignored my comments; she was used to my humor by now.

"What do the experts say this Of the Half Moon means? "

"Apparently he became Pope when the moon was half full, and he died thirty-fours days later when it was half full again."

"Well, that is a stretch." I said this more forcefully than I felt it. But I wasn't going to let my daughter stew over something that she couldn't control even in the most unlikely event there was any truth to the predictions. "Let me give you another interpretation."

"Okay."

"Let's ignore JP I and assume for the moment that JP II is the next one predicted."

"Okay."

"Where was JP II from?"

"He was first Archbishop of Krakow Poland and then he became a Cardinal."

I knew this and, as it happened, another trivial piece of information. "Kelly, did you know that medieval Krakow survived World War II intact?"

"No, but what does that matter?"

"Simply this, the beautiful city of Krakow was saved from the destruction but not the savagery of the Second World War."

"Huh?"

I loved how articulate teenagers could be. "The Plaszow Concentration Camp, the story site for *Schindler's List,* is in Krakow and the death camps of Auschwitz and Birkenau are less than forty miles away. Wouldn't that strike you as a more plausible description of a half moon, a city of both lightness and darkness?" I could see my daughter take this all in. I could see her relax just a bit. Obviously, for the first time in days, she could see the possibility that the world was not coming to an immediate end. "By the way, what's the sign for one hundred eleven?"

"It's *De Labore Solis.*"

Since I didn't know either French or Latin and wasn't sure which language Kelly had just used I asked, "What does that mean?"

"It means either from the toil of the sun or the eclipse of the sun."

I thought that limited it down pretty well but I kept my
44

comments to myself. "And what about number one hundred twelve?"

"Malachy describes him only as the Glory of the Olive."

"Do you know what that is supposed to mean?"

"Some have guessed that the Glory of the Olive will be Christ's Second Coming, the End of Time. Many consider Jesus to be the final Pope of the Church."

"Well, then it seems there isn't anything for you to worry about. No need to finish the paper because the world is going to end."

My daughter chose to ignore my comment and continued. "Others think that the world will be a mess - wars, terrorism and disturbances of nature. Then a new pope will try to bring back really old Catholic traditions and that'll cause a big fight. And there could even be like a Catholic civil war between the people that like the Pope's new rules and those that don't."

"And if the world doesn't end?"

"The optimists?"

"Yes, as compared to those who think we are all doomed?"

I finally got Kelly to smile. To me it was obvious she knew the material. She was simply stymied by what she had learned.

"The optimists think that the 'End Times' might simply be the passing of a particular age or long period in the relationship between man and God."

"I like that ending better. Don't you?" I said. My daughter gave me a relieved smile. "Why not use that in your paper?" I tousled her hair like I used to when she was little.

"Okay, that's a good idea."

I was glad she felt better, because I didn't, this could be just more fuel for a potential fire.

- 15 -

Bartolo had begun to worry. Not only had no one resembling the Archbishop come through customs, customs was practically deserted. With the number of international flights coming into Rome every day, it seemed almost impossible that not one had landed in the last thirty minutes. Even though the Patriarch carried a diplomatic passport, he was still required to go through the maze that made up the customs area because there had been no time to make special arrangements. Normally Cardinal Camperelle would have talked with his counterpart in the Italian government and the Patriarch would have been allowed to deplane first so he could be escorted from the airport in privacy and dignity.

Bartolo wanted to push his way into the customs area and demand to know what was going on, yet this would have accomplished nothing more than providing the police with an excuse to escort him from the building at best or at worst arrest him. Neither was satisfactory with both yielding the same result. While he was being detained by the authorities his diplomatic charge would be forced into wandering around the airport looking for his ride, hardly the result desired and certainly not one of a finely honed diplomat.

When he first entered the priesthood, he had dreamed of becoming a bishop. It seemed to be coming true when he was asked to become the assistant to the new Camerlengo or Chamberlain Cardinal Francesco Camperelle and was promoted to Monsignor. Unfortunately over the years he had learned more than he had wanted to about the Church and its politics. His dream faded. Not so much owing to lack of ability but to lack of desire. His hope was now to be reassigned to the field somewhere. It didn't matter where as long as it was a long way from Rome. He was fluent in several languages so he wasn't limited to his native Italy.

It wasn't that his work was immoral or unrewarding; it was just so bureaucratic, so far removed from the simple life of Christ. He just didn't want it anymore. The Church was 2,000 years old and had, as all human organizations had, developed layers of rule, rulers and regulations, all, it seemed, entrenched over the millennia to the point where change now was almost impossible. More and more he was amazed how the Church that had begun as a decentralized collegial organization had grown into the centralized imperial organization commonly known as the Holy See.

He wondered how a man like Salim Ateek who held one of the oldest and most unusual offices in the Church had reconciled himself to the Church's organizational peculiarities that he had grown to loath. Was there something he had missed? Maybe he was simply used to be the man in the middle. His charge was the current Latin Patriarch of Jerusalem. Though the first seeds of division were sown when Diocletian (284-305) divided Rome into an Eastern and a Western half it took until 1054 for the Great Schism to finally separate the Christian Church. In that year the Orthodox Patriarch of Jerusalem and the other three Eastern Patriarchs formed the Eastern Orthodox Church, and the Patriarch of Rome formed the Roman Catholic Church. Thus Western churches either gravitated around Rome or broke away from her during the Reformation while Eastern churches moved towards the Eastern Empire at Constantinople. Notwithstanding geography, the Latin Patriarch of Jerusalem remained in communion with Rome.

- 16 -

Bartolo was relieved to be finally heading back to the Vatican.

"Your Eminence, I must apologize for the delay."

"There is no need to apologize, Monsignor. I was called by His Holiness on very short notice. I was merely treated as any other traveler. I might add it was a humbling experience I'll need to remember, when I'm tempted to be full of myself."

"Do you know why there was such a delay at customs?"

"Having been born and continuing to live in the Holy Land creates diplomatic issues. In truth I haven't a country. I'm a Palestinian whose family lives in the territories controlled by Israel. When I travel, I must use a Vatican passport. You can see how this would slow down progress with the notoriously slow Italian immigration officials."

"Then you made very good time, indeed."

The Archbishop smiled as he turned to enjoy the view of the Italian countryside.

"One more thing, Eminence. There has been a change in plans."

Still looking out, the Archbishop said, "Oh, what might that be?"

"I am to take you directly to the papal apartments."

"I see, then it is as I feared, the Holy Father is much sicker than has been let on."

Silence ensued for the remainder of the trip.

- 17 -

The limousine carrying Monsignor Giovanni Bartolo and his passenger, Archbishop Salim Ateek pulled up to the private entrance of the building that housed the papal apartment. Waiting for the vehicle was Cardinal Camperelle. As both priests exited, Camperelle turned to his aide and said, "Be sure the guards know they are to tell no one of the arrival of the Patriarch."

"Yes, of course, Cardinal. Will you need anything else?"

"No not right now. But be sure to keep your cell on."

Knowing he had been dismissed, Bartolo got back into the car, which pulled immediately away.

Camperelle turned to Ateek while guiding him towards the nondescript door that led directly to the papal chambers. "Thank you for coming so quickly."

"When the Holy Father asks, one has little choice." Ateek stated.

Camperelle nodded and spoke softly as the two men waited for the elevator. "His Holiness is slipping. Try not to look too shocked when you see him."

"Does he have long?"

The Vatican Secretary of State responded, "The doctors have told us he has at least several more months. God, though, appears to have other plans."

"When are you going to tell the world?" Ateek asked.

"In due time when it is appropriate, but thankfully that's not right now. The last thing the Church needs is a power vacuum."

By now the elevator had arrived on the third floor and the two clerics entered the apartment's public receiving chamber.

"Yes, I see your point; it's good to be sure. The Pope may indeed have the time the doctors anticipate. The course of the disease is anything but a straight line."

Camperelle paused outside the door to the Pontiff's bedroom. "He is still lucid and at peace with himself and the world, though he tires easily. Because of that, I'm sorry to say, we must make your stay as brief as possible. I know that is not entirely fair to you, but I know you'll understand."

"I am at your disposal. Aren't we all here for the same reason, to glorify God and not oneself?"

"I had hoped for something more special for you."

Cardinal Camperelle was surprised by the quizzical look the Patriarch gave him.

"You don't know why you have been summoned, do you?"

"No, Your Eminence. Not that it matters. I assumed the Pope wanted to give me some specific instructions on handling the Church in the Holy Land. I can certainly use all the help, encouragement and particularly prayers available. The Holy Land has seen so little peace over the centuries. It is difficult to imagine it was home to the Prince of Peace while he walked the earth."

Camperelle was pleased by the humility of the man in front of him. Truly his Holiness had chosen wisely. "My dear Archbishop that is not the reason you have been brought to Rome. His Holiness intends to make you a Prince of the Church. Tomorrow, Sunday morning, when you say Mass, it will be your first as one who wears the Red Hat."

A look of astonishment crossed the face of Salim Ateek as the two men entered the Pontiff's bed chamber. It had never crossed the Patriarch's mind that he was here to be made a Cardinal.

50

- 18 -

It was Sunday morning and my daughter had spent the night with a friend. The house was unnaturally quiet as I lay in bed hoping to fall back asleep or to come up with an excuse to skip Mass. I spent several more minutes going through a series of mental gymnastics to justify missing church. To do that I needed to create a believable argument, one founded on some objectively valid reason. The old standby was health. If one is sick, one need not attend. This argument can be taken one step further and still be self-sold. I have worked very hard as of late and I'm very rundown. If I expose myself to the congregation, most likely I will become ill. A mental health excuse is also acceptable. For example, "*I am under so much pressure I just need some time to myself without any outside (read Church related admonishments) stresses.* "As I lay in bed, I found myself failing on all fronts. I hated having to do anything in particular on a weekend morning particularly on Sunday. Going to Mass unfortunately fit into that category. I felt like going ate up the entire morning; from what I wasn't quite sure, as I had nothing planned. Of course I could have gone last night but I just couldn't seem to get going. Why I don't know. Maybe I had subconsciously hoped I would find a legitimate excuse for not going between then and now.

Hard as I tried, I couldn't come up with an acceptable excuse. The idea of just blowing it off was too much for me and my Irish instilled religious guilt. I didn't really think I would go to hell if I missed but … then one never really knows until it is too late. With that happy thought I got out of bed and headed for the bathroom. I was conflicted, but I was going, having decided to stop at the driving range on my way back. I deserved it.

Maybe all my mental contortions were just the result of

needing to talk to my wife about the conversation I had had with Father Schafer. I didn't know what her reaction would be to the news and I wanted to know. Over the years she has been, and for that matter continues to be, an excellent sounding board for me. She has helped in my casework more times than I would care to admit to my superiors, which would be zero. I was certain she could have provided me with some useful insights on the subject of our semi-radical priest.

- 19 -

Mo and I generally attended Mass on Saturday night. Surprisingly this was the second highest attended service of the weekend with only 9:00 am on Sunday morning being larger. I knew from my law enforcement training that once people establish a routine, they stick with it over time. On Saturday night there were people whom I recognized. However, this wasn't the case on Sunday morning. As I sat there, I felt like I was going to church out of town. As I waited, I scanned the congregation to see a familiar face. The only one I saw that was even remotely familiar was not a Saturday night regular. What first caught my attention was his full head of prematurely white hair. The next thing was how tall he was. I guessed well over six feet. I knew I knew this man, but I couldn't place a name with the face. I tried not to stare as my mind ran through its inventory of faces and names. I was getting nowhere when the lector began.

"We welcome you this morning to Saint Charles Borromeo for Sunday Mass. We ask that you turn off your cell phones so as not to disturb the liturgy if they might ring."

Damn, that was it. I could have brought my cell. It would have gone off; it is always going off and I could have ducked out with a great excuse. I would both be protecting the sacred liturgy and saving the world from the bad guys.

As Father Schafer said Mass, my mind continued unsuccessfully on its mission to solve who my mystery guest was. In the old days, before the Second Vatican Council, Masses were said in Latin with the priest's back to the congregation. No one understood what was being said and many, if not most of the congregants couldn't hear. This perfect combination generally allowed for an extra hour of sleep interrupted only by the homily. In Catholic churches it is a homily; in Protestant ones it is a sermon, still it is the same thing, the Bosses representative telling you how you need to live. This phenomenon of the hidden Mass and the incomprehensible words all changed after Vatican II. Now all the prayers are in English and the priest faces the congregation. Everyone can hear and see what is going on. That extra sleep that one could steal is now much hardy to justify and to come by.

As a speaker, I must admit Lukas Schafer is eloquent. Even my cynical mind appreciates what he has to say. Today was no exception, in fact, he was better than usual at least in my unbiased opinion. He was telling the congregation that, "there are a lot of problems in the Catholic Church today and they must be dealt with. The Church needed to return to the simplicity and collegiality of its early days or it would suffer more lost members and would be ignored even more by the rest of society." I enjoyed his points, but I wasn't sure our Bishop would be equally enthusiastic. It seems our parish priest thinks the Church is too autocratically structured and that is one of the primary reasons for its troubles.

Sometime after the homily concluded and communion began, it finally hit me. The guy in the back of the church was Adrian Chalmers. Chalmers owned radio stations. How many I didn't know. All I was sure of was that there were a lot of them. I had heard of the man through Kelly's school. According to those who knew, he was a major contributor to Catholic education. I didn't know much about that but I did know he was on the 500 Richest in America list. As part of my job, I do keep track of Who's Who in the financial world. Additionally, when I was driving a lot during my last assignment, there were times that I listened to some of his stations. However, I didn't listen long as the focus was a bit conservative even for my tastes, and I'm an FBI agent.

Mercifully Mass came to an end, you can see I'm not the holiest guy on the planet. I waited for Father Schafer to make his way to the vestibule of the Church. I needed to find out how he was coming with finding a Muslim cleric to speak at our Ecumenical meetings. I figured I could quickly find out without any further entanglements to my day. However, as I passed from the sanctuary, I could see Adrian Chalmers talking with Father Schafer, and the conversation appeared to be quite animated.

- 20 -

"Lukas, from what we have heard, the Pope is very sick and may be near death."

Schafer looked around the meeting room. The room was filled with around sixty other priests, most of them he considered to be friends including the current speaker Raymond Gates who had just spoken. "Yes, Raymond, I have heard the same thing. It seems the good news we had been hearing was premature."

His comment was acknowledged by a general murmur from the assembled gathering. Those gathered for this meeting were like him in that they were young but were clearly on the fast track to move up in the hierarchy of the Church.

Schafer continued to speak to the group. "Regardless of whether the Holy Father is sick or there is a new Pope. The time is right. The time is now for us to move forward."

"Lukas, we agree with you. But it would look unseemly if we were to issue our paper and then shortly thereafter the Pope passes away."

"Raymond, your point is well taken. However, I'm more concerned that if we wait and the Pope dies our efforts will get lost. The media here in America, as elsewhere in the world, will focus first on the death of the current Holy Father, then on who will fill the papacy, and then finally on the new Pope." Schafer could see the group agree with his conclusion. "Therefore I propose that we don't wait."

Schafer's long time seminary friend rose again to speak.

"Yes, Raymond."

"Lukas, I also agree we shouldn't wait but for another reason."

"What is that?"

"I'm afraid if we wait, we'll lose our resolve or our work will be prematurely discovered. I believe it is imperative that we move now." With that, Raymond sat down.

The room was silent as the priests waited for Father Schafer to respond. "Raymond, as always you make an insightful observation." Schafer paused and looked about the room. His friend was right about not waiting but it was sad that his view came from the negative and not the positive.

Schafer decided to shift the discussion back to everyone's higher aspirations. "What we propose is honorable. It represents a new beginning. We believe there is nothing in it that is contrary to

Church teachings. It is imperative that we make our views known. Delay is not in anyone's best interest."

Schafer looked about the room. He could see they were with him. "However as much as I would love to post our views tonight on the internet we simply don't know the Holy Father's condition and I don't want our message to get lost in the backwash of the death of the Pope."

Schafer paused and looked at the faces around the room. A hand rose slowly in the back, "then how do we proceed?"

"Here is what I propose. We all sign the document and date it tonight. I'll hold it until the time is right. At that point I'll release it, first to the hierarchy and shortly thereafter to the general public. Is this agreeable?"

"Lukas, I trust your judgment. I know that we have endeavored to not pick a leader. We have wanted our organization to reflect what we believe the Church's structure should be. But you should be considered the first among equals, a prime minister of sorts."

"Raymond, do you speak for everyone?"

"Yes, I believe I do." Gates said looking around the room for any disagreement of which there was none.

"Okay, then I will hold the document and release it as appropriate. I'll lead the group as a senior colleague. Not a dictator, and when you tell me or I know it's time, I will step aside for someone else." Schafer again perused the room. "If anyone objects, let me hear from him now." The only noise was the sound of each man getting up to sign the document.

- 21 -

Like most people I hated Monday mornings. It wasn't so much the getting up part as it was with the prospect of dealing with the endless list of work-related trivial musts, in simple English, work's bullshit. As I get older, I find the BS coming up higher and higher on my work waders or at least my tolerance going lower and lower. What also made this particular Monday so charming was my lack of rest. I consider myself lucky in that I enjoy my wife's company. And I quietly pity the guys and gals in the office who don't like their spouses. It must make life long and tough. I consider my wife my best friend, and when she isn't around I flat out don't like it and don't sleep well and this weekend was no exception. Mo had gotten home much later on Sunday that we had originally anticipated so my weekend sleep was fitful at best. And not to mention of course there was always that new work problem; attempting to find out who was trying to use religion to undermine the government of the United States of America.

Adding to the mix were the implications from what I had learned from Kelley's paper. I could definitely see the potential of more fertile ground for societal problems. Personally I don't put any credence in revelation hooey though I know many people do and will act accordingly. To me, it's simple: we have been told that we won't know the time or the place of the end of the world. I figure it'll happen when it happens. Therefore, any of this tarot reading, tea leaf divining, prophetical attributions to things in Revelations is an exercise in hubris and a complete waste of time. But what I think clearly doesn't matter, what does is how others will react and act on certain types of beliefs and associated information. As I pulled out of the driveway, I made a mental note to use Kelly's paper as an excuse to talk with Father Schafer. He might be able to give me some insight into the religiously disturbed and or fanatical. It never hurts to ask.

- 22 -

With traffic it normally takes me about forty-five minutes to get to the office from home, without traffic it never takes more than twenty-five minutes. Not today. A big rig had hit a construction barrier about 5:00 am and as a result the normally slow morning commute had become a how nice to start your week off traffic nightmare. I was into it for just over an hour and I still had a ways to go. What was unbelievable or galling was that the accident had occurred in the opposite direction and it was the looky-loos who had screwed everything up. Unfortunately, this extra time gave me time to reflect upon my fellow man, something I probably should have passed on.

As I sat there inching along I couldn't help but wonder about the other drivers. If I were an observer from another planet I would have assumed that that someone had opened the asylum's doors and had let out all the morons with the only caveat being they all had to get out on the road at the same time. I saw people reading the newspaper, shaving, eating breakfast, with both hands of course, and brushing their teeth while driving, those not doing those mundane tasks were busy given either texting or talking on their cell phones. I kept asking myself how could so many people have so many important things that needed to be said at that hour of the morning and from the car? Over the years I have spent a lot of time interrogating people and most of them didn't have much of value to say and many of them happened to be guilty as hell.

Mercifully, I got beyond the accident and the congestion began to clean and the traffic began to pick-up speed. I checked

58

my watch again for the umpteenth time. Optimistically I had concluded I was going to make it to our new group's kick off meeting on time, but it was going to be close, very close. Not the best way to start out with Alan Mitchell, SACRCTU. I had already received my assignment, but I wanted to hear what everyone else's tasks were going to be. I was considering hitting my siren and flashing lights to improve my odds of being there timely when, my cell rang.

I hit send and at the same time pushed out of my head any thoughts that I had just joined the masses of other inept multi-tasking drivers, "Murphy."

It was Amanda Chehwan.

"Hello, Agent, what can I do for you?"

I listened for a while and finally said, "Yes, I can meet you at Treasury. Give me about thirty minutes the traffic is a killer." As I hung up I might have heard her say something about making it in twenty minutes but that was probably just my imagination. Just in case I hit my flashing flights and stepped on it. It looked like I would meet my new teammates later. Our CIA second in command wanted to meet me at the main offices of the Internal Revenue Service.

If one ever looked at the organizational chart of the Treasury Department, one would see a myriad divisions dealing with economic policy both domestic and international. There were also semi-independent bureaus such as the Comptroller of the Currency and Bureau of Printing and Engraving. But by far and away the largest, best known and least loved of all the functions remaining within the department is the Internal Revenue Service. I parked in a "reserved for customer," spot, I had to be a customer, right? Jumped out of my car and headed for the front doors.

Few people know that all the original functions of the IRS used to be housed in a modest sized building located on

Pennsylvania Avenue. The current headquarters is located in a much larger structure on Constitution Avenue. I might sorrowfully add that the current address will soon change to an even larger headquarters complex in suburban Maryland.

This wasn't the kind of progress I liked to see. To me the cycle of more and more rules, regulations and paper requiring ever bigger buildings to house ever more Internal Revenue employees created the worst kind of perpetual motion machine possible.

However, the information kept by the Service had the potential of providing a great deal of useful investigative information and that was why I had been diverted by Agent Chehwan or at least that's what I had been told. I only hoped I could mine it without boring myself to death. The front doors opened automatically and as I entered I saw before me lay the usual welcoming committee of metal detectors and guards. Beyond that in the lobby I could make out the unsmiling face of Agent Chehwan.

- 24 -

Chehwan looked at her watch as I approached. "You're late, come with me quickly. We have an appointment with the Deputy Director in charge of the not-for-profit section."

With that, she headed off towards the bank of elevators. I couldn't tell if Chehwan was upset with me or merely hurrying to get to the meeting on time either way she was off like a shot making considerable progress considering her limp. I managed to catch up to her just as the elevator car doors were closing. When the doors opened I followed the CIA agent down the hall and through a pair of glass doors with gold lettering indicating it as the Deputy Director for Non-Profits office. Chehwan had pulled out her I.D. and announced that we had an appointment to see the Deputy Director. The receptionist looked at Chehwan's identification as if hundreds if not thousands of CIA regularly came to this office. I, on the other hand, fumbled a bit pulling out my shield. I can't imagine it but one would have thought I was the first FBI agent officer she had ever encountered. Not having had the opportunity to use my rapier-like wit on my new partner, I decided the receptionist needed it. "Perhaps you can photocopy it for greater study," I said. The look I got back was one that said, *you can rest assured that you will be audited every year for the rest of your life and for at least two years after you're dead.*

The icy stare continued and then she finally responded. "That won't be necessary, Agent Murphy. Please take a seat and I'll let you know when you can see Ms. Jenson." The receptionist matter-of-factly pointed to a set of chairs in the corner that looked like they had been most recently used for high school detention.

I headed for the chairs, but not before I caught the receptionist giving Chehwan the knowing pity look. Chehwan came over sat down and whispered in my ear, "Nice start, Sean. I can see where your reputation comes from."

I smiled. "I don't like getting jerked around."

"So I have heard."

I looked at Chehwan but couldn't tell what she was thinking, the perfect CIA expression I might add.

We waited for only five minutes. I assumed that was a testament to my partner. As much as everyone fears the Internal Revenue Service, it would seem the Service or at least this IRS employee didn't want to be on the CIA's shit list. For me, it didn't matter. I was on a lot of shit lists.

We were ushered into an office that reeked of upper government management. It was large and at one time had been nicely appointed, but after an endless series of budget cuts could now be described as threadbare. Fortunately it was a sunny day and there was a large window. Offices such as this usually are as dark as a tomb. For some reason, government-hired architects seem to think of everything but lighting.

"Please have a seat," Ms. Jenson said.

I remained silent while Chehwan began. "As I mentioned to you last week on the phone, it was Agent Murphy who suggested we look at data compiled from certain not-for-profit organization tax returns, form 990 I believe."

"Yes, the tax return number is form 990," Jenson replied.

Chehwan asked, "Just so I am clear, the search parameters also include data from private foundations and political action committees?"

I sat there more than a little surprised as I recalled my own words, from last Friday late in the afternoon, *I would begin by pulling the public non-profit organization data available from the IRS to see what religious based organizations had the most dramatic change in donations. I would then compare this list to those that had become most active on the internet.*

"The answer to your question is yes. I had my programmers write a program that would extract the information you requested. The data search includes PACs, foundations, as well as traditional non-profit organizations. The program has been running since Saturday night, and initial data should be available within the hour."

Chehwan smiled. "Good. I assume your computer people are available for program modifications we might request?"

Jenson responded, "Yes. No problem." I remained silent, feeling more than a little like a pawn.

Again from Chehwan, "Just to make sure; your people know they are to accede to any requests made by Agent Murphy?"

"I told them. They were surprised, but they'll do what he asks."

It was weird being talked about in the third person. But still, I didn't have anything constructive to say.

Amanda then turned and faced me. "Sean, please review the data the IRS has generated. If you want them to cross reference other data, just ask them. I'm going back to the Hoover Building. Here is my cell number. Whatever you find, please tell only me."

Chehwan handed me her card with a number written on its back. While the prospect of grinding through IRS 990 forms was hardly appealing, it beat the hell out of being shot at.

- 25 -

After Chehwan left, Jensen took me down two floors to the computer center where she introduced me to Simon Stallings. "Agent Murphy, this is Simon Stallings, he is our head of IT. Simon this is Agent Murphy, the one I told you about."

Great, just great I thought.

"As we discussed this case has top priority. Do you have any questions?"

"No."

"Very good," I will leave you two now. With that I watched as Jensen headed towards the elevators.

I turned back to the head computer meister "Mr. Stallings, so as the head computer geek of the Internal Revenue Service you are the one to blame." I held out my hand and smiled to indicate that I was kidding.

Simon Stallings apparently possessed the most minimal of social skills. He managed to hand me a computer printout that made the New York City phone book look like light reading and said only, "Here is our first draft," and turned to walk away.

I immediately knew this was too much data. Grabbing his arm I asked, "Excuse me, how did you tabulate the data?"

It seemed he was used to being grabbed as he didn't react. "We ran the numbers looking for a percentage increase of more than fifty percent in contributions."

"Only contributions?"

"Yes." Clearly Stallings didn't waste words.

"How about program revenues or grants?"

"That information will come in the second and third drafts."

Great, I thought, more reams of paper. Maybe being shot at was preferable. "Did you look at the numbers over a set of years?"

"No."

"Tell you what. I want you to resort this data." I could see he wasn't happy receiving this order, but frankly I couldn't care less. "First go back three years and find out what organizations have had income increase by at least four times. After you have done that, run those same organizations through a filter. If the cumulative three year number is less than one million dollars, ignore the entity." I then proceeded to return his paper mountain to him. I could see he wasn't used to being treated this way. I suspected he was treated as the sacred, yet idiosyncratic, guru of the Service. I gave him my card after he put the stack down and said, "Call me as soon as you get the numbers run." With that I turned and left a clearly unhappy Simon Stallings. This will probably the only time in my life that I can stick it to the IRS; however that is not my intent, yea right. Anyway I do need to get back to the office and do some research of my own.

- 26 -

I wanted to do a little data mining myself. The FBI has an extensive data base as well and I had planned on pulling a list of suspected terrorist or terrorist affiliated organizations operating here at home over the same three year time period as I had just requested from the IRS. With luck I hoped I could generate this list about the same time the revised list was available from the Internal Revenue Service.

Traffic was congested as usual and moving very slowly. So I decided to call Father Schafer. Maybe he had luck finding a Muslim imam for my group. "Father, Sean Murphy."

"Hi Sean, good to hear from you. What can I do for you?"

"Well, I was wondering if you had had any luck finding a Muslim speaker for my group."

"It's your lucky day. I spoke to Imam bin-Mohamed of the Islamic Mosque and Cultural Center in the District. He has agreed to speak."

"Great! Thanks, that takes a load off." I paused. I debated with myself. Should I bring up Kelly's paper?

"Sean, is there anything else?"

I wondered if Lukas Schafer was clairvoyant. "Well yes, Father." I explained Kelly's paper to him and finished up by asking him if there was an official Church position on these prophecies?

"Not really, Sean. You know that his descriptions of the various popes were vague and, as such, can be rather easily backed into so as to achieve a desired result." The priest paused for just a second before continuing. "Though it is true there is much to catch the eye and tickle the mind with Malachy's predictions."

"I see."

Since I had the time, I asked, "What do you think?"

The priest laughed and said, "I thought you would ask that question. The Church has had an imperial papacy from at least the time of Saint Malachy earlier in fact."

"When was Malachy's time?"

"Middle of the 1100's I believe. Anyway, when he predicts the end of the papacy, maybe he is really predicting the end of the imperial popes."

I was confused. Of course, Church history had never been my thing. "What other approach could there be?"

"Possibly a collegial style Holy See. You know a structure where input from the Bishops is much more influential than it is today. Something like it was in the very early days of the Church. The Pope would be more of a first among equals rather than a king."

"I see."

"Doesn't sound that way to me, Sean. A current example would be the way the Orthodox Church or the Anglican Church is run. In business one would call it a de-centralized system."

"Is that what you think, Father?"

66

He laughed. "I'll hold off on that and leave you with something to think about. "

"A truly diplomatic response, do you have another minute?"

"Just a few minutes, then I need to run."

"Do you have much experience with what I would call religious zealots?"

"I have worked with a variety of people, some with a lessor faith some with a lot. But that is not what you are asking is it?"

"No, I am asking about people who will use violence or non-Christian means to achieve their ends."

"I thought so. The answer is yes.

"Are they generally sincere?"

"Oh, most definitely."

"Are they prone to violence?"

"Sadly yes."

"Have you met many of these kinds of people?"

"Again, sadly yes. It seems there have been more and more lately."

I didn't immediately respond finally, I said, "thanks Father I know you need to run." With that we hung up and I flipped on the radio. My mind was weighing what Lukas Schafer had suggested, and I almost didn't hear the news bulletin. *This bulletin just in from Rome. According to Vatican officials — the Pope is dead. "*

- 27 -

I mechanically exited and headed for my office. My mind was trying to get around the fact the Pope was dead. I could hardly remember his predecessor. The Pope had become the Bishop of Rome early in his life and with his strong constitution had beaten back a number of life-threatening diseases. As he aged he had taken on an aura. Most popes were respected by the leaders of the other major world religions. But this man had achieved a special level of respect.

The Pope had been a traditionalist during most of his Pontificate, but appeared to have softened in the later years of his reign. Who would take his place? The press was already suggesting those who might succeed him, the Papabili.

The late Pope had served so long that he had selected most of the Cardinals who would now choose his successor. These men undoubtedly mirrored the philosophy of the man who had selected them. But since his philosophy seemed to have changed over the years that left a lot of options open.

Would the Church continue on as before or would the College of Cardinals choose a reformer. If a reformer, would that man be enough of a reformer or too much of one? Would he satisfy the likes of Lukas Schafer or should he? Would he care to? But most importantly would the potential crises I was currently working on be averted by this new man?

I had many more questions than answers and until a new pontiff was chosen there wouldn't be any answers. It was best that I get on with my job. With luck maybe a job I would find myself out of.

I hung my coat on the hook on the back of my door, sat at my computer and logged in. As soon as I was in the system I began typing search parameters. The list I had asked the Internal Revenue Service to create would be useful only if I could generate a comparable one of corporate entities. I began by opening the Securities and Exchange Commission's excellent data base. I planned to run several search criteria. It was possible that if someone was attempting to feed upon the general public's discontent he might also want to profit from it. It was probably a long shot, and it would take some time to find anything at all but still...

- 28 -

The SEC database was only one of my sources. I also intended to run a series of searches using various other government public records. There is an amazing amount of information available on the internet. Among the things available, records on land ownership, vital statistics, as well as tons of data from the U.S. departments of Labor and Commerce. To me the two most useful areas I would need to look into would be payroll and debt-related information.

Why payroll? I made the assumption that anyone doling out money to any organization religious or otherwise would require something of that organization in return. That something would have to include timely reports relating to the progress of the purported mission for which the money had been received. My assumption was also based upon the belief that the distributor of the money, our bad guy, needed to make the donation appear legitimate as well as being used to monitor the use of the funds contributed. If someone were interested in creating chaos or a revolution that person or persons would need a deep base of support. A deep base could be created in either one of two ways. It could be done through a single large organization or a large number of smaller ones. Based upon my prior experience it was more likely that the smaller ones would be easier to manipulate. However that meant a large number of entities. And that in turn would require people to keep in touch with the various organizations, probably a lot of people. Logically I seriously doubted that anyone could find a whole group of people willing to turn the country into religious madhouse. For that reason the employees of the organization I was hunting for would have to believe their jobs were real and the organization they were working for was legit. Legit organizations file paperwork with lots of government agencies. Those reports would give me a list of organization showing a large jump in employees over the time period in question.

The second line of analysis was founded on the first. That is, where there is staff, there must also be office equipment. People needed phones, computers and desks. Unless the organizer was willing to pay cash for all of these things, credit was needed. Companies that supply credit file liens against personal property. I hoped to find a dramatic increase in personal property debt over the time frame in question.

As I typed and entered my final search criteria, I had that uneasy feeling that something was wrong or I was missing something. I knew my ideas were valid, but they amounted to a series of longshots at best. If I were trying to pull something this large off and I'm not a rocket scientist, I would pay cash for anything and everything. If I needed employees, I would lease them and bury my growth in some larger organization. In that way only a few people would be in the know they would all be fellow conspirators. Everyone and everything would be untraceable. I've met a lot of bad guys over the years, and generally the more elaborate the plan the smarter the crook. The plan Chehwan outlined was pretty elaborate, so we were probably dealing with folks with above average I.Q.s who were not apt to leave a trail of financial breadcrumbs but one never knew and sometime arrogant people or people in a hurry make stupid mistakes.

- 29 -

I couldn't shake that uneasy feeling. Dead-ends were an everyday occurrence in my line of work. No one liked them but we all learned to live with and accept as part of doing business.

However, this was different. The longer I sat at my desk thinking about the last few days, the more I was convinced that the best I could hope for would be to use my search data information in conjunction with something else, something I hadn't seen and no one had told me about.

If it were me, I would do whatever it took to keep my organization off the radar. I would do whatever it took, not to generate a paper trail. In that way the bloodhounds at the government wouldn't be able to do what I was attempting to do. There were times when it was easier to hide something in plain sight. This was not one of them. I would do whatever it took to keep my organization private. I wouldn't own anything, no land, no investments, nothing. By doing this, I would stay off the very out-of the-way databases for which I had just spent hours typing search parameters.

As far as my operating entity, I would operate as a church. Hard as it is to believe, churches have little if any public accountability. The theory undoubtedly is that churches have to answer to a higher authority. I would say that the overwhelming majority do just that. But if I were out to cause trouble, I would use a church. I would be the exception to the rule.

If I polled the public, I suspect they would be shocked to learn that churches do not file income tax returns. Other kinds of non-profit organizations do file returns. Thus, only in America can organizations and individuals make contributions to churches, claim a tax deduction without the recipient entity having to pay tax on the money received or even having to make any reports to anyone justifying the use of the donated money. A perfect entity if one wanted to be the wolf in sheep's clothing.

I know you are thinking *well, not everyone can be a church*. Doesn't God or someone of equal importance have to come down and put a stamp on the organization before it can operate as a church? The answer is *not really*. All it takes to be a church is to say one is a church. Sure, a church must file an application with the Internal Revenue Service claiming church status. But once that is done, no one looks at that entity again because the entity filing the application is, that's right, a church.

My train of thought had taken me to a place I didn't like. I needed to talk to Agent Chehwan about this and damn soon.

- 30 -

I called her cell. "Agent, this is Sean Murphy, can we meet?"

Agent Chehwan hesitated, "How about tomorrow afternoon?"

"I don't think waiting that long is a good idea. Can you make it sooner?"

I heard her cover the cell's mouthpiece. It sounded like she was talking to someone else. "Are you at your office?"

"Yes."

"The best I can do is first thing tomorrow that'll have to do."

"Okay," was all I said before she hung up. So much for the social skills taught at the CIA. I had a flood of mixed feelings; I was at the same time relieved, concerned, and irritated.

Irritated was the easiest to explain. I would be giving Agent Chehwan bad news, and I hated waiting around to do this. I didn't sleep well before such events. At least I had accomplished something; sometimes bad news helps an investigation more than good news. At least that is the bullshit one hears in situations such as this. I was also apprehensive. What if my little revelation threw the entire investigation into disarray? Rather than being a star I could just as easily be the goat, internal politics could be a strange master. I could see my transfer to the Nome office coming through before the close of business tomorrow. I knew I would be going alone. Maureen and rustic living didn't mix well. Alaska would be my home, not hers.

- 31 -

I got to the office early. As I had anticipated, I had had a crappy night's sleep. While I waited for Chehwan to arrive, I checked to see if any of my computer searches had generated information. They had not, and so mostly I waited. Shortly after 8:00 am Amanda Chehwan arrived. I broke the silence by offering her a chair, which she declined, definitely not a good sign.

She began, "Sean, what's the big deal?"

"Amanda, I think we have a problem."

"I gathered that." Chehwan said and remained standing.

I decided to dive in and get the bad news out. "I doubt all this computer searching will yield any substantial information." There. I had said it.

"Why is that?' was Chehwan's response. Her reaction was certainly not what I expected. I thought she would have been more animated, but then again it could have been her spy training on autopilot.

"Churches," I said. I could see from her facial expression she knew exactly what I meant. And in that instant I also saw my true role in this investigation. I was to be the guy who was going to be fed to the public if and when things went wrong. This made some sense, of course. I was at a high enough level at the Bureau to be a plausible spokesperson. In addition, I had had some favorable public exposure from prior investigations. Lastly, the public certainly wasn't going to learn of the CIA's role in this, some Congressional rule about the Company not working domestically. It was all logical but it still pissed me off. I was willing to work as a team member, though I preferred the leader's role and over the years I had taken my share of hits for the good of the organization and that was probably why I was tolerated plus I had solved some major cases. What was truly annoying, annoying but not surprising on quick reflection, was to be kept in the dark about it. I hated being lied to. So I was doing the slow burn and her hovering over my desk didn't help. "Why don't you sit down?" I said. It wasn't a request. I continued, "Why don't we go over our respective roles in this little drama." I could see she was debating how to handle this turn of events. Eventually she did sit down. I was still plenty pissed off.

I remained silent, forcing her to begin. "We weren't completely honest with you."

I continued my silent treatment.

"We had already concluded that most likely you wouldn't turn up anything of value."

"So why the hell did you involve me?"

"There were several reasons. One, we thought a fresh set of eyes might get lucky and turn something up."

"Just who is *we*?"

"Alan Mitchell and I."

I had delivered enough bullshit to know it when I heard it. There wasn't one chance in a million that Mitchell and Chehwan knew anything about church financial reporting. Someone else was involved. "And?"

It was Chehwan's turn to stare. After a long pause she responded, "Deputy Director Hanson, as well as Simon Stallings at the IRS."

"How long ago?"

"Six months."

Now some things made more sense. An important investigation and I had been pulled out of the loop before there was a loop. It was no wonder Stallings had shown such displeasure with both Chehwan's order and with my subsequent information request on Monday. "So what have you learned over the last six months, if anything?"

"We hadn't been making much headway until the Agency tied an NSA intercept to a source here at home."

"What source?"

"I can't say."

For the moment I chose to believe her. So there it was. Just as I had begun to suspect, the CIA had been violating federal law by conducting domestic spying for the last several months.

"So Amanda let me guess. You and Mitchell needed someone to find this information that was on the spies approved list. That someone turned out to be me. At some point in my investigation, I was going to discover the appropriate data. In addition, with luck I might have turned up additional data. Correct?"

From Chehwan's expression, I could see I was right but she

remained silent. I rose to leave. I said, "You know I've been compromised, and so it is time for me to leave this charade behind. But before I go, I do have one piece of advice: smarten up! If you can't fool me, you'll never fool the press or anyone else investigating this thing. That includes Congress. I know Congress can be incredibly dull at times, but not even it can be this dumb."

"Sean, wait, please hear me out." My recollection of Bureau regulations left me two official choices. One was to listen to her explanation and then fill out an internal affairs report. The other was to terminate our conversation immediately. I suspected I would choose neither.

- 32 -

"First of all, Congress can be that stupid when it wants to."

I nodded and said, "Go on."

"Second, I hope you can see why we kept you in the dark."

I sensed the CIA agent wanted me to nod or at least show some kind of acceptance. This wasn't something I was about to do. So far as I could see, she was going to be distributing more fertilizer and low quality stuff at that. "Agent Chehwan quit wasting my time. I'm out of here and am going directly to the Director unless you come clean and I mean immediately."

"Okay, just the facts. Once Mitchell and I learned of the church aspect, we figured that was where we needed to hunt."

"I agree, but to do the hunting you were going to … how would one say this nicely? Bend the rules."

"That's one of the CIA's specialties."

"I've heard rumors. Let's get back to the NSA. What did they find?"

"I said I couldn't say."

"Right, it's that domestic spying thing again. How much time in federal prison does that get you?"

"Hear me out, our sources told us the money was coming from the Middle East, we began our eavesdropping there."

"Went after the banks located there and I suppose certain European countries, so you were initially in the clear."

"Correct."

"So what did you find?"

It took just over five months and millions of bits of information, but we were able to establish a money trail."

"Impressive."

"Thank you."

"What did you find?" I wasn't about to let the CIA agent off the hook. I hadn't yet forgotten I had been chosen to be the unwitting front guy.

"You don't have the clearance."

"That dog won't hunt," I commented at the same time I started to rise from my chair.

"Sit down. You can't blame me for trying."

"Oh yes, I can."

"I suppose," Chehwan conceded.

"Please continue and let's keep it believable." I was still ticked off.

Chehwan drew a deep breath. "We began by looking at known and suspected terrorist or terrorist-connected organizations. Eventually we found regular cash flows coming from a variety of organizations. These monies were being deposited into a single Swiss bank account."

"What kind of cash flows?"

"Whole dollar amounts. Curiously the amounts seemed to be roughly equivalent to the size of a particular organization."

"Like a tax."

"Exactly like a tax."

I was stunned. Someone or some organization had managed to get a bunch of disparate terrorist organizations, who hated each other only slightly less than they hated the USA, to agree to be taxed. "Were you able to determine who has such power and influence?"

"No, though we think we are getting closer."

I wasn't completely sure I believed everything I had heard but decided to withhold judgment.

"After Switzerland, where does the money go?"

"We have been working on answering that very question for the last month."

"And this is where we get to the bad side, right?"

"Yes, this is where we move from international to domestic surveillance."

"Well, what have you learned?"

"It appears the money is being transferred to four or five major US banks." I was ready to ask the next obvious question, but Chehwan answered me before I was able to ask. "We haven't found where the money goes next, but feel we are getting close."

Maybe it was her body language, maybe it was the fact she worked for the Company, but it didn't really matter as I didn't believe her.

"Sean, that's it. Now I have a question for you. Are you going to work with us?"

I was impressed with Amanda Chehwan's ability to lie and not blink. No doubt she would have no trouble beating a polygraph. She knew more than she had said. And one of those things was that she had a much better idea of the cash stream than she had let on.

- 33 -

Cardinal Francesco Camperelle was operating on autopilot. He was doing the things he had to, but he still struggled to believe his life-long friend, the Pope, was gone. The Cardinal's mind told him it was so, but his heart had not yet accepted his passing. Camperelle knew he was in a better place, his earthly suffering behind him. Towards the end, his dear friend had slipped in and out of consciousness. It was sad to see, especially for such a vibrant man. The Pope himself had told him of the diagnosis, and together they ran the Church and planned for its future even as the cancer brought the inevitable closer and closer.

What made it so hard was that just a few short weeks ago it looked like the Pope was improving, beating back the disease. Why that changed and so quickly was a mystery. Near the end, his friend had appointed him Camerlengo or Chamberlain, the Cardinal who would run the Church during the period before the election of the new Pope. Though the move was highly unusual, it was not unheard of. There had been several other occasions when prior Popes had made such appointments, but not for several centuries. Camperelle had felt most uncomfortable about the move. They had discussed it at length, almost quarreling at times. In the end the Cardinal acceded to the Pontiff's wishes. Now he had to deal with its realities.

At times like this, it was good to fall back on the centuries old customs and rituals. It made it easier to do what needed to be done. As custom dictated, all the heads of the various Vatican offices had resigned. As Secretary of State, Camperelle had resigned also. In his role as the Papal Chamberlain or Camerlengo, he had asked all the office holders to stay on in a temporary capacity until the new Pope was elected. The finality of it struck especially hard when he destroyed the Pope's fisherman's ring along with the dies used to make the lead seals for apostolic letters and then sealed the Papal apartments. The bedroom and study would be made ready for the next Pontiff.

The burial would take place in three days, well within the allocated four to six day window. He was going to wait the full twenty days before beginning the conclave to select the new Pope. This was what his friend had insisted upon. He didn't know why it was important to wait so long, but he intended to do what had been asked of him. He had already learned that many of the world's leaders planned to attend the funeral. Camperelle found this to be ironic and wondered if his old friend would be glad. During the Pope's lifetime, most of them had taken to turning a deaf ear to his admonitions. He had repeatedly warned of the dangers of a world that ignored God. At first, the secular leaders told him not to worry about such things, and then later they, and many of their fellow countrymen, simply ignored the moral positions he had taken.

80

Now in death, the Cardinal hoped that his friend was at last getting some of the recognition he deserved. However, the recently appointed Camerlengo understood well that none of this mattered. In the end, the only thing he needed to do was to make sure the wishes of his best friend were followed. Both of them believed it was essential that the right man be chosen to become the next Pope. Camperelle didn't know if other Popes had obsessed about their successor. No matter, he had his instructions. He would follow them at all costs.

- 34 -

It wasn't traditional, of that he was sure. He had planned on personally contacting every one of his fellow voting cardinals before the conclave began. That alone he supposed was a good enough reason for the long wait. The message he was to give to each was one he had been instructed to give and had come as a result of much prayer and reflection. He had also been told to distribute a reading to the cardinals for their reflection it came from the Second Epistle of Saint Peter verses ten to fourteen and verses eighteen. He would deliver it in Latin, again as requested. It read:

But the day of the Lord shall come as a thief, in which the heavens shall pass away with great violence and the elements shall be melted with heat, and the earth and the works which are in it, shall be burnt up.

Seeing then that all these things are to be dissolved what manner of people ought you to be in holy conversation and godliness?

Looking for and hasting unto the coming of the day of the Lord, by which the heavens being on fire shall be dissolved, and the elements shall melt with the burning heat?

But we look for new heavens and a new earth according to his promises in which justice dwelleth.

Wherefore, dearly beloved, waiting for these things, be

diligent that you may be found before him unspotted and blameless in peace,

But grow in grace and in the knowledge of our Lord and Savior Jesus Christ. To him be glory both now and unto the day of eternity.

To ensure there would be no misinterpretations he had instructed his aide, Monsignor Giovanni Bartolo, to make sure each Cardinal received the Biblical passage in his respective language, as well as in Latin before the voting began.

- 35 -

"Marvelous meal, Adrian, simply wonderful," John Stevenson said as he approached Chalmers.

"Thank you, John. I was glad you and Janice could make it. I assume she is feeling better?"

"Oh much better; it is simply amazing what the mind can do."

"John, are you sure it was just her mind?" Chalmers asked as he steered the much shorter Stevenson out to the patio. John Stevenson was unknown to the general public but his products were not. He was the most successful producer in Hollywood.

Stevenson looked about and in almost a whisper replied, "Frankly, I'm not sure."

"It must be quite a dilemma for you to admit such a thing coming from the land of liberals and agnostics?" A shadow crossed Stevenson's face but he said nothing. It was generally acknowledged that Chalmers could display all the tact and finesse of a shotgun. This was one of those times. "Incurable leukemia, wasn't it?"

"Yes, she was diagnosed five months ago and was given at most six months to live."

"John, I understand Janice is in complete remission." Stevenson stared out at the Washington skyline thinking. He had told very few people of this new development and Adrian Chalmers certainly wasn't one. Friends had told him Chalmers had a very long reach.

Stevenson cleared his throat, "Your understanding is accurate." As the two men talked, Chalmers had boxed Stevenson into a corner of the patio. Stevenson made a move to return to the rest of the guests, but Chalmers blocked his way

"John, I understand Janice was taking treatments at Georgetown University Hospital."

"She was."

"I thought she would have stayed in L.A. I understand UCLA Medical is outstanding."

"Adrian, Lotus Land has any number of fine medical institutions. It was simply that Janice has family in D.C."

"But weren't you in Hollywood?"

"Yes, but unfortunately I was trapped in a project. After much discussion we both thought it better for her to come East."

"I didn't know Janice was a Catholic."

"Raised as one and then fell away, as they would say."

"I see. Well, whatever produced the remission, I would call it a miracle," Chalmers said, as he lowered his voice and stepped closer.

Stevenson fidgeted, rocking from side to side. Chalmers had clearly stepped inside comfort zone. "Yes, one could call it a miracle."

"John, didn't Janice run into a priest who was able to help her?"

"Yes, she did. A family member suggested that she talk to a Father Lukas Schafer. He is pastor at Saint Charles Borromeo parish in Arlington, Virginia. As it turned out, they became good friends. Janice says their conversations made all the difference in the world. I've only met him a couple of times, but the man is dynamic. Now if you will excuse me, I should get back to my wife. As one would expect she tires quite easily."

"Yes, of course. I too need to return to my duties as host." With that, Chalmers stepped aside.

As Chalmers re-entered the Presidential Suite he signaled to Edward. "Edward I need you to help the Stevensons."

"Is there anything in particular I'm to help them with?"

Edward had worked the Presidential Suites at the Four Seasons for as long as Chalmers could remember. The man had a certain refined quality. It was almost impossible to find that in hotel help anymore. "Yes, Mr. Stevenson's wife is quite tired. She may need some quiet time before re-joining us."

"May I suggest she be able to use the guest bedroom to refresh?"

"Yes, that would be fine."

"Is there anything else sir?"

"Yes please ensure that Mrs. Stevenson is afforded her

84

privacy. I would hate to see her disturbed. They made such an effort to come and I would hate to see them have to leave so early."

"Anything else?"

"Please encourage Mr. Stevenson to mingle, I will check on Mrs. Stevenson later."

"Very good sir, I understand."

- 36 -

"I do miss Margaret and her style. You were right to continue entertaining after her passing."

Chalmers had seen Penelope Wright-Smith, one of Margaret's closest friends approach him as he talked to Edward. He had hoped that she would become distracted by another guest. Unfortunately that had not occurred. "I miss her also," he replied briefly. Chalmers began to tune Penelope out as she prattled on,

"It must have been her upbringing."

"Pardon me?" Chalmers asked.

"Your deceased wife's background, she was a true patrician."

Chalmers couldn't argue about that nor did he want to prolong this conversation longer than he had. His deceased wife's family, the Standish-Lowell family wasn't the first in America, that honor belonged to the founders of Jamestown, though arguably they were the first family of New England. "Yes Margaret was always a very good hostess."

"I'll say, entertaining and connecting was a way of life for

85

her and her family." Barely stopping to catch her breath Penelope asked, "How are Miles and Aileen doing?"

"Both are doing well, all things considered. They took their mother's death hard."

"Yes, I suppose anyone would have taken it hard first their father and then their mother."

Did this woman seriously think it was bad form to grieve? Both his stepchildren were in graduate school. "I thought a tour of Italy would be good for them. It should get their minds off the past and let them think about the future."

"I can't remember what are they studying?"

Chalmers wished he could end this conversation without totally offending Penelope. "Not the most practical of studies. Miles is getting a doctorate in Religious Studies, and Aileen is getting an Art History master's with an emphasis in the Renaissance."

"Then Italy was quite the good idea." Chalmers nodded. Margaret's children were nice kids. Their father had died in an automobile accident about three years before he and Margaret had married. He had married late in life, as they say, and she was five years older than he; consequently, they hadn't had any children together.

"Thank you, I'm so glad you agree." Chalmers could see that Penelope had taken offense to what he had said or maybe how he had said it, but he frankly didn't care. He knew everyone considered him, at best, stuffy and standoffish or, at worst, cold and uncaring. He didn't necessarily agree with them but it was not

86

important. It had nothing to do with achieving his goals. To achieve the results he wanted, all he needed was the right front man, one who was both popular and controllable. He had not yet found the right person, but he had a lead on someone. He knew ultimately someone would be found. And that someone would be the right person at the right time. It could be no other way. He prayed for it daily.

Chalmers knew he should say something to Penelope to help assuage her feelings, but he just didn't have it in him. Rather what he did have in him was an ever increasing need to escape. "Penelope if you would please excuse me for a moment, I need to check on Mrs. Stevenson." Without waiting for a response Chalmers walked towards the guest bedroom.

- 37 -

"Hello," Adrian said as he entered the guest bedroom.

"Who is there? Janice Stevenson asked as the lights in the room had been dimmed.

"Adrian Chalmers."

"Oh Adrian, how nice of you to take such good care of me. I didn't want to leave early, but I tire so easily. By letting me use this bedroom it has allowed John to stay and circulate. It will do him good."

Chalmers made a mental note of Janice Stevenson's comment. "It was my pleasure. Are you doing better?"

"Yes, thank you. The rest has helped me a great deal."

"I'm glad to hear you are doing better. Is there anything thing I can get you?"

"No, I'm just fine. Now you need to get back to your guests."

"Janice you are one of my guests and I would feel remise we didn't visit."

"Well Adrian what should we talk about? Perhaps we could talk about how nice it is that you have carried on Margaret's tradition of entertaining?"

"Janice, I think we would both find that boring." Chalmers hated the tedium of what 'society' referred to as entertaining, the small talk, the drivel, however he had been taught from an early age that it was essential to maintain the family contacts. His father had repeatedly pointed out to him that these contacts had taken years to develop, and they were the family's most important asset. By knowing the right people it was always possible to retain wealth and position.

"Well then how about old times?" Janice offered.

"You know my family story as well as I know yours. It's just that John doesn't know we are so well informed about each other."

"When I was diagnosed I decided to tell John our little secret."

"Did you?"

"You mean that we are distantly related?"

Chalmers paused, "well yes."

"I did. I told him."

"What exactly did you say?"

"I told him the Irish side of my family and yours began in America when two first cousins came here to escape the famine. I also mentioned to him that yours had done better financially; that your grandfather Thomas, your mother Colleen's father, made a fortune during the war. His wealth had come from a variety of sources, but mostly from lucrative government war contracts. With his wealth, old man Thomas had bought all manner of things, mostly real estate, though he did manage to pick up a radio station in Richmond, Virginia, when a man he had lent money to defaulted."

"I see. What else have you told him?" Chalmers asked with a somewhat dry mouth.

"I told him like the good Irish Catholic parents they were he and his wife had had a large family, six children wasn't it?"

"Yes."

"And that when Thomas died, the family's financial pot had to be cut seven ways, six siblings and the federal government. Thomas O'Sullivan had unfortunately died before the estate tax had been lowered, and, as such, the federal government's cut had been substantial. Colleen the rebel of the family had ended up with the radio station the asset no one else wanted."

"Anything else?" Chalmers asked looking hard at Janice Stevenson.

"I just completed your family story."

"Which would be?"

"That in order to marry your mother, your father had agreed to allow his children to be raised as Catholics. Julian Chalmers didn't much care about religion in general or any sect in particular.

Thus it wasn't hard for him to accede to Colleen's wishes as he badly wanted to marry her. As it turned out, you were an only child and thus the first and only Chalmers ever to be raised Catholic. That was hard on you wasn't it?"

"At first, it seemed that at every private school I attended I was in a group of one. I got teased a lot. Later I saw being different as something special." Chalmers stopped and said no more. There was more but she didn't need to know that. As time passed this belief had grown stronger as he had come to believe that God had a special mission for him, a mission that would soon enter its final and most important stage.

"Adrian are you okay?"

"Yes, why do you ask?"

"You stopped speaking so abruptly."

"I did? I hadn't noticed. Chalmers nodded, "and the other thing about you and I?"

"I got better."

"That is understandable."

"Adrian I knew you would see it that way. Why don't you tell me what is on your mind?"

"Very well, let's talk about Lukas Schafer."

- 38 -

Chalmers' angular six-foot-five-inch frame occupied an overstuffed chair with his stocking clad feet stretched out on the coffee table. All of his guests had left, and the hotel staff had just completed their tasks. He was alone enjoying the solitude and the

90

quietness of the late hour.

He was toying with a number of different thoughts and possible courses of action, weighing each one for the desired effect, when the silence was broken by the buzz of his cell phone. He looked at the number and answered it. "Did you get the information, David?"

"Yes sir."

"Good, so Stevenson is broke."

"It seems his reputation is much better than his investment making ability."

"So I take it that he still the go-to producer?"

"Yes, there isn't any question about that. No one seems to know how precarious his finances are. His studio is in hock up to its proverbial eyeballs. The only thing he hasn't mortgaged is his contact making ability. I'm certain he would have leveraged that if he could have.

Chalmers smiled at the news. "It seems we may have a willing partner."

"Mr. Chalmers, from what I have learned, Stevenson will do almost anything to keep up appearances."

"What about the other thing?"

"The priest, Lukas Schafer, seems to be the genuine article sincere, charismatic, in short a perfect candidate. You should know he and his fellow conspirators have written a document, a manifesto if you would, on the changes they believe are needed for the Catholic Church in the twenty-first century. You should check him out for yourself."

"I intend to."

"David, does he have any… weaknesses?"

"He doesn't appear to, though he is an idealist and like most idealists prone to seeing things as they can be, not as they are."

"Excellent work, David, you've given me the information I hoped for. I'll get back to you shortly with new instructions."

"Yes sir."

- 39 -

"Mr. Chalmers is available now, Father, would you please follow me?"

Lukas Schafer understood that the receptionist was not asking him a question. He quietly rose from the expensive leather chair and followed the attractive young woman into Adrian Chalmers' corner office.

Adrian Chalmers rose from behind his desk and walked to him, "Father Schafer, how nice to see you."

"Please call me Lukas."

"Well Lukas, let's sit down and talk." Chalmers guided the young priest towards an informal seating area in Chalmers' large executive office.

Chalmers took his seat. "You look tired, Lukas are you okay? Would you care for some coffee or water?"

"No thank you, I'm fine. Though, I must confess, I am tired. I stayed up to watch the Pope's funeral Mass and burial ceremony on television."

"Hah, yes. I tried to, but I must admit I fell asleep. The Pope was a great man, a defender of the faith in precarious times."

"I suppose that depends upon your point of view. He was certainly a well-intentioned man."

"I will grant you that. I think now is a time of great opportunity."

"That is something we can agree upon."

"Quite."

"Mr. Chalmers."

"Please call me Adrian."

"Adrian, I must say I was surprised when you called. Frankly I was surprised you even knew of me."

"Father, you are far too modest. I believe we've attended a number of the same events. As I recall the last one was the Cardinal's anti-abortion fund raiser."

"Yes I was there but as I recall you sat much closer to his Eminence than I."

"It's just that I am probably a larger contributor than you."

"I'm sure you are."

"You sound as if you disapprove. Are you in the money is the root of all evil club? Money is not evil what is evil is how money can be used. Without the proper help the Good News would be difficult to spread. Wouldn't it, Father?"

Schafer briefly studied Chalmers, The words the man used

were correct, friendly, even jovial, but he himself was not. Under the facade, his demeanor was cold and calculating. "Still in all I was surprised."

"Oh, why is that?"

"For any number of reasons." Schafer waited for Chalmers to respond but nothing came forth.
There was something about this man as he had heard from others. "For one, our religious politics are not the same."

"Why do you say that, Father?"

"I have listened to your radio stations. The content is slightly more to the right than I am."

Chalmers smiled, but it was all teeth and no mirth. "Lukas, I beg to disagree."

"Oh?"

"My audience wants to hear socially conservative programming. I'm filling that need."

"Regardless of the content?"

"I understand your concern but I think there is little harm. There is so much filth and perversion from the left. A little right wing posturing does little harm and is, I believe, on the whole positive."

"Do you think the end justifies the means?"

"Of course not!" Chalmers almost shouted.

"Mr. Chalmers."

"Adrian."

"Adrian, why did you ask me here?"

"I think we are in unprecedented times. The direction of the Church in America, in the world, needs to be reviewed, examined and changed."

"Changed how?"

"Lukas, I understand you have some opinions on that matter."

Schafer was surprised. Had his group's secrecy been compromised? He couldn't believe that one of his fellow priests had talked. He said nothing.

"I can see you are surprised at my knowing about your work."

"Yes." Schafer continued to wonder how Chalmers had learned of his activities, possibly a parish law worker.

"You don't need to worry. No one else knows of your document, your manifesto." Schafer's head was spinning but still he remained silent. "I'm here to offer my help, to make your work known. The time to do it is now. Don't you agree?"

"Indeed I do." Schafer was still stunned but was willing to consider an offer of help. With the Pontiff's death there was a vacuum, one he had planned on filling. He just hadn't known how. Now it appeared that God had provided that answer in the form of Adrian Chalmers. Undoubtedly Chalmers had some kind of hidden agenda. But he needed to move and the offer was too tempting to ignore. He could deal with any potential problems later.

"David, you've read the script?"

"Yes, I have Mr. Chalmers. And it is a piece of crap. That's all that Stevenson seems to produce these days."

"The only taste the American public has is in its mouth. And it's a fact they'll watch almost anything as long there is enough 'T&A' in it."

"I don't think there is anything salvageable about this piece of shit regardless of the sex or violence content."

"David, maybe that's why he is broke." Changing direction, Chalmers asked, "Are you sure about your information?"

"Absolutely, Mr. Chalmers. Stevenson has to produce at least six projects a year to cover the overhead. So he takes whatever he can get his hands on. Recently the problem has been that Hollywood is in one of its periodic slumps, it seems there are very few really good projects out there. In the old days he had the luxury of passing on scripts until the right one came along. Unfortunately, he doesn't have that option anymore. He has produced some real turkeys lately."

"Money losers?"

"Exactly."

"You told me he was still the go to guy."

"He is, from what I have been able to determine his contacts are still pretty darned good, though recently he has burned up a number of favors. His money guys are starting to worry and it's probably only a matter of time before his reputation will begin to suffer. His value is likely headed south and soon he may be of no real value to us."

There was silence on the line.

"Mr. Chalmers?"

"I hear you, David. Okay, let's underwrite his new project, the entire thing."

Now Chalmers' assistant paused, "That could be a lot of money."

"Look, I don't want him out burning up any more favors that I will need or destroying what is left of his reputation as he whores around for more money. Besides, it won't cost a lot."

"Excuse me?"

"All I'm going to do is to put up the front money. The bulk of the proceeds won't be needed until after he does what I need him to do. After that the whole situation is subject to review."

"Understood, I'll make an appointment to see him right away."

- 41 -

Cardinal Camperelle! Cardinal! Bartolo was shouting. Why was he shouting and why was he in the Prelate's dream?

Something just didn't make sense. It had to be a dream. The Cardinal had just gotten to sleep. Sleep he desperately needed. The funeral Mass had gone on longer than he had anticipated draining every bit of the remaining strength he had had. The service was beautiful, steeped in tradition and filled with love for the dead Pope. However, that wasn't the half of it. World leaders, Christian as well as non-Christian, had attended and he, as the temporary leader of the world's largest Christian Church, had met with as most of them.

He was shaking now. Was this an earthquake? Certainly not unheard of in Italy, no, that couldn't be it. The bed was not moving—he was. The Cardinal opened his eyes to see his secretary, Monsignor Giovanni Bartolo, peering down at him.

"Monsignor, what are you doing?"

"I'm sorry, but I thought you should see this." The Monsignor handed him a copy of *La Republica*. The Cardinal reached to the night stand and found his reading glasses. Before he could put them on, his aide began talking again but since he hadn't fully awakened, the words were not making a great deal of sense.

The Camerlengo held up his hand. "Father, please stop talking. Let me read the article you have given me." As he began to read, the sleep vanished from his body. He almost couldn't believe what he was reading. It seemed a group of American priests, led by a Father Lukas Schafer, had issued a manifesto calling for substantial changes in the Catholic Church.

Bartolo waited impatiently for his boss to finish reading. Finally, the Cardinal put the paper down. He couldn't contain himself any more. "What are we to do? There is no Pope. Who will respond? Why have these priests done this?"

The Cardinal sighed. While it was true that this document was not unexpected, it didn't mean he welcomed it either. Yes, he would have preferred that the new Pope have to deal with this. But the Conclave was more than two weeks away. In his calmest voice he answered the Monsignor. "These priests have chosen this time for maximum impact. They simply couldn't have had better timing. No doubt they want to influence the selection of our new leader."

"What should we do?"

"I will issue a statement on behalf of the College of Cardinals."

"What will you say?"

The Cardinal paused. The document as written was not heretical, but situations can take on their own lives. Given an uncontrolled random course of events, a new heresy could be on the horizon and this was the last thing the Church needed now. "I will pray on it."

"Is there anything else I can help you with?"

"Yes, I need to know a couple of things. First, I need to learn everything I can about this American priest, Lukas Schafer. Start by calling his bishop and find out what he can tell us."

"Anything you want to know, specifically?"

"Yes, I need to know who this priest knows or the bishop suspects he knows."

"What was the other thing?"

"I suspect we may see start to see statements of support from other young priests around the world. Send an email blast to all the bishops and find out if they think there might be support coming from their dioceses. Tell them bad news is preferable to no news."

"Yes your Eminence," Camperelle watched Bartolo bow slightly and head for the door. As soon as the Monsignor had departed Camperelle again picked up the newspaper and wondered how this had gotten out so far and so quickly. How could such a small group of relatively unknown priests get such media coverage?

- 42 -

Lukas Schafer was uncertain as to how Adrian Chalmers had made it happen. All he knew was that the document, the new manifesto, was getting incredible press here at home. There was even international interest. Not surprisingly, it was creating quite a stir within in the Catholic Church. Undoubtedly the timing was perfect. The Cardinal's conclave in Rome had not yet begun. Because of this, the Church was being run by a group of caretakers and therefore no concerted response was likely. Spontaneously formed groups were springing up around the country to review the document. He was even getting support from other similar type groups around the world. The demands for his time were piling up. If he tried to meet those demands, he would end up living in airports and still most likely coming up short. His only hope was the mass media. Thankfully Chalmers had opened this door wide. Looking down to re-read the short document he and his fellow priests had disseminated, he again thanked God that it was having the exact effect he had hoped for.

As the Catholic Church enters its third millennium, it is most appropriate for the Church to re-examine its structure and policies. For two thousand years the Church has evolved from a simple collegial organization into an imperialistic, top down organization. This fact has caused the Church to lose her way in today's world.

The trappings of power, ritual and structure have subverted her ability to deliver Christ's message. Quite simply, form has replaced substance. Of course, this is not a new phenomenon to humankind. All one needs to do is to examine the role of the Pharisees in Judaism at the time of Jesus.

Jesus Christ meant for the Pope to be the first among equals, not a king. There was no need, as the role of Kingship was reserved for God. A return to the simple structure as envisioned by Christ will encourage dialogue and diversity. It is clear to all but the blind or the vested. The world sorely needs these traits to be alive and vibrant today.

Matters of custom have taken on the false force of doctrine. Many examples exist but none more notable than the prohibition of priests being able to marry. Many of the Apostles were married, and Jesus seemed to think they were qualified to spread His message throughout the world. It is more than the marriage of the clergy; it is the entire issue of sexuality and reproduction the present Church hierarchy is incapable of handling.

Change is needed and it is needed now. We, signed below, call on the world's Catholics to meet in Washington D.C. within the year to take the appropriate steps to forge a new beginning for the Church's third millennium.

- 43 -

"Are you ready, Father?"

"Please call me Lukas. And yes, I'm as ready as I'll ever be."

"Don't worry, Father, I mean Lukas, you are already a hit. We are anticipating our largest audience ever."

"That does little to comfort me."

The light changed on the camera. "Welcome. Tonight our very special guest is the Reverend Lukas Schafer," Brock Davis announced, turning from the camera towards the priest. The show's host extended his greetings. "I am glad you could join me and our viewers."

"Thank you, Brock; it's my pleasure."

"Tonight's guest is a true phenomenon. CNN USA-Today recently conducted a national poll asking the following two questions. *Have you heard of Lukas Schafer? And do you agree with his manifesto?* "Davis turned again to the camera. "You can see from our chart shown on the screen that over the last ten days our guest went from no recognition at all to be known by ninety percent of the American public. Even more amazing is the response to the second question asked. Of the general public, fully seventy percent agree, the total is ninety percent for Catholics as well as former Catholics, with Lukas Schafer's manifesto."

"Father, how do you explain all of this?"

"Brock, I'm simply amazed. But I do want to make one point very clear. This document is not my manifesto. It is the product of a group of dedicated priests who believe as I do that the time has come to act. I believe it is a sign that Jesus Christ is alive and among us today."

"Has the Church hierarchy contacted or reacted to you?"

"I hope that it is understood, the manifesto is not so much about change but about a return to a more simple understanding of how Christ wants us to live our lives."

"Again, I am sorry but I think our viewers would like some clarification. What has been the response if any from Rome?"

"Our document is not meant as defiance to the current Church authority and as such there is no need for an official response."

Davis continued, "With the Pope dead, isn't there a vacuum of authority in the Catholic Church?"

"First of all, you must remember the Bishops of the Church are the local authority. These men are very much alive. There is no gap in the teachings of the Church."

Pressing the issue, Davis continued, "But what about the Vatican?"

"As you pointed out, the world is awaiting the election of a new Pope. As I recall, the Conclave is set to begin tomorrow. During the care-taker period after the death of the old Pope and before the selection of the new Pope, the old Pope's chamberlain or Camarlengo is in charge. Usually the Camarlengo is an unknown. However, just before the Pope died he appointed his old friend and at the time the Vatican's Secretary of State, Cardinal Camperelle, to the office."

"Will he become the next Pope?"

"While it is true that he was second only to the Pope in Church authority while serving as Secretary of State and he is, in essence, running the Church, there is no way of saying who is going to be the next Pope. Though he is certainly papabilli."

"Papabilli?"

"On the short list to be considered for Pope."

"I see, but have you heard from Cardinal Camperelle?"

"No."

Adrian Chalmers heard all he needed and couldn't have been more pleased. Things were unfolding as he had hoped, better in fact, if that were possible.

- 44 –

"David, are we ready for the next step?" Adrian Chalmers asked.

"Yes. Editorials will begin running tomorrow calling for a National Catholic Convention here in Washington D.C. *USA Today* will be the first, followed by every major daily around the country. The print coverage will be followed by more media exposure. Looks like John Stevenson is coming through on this one for us."

"Do we have a site picked out for our spontaneous event?"

"Yes, I have been able to secure a permit from the Park Service to hold an outdoor rally at the Mall. We can use the Lincoln Memorial as the dais."

"Excellent, very symbolic."

"I'm glad you approve, Mr. Chalmers. Is there anything else you want done?"

"Yes, a couple of things. Be sure to book enough rooms and tell Stevenson to alert the media. I want this event to be front page."

"What about the Papal Conclave? Won't that create an issue?"

"Not at all. The timing is perfect, a never ending news cycle, first from Rome, all secretive, and then an open mass rally from home. The setting and timing is perfect. This is the time to establish an independent America Catholic Church unencumbered by the trappings of old imperial decaying Europe."

"How should I pay for all of this?"

"Use the Hope for America Foundation. The money should be untraceable. I can't afford to have some busy-body, modern-day Woodward and Bernstein snooping around."

"Yes sir."

- 45 -

Cardinal Camperelle was ready, at least he hoped was. He had prayed for everything—wisdom, strength, whatever was required to bring the conclave to a successful conclusion. The opening Mass had concluded, and all his fellow Cardinals had taken their places around the Sistine Chapel. It was now time to call the meeting to order. Camperelle looked around the Chapel from his seat at the altar which for the Conclave served as a temporary dais for this most holy of gatherings. All voting Cardinals were present, including the newest one number one hundred and twenty 120, Salim Ateek.

After and before the informal gatherings and meetings that had preceded the Conclave, he had heard rumors that many considered him as the logical successor to his old friend and mentor the late Pope. It seemed that many of the electors were looking for a caretaker Pope. This was not what he or the late Pontiff had planned or desired. In his very soul he knew the Church needed more than that. She needed a dynamic, forceful man to occupy the Holy See and to lead the Church in the new century. He had come to the conclusion that he would only allow his name to be put forth if he ran out of options, and even then he had no plans to serve. His task, and not an easy one at that, would be to transfer the love and devotion of those who supported him to the man he believed was destined to fill the Shoes of Saint Peter.

Only about one quarter of those present had attended the last Conclave. Fortunately, he was one. With so little collective memory, his fellow Electors would undoubtedly give him a great deal of leeway in how he conducted this gathering. And why shouldn't they? Wasn't he the Cardinal Camerlengo? Camperelle rose to speak. The low murmuring quickly subsided. Camperelle thought it essential for those present to completely understand each other. Prior Conclaves had all been conducted in Latin. That might have worked in the past when Latin was more extensively used in the Church, but not today. He didn't need the Cardinals making critical decisions based upon what they thought they understood while at the same time lacking sufficient language skills to ask questions about what they thought they understood. For that reason he had decided to allow the meeting to be conducted in one of four modern tongues: Italian, French, Spanish and English. To that end, each Elector had been provided with a small headset which would allow him to listen to the debate in the language of his choice. Several of the younger Cardinals had gladly volunteered to serve as translators.

Camperelle began in his native Italian. "Welcome and may God bless you and our holy gathering. I hope you all approve of the use of the vernacular rather than Latin." He looked about the Chapel and thankfully saw only smiles. "I believe more than any time in the Holy Mother Church's history it is important that we be able to clearly understand what is being said. It is essential we discuss and deliberate in full understanding the necessary attributes needed by the next man to assume the chair of Saint Peter. I had been worried that if I gave this address in Latin any number of you would have thought I was ordering a number six pizza with everything on it."

There was laughter. As he had hoped his little joke helped break the tension. Before he could continue, Cardinal Pdozeka of Chicago spoke out. "But please hold the anchovies." The Chapel with its magnificent work of Michelangelo depicting creation and

106

man's relationship with God erupted in laughter.

Camperelle smiled broadly and waited for the room to quiet somewhat, then turned towards the American Cardinal. "Thank you for your suggestion. Now that lunch has been taken care of, I want to introduce our newest member, Cardinal Salim Ateek, the Patriarch of Jerusalem. Please take some time to welcome and get to know him during our breaks."

- 46 -

"In the way of introduction, one of the last acts of our dear friend and former leader did was to name Patriarch Ateek a Prince of the Church. I am sure many of you are aware of the many accomplishments of our newest member. What undoubtedly fewer of you know are the qualities of this man. I can tell you it was more for his character rather than his actions, impressive though his actions have been that the late Pontiff elevated him to the College."

Camperelle spent the next several minutes talking about Ateek. The Camerlengo knew if he was to have any hope of success he needed to praise the man without overly flattering him. The group needed to feel confidence devoid of conceit. Above all he needed to create a dark-horse candidate, a viable compromise candidate, one that would emerge as the next Pope when the Conclave deadlocked. "I will now stop embarrassing our friend, as I can clearly see"' Camperelle pointed towards Ateek" that he has had more than enough of my introduction."

Turning away from Ateek and looking back to all, the Camerlengo changed subjects. "The Church today is confronted with almost unimaginable challenges. Our next leader must be strong enough to deal with this onslaught of change. He must maintain the teachings of the Church while not alienating society in general. Thus, it is essential that we have an open, meaningful discussion under the influence of the Holy Spirit as to those qualities and attributes needed by the next Holy Father. But I get ahead of myself. First we must select the man to lead this Conclave, as well as those who will count the ballots. Each of you has been provided with ballots. Please indicate on the green ballot the one that you choose to lead this most Holy Gathering. On the white ballot please indicate your choices to count the Papal ballots."

Within a short time all one hundred and twenty Cardinals had risen, deposited their ballots in the appropriate chalices on the altar and returned to their seats. Camperelle then asked if Cardinals Ateek and Pdozeka could help him count the votes.

- 47 -

The ballot counting was finally complete and Cardinal Francesco Camperelle had been elected to lead the Conclave. This would be his last and undoubtedly most important duty for the Holy Mother Church. He fully intended to retire after this meeting to spend his last years in quiet contemplation. Standing again at the altar and looking over the works of Michelangelo, he drew inspiration for the task at hand. It was time to sift through the personalities and determine where the power blocks lay. "My fellow Cardinals, I want to thank you for your confidence in me to lead our most holy meeting. As I had mentioned previously, I believe it most important to discuss the qualities and characteristics needed by the man that will lead the Church. Does anyone wish to begin?" Camperelle watched for clues as the different members of the College of Cardinals shifted in their seats. Because three quarters of those gathered were chosen by the late Pontiff, Camperelle assumed their theological predispositions would, in general, be similar. What would be remarkably different would be each one's approach to those predispositions. He knew for his plan to succeed the Conclave would have to deadlock. His only chance of success would be to put forth a compromise candidate at the right time. Timing would be critical.

To get to a compromise candidate, he needed to have three cohesive voting blocks. From prior experience he had found the smallest block would eventually succumb to one of the two stronger and larger groups. When that happened, it would be over. This was not the result he needed. He would have to work hard to make sure the larger groups didn't gain enough strength to put their candidate over the top, while at the same time the third center of power had to hold together so at the right moment it could put forth his candidate, the compromise candidate that he and the late Pope had chosen.

The Camerlengo saw movement from the corner of his eye. Cardinal Giovanni of Milan rose slowly. Giovanni had been a Cardinal longer than anyone else present. However, he was not an old man having been elevated at the age at the young age of forty-one. Coming into the meeting, Camperelle had assumed that Giovanni would most likely be the leader of the European contingent. Though diminished in size from earlier times, it was still the single largest group of electors.

"Francesco, might I suggest we break for lunch? I know it is early but still…"

Camperelle looked around the Chapel for any reactions. He then saw Cardinal Sandoval of Lima rising quickly. "I concur with Cardinal Giovanni. Let us have a good long constructive dialogue this afternoon."

Before the Conclave had begun, his guess was that two main blocks existed: one made up of Cardinals from Europe and another from Latin America. He was unsure as to whether a third group would even emerge; however, for him to do his job properly it was most likely he would need them to emerge. If he failed, there would be just a group of leftover Prelates waiting to be told who to vote for so they could go home.

"Does anyone object?" Camperelle found this turn of events most interesting. It appeared that neither group was ready. He had hoped for this but didn't expect it. Now with luck he would have some time, hopefully it would be enough to do what needed to be done.

Cardinal Pdozeka of Chicago waved his hand. Camperelle tried to hide his surprise when he saw this, an American Cardinal taking an active and early role in the meeting. If there was ever a group of men that hung back, it was the group from the United States.

The priest from Chicago spoke to the group. "It seems such a pity to delay. Might it not be better to talk a little and then break? We would then at least have some food for thought?"

Camperelle tried to suppress his joy. He had the makings of a third group. If he could only couple the Americans with the cardinals from Africa he might have what he so desperately needed. It seemed to be a gift from the Almighty, one he very much needed to nurture. What to do? He needed time, to speak to Cardinal Pdozeka. "I agree that it would be nice to begin as it is a bit early for lunch. However, I would hate to make anyone uncomfortable, and it seems many of our friends are hungry. Let us reassemble at 2:00 pm."

As the group began to file out of the Sistine Chapel, Camperelle called to Pdozeka. "Would you wait a moment? I would like to talk to you a moment about a thing or two."

"Certainly."

"I wanted to get your take on a few things. I know generally the Cardinals from America generally keep a low profile."

"Yes I suppose we do. It probably has to do with simple fact we are Americans."

"And America can be easily resented around the world?"

"Yes even in a group of good and holy men."

"Maybe this time things will be different. As you well know America doesn't have the most Catholics, but for an industrialized country it is remarkably religious, particularly compared to Western Europe. It is also the richest country in the Church and has a history of generously contributing to many groups and causes. I think it would be most appropriate to get more input from you and your fellow countrymen."

"Thank you. This is so nice to hear. In the past I've fought very hard not to have harbored some resentment. Basically, the Vatican has taken my country for granted. It is as if the Holy See would say "Give me your money and we will let you know what to do next. Though I have tried to pray it away I have not been very successful, until maybe today. Your offer is a gift from God, a new beginning thank you."

- 48 -

Brock Davis turned back to the camera and waves his hand. "Ladies and Gentlemen, as you can see there is a figurative sea of humanity stretching as far as the eye can see. Not since Doctor Martin Luther King's, "I have a Dream" speech delivered in August 28, 1963, have so many people gathered here." Davis stopped speaking and allowed the cameras to pan the crowd. This process went on for just over fifteen seconds at which time the producer signaled for Davis to begin again. "Now let's go out into the crowd to find out exactly what is being thought and said, first to Samantha Reis-Jones. Sam, I'm told you have a very special guest." The camera light again went out. Davis turned to his producer and asked, "How long do I have?"

"Five minutes, then we'll come back to you for another ten minutes."

"Okay, what do I have?"

"We are working on the final details, but the lead will be the announcement that Father Lukas Schafer has been officially selected as the group's spokesman."

"Have they chosen a name yet?"

"My understanding is that Father Schafer will announce the name, as well as the group's mission and vision statements at tonight's nationally televised speech."

"When do we get him back on the show?" Davis asked.

"Brock, you are going to love this, tomorrow night. You've scooped everyone."

Davis raised an eyebrow and asked, "How much did my scoop cost?"

"Nothing at all."

"You have to be kidding, nothing?" Davis asked his producer clearly surprised.

"Yes, nothing. Lukas Schafer is apparently grateful you gave him his first shot and he is repaying you."

112

"Loyalty. How amazing in this day in age."

"Brock, remember that he is a priest. He could be the real deal."

"I'll believe that when I see it. Until then … Davis' voice trailed off as he went live again.

- 49 -

"Lukas, are you ready?"

"Mr. Chalmers."

"Adrian."

"Adrian, I am quite nervous. However, I know I'll be okay. God will give me all the strength I need."

"I'm glad to hear of your confidence. I am sure God will give you what you need. I'll continue to pray for you even though I'm quite sure you'll do fine without my humble supplications."

"Adrian, no prayer is ever too small. Besides, without your help the group wouldn't be where we are today."

"Lukas, changing the subject a bit, that is why I called you and asked you to visit with me."

"I see. This location was a little hard to find, but on the other hand the privacy is a Godsend. I can hardly believe I'm saying such things. I know God is with us. It couldn't be any other way; just look at our growth."

"Father, I understand you are going to be on the Brock

Davis show tomorrow."

"Yes, that is correct. But I'm surprised you know this. I thought it was a secret."

"That is something you need to remember. There are no secrets in the media business."

"I have much to learn and I must learn it quickly, for the group's sake," Schafer reflected. Then he asked, "Is my appearance going to be a problem?"

Adrian Chalmers let the question hang in the air for a moment before responding. "No, I don't think so, Brock is a good guy. But in the future, you and I need to work more closely regarding the direction of the movement."

"Adrian, you have been such a great help, but you are so busy and I would hate to bother you with small details."

"Lukas, it would be no bother at all."

Schafer sat quietly for a beat. "I hate to bring this up, but you know we disagree on many issues."

"I can assure you, Father, our disagreements are merely cosmetic."

Schafer paused. "That is certainly good news."

"Father, the look on your face says otherwise."

"Oh no, Adrian, not at all, I'm probably just distracted with the upcoming TV thing."

"Are you sure? I don't want any second-guessing issues."

"Well I had always thought that our views were not so simpatico."

"Trust me on this, Father."

"I do trust you."

"I'm glad. You'll see all will be fine, Lukas. I do though want to go over one other thing with you."

"Oh, what is that?"

"You and I are both aware the American bishops have been very quiet concerning the events of the last few weeks. This can't and won't last. They will have to respond."

"I agree, but not until after the election of the new Pontiff."

"Lukas, I disagree. They will respond soon, most likely right after your national address tonight."

"Adrian, more inside secrets?"

"Perhaps."

"Assume you are correct. Then what?"

"I'm glad you asked. We need to craft a response."

"I suppose you have a point. But I don't want this to become politicized."

"Oh, neither do I. Quite the contrary. However it would be prudent to be ready with something. Something well-crafted and carefully thought out. Don't you agree?"

"Well…"

"Listen, I know your mind is full with tonight's speech and

tomorrow's interview. Why not let me take a first pass at a response. You can review it, of course." Chalmers stopped talking, held his breath and waited for Schafer's reply.

- 50 -

"Father, great speech. Our overnight tracking is showing amazing results. We haven't seen approval ratings like this in years."

"You polled my speech?"

"Of course, I hope that doesn't bother you."

"No I was just surprised; obviously there are many things I will need to learn."

"Look, Father, it's no big deal, it's just information. There isn't any harm in that is there?"

Sounding unsure Schafer replied, "I suppose not."

"Good. Listen Lukas, the reason I called" Chalmers waited for a moment, "you'll recall how I told you the American bishops were going to formally reply to the Movement?"

"Yes, it was only yesterday."

"Well, contrary to what you had originally thought, they're going to issue a statement and it will be tomorrow."

"So be it, Adrian. I still don't see an issue."

"Lukas, you may not but what if they do?"

"It'll all work out. We are all men of God."

Chalmers didn't respond.

"Adrian are you still on the line?"

"Yes, Father," he responded in a barely audible tone.

"Still, we should be ready with our response. You did have a chance to review the preliminary draft I sent you? Didn't you?"

"Adrian, I did and it was okay. I guess I'll just have to trust you on this. Please though let me take a quick look at the final draft before you release it."

"Of course. But I can assure you the final will be almost like the draft you have already seen." Chalmers smiled and hung up.

- 51 -

"Just as I thought," Chalmers said as he spoke on the phone.

"How is that, sir?"

"Those damn fool bishops. There is an honest to God Catholic revival going on in this country, and they couldn't find their collective butts with both hands."

"It is a great help for us though, isn't it, sir?"

Chalmers had returned to his normally controlled self. "Yes, that it is David. They certainly are a group of tight assess. Rather than seeing a great opportunity to lead into the future, they are fighting the Movement and that's not the half of it. Their response lacks imagination. It also seems they are completely disorganized. I would say it is a completely half-assed approach."

"Mr. Chalmers, they are following tradition, aren't they?

"How is that?"

"You know, where the effete meet to sleep."

Chalmers laughed. "Something like that."

"Without being too harsh, Mr. Chalmers, what can you really expect, there being no Pope and all?"

"They lived down to my expectations. I expected exactly what I got. Every word was pious rot. They reminded me of a group of men sitting on their horses all riding backwards. All they can see is the past as they move quickly into the future completely clueless. They love their power. A power, I might add, that is very transitory. David, it is time to press the matter. Schafer must call for a meeting of all parties involved."

"A summit?"

"Exactly, use the usual channels and get it out immediately." There was a pause. "David?"

"Didn't you agree to run this kind of thing by Schafer?"

"What's your point?"

"Won't the priest be upset?"

"Not when I point out to him that we are not responding but rather we are moving forward."

"I don't follow."

"David, responding will only bog us down. I want a Blitzkrieg, not trench warfare. If we do this quickly and do it right, by the time the old boys in Rome elect a new Pope, I'll be in

118

charge of the Catholic Church in America."

"Mr. Chalmers, what about Lukas Schafer?"

"The public won't even see the strings."

"But what if he becomes uncooperative?"

"David, don't worry about a bunch of what-ifs. I have several options from which to choose."

- 52 -

The thing about spies, or operatives as they sometimes like to be called, is that they are consummate liars. I firmly believe that you could pick anyone at random from Langley including someone off the night cleaning crew and attach them to a polygraph. Without a flicker of the needle on the paper, each and every one of them could tell you it was snowing outside even if it were, in fact, a bright sunny day without a cloud in the sky. In short, as a group, they are professional bullshit artists. My assessment included Amanda Chehwan. On second thought, it especially included Ms. Chehwan.

I was meeting with her in ten minutes upstairs. That is where the higher-ups work around here. The meeting was also going to include Alan Mitchell. Just for your information, I consider Mitchell a serious bullshitter but not in Chehwan's league, she was an all-star.

When I walked into the small conference room, Chehwan and Mitchell were already seated. Both gave me one of those looks. I was late and didn't mind one bit. After their little plan for me blew up, I figured they deserved what they got and besides I liked rubbing their noses in it.

"Sean, you are late."

I didn't respond. I just sat down and waited. I knew he was

119

trying his hard-ass routine, but then again it is hard to be intimidating when you don't hold the cards.

Maybe he sensed this. Maybe he didn't, but his tone changed. "Sean, Amanda was just telling me that she is pretty sure the CIA has found the plot's mastermind."

"Congratulations," I said. "Who is it?"

"Mustafa al Bevcar," was Chehwan's immediate response.

I looked at Amanda and then at Alan, "One of our all-time favorite guys."

"That's right, Sean," Mitchell said, "the Joseph Goebbels of the Radical Islamic Movement."

"Doesn't he live in Tehran, out of our reach?"

Chehwan said, "Yes out of reach, at least temporarily, but very much a presence."

"Yes, I suppose that would be the case since I have heard he is RIM's de-facto propaganda minister."

Mitchell spoke up. "Sean, he is a very clever and extremely brilliant. He has the uncanny ability to twist events and actions. He is a formidable enemy. If anyone can pull this thing off, it is Al Bevcar."

Turning to Chehwan I asked, "How about his guy here? Any leads?"

"I believe so. Tonight I'm scheduled to meet with one of my contacts who claims to have vital information. Hopefully he does."

"Who is the special contact? I asked. "Is it the guy you couldn't mention earlier?"

Chehwan smiled and handed me a thin file. "There isn't much, but all of what I have is here."

I looked at her and then to Mitchell; I had this suspicion that she wasn't being completely forthcoming but that would be no surprise being the BS queen that she was.

I opened the folder and flipped through the pages and then look at Mitchell. Chehwan answered my unspoken question. "Alan already has a copy."

Of course he does and I'll bet his isn't three pages long either.

- 53 -

The evening was warm and still with a hint of cherry blossom in the moist air. It was an altogether lovely night, one in which a few final strollers could still be seen walking across the meadow away from the trees where Amanda Chehwan waited. It was the kind of night that normally caused her mind to wander and to consider the many what-if's of life. What if she had been born in another time or place? Would she have married? Would she have had children? She crouched down in the trees and tried to force her mind to clear, to concentrate on the task at hand. It was neither the time nor the place for such questions she had a job to do, and a very important one at that. Still her questions kept intruding, they wouldn't go away. It seemed that as she had gotten older these questions crept into her thoughts with increasing regularity.

Again forcing herself to concentrate on the task at hand, she reminded herself that tonight's meeting was vital. The research had been remarkable. The NSA seemed to ferret out the smallest of details in the most remote corners of the world. The CIA had been criticized and many times for good reason. But in this case, her case, the Agency had its done job, though not as well or as quickly as she would have expected.

She couldn't put a finger on it, but there was something not quite right and she had had this feeling all day. She even made a diary note to discuss it with Deputy Director Hanson. She should have already had the meeting, but held off because she wasn't fully sure how to approach the topic. How do you tell the DDI you think there is a leak? Still, every time she had found a new lead or some kind of break-through, instead of being able to quickly move forward she was always stymied by some kind of roadblock. She had been in the game a long time, and there were just too many of these impediments. It wasn't normal. If she were to guess, the leak was somewhere in the information food chain, either at the NSA or the CIA. The IRS was out, it didn't know enough to be dangerous, and the FBI had been out of the loop. That was one of the reasons she had asked that the Bureau be brought into the process.

The man she was to meet tonight had helped immeasurably with her investigation. Without his ability to sift through mountains of financial data, the investigation would have been stillborn, dropped months ago. Now he claimed he had the final piece to the puzzle. She would soon learn who the domestic contact was in this deadly game of sectarian violence. If as advertised her informant would complete the link from America back to Mustafa al Bevcar.

She didn't like this cloak and dagger, hiding in the bushes thing. Too many things unseen and thus out of control. But her contact had insisted upon it, which was very unusual. As far as she knew, and she had known him for many years, he was an indoors person. Nonetheless she had come alone as instructed. That didn't mean she was without resources; she had her encrypted Agency

122

cell phone, the one with the built-in night-vision camera, as well as her silenced Glock- 29.

Chehwan re-checked her watch. Her contact was late. Since this was their first, and she assumed only, outdoor rendezvous, she didn't know whether late was good or bad. Though her gut told her it was bad and her gut was seldom wrong. She thought she heard movement to her left, back in the trees. This was not the way her source was to come but it was probably only an animal beginning its nightly hunt for food. Just in case she dialed a number from memory and waited for her cell to go through.

"Mitchell."

"Chehwan here," she whispered.

"Is something wrong?"

"He's late."

"Okay, stay ten more minutes. If he still hasn't arrived, abort the meeting. I suggest you keep your camera at the ready until you leave."

"Got it." Chehwan terminated the call but kept the camera active as suggested.

She heard noises again, still to her left but this time much closer. She was sure the only animal making that much noise would be human, probably a homeless person living here. Still to be on the safe side she reached into her pocket with her left hand and removed her pistol. She -also began to shift her position to compensate for the noise. She was about half-way done when she heard another sound much closer than before. Then it came, a blow, massive with lighting quickness. She was caught off balance, unprepared. Someone struck her left arm and sent the gun flying into the night. She staggered back under the force of the blow, seeing a shadow for the first time as her left arm hung uselessly. She spun around quickly keeping her uninjured right side pointing in the direction of the movement she had just seen from the corner of her eye. Her attacker must not have expected her to react as quickly as she had as the next blow glanced off her shoulder and back. Even so the force was enormous and she stumbled backwards, her shoulder hurting like hell.

The shadow materialized into a man dressed in black. He waited for her to react. Under normal circumstances there was no way she could outrun or out-dodge this giant for long. And she felt anything but normal. Her gun was somewhere in the darkness, without it she was defenseless. Her only hope lay in her cell phone. Get a picture of this guy and send it to Mitchell. Hopefully, he would see she was in trouble and then would send help. All she had to do was to hold on for a little while. She balanced herself on the balls of her feet waiting for her assailant to lunge.

Her attacker moved cautiously towards her. As he did she held the camera up with her right hand, snapped the picture and hit the send button. He saw this and sprang towards her. She began to pivot away from his on rushing charge. However as she did her dead left arm banged against her left leg and hit her old injury. Her left leg collapsed instantly and she went down in a heap. Luckily her unexpected fall protected her from her onrushing assailant as he flew over her, grunting as he hit the ground hard.

He quickly bounced up turned ready to strike again. By now the moon had risen giving off an eerie glow. However there was no mistaking the coldness in her attackers face. She scrambled unsteadily to her feet looking to the woods for escape. She pretended to pull out a knife and began to back away towards some cover. When he saw this he hesitated but only for a second.

He then resumed his movement this time with his arms positioned to fend off a striking knife. She felt a rock behind and began to pivot away but as she did she stumbled again this time against some fallen logs and fell backwards. She tried to rise but her legs would not respond. She backed up crab walking dragging her bad leg but time was running out. She began to pray for the first time in a long time and had time for one more picture before everything went black.

-54 -

Alan Mitchell was monitoring Amanda Chehwan's rendezvous. He hadn't liked the idea of her going alone, but could not dissuade her. Now he watched in horror as the first of two pictures came in from her night vision cell phone. It was clear things had gone wrong, very wrong. She was being attacked. He'd immediately called the backup unit. "Mitchell here. GO-GO! Chehwan is in trouble."

"Where is she?"

"Still at the rendezvous site."

"Got it. We'll be there in three minutes."

"Just get there now. She may not have three minutes."

The backup team consisted of two agents and was located about one-half mile away. Though not desirable as a backup location, it was as close as they could get without causing suspicion. It was something Chehwan had insisted upon. Mitchell now hoped her decision would not cost her life.

The driver slammed the SUV into four wheel drive and headed directly cross-country across the meadow aiming directly at the small grove of trees where Chehwan had been waiting. "The park police are going to kill us on this one."

"Better to have our ass chewed about tearing up some plants than to lose an agent."

"Agreed."

The driver wore night vision goggles and was making remarkable progress considering the unevenness of the terrain. Still, the seconds ticked by as they bounced and jumped across the meadow towards the trees. About three-quarters of the way the truck hit a ditch and went air-born. As they landed the driver hit the brakes bringing the SUV to a halt. "Damn! I hope I didn't break anything."

"Only one way to find out, let's go!" His partner yelled.

Just the he looked out his side window and spotted movement in the trees to his far right. "I see something." With that he spun the wheel and the truck did a ninety degree sliding turn. He hit the accelerator kicking up dirt and rocks as he spun the tires aiming directly at the movement he had just seen.

"Where?" His partner asked.

"Straight ahead."

"Got it. Go, go."

The vehicle raced across the remainder of the meadow, violently bouncing the two agents inside. Each man straining to keep their eyes fixed on the location where they saw the movement.

- 55 -

Cardinal Camperelle was exhausted. The voting for Pope was approaching the end of the third day. There would be time for, at most, one more ballot today. Tomorrow was supposed to be a day off, one to reflect and to pray. That is, if he could force the Conclave to take the day off. The European block lining up behind Cardinal Giovanni had almost attained the two-thirds majority on the last ballot. Cardinal Sandoval's Third Latin-American Cardinals were beginning to talk in terms of unity and compromise. Camperelle was afraid that if Giovanni promised to make Sandoval the Vatican Secretary of State, the Conclave would be over, over without the right man being chosen. Time was running out and he was becoming increasingly desperate.

Desperation made for drastic plans. He looked about the

126

Chapel and motioned for Salim Ateek to come to his side. The one-hundred twentieth and last voting Cardinal saw Camperelle call him, and he came from his place in the far back corner of the Sistine Chapel to the dais. The young man moved quickly up the altar steps and leaned over.

"What is it Cardinal Camperelle, are you ill?"

"No, I'm fine. I need you to do a very large favor for me and by extension the Holy Mother Church."

"Of course, what is it?"

"Please make a speech at the end of which you name me as being papabilli." Camperelle could see the look of shock on his face. It was apparent the newest Prince of the Church didn't know how to respond. "Cardinal, you must trust me on this."

Ateek nodded and said, "As you wish." With that he headed back to his seat against the far wall, his face a mask hiding his true thoughts.

The process of balloting was about to begin when Salim Ateek rose. "Cardinal Camperelle, may I say something before the next round of voting?"

"Yes."

"Thank you. For the last three days, as we have been gathered here in this most beautiful of chapels, I have had the opportunity to ponder the meaning of the wonderful frescos we see all around us. I have listened to the different comments and arguments put forth and have compared them to the messages presented in the scenes shown on the walls." Ateek had by now stepped out into the center of the Chapel and was pointing to the works around the room. "We all have worked and prayed hard during our time together asking the Holy Spirit to help guide and enlighten us. I have found of particular significance the magnificent work of Michelangelo depicting the Last Judgment."

Ateek pointed to the wall of the Chapel behind the altar. "Many outside this room have speculated that we are at the end of times. Some of those claiming the Rapture is at hand point to Saint Malachy's list of one hundred twelve Popes."

As Ateek paused, Camperelle looked about the Chapel. He was pleased, for they were paying close attention to what Ateek was saying.

Ateek continued, "It may well be that Christ will come shortly to judge the world. As we are so very aware, only God knows the time or the place of the Last Judgment. Surely the end will come and the need of God's Pilgrim Church on Earth will end. However, until such time, it is essential we pick the best man possible for the job of Holy Father." The Cardinal waited a moment before continuing. I believe there is a man we have not properly considered. He has served at the highest levels of the Church and has, since the death of our Holy Father, run the Church." All heads were now turning in the direction of Francesco Camperelle. "I feel it would be an injustice to the process if we ignore this man and all he has done for the Holy Mother Church. He should be someone we consider." There was dead silence in the Sistine Chapel as Ateek returned to his seat.

- 56 -

Monsignor Bartolo flicked off the television. He had been watching CNN International for days, transfixed by the events in America. He couldn't believe his eyes. In a matter of days, Father Lukas Schafer had transformed, or at least begun, a dramatic transformation of the Catholic Church in America. The simple nobody, a parish priest from Alexandria, Virginia, had become a major personality. Without question he was, for the moment, the most powerful Catholic in the United States. Bartolo wondered if he would fade as fast as he exploded on the scene, but doubted it. Schafer seemed to be making all the right moves. After the American Bishops had issued their response to his Movement, Schafer responded by calling for a Catholic summit. Naturally the Bishops rejected the call. Bartolo knew the rejection was caused by a combination of ego and Church pecking order. Schafer was a parish priest and, as such, was subject to his local bishop; much like an enlisted man in the army is subject to the wishes of his or her commanding officer. Someone so low on the hierarchical food chain could not dictate the actions of those above him. To make matters even more appalling was his popularity, not just in America but worldwide. Recent polls showed approval ratings of over seventy percent, the number for American Catholics was even higher.

Bartolo closed his door and headed to Saint Martha's House. This building was adjacent to Saint Peter's Basilica and during the Papal Conclave was acting as a hotel for the College of Cardinals. Francesco Cardinal Camperelle had summoned him. He didn't know why, not that it mattered. What mattered was whether or not he would break the most sacred of Vatican rules and inform the Camerlengo of what was going on in America. Bartolo was sure the longer the Church remained leaderless, the worse the situation there would get.

The Monsignor didn't know what was in the heart of Father Schafer. Even if one assumed he wasn't a modern day Martin Luther, direction was needed from Rome. The American Bishops had been everything but adequate in their actions so far. Instead of containing the situation they had instead put more fuel on the fire. Bartolo had always believed that if Martin Luther had been given the opportunity to work within the Church structure, there wouldn't have been a Protestant Reformation. Not only that, but many of the practices that Luther rightly disapproved of would have been corrected many years sooner than they had been.

Of course, the only way it would have worked was if the Pope had been willing to meet with Luther. A dialogue was beyond the ability of the local German Church. The parallels to today's situation were uncanny. The Church needed a new Bishop of Rome and the new Pope needed to meet with Lukas Schafer. It didn't matter if it was here in Vatican City or in America, but meet they must. A long deliberation would only allow things to grow more out of hand.

- 57 -

Camperelle had gotten what he needed, time, precious time. Cardinal Ateek's plea to consider him had split off some of the European votes. The last vote of the day had split roughly three ways with Cardinal Giovanni still having the most followed by Sandoval, and then himself. Additionally, considering that a new candidate had been considered the Conclave had agreed that there should be no voting tomorrow and that it should be as originally scheduled a day of prayer and recollection. However once this off day was over there would be at least seven more votes before another day of reflection had been schedule. After that the two-thirds rule would be dropped and a simple majority vote would be all that would be required to elect the new Pope. With God's help Camperelle prayed there would be enough time to swing the Cardinals in the needed direction.

There was a slight rapping at his door. Camperelle had asked his trusted aide Giovanni Bartolo to meet him in his room at Saint Martha's House. "Come."

130

Bartolo stepped into the room, "Hello, your Eminence."

"Monsignor, thank you for coming. How are you doing?"

"Fine."

Camperelle looked at the priest and asked, "Are you sure? You look troubled."

"It is nothing. What can I do for you?"

"I need you to do something very important for me." Camperelle handed Bartolo a piece of paper with a list of names. "I want you to meet with these priests."

Bartolo scanned the list and saw it contained the names of men just like him, senior advisors to Cardinal Electors. "The list is incomplete."

"Not really, it only contains the names of those aides to Cardinals I believe can be influenced to vote in a certain way."

"What way is that?"

"I have prayed for hours, as did our prior Pope. We jointly believed the man that should be the next Pope is Salim Ateek. Your job is to convince the aides listed on the page you hold in your hand that Salim Ateek should be the next Bishop of Rome."

Bartolo was dumbfounded. He couldn't believe what he was hearing. Such raw politicking for the Holy See was, despite his now quite jaded point of view, beyond belief. "Are such actions allowed by Church Law?"

"Monsignor, I know what I ask is quite extraordinary, but we live in extraordinary times. Please trust me on this."

"Even if I can convince my contemporaries, that doesn't mean the Cardinals will vote for the Patriarch."

"You will have to convince them to convince their superiors. At the same time, I will work the Cardinals themselves. With God's grace one hopes, our actions will bear fruit."

Bartolo took a deep breath, before he responded, "I'll do as you ask."

"Thank you, but you still look troubled. Is it what I have asked or is it something else?"

"Cardinal," Giovanni Bartolo answered, "it would be best if the new Pope was chosen quickly." Camperelle did not respond as the Monsignor got up and left his room.

- 58 -

"David, get a hold of that old crackpot."

"Which old crackpot would that be?"

"You know, that breakaway Archbishop. What's his name?"

"You mean E. Roland Smythe with a y and an e?"

"Yes, that's the one."

"What should I tell him when I reach him?"

"Tell him I need a favor."

"Will he know what that means?"

"He will unless he is now completely brain dead."

"Mr. Chalmers, can I ask you a question? Is this guy really

an Archbishop?"

"You bet."

"How can that be? Isn't he a member of some breakaway Church?"

"David he happens to be the head of the Columbia Catholic Church."

"Oh yes, I recall now. Wasn't he excommunicated by Rome?"

"He was. But he is still a bishop."

"What does that mean?"

"According to the Church, even though he has been excommunicated, he remains a bishop with all of the religious powers of one."

"So?"

"So, David, only bishops can ordain priests and create other bishops. A few years ago a theologian, I can't remember his name, found some obscure reason to question whether the bishops of the Anglican Church were really bishops. It seems sometime after Henry the Eighth's schism from Rome and the twentieth century, there might have been a change in the consecration ceremony that made the Anglican Bishops not really true bishops."

"You mean like making Pluto an un-planet?"

Chalmers chuckled. "Yes, a little."

"So what did they do?"

"Several of them ran off to Holland and were re-consecrated by a Dutch Bishop with whom there weren't any question regarding the validity of his powers."

"I understand, Mr. Chalmers, I'll contact him as requested."

- 59 -

"Lukas, it is so nice to see you again."

"Thank you, Adrian. As always it's a pleasure. I don't think things could be going any better. How about you?"

"I am pleased, though I was hoping to have something more concrete to show by now."

"I think you might be a little too impatient,"

"I hear you; perhaps it is my media experience side speaking. It's important to strike while the iron is hot."

Schafer listened but didn't immediately reply. "Adrian, I don't know much else we can do."

"Lukas, there are always options. Here what I think, and mind you, I'm just throwing this out. The American bishops resent you, correct?"

"I'm afraid you are correct in that assessment. Part of the problem is that I'm only a priest, and as such I'm subservient to my local bishop and then all bishops."

Chalmers smiled. "Yes, I know. Additionally they are jealous."

"Oh no, Adrian, they are men of God and would not

134

succumb to such a feeling. Of that I am sure."

"Oh you are? Well listen. These quotes were compiled by my assistant, David and he made sure that each and every one was independently confirmed by a third party." Chalmers read off a series of unflattering quotations attributed to a number of American bishops."

"Those are simply awful!" exclaimed Schafer.

"Here, look for yourself." Chalmers handed Schafer some papers.

Schafer read silently, growing more disturbed by the moment. "I can't believe this."

"Believe it, Father, it is verified. The question is simple, what are you going to do about it?"

Schafer stammered, "I don't know, I just don't know. It's something I would have never expected."

"Look, I have an idea. It may seem a little wild to you at first, but when you think about it, I think you'll agree with me it is the way to go."

"What is the idea?" Schafer asked skeptically.

"Have yourself made a bishop."

"What? Impossible! There is no way," Schafer sputtered.

Calmly Chalmers replied, "Of course there is. I have made contact with the Archbishop of the Columbia Catholic Church, and he is willing to consecrate you as a Bishop of the CCC."

"My God! That is heresy!" Schafer got up and walked about

the room. "That was never, repeat, never my intent." Schafer was practically yelling now.

"I don't think so, Father. It's only if you allow it to be. Your plan is to save the Catholic Church. To do that you need to be the equal of the Bishops of the Church. In this way you can be. You can use this position to force the changes that are needed. The move will create a great deal of pressure to make changes. In my opinion, it's brilliant, bold and brilliant."

Schafer sat back down. He hung his head and said softly, "This is something I must pray on."

- 60 -

If it were possible the truck bounced even violently as it approached the trees. What appeared to be a smooth meadow leading to the edge of the forest was anything but. The ground was punctured with rocks and swales that caused the driver to have to slow down or fail in their mission by having an accident even before they reached the trees. Even though each agent wore night-vision goggles, they could barely hold their heads still to see anything. Finally, they were at the trees, they braked to a halt, jumped out of the truck and ran to where they each had seen movement.

"Stay down and stick close to the trees where you can," the driver and senior team member told his partner. "Someone could be just waiting to nail us."

"Got it." Unfortunately their caution only slowed their progress even more.

The younger agent had moved ahead. As he approached a clearing, he turned and whispered, "I think I see someone lying on the ground."

136

"Do you see anything else?"

"No, nothing."

"Okay, let's do a standard two-man approach, remember be careful."

The two FBI agents split up. The older man headed directly towards what appeared to be a body, waiting only long enough for his partner to indicate that he had secured the perimeter. The moon had risen, and even without his night-vision goggles, the senior agent would have been able to see it was a woman's body lying in the clearing.

She lay on her side with one arm extended as if she were pointing towards something. The driver approached. It was Amanda Chehwan. She was dead. It appeared she had been strangled. He reached down and touched the back of her neck. She was still warm. She had just died.

He waved over his partner. "It's Agent Chehwan. I think there is a chance the killer is still close. I want you to phone this in. Stay here until Alan Mitchell sends someone to relieve you. Don't touch anything and make sure no one, I mean no one, disturbs the crime scene. Got it?"

"Got it. What are you going to do?"

"I'm going to see if I can find the killer." With that the older agent got up and headed off into the night.

- 61 -

I was home when the call came in. From the caller ID I knew it was Alan Mitchell and the reason for his call probably wasn't good since the head of the FBI's religious counterterrorism unit never called me at home just to see how I was doing.

"Yes sir."

"Agent Chehwan has been killed."

Even though the possibility of being killed in the line of duty is always there, it's still a shock when someone you know is the victim. "What can I do?"

"I want you to get over to Rock Creek Park. I want you to lead the investigation."

"Yes sir. Do we know anything yet?"

"Not a god-damn thing. Just that Amanda was killed."

"I see, sir. I'll leave right away." I wrote down the directions as to where in the park she was and then hung up. After standing by the phone trying to digest this turn of events, I went upstairs to tell Maureen what had happened and to not wait up. On autopilot, I then changed into my FBI investigation outfit, grabbed my weapon and night vision goggles and headed to the park. I figured at this time of night it would be a short drive. Mitchell had told me to go directly to the Rock Creek Park police station where someone would meet me. I hoped whomever I was meeting knew where Amanda's body was located because without GPS coordinates it would be a task and a half. The reason was simple: Rock Creek Park is large. I mean something like 1,700 plus acres along Rock Creek Valley. The National Park Service runs it and because it is an urban park, there are numerous recreational facilities including equestrian trails and various sport venues, things one wouldn't find in your typical "natural" park. Additionally, old Civil War artifacts and fortification can be found in there.

Not only is the park big, it is picturesque, meaning there is running water with the associated heavy foliage and rocks. All the things that make it easy for bad guys to hide or disappear. Over the years more than one body had been dumped there. Many hadn't been found for months, some not for years. I turned off Morrow Drive and approached the Rock Creek Park police station.

- 62 -

I rolled down the window and what appeared to be a very young woman came over to my car.

"Are you Sean Murphy?"

"Yes, I am." I handed her my identification.

"I'm supposed to take you up to the crime scene."

"Okay, hop in." As she crossed in front of my car, I noticed she was wearing a brand new FBI unisex outdoor uniform. When she got in I asked, "How long have you been with the Bureau?"

"Just finished training. This is my first assignment."

Great, I thought. A bad guy, a real bad one, bad enough to kill an experienced CIA operative, was most likely loose in the park, and I my immediate backup was a complete newbie. "Do you have your weapon?"

She looked startled but answered quickly. "Yes."

"Be sure you have it ready. Things could get dicey very quickly." That was enough to ensure silence. The only time she spoke was to give me additional directions. Finally, we came upon a clearing.

"From here we have to walk." The young woman pointed to a small grove of trees across a meadow where I could barely make out some figures moving about.

Even in the moonlight, I could see she was right. The only way I was going to drive over there was by four-wheel drive. My official government ride was definitely not up to the task. As we moved slowly towards the rise across the meadow, I looked around. There was only one set of tire tracks, most probably from the FBI. Chehwan had chosen a place accessible only by foot. I wondered why? With her injury, walking across difficult terrain must have been daunting. The only reasonable explanation was that the location was chosen by her contact or the person she thought was her contact.

We eventually reached the spot where the murder had taken place. From first glance, whoever had done it must have materialized out of the woods, probably behind Chehwan, killed her and then vanished back into the trees.

A young male agent came over. By now I felt incredibly old. I was slightly winded from crossing the clearing, and I was in the company of two agents who were only slightly older than my children. The two young agents exchanged a quick hello. They obviously knew each other.

"Agent Murphy, I'm Ben Johnson and you've already met Agent Rodriguez." I nodded as I realized I hadn't gotten the young woman's name; I had been too absorbed in finding out about Chehwan's murder.

"Who are the other two guys?"

"Forensic specialists, just got here," Johnson said.

"Where is your partner?" I figured he was just too young to be on duty without a seasoned agent.

"Agent Young is out seeing if he can find the killer."

"Is that Andy Young?"

"Why yes, it is. Do you know him?"

I thought I knew him as well as anyone. What I didn't understand was what he was doing back on an active case duty.

The last time we had talked he had told me he was on permanent desk patrol. A little boring but not dangerous and not dangerous wasn't bad for old guys like him.

"Yes," I responded. Now there was one old guy and one almost old guy on the case. I was worried. Andy was older than I and in my way of thinking really shouldn't be out on his own hunting a killer, at least not anymore. "How long has he been out hunting?"

"Just under an hour. He told me to wait here and not to let anyone tamper with the evidence."

I nodded. This made sense on two levels. One, the crime scene needed to be preserved. The best chance of finding clues as to who had committed the crime was right here. Secondly, it kept young agent Johnson out of the way. "What direction did he go?"

Johnson pointed in a northerly direction.

"Towards Maryland?"

"Yes sir.

That direction made the most sense, the closer the park got to the Maryland state line, the wilder it got, much better for concealment and possibly an easier escape. "Look, I'm going to see if I can find Andy. I want you to wait here until Agent Mitchell or one of his lieutenants arrives. You will be told what to do next. Be careful. It's possible the killer might double back." With that I headed off in the same direction as my ex-partner.

- 63 -

I didn't go far, just far enough to give myself cover from those who were at the crime scene and any bad guy circling back. I knew I would never find Andy out there in the woods even with my night vision eye apparel. The only thing I was sure to find would be poison ivy. I was guessing on the killer would look back. His means of escape was most likely south in the direction he came. There was also the possibility that he would want to make sure there weren't any loose-ends at the crime scene. Either way the killer would come to me rather than vice versa. Andy would either help flush him out or would stumble out of the forest sometime after the sun came up, tired and frustrated. Even if I was wrong and the killer kept going north being out in the woods kept me away from Alan Mitchell and whatever dictates he would be uttering regarding the crime scene.

I found a series of rocks just outside a small clearing that gave me a good line of sight, as well as pretty good cover. I had been waiting not more than ten minutes when I heard a sound. At first, I thought it was just a creature from the forest. Then I heard it again and it was louder. I listened harder, and unless my mind was playing tricks on me, the noise sounded like two feet instead of four. If I was right, it was human and whoever it was moved quickly in my direction.

I adjusted my goggles and crouched lower. Within seconds, a young man appeared. Without a doubt he was the perpetrator. If I had to guess, he was a pro, no haggard I-need-a-drug-fix or the worried what-am-I-doing-here, over-my-head look. This guy was fit, he wasn't breathing heavily. The haircut was modern-day military.

He was headed in the general direction of the crime scene but it was still possible he was just making his escape. The killer didn't look someone who needed to admire his handiwork but he did look like someone who would have no problems cleaning up any loose ends. Unfortunately those loose ends could be two very young and totally inexperienced federal agents. Whatever his ultimate direction it didn't matter I started to shadow him.

He moved quickly yet quietly and I was starting to lose him

142

when he stopped and dropped into the ferns covering the forest floor. I immediately froze and also fell for cover. I feared he had heard me. But as far as I could tell he hadn't moved in my direction. Then I heard it. Someone else was behind us both making a lot of noise and coming in a hurry.

Andy Young emerged into the clearing, panting hard and looking around for the killer. Even in the low light it was clear to me that Andy had physically changed and not for the better. He swung his weapon widely around.

Nothing good could come of this. I had to act quickly or Andy would be dead. I yelled, "Andy, hit the deck!" I dove to my left to get behind a small berm hoping I wasn't taking Young's place as the next victim. Within seconds I heard three shots. One had to be aimed at Andy, as the other two exploded into the rocks where I had just been.

I crawled along the damp ground hoping my soon-to-be-middle-aged butt was not making a nice big moving target. I decided to move south away from where Andy had been standing. I needed to track the killer and either cut off the killer's escape or warn the two newbies. I hoped Andy had taken cover in time. I moved cautiously towards the killer's line of escape. Up ahead there was a good-sized bush. I crawled to it and used it for cover. I lifted my head and scanned the clearing and beyond, out to where Chehwan's body lay in the moonlight. I saw no one, no one at all, and that included agents Mitchell, Johnson and Rodriguez.

I dropped back down, trying to decide what to do, when two shots tore through the bush where I had just been. I dove to my right and rolled away. The next shots seemed to follow me. I kept rolling until the gunfire stopped. The killer probably had to reload. To be on the safe side, I retreated farther before I popped my head up again. I couldn't see Andy Young, but I could see three silhouettes crouching behind a vehicle out in the meadow.

There was no way the killer was going to get trapped between me and Mitchell's group. Now it appeared his only option was to keep moving away, away from the crime scene.

I had three choices of what to do next. I could stay where I was and the killer would probably escape, it was the safe and maybe the smart play but the most unsatisfying. I could move south assuming the killer was continuing in that direction. Then I only needed to make sure I didn't get shot either by my own people or the perp. Finally, I could lay low and hope the killer would reappear. I decided to take the last option. I hoped the killer needed to stay and clean up something at the scene. After a couple of minutes had passed and nothing had taken place, I threw a small rock to create a distraction, again nothing. I then moved slowly to where I had last seen the assassin dive for cover. Went I got to the spot I found he was gone. The only sign he had even been there was some trampled underbrush. He had at least a five-minute head start. I was pissed, I had guessed wrong and I knew I would never catch him in the dark. More than likely he had better chance of finding me. Being dead wouldn't do me or the Bureau any good. It was time to call it a night. I called out,

"Agent Mitchell, this is Agent Murphy. I'm in the woods and I'm coming out." I sure as hell didn't want one of those rookies shooting at me by accident.

"I hear you, Sean. Come on out."

I slowly rose and headed to the group. "Is everyone okay here?" All three indicated they were fine. "Where's Agent Young?"

- 64 -

I immediately headed back in the direction where I had last seen my former partner. Unfortunately I quickly found him. My heart leapt into my throat. The third bullet had found its mark. I

144

only hoped it wasn't fatal. There was a lot of blood and not much of it inside Andy. As I bent over searching for both a pulse and the wound's entry point, I heard multiple footsteps running in my direction. Without looking I yelled, "Andy Young has been hit. Call for a medevac unit immediately."

It seemed to take a long time, but I finally found the entry point. It was near the heart. Then I checked for a pulse; nothing in the arm. Next I went to his neck. Yes! There was a slight pulse. At least he was still alive. However from what I could see, he wouldn't stay that way much longer. He needed help and he needed it yesterday. I packed off the wound the best I could. The bleeding slowed and I waited and waited for what seemed to be a very long time, but I finally heard a helicopter. I hoped it was coming for Andy. Thankfully it was. Soon the entire area was flooded in a bright light and the backwash of the chopper blades.

"Out of my way, Agent! We'll take it from here." Thankfully the EMTs had arrived. I just hoped they had made it in time. They worked quickly and within moments they had given Andy a transfusion and an IV. Next they had him on a stretcher and were carrying him to the chopper sitting in the meadow just beyond the trees. The helicopter quickly lifted off and headed for the hospital. I hoped they would make it in time. I had followed them out to the meadow and once the chopper lifted off, I found a log and sat down. I was done. It had been a long and very crappy night, one agent dead and another barely clinging to life. The killer had obviously made good his escape and we had nothing. Our investigation had depended on Chehwan's contact. Now we had neither the contact nor Amanda Chehwan. If I were to guess, the guy in the forest was not the contact Agent Chehwan had been waiting for. So, in all likelihood, the contact was also deader than a kipper on a cracker. Not that it mattered, because now we didn't know either the contact or the contact's killer. Once the director heard all of this, all hell was going to break loose.

I just sat hoping to work up the energy to join the others investigating the crime scene. I didn't move for probably half an hour. I was emotionally spent. Having been there before Alan Mitchell knew enough to leave me alone. I appreciated it. Finally I got up and walked slowly towards the body. The medical investigators had arrived and were turning the area inside out. I headed toward Alan Mitchell who was answering questions and directing everyone. As I got closer, he seemed less upset than I would have thought. He and Chehwan seemed close. My guess was that he was relying on his professional persona.

"Sean, how are you doing?" Mitchell asked.

"Pretty shitty." I didn't know nor care whether my current boss new how tight Andy and I had been.

"I understand. It's been a tough night. Come with me. I want to show you something."

I dutifully followed him to the back of the vehicle where the lift gate was up. "What's up?"

Mitchell said nothing but reached in, grabbed something from the truck and turned back to me. He was holding a camera cell phone and he was sadly smiling. "We at least know what he looks like. I've already put out BOLO."

- 65 -

In his gut Cardinal Camperelle knew it was time. It was clear the Conclave was deadlocked and was headed, for the first time in many years, to majority voting rules. There had been six ballots and six times black smoke rose from the chimney of the Sistine Chapel since the Cardinals had taken a day off to pray.

With each ballot his totals had increased while, Giovanni's had

decreased and Sandoval's had remained the same. Obviously he was picking up support from the European cardinals. Though he didn't want to be Pope, he was getting dangerously close to being chosen. At this point in the Conclave, under majority rules, the Pontiff would be chosen if just **50** percent of those voting plus one more selected a single candidate.

There was one more vote scheduled for today after lunch. If no one received a two-thirds majority then, the Cardinals would take a day off for prayer and reflection; after that the implementation of majority voting rules would come into effect.

Almost all the Cardinals had left for lunch. Camperelle walked slowly over to Cardinal Sandoval, allowing the last of the

stragglers to exit the Chapel. "Pedro, do you have a moment to

talk?"

"Why of course, Francesco." Camperelle liked Cardinal Sandoval and believed he would make a good Pope. However, the times called for more than a good Pope. The Church needed the best man for that job. In his heart he believed that neither he nor Sandoval was that man.

"It seems we won't elect a Pope today," Camperelle said opening the conversation.

"Not unless the Holy Spirit has plans we don't know about," Sandoval replied.

Camperelle hesitated. Had the Archbishop of Lima opened the door? "Your support has been very solid."

"I am gratified. But you know…"

"What Pedro?"

"I really do not want to be the Holy Father." Camperelle was surprised. So what an irony God had visited upon them.

147

Neither of the two leading vote getters wanted the job.

"What is it that you want?"

"The Church needs a Pope from somewhere other than the first world. I believe this with my whole heart and soul. We are a world Church, not a western Church. It is time to move on."

"You know, Pedro, I agree."

It was now time for Cardinal Sandoval to be surprised. He was speechless for several moments; when he spoke again, his voice was barely audible. "So you've been holding a place for someone?"

"Yes."

Sandoval nodded, rose slowly and headed for the door. Before climbing the steps leading out of the Chapel, he turned and spoke. "I must go talk to some friends. I presume before the vote this afternoon you will reveal your choice?"

It was Camperelle's turn to nod. With that the Peruvian cardinal left the chapel.

- 66 -

There was a bit of a stir; rumors had flown with lightning speed through the College of Cardinals. Everyone knew something was astir. From the way the men entered the meeting, one could feel a sense of anticipation. Whereas before lunch everyone seemed resigned to an even longer stay in Rome, now it seemed possible, with God's grace, the end was at hand. Camperelle waited for all the Princes of the Church to be seated and to chat for a few more minutes before beginning what he strongly believed would be his second to last official duty as head of the Conclave.

148

Camperelle silently prayed as the other members talked. "Please, God, let me do this right," was all he could seem to say. Finally he rose and the Chapel fell into silence.

"Cardinal Sandoval and I talked just before lunch, and we both learned a most curious thing. Neither one of us wants to be Pope." Not wanting to let the moment go, Camperelle continued on. "We were both holding our positions because we believed we had a mission from the Holy Spirit. Pedro Sandoval and Cardinal Giovanni are fine candidates and each, I believe, would have made a good Holy Father. One hopes they would say the same for me. But what this Church needs today is not good, but great. And being in the twenty-first century, we need a twenty-first century Pontiff. One who reflects the worldwide aspect of the Holy Mother Church. I believe we have such a man in our midst. He should be the Pope. I have prayed many times over this issue since I learned of our late Holy Father's disease. The man who should be the next Bishop of Rome is young and new to us. That is good and that is as it should be. The man I speak of is Salim Ateek." Camperelle dramatically swung his arm in Ateek's direction. Fellow Cardinals, I ask you support this man, currently the Patriarch of Jerusalem, to become the next successor to Saint Peter."

For a moment nothing happened, and then Cardinal Sandoval rose and began to applaud. Within moments all the remaining Cardinals rose as one applauding their newest member. Ateek remained seated, clearly overwhelmed. A chant began. "Vote, vote, let's vote!" Camperelle directed that ballots be distributed. Since acclamation was no longer an accepted method of choosing a Pope, he needed to have the vote. Besides, he didn't want Ateek to decline, and from the look on his face, Camperelle believed that was a distinct possibility.

As Camperelle had expected, the vote was almost

unanimous. Once he had confirmed the totals, he walked across the floor of the Chapel, taking his time to admire the great works of art while at the same time giving Ateek some additional time to compose himself. Camperelle worked his way to where the young Cardinal was seated. Finally reaching the spot, he spoke, "Salim Ateek, you have heard the vote. Do you accept the decision of your fellow Cardinals?"

Camperelle prayed as he waited for the Patriarch to respond. Finally in a low voice, Camperelle heard him say, "Yes, I do. And please, I ask that you all pray for me, and with God's help I can serve the Holy Mother Church to the best of my ability."

"Holy Father, may I inform the world?"

"Yes, you may."

Camperelle quickly gave instruction to have the ballots burned so white smoke would rise from the chimney of the Sistine Chapel.

-67-

Andy managed to linger for another day but he never regained consciousness. I was the only one there when he died. True it was late, but what a sad ending to someone's life. He, for reasons I never completely understood, had become estranged from his family. Maybe it was his illness, I just don't know. When we were partners our families did things together. His home life seemed normal enough but of course one never really knows.

First I had tried to get a hold of his wife but without luck. I then tried his kids with the same result. It was as if they had fallen off the planet or were in a witness protection program. I knew that wasn't the case and that the Bureau would eventually turn them up. I hoped it would before the funeral.

150

As I sat there digesting the fact that he was gone, thoughts swirling in my mind. One minute you are here and the next you are gone just like that. No instant replays, no mulligans. All that you were was over just like putting one's hand in a bucket of water and removing it. All those years of service and I was the only one there to say goodbye.

How to measure a life? Andy had been a good agent. He was honest and hard-working. The man I knew cared for his family and his country. What more could anyone have a right to expect? What could have gone wrong at home? I made a mental note to see if I could find out, though not expecting much success.

Andy had been my mentor and had been with the Bureau for a few years when we were partnered up. He showed me the ropes and kept me from screwing up too bad in spite of myself. To boot, even though he was my superior, we developed a good friendship.

Why had he gone back into the field? This was beyond me. Was he trying to exorcise some demons? From what I knew his physical health problems were behind him. But fieldwork is dangerous and just because you had done it once didn't mean you could just do it again. Andy is, rather was, somewhat older than I am and I know I'm coming to the end of my field career. At some point brain work has to become the measure of one's ability to be an effective agent. What was he doing running around Rock Creek Park at night? His young partner, Ben Johnson, should have at least been out there with him. Were there other issues? I had no answers only questions.

But I did know one thing: this case had become personal, very personal.

- 68 -

The reporters had grown bored. It had been days and

nothing. It didn't matter to them that they were in one of the most holy locations of all Christendom or that people came from all over the world to visit Vatican City whether it was to pray or simply to take in the immensity of Saint Peters and its giant piazza.

There wasn't anything going on and reporters thrived on events. Not only were the Cardinals clearly deadlocked, the real action was taking place in America where, now Bishop, Lukas Schafer was turning the religious world upside down. With little to do, they played cards, slept, read and dreamed of being free to chase some sensational story. It was then the youngest of them, an American intern, noticed smoke flowing from the chimney of the Sistine Chapel. It looked different from the early smoke, but it was so hard to tell. Black, white or gray it was almost impossible to differentiate against the smoggy Roman sky.

"Hey guys, does the smoke look white to you?"

"Nah, black, let's go home. That's it. There won't be a vote tomorrow either. A.S Roma plays Lazio tomorrow and I scored some tickets. Who wants to join me?"

A match between the two Roman soccer teams was a hard ticket to get, so many of the reporters crowded around the speaker making their wishes known. "Listen guys, I think the smoke is white."

"That's nice, but if it is, it is only the Pope. We are talking serious tickets here." It was then the crowd began to roar. The reporters as a group turned and as they did they saw the Camerlengo, Cardinal Francesco Camperelle, step out on to the main Vatican balcony and announce, "Habemus Papami, We have a Pope." With that a tremendous shout of joy rose from Saint Peter's Square. An unfamiliar man wearing white stepped out on the balcony and stood behind Camperelle.

152

"Who is that?" the young American asked.

The reporters said nothing until an Arab covering for Al Jazeera announced. "I believe that is Salim Ateek. He is a Palestinian."

"Who?" Everyone asked in unison.

"Salim Ateek, He is the Patriarch of Jerusalem."

"What is the Patriarch of Jerusalem?"

The reporter from Al Jazeera responded. "For so many of you your history is a mystery."

"The Latin Patriarch of Jerusalem is one of the Catholic Patriarchs of the East."

"Excuse me?" The American inquired.

"In the early days of the Catholic Church the bishops of Rome, Alexandria and Antioch exercised religious authority over large territories. As the Church grew, two additional seats of authority were added, first in Constantinople and later in Jerusalem. The Ecumenical Council of Chalcedon extended the title of Patriarch to these five great Sees, with the Bishop of Rome being the Patriarch of the West also exercising jurisdiction over the Church as a whole."

"That was a long time ago."

"True, today, the Patriarch of Jerusalem is the leader to the few Roman Catholics in Israel and the Palestinian territories."

"And now apparently the Bishop of Rome," the Italian with the soccer ticket connections said.

The huge crowd became completely silent as it waited to hear the name of the new Holy Father.

As Camperelle stepped aside to make room for the new Pope, he completed the traditional announcement introducing the new Pontiff, after which his Holiness would give his first Papal blessing: "Our new Holy Father, Peter II."

- 69 -

"Your Eminence, how nice to see you."

Lukas Schafer mechanically extended his arm to allow Adrian Chalmers to kiss his bishop's ring. He said nothing, merely staring at his benefactor.

"You're quiet, Lukas, is something troubling you?"

Schafer remained still. After a long silence he spoke. "Adrian I'm deeply troubled." Schafer held up his hand as Chalmers began to speak. "Please let me say what I have to say. It may take a while."

"Certainly."

"I am fearful I have lost direction. I'm a simple man and for me life has become too complex. I have made decisions that I can't believe I've made. If someone had asked me three months ago if I would have been willing to be consecrated a bishop outside the Roman Catholic Church, I would have flatly said no. Now look at me. Soon I'll be excommunicated by the new Pope. It will probably be his first official act. I wanted to change the Church from within, first here at home and then later worldwide. That was my dream, to work for change within the system. However, the way things are today, I can just as easily, probably more easily in fact, start a new Church. Every night I pray I haven't repeated one of the classic mistakes of the past. I ask myself over and over, have

154

I allowed hubris to dominate me. I worry that I now consider the Movement and myself one in the same. This is not how it was supposed to be."

As Schafer paused to take a drink of water, Chalmers spoke. "Lukas, it is only natural to have self-doubts. If you didn't have them, then I would be worried. Change is coming and it is necessary you trust me on this."

"Your words have the ring of truth. But I still have my doubts. Besides, there are other things."

"What are they, Lukas?"

"All my old friends are gone. Within such a short time, all the people I began with have been replaced by your people, from the Hope for America Foundation. The Movement has become foreign to me."

"My people have more experience in running organizations that is all. Remember, we talked about it? We agreed that what was best for the movement was to have old comrades in the field. You know their skills are best utilized at the grassroots level. Besides, you can see them anytime you want."

In a most dejected sounding voice, Schafer responded, "My schedule is so full, I barely have time to pray, let alone visit with old companions."

"You are the leader of a great religious movement."

Chalmers was beginning to tire of this conversation. It wasn't the first time that Schafer had expressed such concerns. It was just that he was becoming more adamant every time they met.

"I suppose, but I feel so impotent."

"Lukas this isn't the first time we have had this

conversation."

"I know but it makes me so uncomfortable. I need you or one of your people to make anything happen."

Chalmers put his hand on Schafer's shoulder and said, "Lukas, don't worry. This is the way it is when any organization grows as fast as yours. Why don't you take a day or so off? No harm will come of it. I can arrange a comfortable cabin with a lot of privacy."

Schafer brightened for just a moment. "I would love to, but I can't. I have a youth rally in Chicago I must attend."

Chalmers nodded. "Yes, I suppose you are right, but I would be happy to go in your place."

"Thanks for the offer, but…."

"But?"

"Adrian, it's your personality. You're not good with crowds. Your strength is one-on-one with people. In a crowd, and please don't take offense, you come across as arrogant."

"Father, don't worry, you aren't the first to mention this. Remember my offer does stand though."

"Thank you but no, it is best if I go. Is there anything else we need to talk about?"

"Yes, there is. I want to buy more T.V. time."

"We have had a lot of that already. Don't you think cutting back would be better? We think we need to move from the emotional to the spiritual."

"We will, Lukas, in good time, but I have a contact in the business that wants to help, and I don't want to let him get away."

"Well, I suppose…."

- 70 -

"Did he mention the new Pope?"

"Only once, to say that his excommunication would be the new Pope's first official act."

"But nothing about Salim Ateek's Papal name choice?"

"Surprisingly, no."

"That's not a good sign. Over two thousand years of tradition overturned in an organization that cherishes tradition."

"Yes, David, I know."

"The entire religious world is talking about it and our friend is speechless.

"I hear you."

"Mr. Chalmers, Lukas Schafer is becoming less and less stable."

"Of that I am also aware."

"Do you want me to start looking for his replacement?"

"Yes, but first we need another round of media buys. Contact John Stevenson and tell him I need his help again."

"Didn't you promise him money?"

"Yes, I did and I have given him plenty."

"He is asking for more."

Chalmers' face darkened but he said nothing instead taking several deep breaths. Finally, he spoke, "That little shit. David, this is what I want you to do. Promise him whatever it takes to get the advertising out. But I want you to change the theme of the campaign."

"How so, Mr. Chalmers?"

"I want to emphasize the organization and de-emphasize Schafer. It is time we create an organization that will continue on in perpetuity and not a personality cult that will die with Schafer."

"Got it. Stevenson can do that. It is something he excels at."

"Yes, I know. However, once he develops the campaign, makes his buys and we have the master tapes, be sure he has an accident."

"Yes, Mr. Chalmers, as you wish. At the same time, I'll look for Schafer's backup."

Standing and shaking his assistant's hand and escorting him to his private entrance, Chalmers said "David, I knew I could count on you."

- 71 -

As hard as it was to imagine, my little corner of the world had grown more chaotic, if that was possible. For one, I was sitting with a small group at Andy Young's funeral. For another, my family's local church was in an uproar. Lukas Schafer was now a

158

national religious personality and, depending upon who you asked, was either the savior of the Catholic Church or a heretic. My wife had volunteered at the Church to be on a committee to deal with the fact we had no parish priest. She had originally wanted me to do it, be on the committee, not to be the parish priest, I like my Sunday's free. I ignored her long enough that she finally gave up and did it herself.

My daughter was in a tizzy. Mostly it was the usual senior year, teenage stuff, but it was also because the good nuns at her school were doing flips over the new Pope. Some of the flips had to do with the fact that there was a new Bishop of Rome. This time, however, they were apoplectic. The fact that former Patriarch of Jerusalem, Salim Ateek, had chosen the name of Peter II had them all fired up thinking the end of the world was at hand.

I didn't want to think too much about it, but I had read my daughter's paper on the *Malachi Prophesy.* Whether one wanted to argue about which Pope counted towards the magic number of 112, one couldn't easily explain away the description of 112 which Bishop Malachi had called the *"Glory of the Olive."* I mean, isn't the Mount of Olives located just outside Jerusalem? And isn't it named for all the olive trees growing on it? The Garden of Gethsemane is located at the Mount's base. For those of you who don't recall, and that would include me up until I had read Kelly's paper, the Garden of Gethsemane was where Jesus prayed the night before he was crucified. If all that symbolism isn't enough for you, in the Jewish faith the Mount of Olives is identified as the place from which God will begin to redeem the dead at the end of days. Again for you non-religious types, the end of days means the end of the world.

Personally I felt bad. Physically I was fine but mentally the small funeral was really depressing. And when I say small I mean small. There were five of us in all, a hired minister to say a few words over the urn and Andy's elderly aunt and three of us from the office, all former partners. Neither Andy's ex-wife nor his children showed up. To me Andy was special, a really good guy, tough but fair. I knew his family was very small. That would explain the lack of relatives, but I wondered why so few from work came to see him off. It wasn't much of a legacy. Life is hard and unfair but I think that we all believe there will be a good number of people sad to see that we are gone from this mortal world. It is probably a lot more a wish than anything else. To top it all off I had been put in charge of the investigation into the death of Agent Amanda Chehwan. In my gut I knew Amanda's death was part of something larger, it wasn't just an isolated incident. I couldn't tell you precisely why it was just something I could feel in my bones, and it wasn't a good feeling.

- 72 -

"Sean, have a seat. I want to go over this report." My boss, not being one for small talk, pointed at a document on his desk. He shoved across a rather large report folder. "You can study the details later."

"Yes sir." I waited for Alan Mitchell, head of the counterterrorism unit (SACCTU) to continue.

"Sean, that report was requested by Amanda and I just received it."

The document was what we called an "outside assessment

report." The term "outside" didn't mean that it came from outside the Bureau; rather it came from a special review unit inside the organization. Several years ago in response to Congressional criticism, all United States intelligence agencies created second-look units. At first there had been a great deal of resistance to this kind of unit. I assumed that all our fellow intelligence agencies had had the same general attitude. But over time the units became more accepted, particularly for forward-looking investigations and clearly agent Chehwan's fit that mode. These units contained members from other intelligence agencies. For example, at the FBI our second-look unit typically had members from the NSA, CIA and DIA. I wasn't sure where this was going so I kept my response noncommittal. "That would be typical for an agent as thorough as agent Chehwan."

"As you know, agent Chehwan had been investigating the issue of potential sectarian violence in America."

"For six months, as I recall." I wondered how long it had really been, but I kept my mouth shut.

"Six months of active investigation. In truth, because of her background, she had been researching the issue for years on her own." Some hobby, I thought. Golf or even tennis seemed like a whole lot more fun, but what the hell. "About a month before she was killed, she requested an outside assessment report."

"What's in it?"

"A lot of stuff. Bottom line, they think Amanda was, is, right. We have a major issue here at home."

Just great, my gut was right. I hated it when it was. "Anything in particular you would like me to focus on?" I asked.

"For one, the money continues to roll in."

"Amanda told me that the money was coming into four or five major U.S. banks, but the trail went cold after that. Is that the whole story?"

"Not exactly, Sean." I am not surprised but manage to say nothing. "We also have a pretty good idea of where the money eventually shows up."

"Meaning we are missing the middle piece, and with it, who is directing the money."

"That is correct. Did the assessment group have any ideas?"

"Not really."

"Just great, without the middle we can't do anything. We can't shut it off. We can't tie the money back to Bevcar. We are stymied." I wanted to say screwed but decided not to. Alan Mitchell was too much of a tight ass.

"Your analysis is correct as far as it goes."

"What else?"

"It's action time. Various religious related groups are being established. The purpose of which is to take militant action."

"You mean like bombing abortion clinics and such?"

"That is part of it."

"What's the rest?"

"They seem to be very active in attempting to influence social behavior both through the political process and the courts."

"A lot of that goes on already," I commented.

"Yes, but their focus is narrower. Not just Christianity, per se, but specific Christian sects and associated beliefs."

"I see."

- 73 -

It was essential to find the missing link to Bevcar and buddies and find it soon. Unless we, meaning I, could establish that trail, all the religious based organizations currently accepting dirty donations would continue to do so. With a link, I was certain well established legitimate church related organizations would refuse any further money.

What Mitchell mentioned that really concerned me were both the number and the pace of new groups being formed. I feared that legitimate, yet highly militant, or worse, spurious groups would continue to accept funds regardless of the source. The more of these cabals awash in money there were, the more the road towards religious polarization was likely to continue. The entire situation had begun to remind me of the arms race between the former Soviet Union and the United States. Back then, each side continued upping the ante, building larger and ever more dangerous nuclear weapons. Not because it was economically sane, but simply because they had to be more aggressive and therefore dangerous than the enemy. Fortunately the theory of mutually assured destruction worked. I wasn't so sure we would be lucky twice.

Over time, I had become convinced that the reason MAD had worked was because one side was avowedly atheist. For them it simply made no sense to blow up the only known world. Such was not the case with groups of people completely certain that only their brand of religious belief was a sure fire ticket to eternal salvation.

163

I had two picture phone images to work with, not much but something was better than nothing, but only by a little. Amanda had managed to take two pictures before being killed. Unfortunately, it was twilight at the time and the killer had been running. I had taken the cell phone to our lab to see if the images could be enhanced. The techs told me they thought they could improve the picture quality but it would take some time. When I had asked how long, the answer was most likely three days. I groaned when I heard this. It had already been two, but knew there wasn't anything to be done.

So for the last two days I have been going through Agent Chehwan's papers at work, hoping to find something. Now I was looking through her personal belonging in hopes of finding additional clues. What I have learned so far is that Amanda Chehwan's private life if one could call her non-work life a private life, was exactly like her public life austere, dedicated, and single-minded. Her small apartment might as well have been the annex to a convent. The entire unit, except the kitchen which had linoleum, had hardwood floors throughout. Normally this would have added character to a unit, particularly if the tenant had chosen to strategically place some accent rugs about. Amanda had not. The walls were bare, no pictures of any kind, not even a crucifix. It was as if Amanda, the former nun, no longer believed but still couldn't bring herself to completely forget her past life. The location of her one bedroom apartment seemed to be dictated by the proximity to work and nothing else. Her bedroom contained a single bed, one night stand on which the only lamp in the room was placed, along with a clock radio and a four drawer dresser without accessories on top. Two barstools made up her eating area. She had converted the rest of the space to a computer alcove that I hadn't yet explored. That would change shortly as a computer technician was due within the hour. The living room held a couch, an easy chair, two lamps and a television set.

164

- 74 -

I continued my investigation examining Amada's closets, shelves and bathroom. There was nothing of significance, unless you consider the lack of birth control devices for a single woman of her age important. As I finished inventorying the refrigerator, I heard a soft knock at the front door. It was most probably the computer geek I requested, but then again there was always the possibility it was someone else. I grabbed a towel and in my best high-pitched, now muffled voice I responded, "Just a minute." I walked as quickly as possible to the front door, withdrawing my service piece and unlatched it. The door had a peep hole but rather than getting a bullet in the eye, I decided I was better off inviting whoever was on the other side to come in. In my falsetto I said, "It's unlocked, come on in." Standing behind the door, I waited as it swung open.

At first, no one entered. I did hear what sounded like someone struggling with packages. I continued to wait.

Finally, a head of straggly brown hair popped through the opening. "Agent Murphy, it's Randall Larch. Could you please give me a hand?"

So there I was, standing behind the door, my gun drawn, being an official G-man and this computer tech didn't have the slightest clue that I was lying in wait. I put my piece away and stepped out from behind the door, "Sure, what do you need?"

Randall looked around the room and began shuffling his equipment in the general direction of Amanda's computer. He turned and pointed to a case which in the old days would have held camera equipment, and said, "Please, if you would, grab my hard drive and put it next to Agent Chehwan's computer I would appreciate it."

I leaned over and grabbed the case. The box looked light, so I was surprised when it didn't come off the floor and I headed for it, instead. Larch looked at me, smiled, and said, "I should have mentioned to you how heavy that case is. Doesn't look it, does it?"

This was clearly a joke this guy had played before. "Sure doesn't." However, I was a still a little off balance and had to go down on one knee to stop from making a complete ass of myself. I happened to be looking at Larch as he headed for Chehwan's computer alcove. It was then I noticed something, something that seemed out of place for such a Spartan, utilitarian apartment. There appeared to be a filigreed grate or opening of some kind sticking out from underneath the table top where the computer and keyboard rested.

"Randall, don't move any closer, I need to check something out!" I said in a loud voice.

"Agent Murphy, are you getting back at me?"

"No, and don't be an ass." After a brief pause, Larch again began walking toward the computer. This time I shouted. "I told you not to move!"

Larch stopped.

I slowly approached the computer table, crawling on my hands and knees. I didn't look at Randall Larch, but I assumed by now he knew I was serious.

"Agent Murphy, what is it?"

"There is an ornate grate on the wall behind the computer table."

166

"Isn't that something that would have been common for a building like this in the 1940s?"

"Yes, it would, Randall. It isn't the grate exactly. It's how it is hanging. It just doesn't seem right."

Out of the corner of my eye, I could see Larch squatting down to look under the table. "I don't see anything."

"Larch, pull out your flashlight and shine it into the grate for me, will you?" Almost immediately a light came over my right shoulder. It was then I saw a small piece of filament. It looked like fishing line to me, running out of the grate to the back of the computer keyboard tray.

I stopped and double checked the floor around us. I saw no unusual bumps or bulges, nothing that could be a trip wire or trigger mechanism. I didn't expect there would be, but again one can be too careful when it comes to explosive devices. "Give me your flashlight." Larch placed the flashlight in my hand. "Thanks."

"What do you see?"

"It looks like there is a small fish line running from the back of the keyboard tray through the grate."

In a frightened voice he asked, "Is it a bomb?"

"I don't know. It could be or it could be some kind of security Chehwan used so she would know if someone had tampered with her computer while she was out."

"What should we do?"

I was a little annoyed with Randall Larch, particularly after his little joke at my expense. He was also getting a bit hysterical. I felt like telling him to do nothing and in a couple of minutes I would be happy to put the flashlight somewhere he would never forget, but.... "I think you better leave. Go outside and if anything happens call Alan Mitchell."

Without a word the computer geek scurried out of the unit. With Larch safely out of the apartment, I moved closer to the grate. I had no intention of getting blown up, but I did need to know if I had to call the bomb squad. I stopped crawling as I reached the table. It was clear the thread was attached to the back of the tray. I half-expected to see the wire being held to the tray by a piece of tape. It was not. It was held in place by an eye-screw. This was not good. The chances of a bomb being at the other end of the fishing line jumped geometrically. I got into a crouch and peered into the grate, shining my flashlight about. Within seconds my fears were confirmed. The fish line was attached to an explosive unit or something that looked damn close to one. I carefully backed away. This was a job for an expert, someone who got paid to dismantle bombs. How the Bureau ever found anyone willing to do this was beyond me but it did, and I needed one right now. I slowly backed away from the computer, the alcove and the apartment. As I headed downstairs, I placed a call to Alan Mitchell.

- 75 -

Adrian Chalmers laid the file and his glasses on the table next to his leather easy chair and pinched the bridge of his nose. It had been a long day and he hadn't wanted to read the report, but David had insisted that he do so. His assistant seldom insisted on anything. For that reason Chalmers had acquiesced. Now he was glad he had. His plan, his dream, was coming closer and closer to fruition. Success was hardly assured, but it was within his grasp. Still there were a number of variables and with each variable came a lack of control. He knew it was essential he remove all of them. Perhaps the trickiest one of all was to maintain control of the

Movement.

Lukas Schafer was becoming ever more erratic. Though widely popular with the public, the man was a mountain of self-doubts. Chalmers was wearying of constantly reassuring him. Chalmers was beginning to believe there would never be enough he, or for that matter anyone, could say to assuage Schafer's feelings.

Administratively, Chalmers controlled the Movement, having control of the most important organizational positions. However, the organization was still so new that it had not yet attained a self-sustaining existence nor would it be likely to reach this plateau for a number of years. Years Chalmers could not wait to pass. The time for his plan, his dream, was now. Sadly, he knew his personality was not such that he could directly take Schafer's place. Had that not been the case, Lukas Schafer would have met martyrdom several weeks ago.

Now it seemed that David had found a suitable candidate to replace Lukas Schafer. The question Chalmers had to address was how to approach this person. Should he go directly to him or should he use an intermediary? Each option had certain advantages yet disadvantages as well.

-76-

Chalmers reviewed the executive summary again. Raymond Gates, Jr. had known Lukas Schafer since the sixth grade at Saint Mary's Elementary School. Raymond and his family moved in next door to the Schaffer's during Christmas break.

Raymond's parents felt they had been lucky in their choice of house purchase believing young Ray would make a friend who would help him meet others at his new school. Apparently this did happen at least to some degree. However, the consensus was that Gates believed that Schafer had used him. It seemed theirs was a one-way relationship. Gates' friends would become Schaffer's but not vice-versa. This pattern of control seemed to be a key element of their relationship ever since.

The also attended the same Catholic high school. Gate's father died of a heart attack during the summer between his junior and senior year.

Lukas Schafer went into the seminary directly out of high school. No one was surprised. Everyone, however, was surprised when a year later Raymond Gates followed him into the seminary. Because Gates had taken the year off, to work construction to help support his family, he was a year behind his friend. Normally, a year in a small school such as the seminary wouldn't have made much difference in a relationship as old as theirs. It did though allow each to develop a separate circle of close friends.

They followed similar paths after ordination and kept loosely in touch over the years. It was hard not to, for there weren't many young priests in the diocese or, for that matter, in any diocese in the country. Both believed in the need for change in the Catholic Church and for that reason joined together with a group of other young priests on a regular basis to try to influence their local bishops. From this group, the Movement had evolved. Schafer, its leader, had gone on to great notoriety while Gates its second in command, had been left in an important but obscure role.

Chalmers closed his eyes. He needed to concentrate. He remained this way for a number of minutes mulling various options. Finally he smiled. He had it. The solution was so simple he chided himself that it took so long for him to come up with the answer. It must have been the hour or all the other things on his mind. Why, he would simply have Lukas Schafer do it for him, how wonderfully ironic. Bishop Schafer wouldn't even know he was interviewing his own replacement.

- 77 -

Monsignor Giovanni Bartolo had been stunned. He took some small comfort in the fact he was not alone. The world was stunned or shocked, depending upon whom one listened to. The new Pope had picked as his papal name one that he had thought would never be picked. The entire Church was asking what it meant. The choice had certainly unsettled the tradition rich and conservative organization. He thought it could portend something but he simply couldn't concentrate on what it could be. Bartolo knew almost nothing about the new Pope. However, it didn't matter. His mentor and superior, Francesco Cardinal Camperelle, thought highly of the man. Whispered rumors around the Vatican told of how Camperelle had even orchestrated the election of Salim Ateek. Knowing Camperelle as he did there could be some truth in what was being bandied about. The new Pope's first official act had been to reappoint Camperelle as Vatican Secretary of State. None of that mattered, really; Bartolo was ready to resign. The political world of the Vatican was now far too much for him. He was burned out and needed a change. He hoped Camperelle would understand this and immediately grant him his request when they met at this morning's meeting.

Bartolo had toyed with the idea of resignation for months, and now after praying for hours it was what he felt he needed to do. He hoped this would be his last walk across the Vatican in an official capacity. For that reason, he took his time. The luxury of time he seldom granted to himself. Time for once to reflect upon the meaning behind the immensity of Michelangelo's giant Basilica and its square, the Piazza San Pietro, its very size reflecting upon God's greatness and man's individual smallness. He stopped for a group of tourists who were headed for the Vatican museum. As he stood warming himself in the afternoon sun, he now realized all he wanted was a few weeks off and then to be transferred to a small parish in his native Tuscany. Standing alone, reflecting, he lost all track of time. It was only his beeper going off that brought him back. Looking at the number and then glancing at his watch he discovered he was late for his appointment with the Cardinal. He thought. This was surely an ill omen. Late for the very meeting he needed to go well. He began to pray again as he hurried to meet Camperelle.

- 78 -

"Sean, you were right in calling in help. It was hot and if you hadn't spotted it, your family and Randall Larch's would have been applying for survivor benefits."

Alan Mitchell had walked into my office and began talking without as much as a how do you do.

I was glad to hear that my discretion was the better part of valor. I was getting too old for this crap. This assignment had started out, at least the way I perceived it, as a thinking man's job: investigate, analyze and research. True, I had done a little of that work and needed to do much more. However, I had also found myself running around Rock Creek Park in the middle of the night being shot at and now becoming a potential bombing victim. No thanks. "Find anything special?"

"Yes, we did. The device was not only set to blow up anyone within fifteen feet of the computer, it was designed to take your picture before the explosion and send it to, presumably, to whoever was responsible for planting the device in the first place."

"For their scrap book, I suppose." His victims-b-us scrapbook?

"Apparently the bad guys want to be certain of who they take out," replied Mitchell.

172

"Well, we have used disinformation before."

"And it seems these guys know it."

I looked at Alan Mitchell a moment before I asked my next question. "Does that little piece of information help us in any way?"

"It does. It tells us that whoever is behind this isn't your garden variety nutcase. To me, this confirms our prior assumptions and limited information."

"You mean we are talking about an adversary with connections and a sophisticated background."

"Exactly, Sean."

"Changing the subject. Did we get anything from Amanda's computer?"

"We think maybe yes. The drive had been wiped but…."

"But thanks to our friends at the NSA we can still extract some data."

"Sean, I want you to come with me to Fort Meade and see what the computer forensic team has found. Fortunately they can see us if we leave right now."

"Thanks, sir." I meant it. At least I now had two potential lead possibilities, Chehwan's computer and her cell phone pictures.

"Sean, where do we stand with getting something from Amanda's cell phone pictures?"

"Still waiting, but I expect something very soon from the

techs."

"Still?"

"Yes."

"They know this is top priority don't they?"

I answered simply, "Yes and I mentioned your name."
Though I'm not sure if this helped or hurt.

"Well okay, let's go."

Mitchell started out my door. I followed, quickly grabbing
my coat from behind the door. Alan Mitchell sure wasn't one for
social graces. He got to where he was at the Bureau by being good
at his job, not being good with people.

-79-

"Ray, good to see you!" Lukas Schafer acted happy to see
his old friend as he rose from behind his desk and gave him a bear
hug. "Sit down, please sit down." Schafer pointed to a set of
comfortable overstuffed chairs in the far corner of his office.

Gates sat down, but said nothing.

"Ray are you okay?

"Just fine, just a little distracted."

"Why is that?"

Gates stared at Schafer, "Oh I don't know. Lately it just
seems that every time we get together I think back to when we first
met."

"You mean when we were in grade school or when you
were chasing the cheerleaders at old Saint Vincent's High School?

174

"A little of both I suppose."

"As I remember you were pretty serious with one girl weren't you?

"Sally La Caoselle. I don't know how serious I was but she was fun."

"Fun?"

"Oh Lukas, after all these years. Not in that way, she was just nice to be around. She cared."

"What ever happened to her?"

"I lost track after we broke up. I suppose she is married and has a family."

Schafer paused and changed the subject. 'How is your mom doing?"

"About the same."

"I was afraid of that. She never did recover after your dad died. Did she?"

"Not really."

"You know I pray for her daily."

"Thanks, I hope your prayers are more effective than mine. But that is past, now is now. What did you want to talk to me about?"

"I wanted to go over some of the points in your draft response."

"Which draft? I have sent you quite a number lately."

"The Movement's official response to the new pope. Could there be a more important one?"

- 80 -

"Father Gates, I understand you and Lukas Schafer are old friends."

"We have known each other for years."

"Yes, he said the same thing. You know he speaks very favorably about you. He says you are an excellent assistant."

Chalmers studied Raymond Gates. Adrian had known this man since the very beginnings of the Movement. It was interesting how he seemed to be a mirror reflection of Lukas Schafer. They were similar in many external ways—height, weight—yet dissimilar in so many internal ones—temperament and attitude. Though Gates masked it well, Chalmers could tell Gates didn't care much for Lukas Schafer or at least what he had become. David's report suggested that he chafed at being a perpetual number two. Pushing a little harder, Chalmers spoke again. "It must be quite the challenge keeping up with Bishop Schafer."

Without emotion Gates responded, "I'm used to it."

"But still, I feel for you."

"It isn't as hard as you might imagine. Lukas Schafer is quite predictable. It is easy to stay ahead of him. My concern is to ensure the Movement outlasts our personality boy."

"You disapprove?"

176

Gates paused. "Not so much, but the organization needs to be founded on something more than emotion."

"Enthusiasm is a good thing, isn't it?"

"Mr. Chalmers, I sense you are probing me. Let me make myself clear. Lukas Schafer is both the best thing that could happen to the Movement, and the worst. In my opinion, we are about out of the best phase. It is essential we move forward as something more than a holy hosanna, touchy-feely club. To make a lasting difference and to be continuously effective, this organization must mature. It needs to embrace new attributes. I personally doubt Lukas Schafer is up to this phase of the program."

"What might those qualities be?" Chalmers inquired.

"Mainly it needs a sound distinctive theology, a unified belief system supported by a central authority."

"Sounds a lot like the Catholic Church," Chalmers said.

"The Church has lost its moral way. The only reason it remains a force today is its structure. An entity that has evolved over two thousand years and that is still functioning is worthy of copying." Gates folded his arms.

"I see, Raymond. How are you going to ensure such maturation?"

"Wait and see."

"Excuse me?"

"I effectively control the organization."

"To correct you, Father, it was I who built the organization, and I've made sure my people are in the key positions."

"Adrian, you can think what you like. But I'll say it again, all the people in those positions I consider key are loyal to me."

"What of loyalty to Bishop Schafer?"

"There are different kinds of loyalty." Gates said. "Trust me, if you want something done, see me."

Chalmers smiled, "Do you think can run The Movement?"

"If need be, yes."

"I see. On another subject, "have you gotten all the promotional materials from John Stevenson's office?"

"Yes, the last of it arrived yesterday."

"Raymond, have you had a chance to review it?"

Gates again paused. "Yes, the first of it, I haven't had chance for the stuff that just came in."

"Well, what did you think of what you saw?"

"Adrian, I thought it was good. I liked it. The emphasis has finally moved away from that of a Lukas Schafer personality cult to extolling the values of the Movement."

"Well, I can assure you that you will like the part you haven't reviewed. The entire piece moves in the direction you want."

Gates' eyes twinkled and he smiled broadly almost shouting he said, "That is good news!"

Chalmers eyed Gates. This normally stolid man had exhibited more personality in the last few minutes than he had in any time since he'd known him. Though he had had some doubts, they were all gone now except one. David was right. This man would do quite well.

- 81 -

The drive through suburban Maryland took about forty-five minutes. Alan Mitchell didn't say a word during the entire trip. After turning off the main road it took another fifteen minutes as we wound our way to the NSA building we were looking for. We parked the car and showed our credentials to the sentries at the front door. The guard ran our identifications through the computer, and we were allowed to enter the building. We were asked if we needed directions. Agent Mitchell said that he didn't and headed off down a long hallway. I followed, not knowing if he was really sure where to go. I had been here several times and managed to get lost each and every time. What I was sure of was that he suffered from the very male disease of not asking for directions, ever. And people wonder why it took Moses forty years to lead the Israelites out of the desert. I can just imagine Moses talking to his brother Aaron. *"Hey bro, do you think we should've checked back at the last oasis whether we needed to go north or east? Nah, no need. I'm sure I know how to get there. First we go south for thirty miles and then turn east. It's just ten more miles and we hit the Red Sea, from there we turn north and before you know it we will be in Israel."* It seemed forever, but Mitchell finally grunted something about finding the lab. He opened the door and we went in. I followed him to the receptionist who told him that we would be helped in just a few minutes. As we sat down, I wondered if the time here was like airline time. You know, fifteen minutes can be anywhere from half an hour to an hour and a half.

Remarkably, within about five minutes a young technician

wearing the proverbial long white coat approached us. "Are you agents Mitchell and Murphy?"

I looked around. There wasn't anyone else in the room. So who else could we have been?

Alan Mitchell answered for both of us. "Yes."

"Please follow me," the young woman said. I followed my boss, grateful that apparently the NSA didn't want to piss off Alan Mitchell by making him wait around.

The tech placed her hand on an entry pad and a keyless, handle-less door opened with a whooshing sound and then closed with a thud immediately after I the last in our trio, entered the hallway. We walked past lab after lab filled with various kinds of test equipment and white coated workers. The hallway turned left, and we followed it walking past more labs still filled with the same ubiquitous worker bees, but this time the rooms were filled with computer equipment. Finally, she led us into a conference room and told us someone would be would be with us in a moment.

- 82 -

Bartolo was out of breath when he burst into the Cardinal's office saying, "I am sorry for being late, Your Eminence."

Seated at his desk, Camperelle looked up at him over his glasses. "No problem, Monsignor. Please sit down. We have much to discuss." Bartolo took a seat across from the Cardinal.

"What did you want to discuss your Eminence?"

The Secretary of State put down some papers and waved at them. "Quite a mess in America right now, isn't it?"

"Yes, unfortunately much happened while the Pope was

180

being elected."

"Yes, the power vacuum made a difficult situation worse. One would have thought the local bishops would have done a better job of dealing with the situation." Bartolo remained silent. "Unfortunately there is a certain lack of talent and ability in that group." Camperelle paused and exhaled. "Well, for that matter, most local bishops lack the ability to deal with the changing world. No matter. I believe we have the man to do that for us now."

"Peter II?" Bartolo said in a barely audible voice.

"Father, you disapprove of the name he took?"

"It is not for me to approve or disapprove, though the choice concerns me."

Camperelle got up and began to pace. "A name is just a name. What concerns me is how the world might interpret his choice. I fear that it may be seen by some as a sign foretelling the end of the world. And as such use it as a justification to do unspeakable things in the name of salvation."

"Maybe it is the beginning of the end!" Bartolo blurted.

"That may indeed be the case. However, I certainly wouldn't know, and neither would those making such predictions. We must remember the words of Christ, *"Neither the time nor the place."* Camperelle stopped and returned to his desk. "Nonetheless, until the world comes to an end, we have a job. That job is to bring Christ's message to the world, to help do that we need to tell the world about the new Pope. I need your help for this most important job."

Bartolo was trapped; there was no way out. He could barely respond, "What do you want me to do?"

If he noticed, he showed no reaction and Bartolo quickly regained his composure. "Father, I want you to get the word out. The world must know of the new Pope, his qualities, the things he has done, said and written. He is the right man at the right time. The world must know this."

Bartolo was initially crestfallen and quickly overwhelmed. How could he accomplish what the Cardinal wanted? He might as well have been asked to convert all Islam as to do this thing. "How should I begin? Your Eminence, I'm sure I can't do this," Bartolo protested.

"Of course you can. Begin with the story of how he defused the situation at Jericho on the West Bank, or possibly tell how he came to write his book, *How I Found Peace in a Troubled Land*."

Bartolo nodded. "Yes, either would be a good beginning, but the West Bank story was the most initially compelling. I felt it was quite a moving story. It revealed the character of this unknown but potentially impressive new Pope."

"I've read it as well and agree with you."

"It is a relatively recent tale as I recall."

"Yes, as I remember it, though you will of course, have to double check; it was just after he had been named Patriarch. He was visiting friends and family in his home town of Jericho when violent clashes between the local Jewish settlers and the Palestinians broke out. I don't recall the cause, not that it really matters. It doesn't take much to get those two groups to go at each other then or now."

182

- 83 -

"I will have to double check. As I recall it," Bartolo said, "fighting had broken out in Jericho and as soon as he had heard of it Archbishop Ateek headed there from Jerusalem. Jericho was his home and is one of the oldest cities in the world and, like so many places in the region, important to Jews, Muslims and Christians."

"To the Jews, it was the first city in Canaan. Joshua arrived there after forty years wandering in the desert. It was at Jericho that God instructed the Prophet to have his troops march around the walls of the city once a day for six days. The force was led by seven priests walking beside the Ark of the Covenant which contained the Ten Commandments, and as they walked they blew their ram's horns. On the seventh day, the Jews circled the city seven times, and when their horns were blown, the city walls fell, the Canaanites were defeated and the city was theirs."

"To us Christians, it is reputed to be the site of the Mount of Temptation where tradition says Jesus was tempted by Satan," said Camperelle.

"To the Palestinians, it is the site of Caliph Hisham's Palace which dates from the seventh century and the beginnings of Islam. It was a place where the true followers of Muhammad had come following his death in 632," Bartolo continued.

"And sadly, in modern times it has become the location of innumerable refugee camps," Camperelle added.

"I remember the Archbishop saying that he became involved "because he believed he was the only truly impartial person in the area and for that reason he hoped he would be able to mediate disengagement.'"

"When he arrived at the scene, two mobs were fighting each other. Molotov cocktails and rocks were being tossed back and forth. The Israeli security forces and Palestinian freedom fighters were coming down the main road from opposite directions towards each other." Unbelievable as it seems, he entered the fray by driving into the no man's land between the two sides. The very fact that someone had done this caused a pause. Filling that pause, Ateek, in full bishop's regalia, climbed onto the roof of his Land Rover with a megaphone in hand. First in Hebrew and then in Arabic he addressed the mob asking for them to send representatives to meet with him in the middle of the field. Remarkably each side complied. He managed to get the two sides to talk. For this reason the confrontation cooled by the time the IDF arrived, and because of this, there was no need to immediately use tear gas or other riot control techniques. Sensing a change, the heavily armed Palestinians chose to do nothing and waited warily in the distance. Under the gun, literally, Ateek managed to get the leaders to agree to meet again. Once this news had gotten back to both sides, what once had been a surely angry mob became crowds of people returning to their homes."

"The representatives met at Ateek's home for further negotiations. The reasons why were complex and have been debated, though both sides seem to agree that much of it had to do with the Bishop himself. The results were amazing: a new informal and badly needed backroom channel was opened. The channel managed to last for a number of years. During those years the calm led to economic prosperity with even a casino opening in the area."

"Good, good. Be sure to get it out as fast as you can. After that, let's explore how his writings can be disseminated," the cardinal said.

184

"Yes, Your Eminence." He rose to leave, his heart still heavy from not being able to resign.

Camperelle then rose and put his hand on Bartolo's shoulder. "And Giovanni, once this task is completed I am transferring you to San Domenico Church in Sienna." Bartolo couldn't believe his ears. How could the Cardinal know? Flabbergasted, all Bartolo could say was, "Thank you."

- 84 -

It was dusk and John Stevenson was heading to his home in Malibu canyon. He was pushing his vintage convertible Jag hard, trying to take each turn and corner as fast as he could. Maybe with luck he could purge his feeling of being soiled. He got that dirty grimy feeling every time he dealt with Adrian Chalmers or one of his minions. Maybe the feel of the wind rushing past him would clear his soul. However, he was having no luck. The man and all he stood for, or the lack of what he stood for, clogged his every thought.

That Bastard is what John Stevenson had come to call Chalmers, in private anyway. It wasn't one thing, it was the entire package. The man was completely insufferable. And compared to his asshole assistant, David with no last name, Chalmers was a saint. Chalmers had promised him a substantial amount of money to make Lukas Schafer and the Movement famous. He had done exactly that and to boot he had done it to his detriment. He had had to turn down and postpone several promising projects because of Chalmers' demands. Normally, he would have told Chalmers to shove it when first approached, but he needed the money, badly needed it. At the time, several of his recent projects had been very successful artistically but had turned into commercial flops. Normally, that would not have put him into such an economic pinch, but his wife's illness had cost him a small fortune, no make that a large fortune.

A generally unknown price of working in Hollywood is the inability to purchase reasonably priced health insurance. Now several very well-known medical institutions were hounding him for money. Thankfully for his reputation, all were on the East Coast. The truth be told, that was why he had had his wife treated there rather than at home. However, geographic information isolation would last only so long. Now that bastard was refusing to pay what he had promised. True he had paid some, but not nearly all the money Chalmers had said he would. This was even after he had handed over all the things that little prick David had asked for. Hell, not asked, demanded. He had been such an idiot. He should have held onto the master tapes until Chalmers had actually forked over the cash.

-85-

It was almost dark with the sun low in the sky, making it difficult to see particularly when the road turned to the west. He eased off as he approached home. The high pitched whine of the Jag's engines was replaced by a well machined quiet humming.

Thankfully, his wife health had improved. True their marriage had been Hollywood rocky almost from its inception. However now after her illness they had grown closer. Their marriage was not only peaceful it was happy. For some there were second chances.

As Stevenson slowed further to negotiate a tight turn a large 4x4 pick-up truck approached him from behind. When he looked into his review mirror, all he saw was grillwork. He began to speed up to get away, but the truck kept pace. As they approached a straight portion of the road, the last one before he turned off to his home, the 4x4 bumped him. He almost lost control but managed to keep his Jag from fishtailing into oncoming traffic. Tension rose in his body as Stevenson sped up. The truck

186

kept pace and bumped him again, harder this time. Fortunately he was prepared and managed to keep his car going straight.

The straightaway section of road was almost gone, and there was no way such a big vehicle could keep up with his sports car in the upcoming turns. He would shake this guy and be home before the idiot knew it. Stevenson eased into the first turn and then gunned out of it turning south. Next, a tight U- turn followed. Stevenson stepped on the gas and the brakes simultaneously making the 180 degree turn as fast as he ever had. Checking his review mirror, he was surprised to still see the truck close by. The 4x4 held tightly to the road.

He had to shake this guy because the turn-off to his home was only a quarter mile after the turn, and it was a sharp left turn across a narrow bridge. He was preparing to power through the turn when another truck appeared out of the setting sun right in front of him. Instinctively he slammed on his brakes and turned to the right hoping to avoid contact. Unfortunately he hadn't reacted in time. The oncoming truck hit him pushing him dangerously close to the edge of the road. Gravel flew in all directions. He could feel the Jag begin to go over the edge of the narrow shoulder. In response he swung the wheel into the skid. As he did so, he got a clear view of the creek a good seventy-five feet below. The car started to come back from the abyss turning into the skid had worked. It then he was slammed from behind. Any motion the car had made away from the edge was instantly lost. The car lurched forward. For a moment the car seemed to freeze in midair. Then it headed over the bank and began hurtling towards the darkened creek bed below.

- 86 -

"David, how good to see you," Adrian Chalmers said as he rose from behind his desk to shake hands. "Please have a seat." Chalmers pointed to one of two wing chairs set in a corner of his

187

hotel suite. The two men sat. "David, before beginning I want to thank you for the nice job you did for me with John Stevenson."

"You're welcome, Mr. Chalmers. It was my pleasure."

"Let me I assure you, I appreciate your enthusiasm."

The two men sat. "David, let me get to the point. The Movement has become everything I had hoped for, maybe even more."

"You have a right to be proud."

"David, I believe we are at a turning point in this country and in the world. The days of lax religious attitudes in the Western world are over. The godless society is at an end. I am positive that it'll happen in America first and then spread around the whole world. An individual's religion will mean more than it has in years. People will fight over the right kind of God. I can feel it."

"Yes sir, I can see how you would feel that way."

"David do you disagree?"

"Sir just let us say I have my doubts."

"I see. Well you are wrong."

"That may well be but I like things I can touch and feel. I am a realist. The esoteric makes me uncomfortable."

"David, whoever controls the largest religious body will be able to control the United States and, by extension, will be able to have global influence."

"Don't we already have a world religious leader?"

Chalmers laughed. "You mean the Pope? Don't be absurd,

maybe fifty years ago but not today. It's a new world and I intend to control it."

David sat thinking. Chalmers certainly had large plans. Finally he spoke. "What do you want me to do?"

"I believe The Movement is the organization that can be used to control religion in America and by extension around the world."

"That is a mighty tall order. What of the established churches and the non-denominational Christians?"

"The Movement is it!" Chalmers almost shouted. "I have designed it so that it'll have mass appeal."

"How so?"

The organization is both traditional and charismatic, so it should appeal to members of non-denominational Churches."

"But…."

Chalmers continued. "Fundamentalists are more vocal than they are numerous. That is why I built the organization using a Catholic base."

"Mr. Chalmers, it's true the Catholic Church is the single largest denomination in the United States."

"Exactly, throw in a few Episcopalians and Orthodox believers and what more do you need? The bodies will be there and with it the control."

Prior to this meeting David had only guessed of Chalmers' plan. Hearing it directly from Chalmers's it seemed quite ingenious. "The public opinion numbers do seem to support your premise. But let me play Devil's Advocate for a moment."

"Go right ahead."

"It is a pretty large tent, and I have a hard time imagining these disparate groups sticking together over time."

"What you say is a concern, unless I change the matrix."

"Sir…"

"I need to break the Catholics away from Rome."

"A schism, in this day and age, surely you don't mean it?"

"Yes I most certainly do. David, the time is right. I know it, I can feel it. Most American Catholics are followers. Control the top and you have them, or almost all of them. Without Rome, the differences with most other religions simply fade away."

"But do we control The Movement?"

Chalmers jumped up. "That's the question David! That is it! I need to make sure the organization is mine."

"I thought it was?"

"So did I. However, there was something Reverend Raymond Gates said to me that made me question my assumption. While it is true I've picked the top leaders, I need to make sure their deputies are loyal to me and not to Gates or Schafer."

"So, you want me to find out who you can count on and who are those loyal to Gates or to Schafer, right?"

"Right, and do so quickly. Time will start running out, I can feel it."

David rose and left the suite. He had more to do now than he had originally anticipated.

- 87 -

As Agent Mitchell and I sat in the windowless conference room, waiting for only God, and of course someone Alan Mitchell had arranged to meet, I had time to reflect on what I knew and what I didn't know. On the negative side of the ledger, I had read the report Amanda had given me and frankly it wasn't much help. Though it would have done the editors at *Readers Digest* proud, it was a condensed version if there ever was one. A general story without those important little details needed to solve cases. Positively, if one could really say that, I had learned the threat as described was real; the outside assessment report had confirmed this. It didn't take a mental giant to figure out Mitchell's report was not nearly as abbreviated as the one I received. However, being with the Bureau as long as I had, I believed the additional information contained in his report would only confirm that the intelligence boys and girls had gone off the reservation. Meaning there was enough data there to hang a number of high ranking civil servants, but probably nothing useful to solve the case.

I then reflected upon the players, at least the ones I knew in this little Kabuki dance. First, there was the recently departed Amanda Chehwan, employed by the CIA. There was also what must have been her boss, Deputy Director Hanson. The very fact that her boss was so high up the Langley food chain, in my mind, added credibility to the assertions of potential sectarian violence. It was also idle speculation as to whether his report had the same number of pages as Mitchell's report. I made a mental note that one of the next things I needed to do was to pay a visit to Director Hanson.

Then there was Simon Stallings at everyone's favorite government agency, the Internal Revenue Service. I figured him as a resource and nothing more. Mitchell and Chehwan needed data, and the only place to get it was from the IRS. He was most likely a dead end for any new data.

Next in my little hit parade was Alan Mitchell, the happy head of the Bureau's counterterrorism unit. I figured him as a solid FBI guy, but one who knew how to play politics, meaning if something blew up and the Bureau was going to take a hit, I, or someone not Alan Mitchell else, was going to be burned. By the way we had just been treated, or more precisely, the way Mitchell was treated, I was sure the NSA contact was his and not Amanda's. My reverie was stopped as a tall man, mid-fifties with short cropped hair, entered the room.

Alan and I stood and took turns shaking hands. Confirming my analysis, Alan spoke first. "Sean, this is Dennis Hamilton. Dennis, Sean Murphy."

Hamilton asked us to sit down.

Mitchell was the first to put in, "Dennis, did your technicians find anything?"

"Yes Alan, they did. Most of the drive had been cleaned, but we did find this." We each were handed a sheet of paper.

I looked at the page. It contained numbers, lots of numbers. In what appeared to be no particular order.

"Mr. Hamilton, do these mean anything?" I asked.

"No we couldn't make heads or tails out of them. Of course, our primary job is to find the data and not to analyze it."

"Thanks, Dennis. It's definitely better than what we had before. I'll give it to our guys and see what they come up with."

192

Mitchell got up. And with that I concluded our meeting was over.

- 88 -

As Mitchell and I returned to the office, I called Langley to make an appointment with Deputy Director Hanson. I reached his assistant, David Brown, who told me that Director Hanson was extremely busy, and it would be at best sometime during the following week that we could meet. He did offer to meet with me himself, the next day instead. I had heard enough interagency refusals to last a lifetime. Normally I play the game, sort of, but there simply wasn't time. I asked Brown to wait a minute as I handed the phone to Mitchell.

"Says he can't see me until next week."

Mitchell nodded and took my cell. "Mr. Brown, this is Alan Mitchell. I want to speak to Director Hanson immediately."

Mostly it was a pain in the backside, but there were advantages to working for a dedicated hard-ass who I suspected knew where all the bodies were buried. This was one. I could just image Hanson's assistant feeling a bit of warmth on his old posterior.

Within seconds I heard Mitchell speak again. "Dennis, one of my guys, Sean Murphy, needs to talk to you. It's about the Chehwan case. Mitchell's hand tightened around the phone as he spoke. "Yea, I know. No, it can't wait. It has to be today. Thanks."

Mitchell handed the phone back to me and said, "He'll see you at three in his office. Don't be late. He's very busy." So I've heard.

I looked at my watch. I figured I would just make it. "I'll be on time."

"Good."

"While you are talking to him, I'll turn the NSA page over to our guys. Hopefully they'll come up with something."

"I'm sure they will. I just hope it's timely."

"Me too."

We completed the drive talking about the numbers. Well, I mostly talked. Mitchell didn't. I was grateful.

Mitchell parked his car and headed upstairs. I headed down into the nether reaches of the parking garage to find my government issued sedan.

- 89 -

I drove with one eye in the review mirror, not so much that I was worried about getting a ticket. I was pretty sure I could talk my way out of one, national security and all. I simply couldn't afford the time it would take to explain national security to the local constabulary. I pulled into the Langley's main gate and told the guard with whom I had an appointment. Fortunately, my name was on the list and I was directed to visitor parking in front of the main building. I again showed my credentials to the guards as I entered the lobby and hurried to the elevator and rode it to the fifth floor, one below the top.

Exiting the elevator, I didn't find it hard to know which way to go. One thing you can always count on in the wonderful world of federal bureaucracy is that the size and location, as well as the appointments of an office relate, directly to the rank of the civil servant. Given I was visiting the second in command of the CIA, there was only one direction to go.

194

Deputy Director of Intelligence Harold Hanson's office said it all. It was large and plush with an impressive reception area. I approached the receptionist, handed her my card and told her I had an appointment. She thanked me in the noncommittal way one would expect and asked me to take a seat pointing towards the corner of the office. I did as instructed and settled myself into an overstuffed chair and began my wait. It wasn't bad at first. I was tired and the chair was comfortable. I had also convinced myself the wait wouldn't be long since I had an appointment. Heck, even at the DMV having an appointment meant something. As time dragged on I realized I was wrong. Finally, after almost an hour and a half, a nondescript man of indeterminate age approached me.

He extended his hand. "Mr. Murphy, my name is David Brown. We talked earlier. I know you've been waiting some time for the Director. He has been tied up in a series of unexpected meetings. He has assured me that he'll be with you shortly. Is there anything I can help you with?"

"Sorry no, I need to see the Deputy Director."

"Very well."

I waited another half hour before I was summoned into the DDI's office. Mitchell had spank but…

- 90 -

As I had suspected, there was an office between the reception area and the DDI's. Sitting in this office was David Brown. As a receptionist escorted me to the inner sanctum, Brown rose and followed me. "Mr. Hansen, Agent Murphy."

"Thank you, Jennifer."

"Will there be anything else, Mr. Hanson?"

"No, be sure to hold all my calls."

"Yes sir." The receptionist who appeared to be too old for her name left us.

I had never met the DDI. My first impression was that he had the aristocratic look that came from attending the right Ivy League university and was beyond the Social Security retirement age. He turned. "Please sit down gentlemen." Brown, who had followed me into the office and I sat.

"Sean, may I call you Sean?" He also had the mid-Atlantic English accent as he began with the old standby.

"Only if you can tell me something I need to know."

Hanson smiled broadly and said, "Of course, we are all here to help each other, aren't we?"

"Of course we are, sir," I replied giving him the same toothy smile in return. Even though Hanson acted friendly, I knew he was a consummate operative worthy of his rank and that he would actually reveal nothing unless forced to for some reason.

"Sean, I asked David" Hanson pointed towards his assistant "to sit in on this meeting with us." I looked at Brown. I hated the idea, but what could I do? I merely turned back to the DDI and nodded.

"Now Sean, what can I do for you?"

"First of all sir, I would like to say how sorry I am that Amanda, agent Chehwan, was murdered. I could see from our short time together that she was a true professional."

"Thank you, I already miss her."

Brown remained silent. Under that average exterior I

suspected there was a cold as steel interior.

I continued, "Mr. Director I have a few questions I would like to ask."

"Fire away."

"This may seem like a stupid question to you, but I have to ask it. Do you consider Agent Chehwan's theory to be credible, or is it merely an ass covering exercise by a couple of agencies doing things they weren't supposed to?"

"In short, yes, I consider the possibility of some outside power manipulating and fostering a sectarian divide here as real. And just so you know, we also may be covering our butts."

I was glad to hear the man say what he had. I stole a glance at Brown who remained impassive.

"Fair enough. Without seeming too rude, may I ask why Mr. Brown has joined us?"

"Easy, Sean. There is no conspiracy going on. I'm getting older. David here helps me remember things."

"Amanda gave me the report on her operation. I wanted to compare it to yours."

"How do you know I have one?"

"Because you do," I answered simply.

"And if I have it, why should I give it to you?" Hanson had the slightest hint of a gleam in his eyes as he said this. I couldn't be certain, but I think I was his late afternoon entertainment.

"Aren't we all on the same team, seeking truth, justice and the American way?"

Hanson startled me by laughing loudly. "That was the correct answer." He turned to his assistant who I had begun to think of as an automaton. "David, please bring Sean the report, the complete report."

"Excuse me for asking, but how many versions of the report are there?"

"As many as are appropriate."

I smiled and said nothing.

By now Brown had left the room. Hanson looked in that direction. "You know, Sean, it's hell getting old. In the past I wouldn't have needed David's help. I liked it a lot better that way"

I finished off, "Because it kept the secret society smaller?"

"Precisely, my man. While David has been quite helpful to me, I really wish he weren't needed."

"I can appreciate that."

We waited in silence for his assistant to return.

"David, what took you so long?" I was glad Hanson asked because it did seem that Brown was gone an excessively long time.

"Sorry sir, I misplaced it. It took me a few minutes to locate it again." He then handed the report to Hanson who looked it over before handing it to me.

"Here you go, Sean. This is a complete version." I didn't know if what he said was true. He did seem sincere, but he was an agent's agent.

"Thank you. May I call you if I have any further questions?"

198

"Yes, of course. Just remember I'm a busy man" We all rose, shook hands and then Hanson handed me his card and said, "Add one number to the one shown. That'll get you my private line."

I don't know why, but for some reason, I turned to look at Brown. For the very first time, I saw a reaction. To me it seemed Hanson's assistant was clearly unhappy. My only guess was that he didn't like being relegated from his gate-keeper role.

Hanson apparently saw this also. "David, do you have a problem with this?"

Hanson's assistant paused for a moment. Cleared his throat and pulled at his earlobe before responding. "Why of course not, sir. I was just wondering how I could back you up if you were the only one in contact with Mr. Murphy here."

Hanson replied, "Thank you for your concern. I'll be sure to keep you in the loop."

The CIA director turned back to me, extended his hand and said, "I wish you good luck."

- 91 -

I looked at my watch as I got in my car. It was certainly too late to go back to the office. So I decided to go home and look over the next version of the report I had just been given. As I pulled out of the parking lot and began heading north, I flipped on the radio. I was tired and hoped I could find something on that would keep me awake. I hit the radio's scan button and waited. I really wished the car had satellite radio. I found the reception out here on the AM band was spotty, and FM was filled with music I neither liked nor understood. I decided to stick with the fuzzy talk radio, the sole province on AM these days. I know I should have been grateful to even have a radio. In the old days, the Government considered them luxuries, and none of its cars were equipped with them. Air conditioning also fit the same category. Finally these luxuries became part of the standard government issued sedan. Rumor has it that someone at the GAO had concluded that more federal officers would actually buy these cars at the end of four years if they were so equipped. I can't imagine what moron would want one, and I personally knew of no one to have ever requested such a thing, but at least I had air conditioning and a radio.

It was near dusk and the scanning process had run around the dial about three times before it finally stopped. The cause of such poor AM reception was either the setting sun or the radio equipment at Langley. I didn't know which. As I drove home, it took me a few minutes to focus on the words coming from radio program, but when I finally did it caused me to pause.

The host of the show was expounding upon the need to follow Jesus Christ, which to me sounded well and good since, in general, I thought most people did a poor job at that particular task. He went on to say how thankful he was that his radio station, which had been on the verge of bankruptcy, had been saved by an anonymous, yet substantial, donation. He believed it to be the work of God. His station had been saved for one reason, and that reason was to spread his particular message. This is where it got scary.

His view of the Almighty happened to involve more intolerance than I had heard in quite some time. Apparently this speaker believed that his was the only way to salvation and if one chose another way, he was basically an infidel. Of course, infidels were the same as sub-human. Naturally, one could do just about anything they wanted with such creatures. The way this guy sounded, animals should have greater rights and protection.

My stomach was becoming more upset by the mile as this

presenter plied his bilge. The final acid drip test was when he invited others to phone in to voice their opinion. I could hardly believe my ears. The callers more than echoed the radio host. They went further. In the end, they all agreed that getting guns and para-military training was a good idea so as to be able to protect the true faith.

I turned off the radio in a cold sweat. True, this might be hillbilly country, but that made it worse. This region was generally a follower to other regions around the country. If it was this far down the road, where was the rest of the country? I asked myself why I hadn't heard more. Guessing, it was probably because other regions felt the same way, only the callers and leaders were more sophisticated in the way they presented their points of view.

The rest of my drive home was anything but relaxing.

- 92 -

It was dusk, the time of day Adrian Chalmers liked best. He liked it because it was when he could read or reflect on the day, or life in general uninterrupted. Today he was thinking back reflecting on where he had come from, who he was, and where he wanted and needed to go.

His family had been in America almost since the beginning. During that time its fortunes had swung like a pendulum. There had been prominent times and something quite the opposite. His birth had coincided with an upswing in the family fortunes. His grandfather and his father were both prominent Washington D.C. attorneys with what he would freely admit were important connections. With those connections had come a level of financial comfort and modest wealth.

His father Julian Chalmers had, like so many of his generation had put his life on hold because of the Second World War. While working for the Navy, Julian met his future wife, Colleen O'Sullivan. They were drawn to each other almost immediately. Chalmers had an inherited streak of stubbornness.

Both his parents had the trait. He had often speculated that was what had drawn them together. Both families hated the idea of their marrying. The Chalmers were, had been, and it was thought, always going to be Protestants. The O'Sullivans were Irish Catholic who had come to America at the time of the Civil War to escape the famine.

He had had a very busy day and it wasn't done yet. David had delivered the report he requested that afternoon. He had wanted to drop all his appointments to read it, but he dared not. It had taken all his patience to wait, to not raise any suspicions, suspicions that might come from an inexplicably cancelled appointment. Now finally he could review the report, so brief but yet so critical to the final phase of his plan.

The report confirmed what he had only speculated upon since his conversation with Raymond Gates. *The Movement* had been tremendously successful in an unbelievably short period of time. Lukas Schafer, its leader, was an idealistic dreamer. The course of events had swept him away. He was now in a place that, just a few short months ago, he not only would have been unable to imagine, he would have rejected outright as sacrilegious. As the founder, he was admired and loved throughout the organization. However, because he had relied upon others to build the structure of the organization, the depth of his support was problematic.

As Gates had alluded to, there appeared to be a shadow organization within *The Movement.* Chalmers' loyalists were nominally in charge of all the branches and departments. However, the assistants, deputies, whatever one wanted to call them, were Raymond Gates loyalists. Chalmers had been mistaken and he hated it. He had believed his selections would have chosen more wisely. The report made it clear they had not. He could take some small solace that it was the result of rapid growth, but it was stupid. He needed to change this. The shadow must go. The easiest way would have been to take care of Gates. But that solution was out as he needed Gates as a counter-balance to Schafer.

Time was short, but at least he still had some. The task was straight forward; he needed to implement a reorganization of *The Movement's* organizational chart. Fortunately, he did have a list of people he could count on to fill a number of positions. His task would simply be to create the appropriate openings.

- 93 -

It had been a long day. I had fully intended to read the report Hanson gave me. With good intents I had even picked it up several times. Each time my mind clouded over. It didn't take me too long to figure out I needed to do some mundane household task to let my mind drift and then go to bed. In that way, I would be able to start again fresh in the morning.

I poured myself a glass of red wine, secure in the fact that not only would it help me sleep, but that it was also good for me, being filled with anti-oxidants and all, whatever those were. I decided to pay a few stray, pressing bills that still couldn't be paid electronically. Most of our expenses went on the old credit card. Each month this bill was paid automatically from our checking account to which my paycheck was automatically deposited. I had fully embraced this modern technology. Not only did it save time, but I got air miles. I figured if I could charge four years of my daughter's soon-to-be-very-expensive college education, I would have enough miles to fly free to Europe. Of course, after four years of her college bills I doubted whether we could afford to vacation in our own back yard. But I had hope. In reality, it probably didn't matter because by the time I was ready to cash in, there wouldn't be any airlines accepting my points.

I pulled out our joint check book and paid those non-twenty first century businesses that still insisted on receiving checks. Since I paid so few bills anymore, each time I did it, it was almost like the first time I learned how to write a check. I remember my mother taking me down to the credit union and saying I was now old enough to have a checking account. Back then the special thing was the type of checks one could order for free. I chose the athletic series. My checks had pictures of athletes who had last competed in the 1930's. When I think about it today, I'm sure the reason was that those were the athletes that needn't be paid for the use of their likeness. Today some journeyman hitting a buck ninety makes close to a million and gets paid when his picture is carried in *Under Achievers Today*. My mom explained how to fill out a check and told me what the different numbers on it meant. She wasn't a banking expert, but she had been a teller.

 Thankfully the job was brief and I headed to bed. I really needed a good night's sleep.

- 94 -

 I went out like a light, or at least I think I did. Normally this wasn't the case. I can't tell you the number of nights my dear wife would crawl into bed next to me and within seconds be sleeping soundly while I spent time churning over the day's events. Or if those weren't sufficiently disturbing I would shift to the tasks I had planned for the upcoming day.

 It was about 5:00 am when I awoke with a start. I sat up straight in bed. It was clear. I knew what the numbers were that had been recovered from Amanda's hard drive. It was so obvious. They were bank numbers, bank routing numbers as well as ones for individual accounts.

 I tried to get out of bed as quietly as possible, hoping not to wake Maureen and headed downstairs to my home office. Office was a nice term; it was really more of a space Mo and I shared to do necessary domestic paperwork. I grabbed the paper I got from the NSA and stared at it. Just as I thought, seemingly random

204

numbers were actually bank routing numbers and the associated bank account codes. It appeared that some number sets were either fragments or references to something else, but from what I could tell the majority were just like on the bottom of a check.

With this discovery, I had that adrenalin charge that comes with making a breakthrough. I knew there wasn't one chance in a hundred I could go back to sleep. I headed to the kitchen to fix myself a quick breakfast and decide how I would proceed. Of course, I needed confirmation of my theory. I could use the Bureau or the NSA to do this. Since the numbers had originated with the NSA I figured my fellow federal agency would be the best place to begin. Not of course because it was going to be so extra helpful but because I could more easily learn whose accounts we were talking about. After that, a trip to the super-snoopers at the always pleasurable IRS would be on tap. I needed to know what was going within those accounts and at the moment I couldn't think of better place to go. Naturally, I would need a court order before beginning. I decided to ask Alan Mitchell for help. I picked up the phone and dialed him at home. I figured there wasn't any point in not sharing my good news, particularly at this hour.

- 95 -

Mitchell was waiting for me outside the NSA's main entrance. "Sean, I hope you are right on this. I called in a lot of favors and woke up a lot of people. The entire day shift is either here or will be here shortly. If this is a screw up, I hope you realize that paybacks can be hell."

"Paybacks?"

"Yes, follow me. I'll tell you as we go." Now this concerned me. Alan Mitchell was not known as a chatty sort. The brevity of his conversations was legendary. Rumor had it that he never had conversations longer than five minutes. If he had a story to tell, there was a definite reason, one I was sure applied to me and the current situation.

We entered the building and stepped around the metal detector. No point setting the alarm off. The guard was ready to hit the panic button when we flashed our ID's and slid them through the reader and began moving towards the elevator bank.

"Gentlemen excuse me. I need to take another look at those ID's and while you are at it please put your weapons on the table."

I did as requested but I wasn't sure what Mitchell was going to do. I was pretty sure no one had talked to him like that in years.

"What's the problem?" was all Mitchell said when the watchdog approached.

"Sorry, but we have been having computer problems. I need to confirm you are who your identification says you are."

I couldn't imagine how the NSA could have computer problems, and I was ready to ask the question when Mitchell did it for me. "What kind of computer problem?"

"I'm not one hundred percent certain, but it seems we are victims of a computer virus."

I spoke up. "I thought that was impossible. Isn't this place supposed to have firewalls protecting firewalls? I didn't think anything could get in here from the outside."

The guard had taken our plastic ID cards and was doing something with them. Whatever it was, it worked. He returned our documents. "Welcome gentlemen and sorry, Mr. Hamilton is waiting for you in the main conference room on the second floor. Do you need directions?"

"No," was all Mitchell said, as he again headed for the elevators with me in tow holding both plastic cards.

"Sean, a couple of years ago a NSA special agent thought he had stumbled across a plot to break into the Federal Reserve Bank in New York City."

"Okay," I said noncommittally. The elevators doors opened and we stepped in, hitting the button for the second floor.

No one else was in the elevator so Mitchel continued, "Anyway, the NSA guy thought some Russian Mafia guy wanted to make a gold withdrawal."

"Sounds like a Bruce Willis *Die Hard* movie."

"Well, apparently the NSA guy had never heard of this *Die Hard* movie. Anyway, the Bureau gave it a full court press, staked out the New York Fed building on Saturday night and all day Sunday."

"Sounds like a lot of overtime."

"You can bet your buns. It was a ton of O.T."

"Nothing came of it, right?"

"What do you think?"

The second floor elevator door opened and we turned and walked down the hall. "How come I never heard of this?"

"This was such a screw-up there were only two things the Bureau and the NSA could agree upon."

I looked at Mitchell, "To bury the story so it would never see the light of day, and to send the NSA guy packing to some god-forsaken spot, like the middle of the Sahara Desert."

"Close, actually he was transferred to a NSA listening post in South Sudan," Mitchell said as he opened the conference room door. I got the message. I sure hoped I wasn't on my way to the Bureau's domestic equivalent. There were at least ten people waiting for us inside.

Mitchell, ignoring the crowd, spoke directly to Hamilton. "Dennis, what is with your computer problems?"

"Alan, I know it is a little hard to believe. But it appears we have been hacked."

"From the outside?"

"Nothing is impossible, but there isn't one chance in a trillion."

"An inside job?"

"That is the only other reasonable explanation."

- 96 -

"Your Holiness." Cardinal Francesco Camperelle said as he entered the Pontiff's office.

"Francesco. Yes, please come in," the new Pope said warmly. "Sit, sit."

The Vatican Secretary of State sat in his customary seat. "What can I do to help you?" Had this been his old friend, Camperelle would have known what the Holy Father would have wanted. But now, with this new man he was clueless. To Camperelle, with so many years of Vatican insider experience, this uncertainty was more than a little unnerving.

"The Church's situation in the United States is precarious and we must do something."

"I can't disagree with you, Holy Father. For years we have treated the American Church with benign neglect. The recent scandals caused us to back even further away. However, as prudent a policy this seemed until just a few years ago it is clearly not the best course of action today. "

Looking at his Secretary of State, the Pope commented, "Yes, times have changed and significantly so."

"Indeed they have. I believe only Jesus could have guessed of such events."

The Pope nodded, "yes, I suppose so, but…"

Camperelle was a little taken aback. The new Pope had just commented on the policy that he and the prior Pope had been involved in. He thought about saying something but chose to remain silent. Change as much as it was needed was clearly going to be a challenge.

"It is time the Holy See becomes more pro-active. The United States is simply too important to the Holy Mother Church. It's not only the country with the most Catholics in the world, it is the richest.

"Yes, Your Holiness. What do you want of me?"

It was as if the Pope had not heard Camperelle. He continued speaking, "The Church must take action. It must be immediate and it must be dramatic. Every day that we wait creates a bigger problem"

"Yes, Your Holiness. What do you want me to do?"

"The United States is where I must go. Please do whatever

diplomatic things you need to do to make this so."

"Yes, Your Holiness. Is there anything else?"

"No, just the sooner the better, please."

- 97 -

"Dennis, do you know what was hacked?"

"Alan, no we aren't certain as to the extent of the intrusion."

"I see. Well, there isn't anything Murphy and I can do about it. I suggest we finish up our meeting as soon as possible so all you folks," Mitchell looked about the room for the first time, "can get about your investigation."

"I agree. Let's all sit down."

I sat down, still wondering whether I was going to have to go home and tell my family of my unexpected transfer to shit-hole America.

Hamilton looked first at Mitchell and then at me, "Alan you should be proud of Murphy. He came up with something that had stumped our computers."

I can't tell you how relieved I was to hear those words. America was a great country, but there were some bad places, especially for a dedicated urban boy like me. "Thank you sir," was my only response.

Hamilton nodded and continued. "We have isolated a number of the banks and account numbers."

"How many accounts could you isolate?" I asked.

"Not as many as you would think. There was a lot of

210

repetition. I'll get you a list as soon as we are totally certain."

Mitchell interjected, "sounds fair enough."

Still basking in relief, I asked, "Was there anything else?"

As Hamilton responded, I wondered why the crowd, this was American and we loved our bureaucracy but... "There was indeed. Janet, please tell us what your group found."

At least we were going to hear from one member of the silent majority. A middle-aged, rather ordinary, but nervous looking woman rose and headed to the lectern. She began in a barely audible voice, "My name is Janet Costers, and I'm sorry if I seem a little ill at ease. You see, I'm standing in for my boss, Mark Ruben, who normally does this kind of thing."

I turned to look at Mitchell who was already staring at Dennis Hamilton. "We don't know, Alan. Mark phoned in several days ago saying he needed some time off."

"Is that unusual?" Mitchell asked.

"Yes. The only time he normally takes off is his annual vacation, and during the weeks leading up to his leave his tendency is to drive everybody crazy."

"Why is that?"

"He tries to get all his work handled before he leaves regardless of the level of priority. He apparently hates coming back to a pile of unfinished things."

Mitchell returned his gaze to the front of the room. Thankfully Ms. Costers had relaxed a bit and seemed more comfortable making her presentation. "Actually there are number of things we noticed. The vast majority of the bank numbers were in sequence. However, one banking number, at least we think it is a banking number, is different, out of order if you would."

"What else? You said there were a number of things," it was Mitchell's turn to interrupt.

"There were three other number sets. These sets matched nothing. The only thing we have been able to conclude is that two of the three numbers are alike. What the other one is, we are still clueless."

As she was speaking, another conference room committee member handed out a single sheet of paper. "I suppose these are the orphan numbers?"

"Yes, they are, Mr. Murphy. Do you see anything?"

I sure wanted to be the wonder kid again, but all I could see was gibberish. "No, sorry." I definitely had had my fifteen minutes of fame.

"Well, we are going to run a number of algorithms and see what we come up with."

"What's the time frame, Dennis?" Mitchell asked.

"Alan, could be a few days, could be more. We'll let you know as soon as we get something."

"Okay, Dennis. I think we have learned all we can. We should let you get back to your problems." With that Alan Mitchell rose and walked out of the conference room. I smiled weakly as I jumped up and followed Mr. Personality out the door.

- 98 -

212

"Monsignor, please sit down," Francesco Camperelle asked his aide Giovanni Bartolo. "I'm afraid I have some bad news."

"What is that, Your Eminence?" Bartolo asked as if he already knew the answer.

"I know I promised you a parish in Sienna, but I'm going to have to delay those plans."

"I'm not surprised," he said resignedly.

"I really hate to do this, but the Holy Father has tasked me to arrange a foreign trip immediately and I desperately need your help."

"Where?"

"His Holiness wants to go to America. He needs our help translating his wishes into diplomatic reality."

Bartolo pondered the Cardinal's words, but didn't immediately respond. "Giovanni, is there a problem or something I should know?"

Again silence. Camperelle could see Bartolo was struggling. "Father, what could be so bad? The truth is always best. What is it?"

In a barely audible voice Bartolo began. "Your Eminence, while you and the rest of the Cardinals were sequestered in the Sistine Chapel, I had the chance to talk with many of my contemporaries. It was one of those times where one found both happiness and sadness."

"How so?" Camperelle asked.

"I know you have known for some time about my

dissatisfaction with the politics of the Church."

"Yes," was all the Cardinal said.

Growing more confident, Bartolo continued. "The happiness I experienced was finding that I was not alone. I also found sadness. An overwhelming majority of my fellow aides feel as I do. They are tired of the intrigue and the worldliness of what we do. In short, they want a change. Some like me have looked to parish ministry; others have contemplated leaving the Church altogether, while others have looked to the monastic life as a solution."

Camperelle was disturbed by what he was hearing. This was something he hadn't truly expected.

"You look concerned. Do you want me to stop?"

"Of course not. I am surprised that is all."

"About what?"

"I knew of your job fatigue and wish to work in a parish. What I was unaware of was the depth of the problem with your contemporaries."

"Surely you must have suspected, why else would you have pushed to have Archbishop Ateek elected Pope?"

"The situation is just further along and deeper than I thought it would be that is all. Please continue."

"From our conversations and my associates we learned how divided the Cardinals were. We were concerned that the Conclave would fail. That it would drag on and on as a majority failed to materialize. Eventually we assumed a caretaker would finally be chosen as someone had to be picked. All of these concerns vanished when the new Pope was announced. There was new hope. My contemporaries believed that this man will change things. They see a new beginning for the Holy Mother Church."

Camperelle thought back to the Conclave. He had allowed his name to be thrown into consideration. He had done this to buy time so he could line up support behind the new Holy Father. He hadn't realized until this moment, how close he had come to becoming Pope. He was the compromise candidate. But in God's will, things had indeed worked out. So what was bothering Bartolo? "I don't understand. What are you telling me? Aren't you getting the kind of action you wanted?"

"You are telling me that His Holiness wants to go to America. I fear for his life."

"It is America, not a war zone."

"It is a country that believes in the divine right of guns. It is not a safe place, particularly in light of what can only be called a developing schism."

"Christ died for us. One can't expect the Holy Father to shy away from danger. Can one?"

"If something happens to this man, I fear there is no one that can replace him, no one. You can be certain the Church will break into hundreds of pieces." By now Bartolo was almost shouting. "The Holy Roman Church will cease to exist; of that you can be sure." With that Bartolo fell silent.

Camperelle knew two things: one, Bartolo was most probably right. If anything happened to the new Pope, the future of the Catholic Church would be dramatically different and not different in a good way. Two, he also knew he had to do as the new Pontiff requested.

- 99 -

I basically chased SAIC Mitchell all the way down the hall to the elevator. We walked silently until we got to the Bucar, our trustee Bureau sedan. I considered saying something but thought better of it. We were at least five miles away from the NSA before Mitchell finally spoke. "Sean, pull over up there."

"Okay." I pulled off the road into the parking lot of a coffee shop.

Mitchell got and headed towards the restaurant.

I got out of the car and joined him. However, he didn't say anything further until we were seated and had ordered some coffee.

"Sean, you need to be very careful."

"Because you think there is a leak at the NSA?"

"It could be either at the NSA or the CIA, but I would bet my paycheck there is one."

I drove along thinking about what Mitchell had just said. I couldn't help but agree. There was a bad apple out there; maybe two, one at the CIA and another at with NSA.

"Do you think the hacker was after Chehwan's data?"

Mitchell thought for a minute before answering, "I don't know."

This surprised me, "I would have thought you would have said yes definitely."

"Unfortunately, there are a lot of possibilities. The hacker may very well already know everything about Chehwan's

216

investigation. It could be whoever hacked was merely following through moving on the next part of the plan. The plan, I might add, that we basically don't know anything about. On the other hand, we could be in better shape in that the bad guy isn't that far ahead of us and was looking for information. Another option would be that it is all a smoke screen. The real plan is something completely different than what we have been investigating and the hack was merely a red herring."

I could see Mitchell's logic, and I was impressed with how thoroughly, quickly and completely he had analyzed the situation. I understood why this man was a legend with the Bureau. "I hate being behind the curve."

"So do I. Sean, it's time we change the dynamic."

"I agree."

"What's your plan?"

"As soon as I get back, I'm going to tear Amanda's report apart. Then I'm going to rattle a few cages if those picture enhancements aren't done yet."

"Good choices," Sean there is one other thing you need to look into."

"You want me to find out anything I can about Mark Ruben and find it ASAP."

"Exactly, if the NSA gives you a bunch of crap, let me know." I liked hearing this. Alan Mitchell's pay grade and pull was way higher than mine. We sat quietly finishing our coffee each lost in our own thoughts.

When Mitchell finished he said, "Sean, let's go." As we headed back to the car about half across the parking he stopped and said, "Oh and be sure to have your car checked for bugs." We rode the rest of the way back to headquarters in silence.

- 100 -

"Mr. Chalmers, meeting like this in the middle of the day is very dangerous."

"It couldn't be helped, David. "I shouldn't have to assure you, all necessary precautions have been taken."

"Still," David's voice trailed off.

His voice rising with irritation, Adrian Chalmers responded, "I have an appointment out of town that I couldn't reschedule. Now, so we can keep this brief since you appear to be a little nervous, show me what you found."

David's normally placid face gave just a glimmer of irritation and then it was gone. "Mr. Chalmers," David pulled from his brief case a single sheet of paper. "Here is a list of those key players loyal to Raymond Gates."

Chalmers grabbed the paper and quickly read it. "Are you sure? I thought there would have been more."

David hated dealing with amateurs; most of the time he could handle them. However, Chalmers' shtick was wearing thin, very thin. "There are more. But we only have to replace these three." David pointed to the top three names listed.

218

"You think everyone else will fall in place?" David had been a vital in helping Chalmers and he had enjoyed the man's work ethic and efficiency however, his assistant's arrogance was growing over time and this was becoming a problem. He hated to ask the question, but he needed to assure himself of the answer.

"Yes, trust me on this."

Chalmers sat saying nothing, calming himself. He was close, so close to his goal. He knew he had to put up with David for at least a little longer. In a calm voice he asked, "What do you recommend?"

"I think *The Movement* could use some martyrs."

Chalmers did enjoy David's practicality. "Accident or attack?" Chalmers knew what he wanted, but he was curious to see what David would suggest.

"A tragic accident. Things are still a little fluid with *The Movement.* A murder might cause some people to make some decisions we would rather they not make. Besides, any death in the line of duty will help the organization and multiple deaths are even better."

This was exactly what Chalmers thought. An accident would draw the organization together without the risk of alienation. It might even draw more people and publicity. Besides, he had two very good candidates to give their last measure of support to the organization. At this point he just didn't know which one would be the lucky man. He knew it would be fun finding out. Chalmers calmly said, "Small plane crashes are always good."

Without saying a word, David nodded his approval.

"David, there is a rally the day after tomorrow in the Quad Cities. It would be quite reasonable to use a private plane for our people to get there, busy schedules and all. Do you see a problem?"

"None, Mr. Chalmers."

"Then please take care of it."

- 101 -

It was mid-afternoon and, for the last several hours, I had been banging away reviewing Amanda's report and the few notes of hers that had managed to be found. During this time, my level of frustration was directly opposite to my level of success. I was very frustrated. What I had learned was there was practically nothing left to learn. It was true the report had lots of words. In fact, it had pages of analysis spelling out various hypotheses which would later be disproved by still further analysis. What made the task even more difficult was her writing. It was stilted and dry, even by the Bureau's dry standards.

I was staring at my monitor hoping for inspiration, when an email telling me to come to the lab annex right away popped up. Normally a command like that gave me an attitude, but since I wasn't getting anywhere and I needed a break, I put on my coat and headed downstairs to the lab. Hopefully I was in for a change in luck. The lab annex was not located in the main FBI building but was across the street. The email said someone would meet me at the main entrance. This all seemed a little unusual, but then again, I did work for the Federal government. There was a subway that connected the two buildings. Normally, I would have taken it, especially today because rain was in the forecast. But since I was to meet someone at the front door, it was quicker just to cross the street.

While the day had begun nicely enough, it hadn't stayed that way. The sun had been bright, but not too warm and without humidity. As Mitchell and I drove back from Maryland, the sky had begun to show signs of the Washington summer, with the Government buildings beginning to take on a hazy shroud. When I exited headquarters, I was hit with a wave of summer-like humidity and I began instantly sweating. I ducked back in and contemplated again the possibility of using the tunnel down in troglodyte land, but the email had been time specific. So rather than piss off some faceless tech person, I headed out with my dark blue suit and white shirt on.

There weren't a lot of people out as it was too early in the day for the federal work force to head home and too early in the year for your garden variety tourist. The traffic was heavy enough for me to quickly pass on my initial plan of making a dash across the street. Instead, I headed for the corner to be a good boy and cross at the light. I waited my turn and began to cross. Out of habit I checked both ways. Cars several deep had come to a stop with most of the drivers glued to their cell phones. I was three-quarters of the way across the street when I noticed the light had changed. This made no sense. In the name of making the Capital more pedestrian friendly, the city had installed traffic signals with crossing timers. I was sure the timers were set to allow wheelchairs to cross with time to spare. I wasn't in a wheel chair and I wasn't crawling, so there was no reason the light should have changed. I don't know if it was instinctive or I heard something, but I looked left in time to see a black sedan bearing down on me. Thankfully I had always been quick, not fast, but quick. I reacted to the motion and jumped forward. I managed to come down with a thud slipping and landing on my butt on the very edge of the sidewalk right next to crossing signal. This was a lucky thing because the sedan had continued towards me, not slowing at all. At the last minute the car was forced to swerve, undoubtedly because of the location of the signal post. The vehicle was up against the edge of the gutter and only missed me by inches.

I sat there on the sidewalk, not moving, stunned. This was the third time someone had wanted me dead since I had been given my latest assignment. I was shot at in Rock Creek Park and there was the bomb in Chehwan's apartment though it could have been meant for any lucky Fed. This time it was personal. I had definitely pissed off and/or scared someone. Unfortunately for me, I didn't know who it was or which it was.

I continued to just sit there trying to get my heart out of my mouth and wanting to make sure all of Sean was there and working within tolerances. I wasn't sure as everything was deadly quiet. People and cars were moving about but they did so silently. Maybe I was beyond okay sitting in God's waiting room and not really knowing it. I hoped I was okay and I thought I was sitting there just breathing deeply, and trying to calm myself, but....

- 102 -

Finally and thankfully, sounds started returning, first softly and then much louder like waves crashing on the shore. It was then I heard what I thought was the sound of tires squealing. It suddenly occurred to me that whoever had made a pass at me might be returning to finish the job. Clambering to my feet, I headed for the front door of the lab as fast as I could, which wasn't very fast. I had definitely sprained my left ankle. Looking over my shoulder, I thought I caught a glimpse of a dark sedan coming in my direction. This being Washington D.C., a dark car accelerating down the street was hardly out of the ordinary. Not wanting to take any chances, I broke into what I could only, with a great deal of charity, be described as a sprint. Thankfully the front door was close, so I didn't have to run far. As I burst through the front doors and dove onto the marble floor, I thought I heard popping.

It had taken a few years, but every federal building in the Capital has been equipped with metal detectors and armed security personnel, both of which starting making noise. The guards were yelling and the equipment was bonging. As soon as I hit the floor, I managed to roll over on my back grabbing my gun. I was sliding away from the doors with weapon aimed out towards the street. The security guards were ready to treat me as public enemy number one when the front door glass simply disintegrated. The guard closest to me went down, grabbing at his chest. Unfortunately for him, I had been right about the popping sounds.

As quickly as it started, it was over. Whoever had attacked me chose to leave and fight another day. I crawled over to the downed man. He was clearly in a bad way, losing a lot of blood. His partner appeared dazed as he approached us, waving his gun. He was yelling something, but it was incomprehensible. I decided to raise my hands. After getting lucky outside, I didn't want to get shot by accident inside. This was apparently what he wanted me to do. Of course, it didn't do anything for his wounded mate. I could see from his look he really wanted to do something. I was afraid his something, was to shoot me. I tried in vain to explain I was a Fed, but it just wasn't sinking in. Fortunately, all hell broke loose next.

The lobby filled with police. Thankfully they looked like they knew what they were doing. A man about forty-five approached. I managed to convince him of the possibility I was FBI. Once I pulled out my credentials and showed them to him, I was accepted as a good guy. About the same time, an EMT arrived and began caring for the injured officer. Though I was afraid they were too late.

It was over. It seemed forever, but when I checked my watch it wasn't more than six minutes since I had exited my building across the street. "Sean, are you okay?" I looked up. It was Agents Johnson and Rodriguez.

"Yeah, I am."

"You sure?"

"Yeah, I'm sure, why?

"Well, you look like hell and there is a bunch of blood on your jacket."

"I always look like hell and the blood belongs to the poor guy they are now hauling away on the stretcher." I pointed with my thumb.

Both agents gave a forced chuckle. Rodriquez asked, "What happened?"

I explained to them how, getting an email message set off a chain of events culminating with me with a sprained ankle sitting on the marble floor in a ruined suit.

"Well, at least the Bureau will get you a new suit," Ben Johnson cracked. "Up to $**300** hundred dollars," Rodriquez added.

I looked at both agents and said, "Just what I need, two comedians. Make yourselves useful and help me up." The two young bucks had me up within seconds. I tried putting weight on my left ankle. It held. Fortunately the sprain was a mild one.

"Sean, your leg okay?" Johnson asked.

"It'll hold. Can you guys do me a favor?"

"Sure. We were just going off shift."

"Walk me down to the photo lab, okay?"

"Why not? Wouldn't do the Bureau any good to have an old fart like you collapsing someplace in the bowels of the building you might lay there for days," Rodriquez said.

"Yeah, and the only way old Sean here would be found would be when the smell got bad enough," Johnson added.

I headed to the lab with the FBI's modern day version of Burns and Allen.

- 103 -

While Johnson and Rodriquez walked and I shuffled, I filled them in on the course of my investigation since we had first met the night Amanda died at Rock Creek Park. By the time we got to the lab, my ankle was screaming at me, but two good things had happened. One, I had managed not to fall down, and two, I was pretty sure it would hold me up. That is, at least until I got home, where I could soak it in hot water and get my hands on a crutch or cane. I had been injured before.

"Anything else you need, Sean?" Johnson asked.

I told them no and that I appreciated their help. With that, my escorts departed. The receptionist had given us a strange look when we first arrived. Maybe it was my somewhat disheveled appearance, but I wasn't sure. However, after I asked to see the head tech, I got a real frosty response.

"Do you have an appointment?"

"I thought I did, but no. It is a long story."

Obviously she didn't want to hear a story of any length, "Ms. Holland is tied up in an important meeting and is not available."

Some people shouldn't be allowed to have power, any kind of power. This receptionist was clearly one. I understood that her boss could be in a meeting and I knew I didn't have an appointment, but why this Attila the Hun clerical person couldn't offer me another option, an assistant, a cup of coffee, was beyond me. Anyway, I wasn't in any mood for crap. "I'm sorry to hear that but I still need to see her."

In an even more snippy voice, she responded, "I told you she is busy."

I had a rule, never throw a name around. But every rule had its exception, and it was time to make an exception. "My name is Sean Murphy, and I'm leading an investigation into the death of a federal officer, Amanda Chehwan. There is vital information in the lab I must see. Is there someone else I can talk to?"

"No," was all she said as she turned back to her computer monitor.

That response, combined with almost being killed, did it. "Listen, if you like working here or even if you don't, this job is better than the one Alan Mitchell will find for you if you don't get Ms. Holland here within thirty seconds."

The look on this woman's face remained impassive, but not as certain as it was just seconds before. "Like I said, Agent Murphy, Ms. Holland is busy in a meeting."

"Listen, unless she is with the President, you will get her and get her now," my temper was really up. At the same time I leaned over the counter and grabbed her phone and dialed Mitchell's office. "Alan Mitchell please," was all I could get out before the receptionist depressed the switch hook and sullenly hurried off.

- 104 -

I stood waiting at the receptionist's workstation, not daring to walk anywhere. It would truly have been bad form to be lying on the carpet when my new friend returned with her boss. Within just a few minutes, Ms. Holland and the receptionist returned.

"Agent Murphy, how may I help you?"

"Thanks for seeing me, Ms. Holland."

"Call me Betty." As cold as the receptionist had been, her boss was all peaches and cream. What a Jekyll and Hyde office.

"Well, Betty, your lab has been running enhancements on two camera phone pictures I gave them."

"Oh yes, the Chehwan case. We have given it our top priority."

"Could you tell me what you have learned?"

"Certainly. If you would please follow me, we can meet in my office."

I almost keeled over after I took my first step. The lab director noticed this and asked me if I needed to stay in the lobby. "No, I think it would be best to meet some place private," was my response. I had suddenly become very cautious about almost everything. Holland then asked me how I hurt myself. I told her that some unknown assailant had helped me get in my present "comfortable" situation. We finally arrived at her office, and I gratefully slumped into a guest chair.

Holland took a seat and began, "I'm sorry to say that we haven't been as successful as I would've liked."

"How's that?"

"We have done what we can do. Unfortunately, the resolution has only been marginally improved."

"I see. Why?"

"There are several reasons: the time of day, the angle of the camera and the unit itself."

"I thought she had a state-of-the-art cell."

"State of the art several years ago. It appears Agent Chehwan never upgraded her instrument." I paused. I was clearly disappointed, and it must have shown. "Let me show you what we have come up with."

"Okay."

Holland reached into her credenza, searched for a file and found it. She opened it and pulled out two photographs and handed them to me. "Here"

I took the pictures and looked at them. Nothing, it was two pictures of some unknown male only slightly clearer than the ones I originally had seen. It could have been almost any white guy in North America or for that matter Northern Europe. I looked up and shook my head. "Not much better are they?"

"I'm sorry, but no."

"May I keep these?"

"Sure, no problem." She took them and started to put them into an envelope.

"Excuse me, Betty. Let me look at them again." She handed the pictures back to me. I looked at them again. Yes, on reflection there was something different this time. I couldn't put my finger on it, but there was something. At least that was something.

I drove home with one eye in the rear view mirror, random clues rolling around my mind. Whoever was after me was an insider, of that I was sure, well pretty sure. If not an insider, it had to be someone both tech savvy and well connected. What was truly bothersome to me was I knew nothing, but apparently someone thought I was much further around the curve than I was.

I was worried. I wasn't safe. This wasn't desirable but understandable because I was in line, but my family could easily become collateral damage. Tomorrow I had an appointment with Simon Stallings at the Internal Revenue Service. I needed access to some of his financial data. No doubt it would probably take a warrant, but I saw no difficulty if the request came from Alan Mitchell, which was fine since I needed to talk to Alan anyway on a personal matter. My family needed protection, and he was going to provide it, he just didn't know it yet.

I was sore all over, and that made it hard for me to think of the case and pay attention to the road. The pictures I had been shown kept rolling around in my mind. Of course nothing stuck, they just kept whirling. The radio was on, but I hardly noticed it until a report came through about a plane crash.

"Reports are coming in to us from our reporter who has been attending The Movement's mid-Western rally for Christ that several high-ranking organization members are missing and presumed dead. They were to have arrived in the Quad-Cities earlier today via private plane. The plane is now long overdue, and officials at the regional airport have confirmed contact was suddenly lost with the plane. At the time, the craft was over central Illinois. Severe thunderstorms had been reported in the area. It is unknown if weather was a factor. We have unconfirmed accounts telling of wreckage south of Galesburg that could be a downed private plane. To repeat, we believe three senior members of The Movement are missing and presumed dead. Our correspondent further tells us the impact of this disaster has created an enormous emotional response from the rally participants. We will bring you

*more news of this breaking story as soon as we have more for
you."*

I flicked off the radio and wondered how many important
or near-famous people had died in small plane crashes. It sure
seemed like a lot. Personally I refused to fly in them.

- 106 -

Camperelle needed to keep the probability of a Papal
pilgrimage to the United States as confidential as possible for as
long as possible. The fewer the people, the shorter the time, the
better it would be. Certainly it would not assure the Pope's
complete safety, but it couldn't possibly hurt. Normally, he would
have first broached the possibility of a visit with the American
Ambassador to the Holy See. The Ambassador would then inquire
as to certain logistical issues before getting back to his Department
of State. Precisely what happened after that, the Cardinal wasn't
completely certain since each country's governments had its own
individual peculiarities. What he was certain of was that in the
process a lot of people would learn of the impending visit.
Eventually, the American Secretary of State on behalf of the
President would privately offer an invitation to the Pope to come
to America.

The Vatican's response was centuries old and steeped in
tradition and by nature slow. Many of its protocols had originated
at the time when the Pope was both a temporal king, as well as, a
spiritual leader, when the world moved at a much slower pace.
Camperelle also was aware that before the general public was
informed of the Pope's "acceptance" hundreds of "Vatican" insiders
would become aware of the planned trip, creating a veritable
potpourri of security issues.

Today's circumstances dictated that he make direct and

private contact with the American Secretary of State. Camperelle wasn't sure how Monsignor Bartolo had managed to acquire a private phone number to the American Secretary, but he had. The American Secretary was new to the position, having just been confirmed by the United States Senate after a long and distinguished career in the Foreign Service. One of his prior jobs had been chargé d'affaires at the American Embassy in Rome. Camperelle could only assume it was during that time Bartolo and Secretary of State Lucia had become well enough acquainted for Bartolo to have access to such a phone number.

Camperelle looked at his watch. It was late 2:00 am. But only 8:00 pm in Washington DC. Was it too early? Camperelle wanted to reach the Secretary after work and before bedtime. He had already checked with the Papal Nuncio, and to his knowledge the Lucia had no published late night plans for tonight. As the number two man in the Vatican began to dial, he wondered if Carlo Lucia was Catholic. Without a doubt, the man's family at one time had been Catholic, but who knew today. Surnames didn't mean much, particularly in America when it came to religious beliefs or the lack thereof. Nonetheless, Camperelle knew it would be easier if Lucia were a practicing Catholic.

"Hello, Lucia speaking."

"Mr. Lucia, Francesco Camperelle speaking."

There was dead silence on the line. "Sir, I don't know how you got this number, but impersonating a foreign official is a very serious offense."

"Mr. Secretary, please do not hang up. I want to assure you this call is genuine." Again silence. "I can offer you two forms of proof."

"Go on," was the wary reply.

"First, I got your phone number from my assistant, Monsignor Giovanni Bartolo. He tells me he knows you quite well."

"Yes, we are old friends."

"He says to remind you that Palermo will never beat Siena."

Camperelle could hear laughter on the line, no doubt a good sign,

"And what is your other proof?"

"Please phone the Vatican through your normal diplomatic channels and ask for me. Monsignor Bartolo will answer."

"At this hour?"

"Yes, please Mr. Secretary, it is crucial you satisfy yourself of the authenticity of my call. It is critical that we speak privately." Camperelle anxiously listened, and finally he heard Lucia dial another phone. "Night desk, this is Lucia. I need you to call the Vatican. When whoever answers the phone at this hour answers, request the Vatican Secretary of State's office; once your call is picked up, please drop off the line."

Camperelle waited and waited. The minutes crawled, the line open but silent. Normally a patient man, he was ready to scream when Lucia picked up the instrument and began speaking.

"Your Eminence, I am sorry for the delay, but I am sure you can appreciate that I needed to assure myself of the genuineness of this call."

"I understand completely. This call is quite unusual."

- **107** -

232

"That is an understatement. Now what is so important that you need to call me in the middle of the night?"

Camperelle paused. He still had no clue whether Lucia was Catholic or not. "Mr. Secretary, there are some extraordinary things going on with the Catholic Church."

"Yes, so it would appear."

This conversation was harder than Camperelle had imagined. What to do? What approach to take? The Cardinal weighed several approaches before he decided just to go with the direct one. "His Holiness is worried about what is happening to the American Catholic Church. He is concerned about a schism."

"I would be too."

"Mr. Secretary, the new Pope wants to come to America."

"Why?"

"He wants to prevent the American Church from splitting from Rome."

"Father, this kind of trip presents certain difficulties. As you may or may not be aware, we are in the midst of a religious revival. Various groups are competing for membership and influence."

"Mr. Secretary, I'm familiar with what is going on. However, I don't see how that should affect the Pontiff's visit."

"Our Constitution requires the separation of Church and State."

"I know that."

"Our courts and our traditions demand that the secular

government show no favoritism or preference to any particular religious belief or organization. If I allowed the Pope to come to America, to repair the rift between the American Catholic Church and Rome, the Administration could be accused of violating this principle."

"Mr. Secretary, the Church is aware of the proscriptions of your Constitution. His Holiness has no desire to create diplomatic issues." The line went silent. Camperelle wanted to say something, anything, but his years as a diplomat held him back.

"What did the Pope have in mind?"

Camperelle was relieved. Lucia could have just rejected the request but he had not.

"The Holy Father is flexible."

"That's nice to know. Just tell me what he wants and I'll see what we can do."

"He wants to come and meet with the leaders of *The Movement.*"

"Is that all? How do you know they will even meet with him?"

"I don't know for sure but…"

"I get it; they were once good boys and will most likely still defer to the Pope. Anything else?"

"He also wants to participate in a number of religious rallies around your country."

"Father, this request is problematic. It will take me some time to think about it."

Camperelle was horrified. The last thing he needed was to
234

get caught up in the diplomatic time wasting game. Eventually a positive response would probably come, but it would be too late for the Church in America, "Time is something we simply don't have. I am certain that left unchecked; the American Church will split from the Vatican."

"That is not my problem or America's problem. In fact, it might solve some issues we have had here for years."

"I know that, but there is something more to this, something more important than earthly politics."

"You mean eternal salvation," the Secretary of State said rather dryly.

"Yes, Mr. Secretary."

Again silence.

"Your Eminence, I understand your concerns. However, I am simply not at liberty to accede to your request. I must think on the matter and consult with the President. I'll get back with you. You must remember my position is one in which I must deal with the problems of this world not the next."

"Mr. Secretary, I implore you to move with all urgency. It is a matter of the gravest consequences."

"I understand your position. I will get back with you. Good night." With that the line went dead and with it a great deal of Camperelle's spirit. He hadn't actually expected an invitation to be immediately extended, but he had hoped for a much friendlier response.

- 108 -

Prophecy

I arrived home to find an empty house. I didn't recall Mo and Kelly having any plans for the evening. Normally I wouldn't have been too concerned because it wasn't really all that late, but after today's little encounter, that wasn't the case. After I managed to get myself upstairs to our bedroom where I found an ace bandage to wrap my ankle, I started phoning. I tried first my wife's cell and then my daughter's. From both I got the happy voice telling me their cell were turned off or otherwise unreachable. I didn't bother with leaving a message. Either they were okay and anything I would have said would have only upset them, or they weren't all right and they already knew there was a problem. I then reached Sean, Jr. to learn he was fine and no, nothing unusual had happened and that he would have loved to talk longer but he was off to the library to study. I'm not sure I believed the part about studying, but I was in no mood to push the issue. I next tried his brother Thomas. I couldn't reach him, but that wasn't too surprising. Tom seldom carried his cell phone with him. Probably the only kid not to, but then again he had always traveled to the beat of different drummer. I called it middle child syndrome. Having called the obvious choices without any luck, I then spent the next hour first trying to figure out whom I could call and then discarding the candidates. With each passing minute, my anxiety grew, and with it my acid indigestion. Finally, the phone rang. Was it them? Was it someone worse? I didn't let it ring twice. It turned out to be one of those push-the-button BS political surveys. The candidate was lucky there was actually no human being on the other end of the line. I was about ready to call the police when I heard a noise downstairs.

I jumped up and immediately fell over. In my haste I had forgotten about my injury. As I struggled to my feet, I grabbed my gun and started out the bedroom door. I descended the stairs as quietly as possible which frankly wasn't all the stealthy, but fortunately there was a lot of noise coming from the kitchen, but not much talking, I crept as close as I could. A swinging door separated the hall I was in from the kitchen. I was either going through it or waiting for someone to come my way. I had no intention of waiting. I slowly pushed the door open, keeping my gun hidden behind the jam.

I saw my wife putting down a bag of groceries. Behind her was my daughter, holding a case of drinks. On top of all that, Tom was bringing in more things from the garage. "Hi Sean, look who's here." Her head tilted in Tom's direction.

I stood there, mouth opening and closing without words coming out. "Everything okay?" Mo asked.

I finally managed to blurt, "I tried to call you."

"You did? I didn't get your call or a message. There must still be something wrong with our account again." My wife, who doesn't get easily upset, was almost yelling. "I can't tell you the number of times I have talked to the damn phone company. Nobody can seem to figure it out. I don't understand it at all. We haven't had any issues or problems for years. Then within the last month nothing seems right; account problems, service interruptions you name it."

Not able to say much else but wanting to calm her down, I managed to croak, "I just had a tough day at work and was worried, that's all."

My wife came over and gave me a kiss. Before she got there, I managed to ditch the gun while making a mental note. The phone company was going to hear from me. And I wasn't nearly as reasonable as Mo was.

- 109 -

Later that evening as we got ready for bed, I gave my wife the sanitized version of my day. I touched lightly on my sidewalk gymnastics. She didn't say much and tried to put on a good show, but I could tell she was worried about me. Thankfully, she hadn't figured out that I wasn't the one I was worried about. The trick was that I needed her to be cautious, but not worried about herself and our daughter. The boys, I figured, were safe as long as they stayed at school.

"Mo, I'm going to talk to the phone company."

"Why? I can take care of it."

"I know, but a call from the FBI might motivate them more than a call from…"

"….from a housewife."

"Don't you mean homemaker?"

"And Sean, don't you mean threat?"

She had me on that one, Mo and I had been married for a while. "Okay, call it aggressive persuasion."

"All right. Is there anything else?"

"Just be a little more careful, that's all."

"You mean careful, eco-terrorism careful?"

"Yeah," I said quietly "Yeah."

Mo nodded and then asked, "What about Kelly?"

"I've thought about that. I'll call in a few favors and make sure she gets some protection."

"Okay," was all Mo said, but I knew it wasn't okay.

I was about ready to fall asleep when Mo said, "I forgot in all the uh…"

"…confusion," I responded.

"Yes, we can call it that, confusion. Lukas Schafer called."

I was surprised. Why would our old parish priest call? "What did he want?"

"He wanted you."

"He must really be desperate if he needs to talk to me. I thought he was in religious hog-heaven these days."

"Didn't say, but he did give me a number to call," were Mo's final words before nodding off.

- 110 -

I hadn't slept well, too many disjointed thoughts running around and around in my mind including my family's safety and the surprise call from Father, rather Bishop Lukas Schafer. It didn't help either that I had an appointment with the Internal Revenue Service that morning. It was weird, I was going to the IRS to get information, not to be audited, but still it was the IRS and there was just an atmosphere about the place. I had hoped to make my stay at Treasury as brief as possible. Attaining that goal was fast becoming mission impossible. I had a 9:00 am appointment. It was now 9:30 am and the receptionist hadn't yet even bothered to assure me that Mr. Stallings would be with me shortly.

"Mr. Murphy, sorry to keep you waiting," the man extended his hand, "Simon Stallings."

"Mr. Stallings, Sean Murphy, we've met before with Amanda Chehwan."

"Yes, I recall. Quite a tragedy. Please call me Simon." To me the words were friendly, but the man's tone was decidedly cold.

"Fair enough Simon, call me Sean." I responded and handed the man my card.

"Sean, I understand you have some more information you would like us to research." Before I could respond, Stallings had spun around and was headed toward the door from which he had only just emerged. He continued speaking. "Please come back to my office; we can talk more freely there."

I followed Stallings through the magic door. Behind which was a short hallway, with several small windowless offices off it. At its end was the one apparently belonging to Stallings. We entered, he pointed to a side chair and he took his seat behind a gray government desk and stared at me. Apparently it was my turn to speak. I took my seat, and I could have been mistaken, but I believe my chair was lower than Stallings'. I distinctly felt I was looking up at the man. "I need you to run down some account numbers for me."

"Do you have them with you?" Stallings asked.

"I will have them emailed to you later this morning."

"From where will these numbers be coming?" I couldn't tell for sure, but it appeared there was a trace of emotion behind the question.

"CIA agent Amanda Chehwan's computer by way of the NSA." I could plainly see this answer was not what Stallings wanted to hear.

"I see," was his rather evasive response.

I started out by hating to have this meeting; by now I had moved onto pure loathing. I needed to escape. Hoping to cut short the agony, I tried to cut to the chase. "Simon, you don't need to worry about the numbers. They'll be sent to you via secure email. Alan Mitchell, my boss, is as we are speaking, getting a court order. The IRS will have all the necessary legal permissions."

"I assume you are referring to the Alan Mitchell?"

"Yes as far as I know there is only one."

"Quite, I appreciate your thoroughness," he said dryly.

"The Bureau doesn't want, and I particularly don't want, any screw ups. All the legal I's will be dotted and T's crossed."

"What are these numbers?"

"Bank account numbers, sequential bank account numbers. All except one set of numbers. We think it is a bank number, but we aren't entirely sure."

"So for those known bank numbers, what do you want?"

"Simon, I need you to tell me whom they belong to, how much is going through the accounts and whether or not those numbers agree with the tax returns being filed, if any."

"I see. How about the other number?"

"I was hoping you could determine if it was a bank number

and if not what it might be."

"Wouldn't this be something better suited for the Federal Reserve and its computer technicians?"

"If you and the Fed didn't have a reciprocal data sharing relationship, it would be. But I believe the Service is better suited to provide the Bureau with the needed data."

This remark seemed to please Stallings, at least it seemed that way because he smiled, though it was a cold smile. "A little detective work; should make for an interesting change around here. If it is a bank number, I suppose you want to know everything about it?"

"Yes, I would."

Stallings sat there and said nothing more. Several moments passed before he replied. "Sean, I believe we can help you. Provided, of course, we get proper authorization. You know it isn't like the old days when the legal niceties were sometimes ignored."

"You mean for national security reasons."

"Yes, exactly."

I needed to leave. This cat and mouse minimal response game had worn me out and to boot my ankle was throbbing away. Additionally, I had grown tired of gazing up at the man from the IRS. "Well, Simon, this request is coming to you because of national security issues. So I expect you to put your best people on it." I could see Stallings didn't like the role reversal and how

quickly it had happened, but I didn't care; in fact, it was the first time I had enjoyed anything about this meeting. Also, by now I had gotten out of my chair and was headed for the door. Just as I was about to leave, I turned.

"Oh, and by the way, I need this information ASAP. I'm sure you understand."

With that I headed for my office, grateful to be away from that cold fish of a man.

- 111 -

Not that I was free of unpleasant inter-agency bonding tasks for the day, my next stop was Fort Meade and the NSA. I had a scheduled meeting with Dennis Hamilton, or at least I was told it was with him. With the way my luck had been going, I figured it was going to be staffed out to some rookie fresh out of training. If there is one thing that all agencies share is an intense dislike of any other agency investigating or even questioning potential internal problems.

I managed to get to my meeting on time. This was no mean accomplishment, considering the traffic. As a reward, I was asked, more like commanded, to sit, read, cool my heels in Hamilton's office lobby. I had been waiting almost an hour when a young man appeared from, what seemed, out of nowhere and asked that I follow him. I followed him down several twisting corridors and then onto an elevator which we rode to, apparently, the basement. He ushered me into a windowless office and left after saying I would be attended to shortly. As I sat there, I wondered what "shortly" meant. Was this glacial time, airplane waiting time or just normal business government time? Half an hour later, I decided it was at best airplane waiting time.

As I sat there, my mother's words came back to me about having only so much time in this life and that God didn't approve of wasting it. I decided my mother's words were indeed sage words of wisdom and to avoid a guilt trip I had taken out my cell with every intention of getting some work done. However I couldn't get any reception; I was either so low in the bowels of the building or there was some kind of shielding. It didn't really matter, I was stuck. Having nothing else to do, I began to go over what I knew.

First, there was credible evidence that someone was trying to create a pattern of sectarian violence in the United States. In the past I would have said Americans don't care enough about religion or their particular brand of God. However, I wouldn't say that today. The rise of *The Movement* was just one example. There were other examples. America had had its share of church bombings, and those had continued at about the same pace in prior years. What was new were individual killings and assaults in the name of God. So far the FBI, with the help of local authorities, had kept this information reasonably under wraps. It wasn't likely that this would continue in our 7/24 news-cycle world. Inevitably the press would pick up this, and then it would be *Katy bar the Door*.

People can get upset over things, but without money nothing usually comes of it. But money was coming into America ostensibly from the Middle East and was being orchestrated by one of the world's great psychopaths, Mustafa al Bevcar. I was sure that most, if not all, of the fund's recipients didn't realize they were being used as bit players in an overall scheme that was fundamentally destructive to the United States.

Because money was the grease on which all things spun, it made sense to follow the cash. That was why first Alan Mitchell and then presumably I were brought into the investigation. The Bureau did some things well and others needed improvement. However, one of the things the Bureau did do very well was to follow the money. Unfortunately, the money trail was skimpy at best. In America almost every institution was required to report its financial condition to the government. Even the government itself had to report its finances to the public through the Congress. For reasons unknown to me, there was one exception, and the exception applied to churches. Churches reported to no one, not even God, at times.

After 911, Congress had ordered multi-agency task forces where appropriate. It was generally believed that if the different intelligence agencies had communicated prior to the events of September 11th, it was quite possible that events of that day would never have occurred. Amanda Chehwan, an agent of the Central Intelligence Agency, had been the lead investigator until her death. That position had now fallen to me. Besides myself and Amanda, my boss Alan Mitchell and her boss Deputy Director Hanson knew the complete story, such as it was. Simon Stallings at the IRS and Dennis Hamilton here at the NSA were also in the loop to some degree.

We've learned that Chehwan had managed to pull together certain financial information from an unknown source. I personally believe that source works for the NSA. On the night she was killed, Amanda was to have met with her source. According to Alan Mitchell, the source was going to provide her with vital information. Information to link the external cash flows from the Middle East to people or institutions here at home. I also believed that none of the information had been legally obtained and therefore would be of no use in a court of law. If Amanda's scenario was correct, this issue would be the least of our problems.

Now an employee of the NSA, Mark Ruben had gone missing at around the time Amanda was killed. Not only that, but it appeared the computers at the NSA, or at least some of them, had been hacked to some, so far unknown, degree. In my mind, this clearly had to have been an inside job.

Summing it up, I had a lot of questions but no answers. Unfortunately for someone, that was still good enough to make me a target. As I sat there mulling over this final thought, I thought I heard something. I looked up, and Dennis Hamilton was looking down at me.

- 112 -

To say the least, I was startled and blurted out, "How long have you been standing there?"

"Just got here," Hamilton replied with a smile.

I didn't believe him. After all my waiting, I ended up keeping the head honcho, or at least a head honcho, waiting. "Sorry, I was going over the case in my mind. I was lost in thought and didn't notice you."

"That's okay. I know you have been waiting for some time. For that I must apologize, but I got called into an unexpected meeting by my superiors, and I'm sure you know how that goes. Let's see if we can sort this thing out."

I followed Dennis Hamilton into a small interior, windowless conference room. The walls were heavily padded and without form of artwork or other common wall hangings. Hamilton must have seen me look about. "Secure room."

"I see, Mr. Hamilton."

"Call me Dennis."

"Thank you, Dennis. I wanted to let you know how much I appreciate your help and cooperation in this matter."

"I believe we have a real problem and it needs to be solved. Any help is greatly appreciated."

I found his point of view refreshing and hoped it wasn't just so much political nice speak. I was about to find out. "Dennis, I wanted to go over two issues with you."

"Let me guess, Sean. Mark Ruben and what we have

learned about my department being hacked."

"Exactly. Was it only your department?"

"No, there were two others."

"Which ones?"

"Odd really, personnel and communications."

"Communications?"

"Yes, our internal email and voicemail logs."

"Was it an inside job?" I asked.

"Sean, we can't say for certain. But if not, it certainly had to involve someone who was or had been recently connected to the Agency in some way."

"Meaning it could be someone working for the Bureau or maybe the CIA?"

"Yes, quite possibly."

"Any guess as to why those two departments?"

"No not really, but we are still working on it. I know that doesn't help you but it is where we are. I will get you whatever we find as soon as we find it.

I certainly hoped he was telling me the truth and not just blowing sunshine up my skirt. Changing the subject, "What can you tell me about Mark Ruben?"

Hamilton shuffled some documents he had and pulled out what appeared to be a personnel file. He quickly reviewed the file and began speaking. "Mark Ruben, born 1958, has been with the Agency over twenty-three years, single with no apparent hobbies or vices."

"Anything particularly unusual about the man or his background?"

"He was born in Beirut."

"So he isn't an American, or rather he is a naturalized citizen?"

Hamilton, referring again to his file, "No, his parents worked for State and were stationed in Lebanon at the time he was born."

"Do you have a picture of him?" Hamilton handed me a passport sized picture of a middle aged man who was losing the hair loss war. I studied it for a moment and then said, "May I keep this?"

"Sure."

I placed the picture in my inside coat pocket and asked, "Any siblings?"

"No," Hamilton said simply.

"Parents still alive?"

"Both parents are dead. They were killed in an auto accident while he was in college."

I wasn't sure, but the way Hamilton said auto accident, it sounded as if there were some doubts about its nature. "Where was the accident?"

"In Jordon. They were returning to Amman from Damascus."

"I see where did Ruben attend college?"

"Undergrad at MIT and grad school at Columbia."

"Has he always worked in Financial Analysis?"

"No, prior to working the financial end of Cryptology, he worked in our Middle East section."

"As I recall, the NSA has both geographic analysis groups and specific discipline analysis groups. Is it unusual for individuals to cross between disciplines?"

Hamilton looked at me and paused before continuing. "Not for our brightest employees, the ones we believe have management potential."

"So Ruben was a comer?"

"I thought so."

"You sound as if something changed."

"About maybe, three and a half or maybe four years ago, his behavior became erratic."

"Did anything special or different occur around that time?"

Again Hamilton consulted Ruben's file. "Nothing that we know of, though he had been to Jordan."

"Was that unusual?"

"No, not really. Depending upon their expertise and our needs, there are many times we send staffers to various regions of the world. In Mark's case, he had some familiarity with the region and it was as it is today a hot spot."

I waited a moment before asking my next question. "Does the employee request or is he required to go to some of these places?"

"Sean, because of the skills we need and the type of personality required we don't force staffers to go to places unless they are interested, particularly to places like the eastern Mediterranean and beyond."

"So it was something he requested?"

"Yes, and in Mark's case, it appears he also took some personal time while he was there." I must have made a quizzical look. "Oh Sean, there is nothing usual about that. Many of our staffers do this. It is a cheap way of getting a nice vacation. A perk of the job, government pay isn't the best. You know there are many cultural sites of interest in Jordan."

Switching the topic, I asked, "In what way did his behavior change?"

"Sean, the NSA has two distinct functions. One is to gather data and the other is to interpret data. It is our policy to keep the two functions separate. The rationale behind doing this is to keep opinion from clouding factual information gathering. Ruben was working in data gathering."

I interrupted Hamilton, "let me guess, he began to do uncalled-for analysis."

"Everyone does, but he went to an extreme degree. As time went by, he became very insistent."

"I see. Do you know when he might have come into contact

250

with Agent Chehwan?" I took a leap when I asked this question but it seemed to be where we were going.

Hamilton looked and me and said simply, "Three years ago."

Those three words hit home. I had only one more question to ask. "And what was Mark Ruben saying that he was so "agitated" about?"

"That there was a Middle-Eastern based plot to create sectarian strife in the United States."

- 113 -

I left Dennis Hamilton, thanking him for his help and again asked that if he learned anything new to let me know immediately. Hopefully, in his case, I believed him, as much as I believed anyone in the spook business, when he said he would. Before I headed back to DC, I pulled out the picture Hamilton had given me of Rueben and the two "enhanced" pictures Chehwan had taken the night she was killed. I sat in the front seat and compared them. It didn't look like Rueben but it was so hard to tell. Maybe some more computer analysis might clear it up. My gut said it wasn't but I would rather have something more objective to go on than my personal plumbing. I turned on the Bucar and headed back towards DC as I went I put the rest of my thoughts in order.

Most likely three years ago Amanda Chehwan made contact with Mark Ruben. Whether or not they knew each other before was unknown and probably unimportant. Of the two, it didn't really matter who first came upon the plot. My guess was that it was Ruben. How this happened might be important as it could provide a lead. Nonetheless, regardless of how it happened,

251

he believed the plot was real. He became very concerned and then when no one would listen, he became increasingly agitated. During this time, Chehwan and Ruben somehow met. She believed him and took over the investigation with Ruben providing her with information she couldn't obtain legally or illegally.

Ruben clearly had gone off the reservation. First, he had conducted unauthorized domestic spying, and second, he passed classified data. True, it was to a member of the American intelligence community, but still he had committed a major breach of security. Amanda had managed to bring acceptance to what had previously been one wild-ass theory. She had been killed while supposedly meeting with Ruben, and now Ruben had apparently disappeared.

At this point, I could only see two possibilities. One, Ruben had been turned and in the process killed Chehwan. If this were the case, he would most likely be long gone. The other option, and the one I thought more likely, was that Mark Ruben was dead and whoever had killed him had also killed Amanda.

I needed to know more about Mark Ruben.

- 114 -

Carlo Lucia sat in his spacious office starring off into space. He had to do something. He had procrastinated as long as he dared. Of that there was no question. The Catholic Church in America was coming apart at the seams. The Pope had made an unofficial request to come to America.

If he were Pope, he would have simply boarded his jet and flown to the United States, the diplomatic consequences be damned. The Secretary of State could just picture it. The Pope's 747 rolling up to the jet-way at JFK and some INS official standing at his customs desk asking if the purpose of his visit was business or pleasure and then refusing entry to the Bishop of Rome. True, there were numerous real security concerns, but Lucia believed this was the last thing on the Pontiff's mind.

The logical thing would have been to contact the FBI Director, lay the mess off in his hands and be done with it. Not only would it have been proper protocol, it would have been fair turnaround for the many times the man ran down State Department Security. A fitting hot potato for someone Lucia just didn't like. Going through channels would have fit the Government bureaucratic model, but that was about it. Being new on the job didn't help either. Lucia needed to talk this out. It was time to call his oldest friend in Washington. The Secretary of State quickly dialed the number he knew by heart. It only rang a couple of times before it was answered.

"Harold Hanson."

"Harold, Carlo Lucia."

"Carlo, how are things at Foggy Bottom?"

"Almost everything is going through its proper and traditionally slow paces."

"So what isn't?"

Carlo loved the way his old friend could see right to the point. "I got a personal and direct call from Francesco Camperelle."

"What did the Vatican Secretary of State want?"

"The Pope wants to come to America."

There was a pause on the line. "When?"

"My impression - seven hours after I said yes, he would be here."

"Why did he call you directly?"

"Security concerns."

"I see," Hanson responded, "certainly creates a number of issues."

"Yes, it does." Lucia was about to speak again when he heard first noise in the background, then what seemed to be muffled dialogue, and then nothing. It was several moments before Hanson came back on the line.

"Sorry, Carlo, my assistant David Brown needed me to sign some documents. I don't know why he insisted on interrupting me. The man is efficient, almost too efficient if you know what I mean. He can be a real busy body when he wants."

"Was he listening in?"

There was a pause before Hanson responded. "Why, I don't think so." There was another pause before the Deputy Director of Intelligence spoke again, "You know he is authorized to listen to calls on a random basis, CIA security protocols and all."

Lucia thought he noted an uncertainty, or at least some discomfort in his old friend's voice, but decided to drop the issue. "Harold. Do you have any thoughts, or better yet, have you heard anything?"

"I've heard nothing, but that isn't unusual. The Vatican has to be the tightest run organization in the world. Nothing, absolutely nothing, accidentally slips out. Even when it appears to be the case, it is not."

"Hell Harold, the Church has had over 2,000 years of practice. It has outlasted empires, presidents and dictators and your odd suicidal prone despot. I wouldn't expect anything less."

"True, I just wish I could be as leak free. That's all."

"You think your spy group is leaky, you should be over here on the SS Titanic. Herding cats would be twice as easy." Lucia paused for a drink of water. "You know I need to decide soon. What do you think?"

Hanson chose his words with care, "Carlo, why not let the man in, but as a private citizen, not the head of state?"

Lucia digested what Hanson had suggested. There was a great deal of merit to his suggestion. One, it allowed the Pope to come, but not in a way that would get the ACLU all excited over potential Constitutional bitches regarding the separation of church and state. Second and most of all, the safety concerns would lay with the Catholic Church and not the Administration. "Harold, great idea, I think it works. Thanks, I really appreciate it."

"Carlo, will I see you Friday for cards?"

"That is my plan, but in this world plans made that far in advance are often subject to change."

Both men laughed and simultaneously hung up.

- 115 -

"Your Holiness."

"Yes Francesco, what is it?"

For once Camperelle was able to bring some good news to the new Holy Father. It seemed as of late, all he could do was to add to his burdens. "I just received a phone call from the American Secretary of State."

"What did he say?"

Camperelle could almost see Peter II brace himself for more bad tidings. "He said you could come to America, if you came as a private citizen and not as a head of state."

Camperelle watched as the Pope broadly smiled and nodded, obviously enjoying this unexpected turn of events, even if the offer itself created another set of problems. "Very clever of Mr. Lucia, very clever indeed. He has created a no-lose situation. I can come and possibly help, but I'm to keep a low profile so if there is a failure…"

"You will not fail, but yes, a low profile is mandatory. No mass rallies of any kind. And yes, I agree with you. It is indeed a clever solution. It solves America's peculiar constitutional issue while at the same time providing you with an opportunity to fix the problem caused by *The Movement*."

"Francesco, *The Movement* is just one piece of what is going on over there. Religious intolerance seems to be growing exponentially."

"Yes, I have read the reports, quite disturbing. Why do you suppose this is happening now?"

"Money," the Pope responded.

"Money?" Camperelle had his own thoughts on the matter but wanted to see what his new leader thought.

"The importance of religion to those living in the developed world, particularly Western Europe, as you and I know from experience, is low."

"Your Holiness, I wish it were that high."

The Pope wanly smiled at Camperelle's sad little joke. "Nonetheless, America has been a modern anomaly. Religion still means something there."

Camperelle, wishing to draw the Pontiff out, responded, "Yes, that is true, at least to some degree."

"Yes, to some degree. Francesco, I think it is one of God's little jokes on us. It is true; the depth of the country's fervor is subject to debate. But therein may lay the reason for the tolerance most Americans feel towards those who do not believe as they do. Think of those countries where people believe deeply. Many times the population seems more than ready to dispose of their fellow citizens in the name of God."

"Yes, Your Holiness. There is a fine line between indifference and tolerance."

"Yes, there is. Now please make our arrangements so we can walk that fine line."

- 116 -

"I hope the setting is more to your liking, David," Chalmers said with a hint of sarcasm. "As I recall, you were rather unhappy about the timing and location of our last meeting."

David looked at Adrian Chalmers and fought his anger. More and more he had to remind himself to remain calm when around this man. David's rage had risen over time in direct relationship to the growth in Chalmers' arrogance and lust for power. In a low voice, David merely said, "I was only concerned about security."

"Be that as it may, what do you have for me?"

"Before I answer that, I wanted to discuss another matter with you."

"What?" Chalmers practically shouted, "Isn't the money good enough for you?"

David waited for Chalmers to calm down. "The money is fine for what we agreed I would do. However, now I bring you something more, something that'll bring you within reach of your goal."

"So you want a bonus for this special news? Is that it?"

"Yes, you might say that."

Chalmers said nothing. He wanted to make David wait. He had, in fact, been waiting for him to ask for more money. Money was all that motivated this man, and money would eventually be his downfall. At the right time, but now was not that time. "How much more?"

"I was thinking $1,000,000."

"In the usual bank, I presume."

"I haven't decided."

Chalmers starred at David. The amount was a little more than he had expected. Undoubtedly, what he knew was worth it. The man had always fairly priced his information. One could always say that about it. Still, $1,000,000 was a lot of money. Then on the other hand, how long would he live? He might not be able to spend it all. "$1,000,000 is a lot of money."

"Not much for a man like you."

258

"True and I can say you have always been fair with your pricing. Okay, $1,000,000 if I think it is worth it."

"Oh, you will."

"David, I certainly hope so. If it is, where should I send the money?

"I will let you know very shortly."

"Okay Now, what is the information?"

"The Pope is coming to America."

This was just the news he had been hoping to hear. However, for $1,000,000 he could hear the same news shortly on any of the news networks. "Why is this tidbit worth a bonus?"

"Because I'll be able to get you his itinerary."

"That will be all over the news. So far, your information isn't adding up."

'I said I will be able to get you his itinerary, his real itinerary. Oh by the way, he is coming as a private citizen. There are to be no rallies or large outdoor Masses. And…of course, security will be very tight."

"Very interesting, I stand corrected, David. You have earned your bonus."

David merely nodded and said nothing as he left, his expression not revealing his innermost thoughts.

- 117 –

I made a quick call back to Dennis Hamilton's office to get

the address to Mark Ruben's residence. The address they had was Laurel, Maryland, formerly a small town but now, like much of Virginia and Maryland, close to D.C., a growing suburb. It was convenient to Fort Mead, so apparently many federal employees had chosen to live there. I caught route 128 and headed west. The countryside is as you would imagine, old homes and small farms interspaced with new carefully planned, environmentally friendly subdivisions. You know the kind, with pathways and other amenities that are supposed to bring neighbors together but seldom do. The reason obvious to all but city planners, who apparently have yet to realize that their new citizens spend the greater part of their days either on the job or commuting to it.

Ruben's place was west of downtown, and as I drove to it, the scenery became more rural. It was times like this that I really wished I had an onboard GPS system. But the government, in its infinite wisdom, saw the units as luxuries, and it would, of course, be unthinkable for federal employees to work in the lap of luxury. Consequently, it took me a while, but I finally located where Ruben lived.

Mark Ruben lived at the end of country lane in a small cottage tucked back in the woods. Old growth hardwoods abounded, as well as ferns and my all-time favorite poison ivy. As I approached, everything about the place said, I like my privacy, go away. To me, the grounds and house had that not-lived-in look. There weren't any vehicles of any kind around. But of course, a lot of country places have a similar look. I parked the car and before I got out, I grabbed my weapon from the glove compartment, better to be safe than sorry.

As I stepped out from the car, I noted there were no human sounds, just a lot of forest noises. Looking down for tire tracks, I noted nothing fresh. The ones there were days old, at least. I then headed around the back of the house, being sure to keep enough cover between me and any direct line of fire from the cottage. From what I could tell as I circled the house, the emptiness was more than an appearance; no one had been around for some time.

The front porch and steps creaked as I walked to the front door and knocked, stepping back from the door just in case. However, there was no answer which was a bad thing. There were no shots either, which was a good thing. Still no answer, even as I repeated pounding loud enough to wake all the woodland creatures within half of a mile. As was typical in a cottage such as this, there was a window off the porch. Peering carefully through, I saw no activity. It was a little dark in the room, but the place did look deserted.

I headed back to the front door, figuring I would probably have to pick the lock to gain entrance. I tried the handle just in case. Nothing is sillier than spending a bunch of time trying to pick the lock of an unlocked door. As I grabbed the handle and depressed the lever, I noticed bits of shiny metal near the key hole. The lock had been recently picked and the front door was, to my surprise, unlocked. It swung open, squeaking the entire way.

Swearing under my breath, I waited outside. There wasn't one chance in a million that if someone was in the house, he could have possibly missed the front door opening. Nothing happened, other than having my blood pressure reach new heights. Taking a final look around, I headed in.

- 118 -

By now I was certain or at reasonably so that there wasn't anyone present, or that at least was alive. The cottage was musty, and there was a general level of dust on all the furniture. Every time I took a step on the hardwood floor, there was some kind of noise; clearly the place was old and the floor joists complained every time I took a step. I quickly moved into the kitchen and opened the refrigerator door. There weren't a lot of items, but it didn't exactly look like someone had cleaned it out planning on being away for a while. I pulled open the vegetable drawer and with it got a real whiff. Everything was bad and moldy. I continued my inspection, checking out both bedrooms, one of which had been used as an office. The bathroom came last. I didn't find a body, for which I was glad on many levels. I noted there were plenty of clothes in all the closets and the bathroom medicine cabinet had the usual assortment of medicines, ointments and creams, and interestingly enough Ruben's toothbrush.

Heading back to the living room, there didn't seem to be much doubt that if Mark Ruben had taken off, it was not planned. There were just too many things in the house that said he had no plans to take a trip. It was time to take a closer look. I went back to the car and got my small flashlight and to begin looking for clues.

I wasn't having much luck. That really wasn't fair to say. Actually, I wasn't having any luck at all. The place was normal, boringly so. There were a number of what I would call knick-knacks. Not really typical for a male-decorated house. There were a lot of books, all neatly organized and filed away. At first glance the topic range seemed generally limited to religion, the Middle East and archeology. The man was obviously a neat freak. Everything seemed to have a place, and from I could tell, everything was in its place. Drawers were organized; papers were straight and stacked. True, it appeared the front door lock had been tampered with, but there simply wasn't anything else in the house to indicate anything was out of the norm. I was going to leave when I decided to take one more look in Ruben's office. I wasn't about to try to do anything with the man's computer, but I wanted to check out his setup so I could have tech come out from headquarters. I finished my little research and headed back down the hall when I noticed something about the rug. It wasn't square.

At my house, something not perfectly lined up wouldn't

have meant a thing. But that wouldn't be the case for Ruben. The rug in his front room was turned at an angle. The arrangement brought it much closer to the front window and door and left a gap by the swinging door leading into the kitchen. Looking more closely, I noticed it was also bunched up at the couch and coffee table. It looked like someone had hurriedly tried to pull it without bothering to adjust the heavier pieces of furniture.

I walked slowly over to the corner by the window and pulled it back. That section of hardwood floor was more lightly colored than the surrounding wood. The rug had obviously been pulled to conceal the fact that the floor had been marred there. I again took my flashlight and began to examine the spot. There could be a number of legitimate answers to the question as to what had caused the discoloration, including rain coming in though the nearby open window or a cup of hot coffee being dropped. But still, why was carpet bunched up around the heavy furniture pieces, particularly by someone obviously as organized and precise as Mark Ruben?

I ran my flashlight back and forth a couple of times. At first I didn't see it. But as I expanded my search to the edges of the marred zone, I saw something. It appeared to be a drop of some kind. Again, there wasn't anything insidious about drop marks. I had plenty in all the rooms at my house. However, this one was that particular color of brown that dried blood leaves. I wouldn't bet my last dollar on the drop being blood, but then again considering the circumstances, I wouldn't bet against it. Blood, even Ruben's, in and of itself didn't mean foul play, but my gut told me something bad had happened here.

At this point, I decided I didn't need to continue to contaminate this potential crime scene. I backed out of the house and called headquarters, told them what I had found and asked them to send help. I planned on waiting until the forensic team arrived. I figured it would be at least an hour and half before they could get here. Wasting time bugged me, so I decided to see what I could find outside.

The cottage had a detached garage behind it. I headed for it and opened the unlocked door. The garage was empty, which wasn't surprising. Quickly glancing around, I saw nothing of immediate interest. I closed the door and headed away from the house. The ground sloped away down to what appeared to be a creek. I followed a slightly overgrown path towards the sound of water. About forty yards out, I came to a bluff that dropped five or six feet to a swiftly running stream. It was an idyllic spot; running water, chirping birds, buzzing something.

The buzzing sound puzzled me. I looked up and down the creek bed for the source of the noise. In the direction away from Ruben's, there seemed to be a swarm of some kind of bug. I couldn't quite tell from the distance. I didn't see a ready way down to the creek. The only way down was to climb. I hated this. It looked like I would be lucky if I didn't ruin another pair of slacks and shoes.

Fortunately, I managed to get down to the creek with some dignity. As I approached the swarm, I could see the insects were flies. This wasn't a good sign. I looked around. I needed to see if anyone was here. I was alone and was beginning to have a real bad feeling. I grabbed a branch that had a few leaves still attached and preceded to shoo the flies away. At first they weren't terribly interested in leaving, but finally I broke up the swarm that had been hovering near some thick undergrowth. With the flies gone, I used my stick to gently move the leaves and branches aside. It didn't take long. Within moments I found what had attracted the flies. It was a body that looked, as much as I could tell considering its condition, to be that of Mark Ruben.

264

- 119 -

"Francesco, have all the necessary arrangements been made?"

"Of course not, Your Holiness. All that is needed could never be done in such a short time."

"Do the large things. The small ones will fall into place."

"I'm having trouble doing the large ones," Camperelle wanted to yell but didn't.

"Do your best. It's in God's hands."

"I would feel better if it were in some mere mortals hands."

"You doubt the Lord?"

"Of course not, I would just feel better if you had more protection."

"More protection and more..." the Pope asked.

"More everything. Coordination, communication..."

"Francesco, it will be all right." The young Pope laid his hand reassuringly on the Cardinal's shoulder. "You have set up meetings with as many American Bishops as possible, correct?"

"Correct. But I think we should schedule something with *The Movement*."

"I will meet with Lukas Schafer, but when and how will have to be determined when we get to America. You will have to trust me on this."

"I trust you completely, Holy Father. It is everyone else that worries me. This trip is very dangerous. You could be killed."

"If that is God's wish, then so be it. I must go and what happens then happens. But please join me now for dinner. There are other things we need to discuss."

The Vatican Secretary of State merely nodded. Of course, the Pontiff was correct. It was God's will. He just hoped and prayed that it was God's will to keep the new Pope on this earth at least a few years longer.

- 120 -

I turned away. The body had begun to look and smell like, well like just what you could imagine. I felt sorry for the M.E. boys, but it was something they had signed up for. Frankly, I was glad to leave the crime scene as it was, uncontaminated by my presence. There wasn't anything I could do. Mark Ruben was beyond any help I could provide, other than prayer.

I made my way back to the car and called in my report. As expected, I was instructed not to disturb anything and to wait until the examiners arrived. I'm not sure why the dispatcher had to give me these pearls of wisdom. What in the name of whatever is holy did she think I was going to do? Run down to the local cop store and buy nine miles of yellow tape and start stringing it all over the property?

Before I had hung up and after I got my dopey instructions, I requested a computer technician and someone from the bomb squad. I had had enough fun playing at Amanda's place. This time I wanted someone else to go back into the house to deal with whatever might be there, someone who happened to be both trained and paid to do that kind of thing.

266

I stayed by my vehicle as I waited. It was parked in such a way that it afforded me the best view of the property. I could see the house, garage and most of the property above the creek, as well as down the lane to the main road and the open field beyond. Help arrived much sooner than I had anticipated.

At first I only heard it, but within minutes a helicopter was putting down in the pasture by the highway. I grabbed my binoculars to see who my first guests were. I figured it had to be someone fairly high up the food chain. Not everyone gets to ride to a crime scene by chopper. However, I was still surprised when Alan Mitchell and then Dennis Hamilton stepped out of the aircraft and began walking in my direction.

- 121 -

"Sean, how are you doing?" Dennis Hamilton extended his hand to shake mine.

"One hell of a lot better than poor Mark Ruben."

"Can you show us where the body is?" Mitchell asked.

Interesting question, I thought. Of course I can show them. I was just down in the creek where I found him. "Yes Alan, are you sure you want to go down there?" I figured why not ask him a stupid question. What did I have to lose? Maybe he would say no. I simply didn't want to go back down there. As it was, I would probably have bad dreams about what I had seen for weeks.

"Yes," was all he said, but the look he gave me said a lot more. Frankly, I didn't care. I had a bit of a wiseass reputation, and I hadn't filled my quota lately. I led our little group back to the creek bed and to the spot where the body lay.

"There he is, sir." I pointed toward the body. At the same

time I pulled Ruben's picture from my coat and handed it to Mitchell, who merely grunted.

Hamilton and Mitchell slowly approached the body. I decided to hang back. The wind had shifted since I had been down in the creek bed before wafting the stench away from us. I suspected this change of direction was only temporary. If I was right, I wanted to be as far up-wind as possible when it happened. I could see Mitchell and Hamilton look back and forth, first at the body and then at the picture. They were nodding. To me it looked like they were almost satisfied that I hadn't jumped to some stupid conclusion about who the DB was. Then the breeze swung around, and before you knew it, they were heading back to higher ground, and I was right behind them.

"Sean, it's Ruben," Mitchell said and handed me back the photo.

"Yes sir."

Hamilton had moved away from Mitchell and me and was talking on a phone. "Sean, Dennis is calling in some special help. His technical team will work with ours. Between the two of them hopefully, they will turn something up."

"As do I, I could use a break about now."

"You can head home once our team gets here and you can fill them in on what you found etc. etc. No need to stick around after that, just make sure you give me a full report ASAP. We'll chopper back in a few minutes." Mitchell nodded his head in the direction of the helicopter.

I wondered if somehow he thought I had forgotten how they arrived, it being so small and quiet and all. "Yes sir." So far it had been a real easy conversation with my boss. All I had had to do was nod and say yes. It had the added benefit of keeping me out of trouble. By now Hamilton had returned. He shook my hand again and turned to leave. The man was clearly upset. Mark Ruben must have been special.

- 122 -

Adrian Chalmers again looked at the paper in front of him. David delivered as he had promised; and as promised Chalmers had transferred the required sum as he had been instructed. A million dollars was a lot to pay for information, even to a man as well off as Adrian Chalmers. Then again Chalmers knew the money was only a loan, albeit an interest-free one, but a loan nonetheless. As cunning and ruthless as he was, David could best be described as a financial neophyte. Chalmers was convinced that David believed that no one, Chalmers included, could access his bank account. Thankfully, David had not done the usual things experienced people did with their ill-gotten gains such as using front corporations and making extensive transfers among financial institutions to hide the trail of their money. He had left all his proceeds in the same bank since the very beginning. The only deception he had tried was his futile, "I'll let you know where to send the money ploy" Had he tried to move the money around he might have developed a suspicion that there were strings attached to what he believed to be his money. Chalmers knew this was a loose end. One that was necessary to leave open now but would shortly be closed.

Chalmers turned back the paper. He began to study to commit to memory the Pope's United States itinerary. The time had come to choose. To choose who would live and who would die. Chalmers wanted an elegant end to his years of planning and scheming. He wanted it to happen now, in one day, and if it could be done in one single grand action, so much the better. It would be a day of celebration, of great achievement to be celebrated throughout history. His *Hope for America Foundation,* and by extension Adrian Chalmers, would have the power he always coveted, to make things as they should be to write the right kind of rules for this country.

Chalmers sat quietly, formulating a plan. Yes, a single stroke that was the answer. Had this been a public trip, a single action would probably have been too difficult. This would not be the case of private citizen Salim Ateek, now known to the world as Peter II, Bishop of Rome. The new Pope had unbelievably, in Adrian's mind, scheduled a meeting with Lukas Schafer and a few close associates at the end of his trip. Yes, definitely it would be at this meeting that some of these holy men would have a chance to meet their Maker. Of course, along with these men of the cloth, the evil assassin, the perpetrator of this hideous crime, would also have to die. A necessary closure needed by both the public and himself.

- 123 -

I waited around long enough at the crime scene to get a feel as to the quality of the investigators. I could readily see both agencies had sent their A teams. I exchanged pleasantries with both of them and was assured I would get whatever information they turned up in real time. With that, I headed back home to Washington. Thankfully, it didn't take me long to make the drive. Most of the late rush hour traffic was clogged heading north. By the time I hit the Potomac, the southbound commuters had just about cleared out. I pulled into our garage. Mo's car wasn't there.

That didn't mean much these days. My daughter had probably taken it to one of her many social or school-related events. I swear she did more things than any ten adults I knew put together. I announced my presence to whomever that I was home.

"I'm upstairs. I'll be right down," I heard my wife shout. As promised, I heard her come down the stairs before I had a chance to sort through the mail.

"How was your day?" My wife asked.

Not wanting to spoil our evening, I gave her the short, less ghoulish version of my encounter with Mark Ruben.

"A young life cut short, how sad," was her only comment.

Wanting to change the conversation, I asked, "Where's Kelly?"

"At the Patrick's. Some dance committee thing. At least, that is what she told me."

I didn't immediately say anything. I didn't like her last comment. "Listen, Mo, I don't want to get into a fight but what do you mean, "*at least that is what she told me.*"

"You know our sweet, lovely, youngest child has become a bit rebellious."

"A bit?"

"Well, a lot. Takes after someone I know. You know it was bad before you called in your cop favors. Now she hates everything, thinks we are spying on her."

"Do I need to talk to her about it?"

"Sean, it couldn't hurt, but it probably won't help the way her teenage brain is functioning."

Mo was clearly frustrated and drained. "When she gets home, I'll talk to her. I'll tell her that as soon as this case closes, life will return to normal."

"Yea Sean, whatever normal is."

"Yeah. I know."

Mo went to the refrigerator and pulled out dinner ingredients. She handed me what I needed to make a salad. We worked in silence, each with our traditional responsibilities. Mo would fix the main course, and I would then be in charge of cleaning up. We made mostly small talk during dinner. The quiet wasn't uncomfortable; we were both tired and simply didn't have much to say. Before I got up to clean, Mo asked, "Have you had a chance to call Lukas Schafer?"

"Thanks for reminding me. I forgot to call."

"Why not call now? It's not too late."

"Good idea." Mo handed me the phone and a piece of paper with a number.

I really didn't want to call, and I knew that Mo knew this. She was good at making me toe the line. I punched in the numbers and waited. The call didn't go through. All I could hear was a series of clicks. I hung up and redialed, again a series of pops and clicks. Finally the call connected and the phone began to ring. It continued to ring, five, six, seven times. I waited for a phone machine to pick up, but nothing happened. I finally hung up and turned to Mo. "I just remembered something else I forgot to do."

"Contact the phone company," she said with a knowing smile.

"Very clever way of reminding me."

"I know. And you still need to talk to Lukas."

"Yes, I know."

- 124 -

Adrian Chalmers picked up his private secure phone. It was time to make the call. He relished times like this. It was the drama of life, the choices made. First the uncertainty, followed by the exploration of the options and then finally the resolution. It was raw, human emotion at its unbridled best.

What would the outcome be? Who would live and who would die?

The phone rang only twice before it was answered, "Raymond Gates."

"Reverend Gates, Adrian Chalmers."

"Hello, Mr. Chalmers."

Chalmers waited to see if Gates would say anything more, but there was only silence. "I want to express my condolences. I understand you were close to the men who died.

"Yes, they were my best friends, as well as vital members of *The Movement.*"

Chalmers hesitated. He didn't want to rush the game. He wanted to play it, savor it, to the end. "Yes, I know they were your lieutenants. Small planes are so convenient, but at times so deadly."

Again, silence from Gates. Chalmers simply waited. Finally, "what can I do for you Mr. Chalmers?"

"I was thinking about how brief life could be. About how many people never live long enough to fulfill their destiny. Tragic, if you know what I mean?"

"God has his ways."

"Yes, he does. But that doesn't mean man doesn't have

choices and options. Choices and options presented by the Lord."

"Mr. Chalmers, please make your point you must have one or you wouldn't have called, but remember I will not do anything immoral."

Chalmers smiled to himself. He had him. "If you did, you wouldn't be the man I would want."

"I'm glad you understand. That being said, I'm at your disposal."

"Raymond, I'm so happy to hear you say that. I can't tell you how pleased I am to have your total support. I'll be in touch with you shortly. Until then, goodbye." Chalmers didn't wait to hear Gates' response. Placing the phone in its cradle, he knew he would soon have to make his final selection.

- 125 -

I had planned on contacting TPC, the Phone Company, as soon as got into the office but was surprised to find a preliminary report on the Ruben investigation. There had to be a tremendous amount of heat on this one. Seldom did anything arrive this quickly, even from the A team. According to the NSA, FBI joint investigative committee Mark Ruben's computer along with the rest of his personal possessions had been subject to intense scrutiny. Almost nothing had been found. The man's clothing and possessions were clean. His residence had yielded only one piece of paper with a series of numbers. Whoever had scrubbed his cabin must have missed it. The paper was small and had gotten lodged behind Mark's upper right hand desk drawer. Sadly, forensics

274

couldn't find any specific clues. As far as his computer was concerned, it had been wiped slick. Nothing was retrievable even under the most intense and top-secret NSA searching techniques. It should have been apparent to even the slowest investigator that the laundry job done on Mark Ruben and his goods was a professional one. Hopefully, I wasn't the slowest agent in the Bureau's stable.

However, as of late I'd been feeling more than a little bogged down.

After I had digested the report and had re-read it a number of times I finally was able to call our friends at the TPC. I knew their customer service rep would definitely recognize the DC exchange, and most likely the call was originating from the Bureau. I hoped a little intimidation might go a long way, or at least get a modicum of "service."

I dialed and got the usual assortment of electronic number options. I continued to punch buttons with ever growing frustration. Each time thinking I had finally made the connection only to find I was wrong. Finally, I stumbled upon an option of staying on the line for the next available operator. I selected it and waited... and waited.

Finally, a live human being came on the line. I gave the woman my name, billing address and phone number. All of which she dutifully typed into her computer terminal. "How may I help you?"

"I need to know when, or at least approximately when, you sent out a crew to my house."

"What was the problem?"

"There wasn't any problem. The phones were working fine." I explained to the disembodied voice.

"So then might I ask why you are contacting us?"

"Because, now the phones don't work worth a darn."

"Please explain."

I could hear her entering data into her computer. As she typed, I explained what the difficulty was.

"I see. Mr. Murphy, I don't see any work order for your address. Are you sure about the dates?"

"There are a lot of things I'm not sure of. In fact, as I get older it seems I'm less sure all the time. But I know the difference between the phone working and not working and when the problem started."

The woman paused. I was afraid she wouldn't appreciate my humor and the next thing I would hear would be a dial tone. Mo has said more than once that my sarcastic side is not that appealing, but what does she know? She married me. "Mr. Murphy, I have crossed checked against your neighbors and other closely associated phone numbers. I can find no work orders. From the company's point of view, your phone should be functioning nicely."

I was beginning to grow concerned. "I don't want to be a pain, and before you answer, I want to let you know I work for the FBI. Are you sure?"

"Mr. Murphy, or should I say Agent Murphy, I'm aware where you are calling from. That is why I double checked the information I just gave you."

"I see." I wasn't enjoying where the logic of my thoughts was taking me.

"Please describe the problem again in as much detail as you can give me."

I explained how calls either took forever to connect or simply didn't connect. Accompanying the delay were a series of strange clicks and tones.

"To me, Mr. Murphy, and I want to make very clear that my statement is unofficial, it sounds as if someone has tapped your phone line. Now this is important. I want to assure you we, at the phone company, have no records of anyone authorizing any kind of surveillance."

Waves of panic were washing over me. Her response was both reasonable and logical. "Thank you for your help. Assuming again that we are speaking unofficially, where might I look to check to see if my line has been bugged?"

"Most likely at the main utility or electrical box at your house."

"Not at the company's switch gear box?"

"No, too many chances that one of our repair technicians would stumble across it."

"That makes sense. Anything else to look for?" I asked.

"The tap will need some kind of power source and the ability to transmit data to whoever has bugged your phone."

"Thanks for your help."

"Good luck, sir" was her response, one I barely heard as I grabbed my coat and headed for the door. I needed to get home as soon as possible.

- 126 -

I was in a cold sweat as I drove home. I managed to set a speed record getting there, committing any number of moving violations in both D.C. and Virginia. Frankly, I didn't care. If someone in law enforcement had stopped me, I would have flashed my credentials and given the guy the standard I-need-your-professional-courtesy speech. I was prepared to do this as many times as needed. If that didn't work, I think I would have drawn my weapon. I bounced into the driveway and headed for the side door.

Thankfully, no one was home. I took off my coat, dropped my laptop on the kitchen, table, grabbed a flashlight and headed first for the attic. I wasn't exactly sure where I was going to find the equipment box the service rep told me about. I pulled down the folding stairs and climbed up. I hadn't been in the attic for over six months. However, it was exactly as I remembered it, a mess still awaiting my new year's resolution to clean it. Dust and cobwebs were everywhere. It didn't take long for me to determine this wasn't where to look. Nothing was moved or cleaned. If someone had been up here working, that person would have had to be a magician not to disturb anything. My next stop was the basement.

The basement was the more likely candidate. Stuff was always being moved in and out of it by someone; the kids, Mo or me. We had piled boxes on top of each other, mostly containing possessions from our married life, but some from times earlier than that. We had filled every conceivable corner in the basement as well as most of the available wall space. In an earlier time I could have gone straight to the electric or phone box and looked there. However, with the advent of wireless electronics, the tap could be anywhere. I began with the corner closest to the stairs. My plan was to move clockwise until I found the bug or got back to the

278

stairs.

I had been working steadily for about an hour and had gotten half way around the room into the third corner when I spotted some metal shavings. If I hadn't been looking, I would have either missed the pieces or simply ignored them as standard un-swept trash. My heart raced as I slowly and carefully began examining each box before I moved it; for all I knew the bug could be in one of the boxes. I had removed four before I could see into the corner. I shined my flashlight into the darkened space and saw nothing. Moving the light up the wall towards the ceiling, I also came up empty. Three almost identical large cartons remained on the floor. One was stacked on top of the other two like a mini-pyramid.

From the exterior, nothing seemed out of order for the three moving cartons, no unexpected cuts, dings or tears. However, the dust patterns surrounding the slightly smaller top carton indicated it had recently been moved. I picked it up and placed it gently in the center of the room under one of the fluorescent light fixtures. I began examining the box in the back.

Written on it were the words "Christmas stuff." The shards I had seen could definitely have come from a broken ornament. The flaps had the look of being opened and closed many times. This wasn't surprising since we had probably had it for over twenty years. The box wasn't sealed and the flaps sagged slightly inward. I shined the light and what struck me was what I didn't see. There weren't any cobwebs or dust. The boxes were clean. The inside of our Christmas boxes were never clean. I looked under the lid and didn't see any wires or filaments.

I slowly opened first one lid and then the other. Something seemed out of place. I always packed these boxes, and the way the inside of box was arranged didn't look like my work. The box holding our large top of the tree ornament was crushed down. This isn't something I'd have done, especially considering how much the sucker had cost. Again shining the light looking for trip wire, I didn't see anything. I then removed the ornament box from the stack.

There it was. A hollow space had been created among the boxes, and a small electronic box hooked to a battery pack had filled it. Someone had been listening to our telephone conversations and God knew what else. It could have been going on since the first of the year, but most likely considering the evidence, since March, which was about the same time I had been assigned to the counterterrorism unit.

I wanted to pick the thing up and smash it into a million pieces. That would have felt good in the short run. However, in the long run I needed to make whoever planted the bug think I didn't know about it. With luck, I could set the person or persons up. I had had some training and the unit looked fairly sophisticated, third or fourth generation. So I was going to have to use some kind of false lead approach. My head swam with possibilities and options, mixed with anger about my family and my space being violated.

As I stood there fuming, I thought I heard a noise coming from upstairs, probably Mo or Kelly. However, not wanting to take any chances, I quickly put everything back as I found it and headed upstairs.

It turned out to be Kelly, some special half-day thing. I swear her school has more special days than I can believe. No wonder kids are unable to concentrate for more than a short period of time these days. No one ever asks them to or trains them. Of course, I was having trouble concentrating. Though my excuse was better I thought than VGML, video game memory loss.

"I'm going to have to go back into the District," I said to Mo who had also arrived right after Kelly.

"Okay, but I thought you were going to work from here."

She pointed to my laptop sitting on the kitchen table.

"I was, but I'm drawing blanks. I'd hoped the change of scenery would help my creative thinking skills."

"Oh, you have creative thinking skills?" Mo sarcastically commented.

My look must have said it all. Normally I would have had some clever response. Mo just came over and gave me a kiss, "Good luck and let me know about dinner."

- 127 -

As I drove into the parking garage of the Hoover Building, I called Alan Mitchell and told him of the bug. He promised me he would think about the best way of handling the situation. I thanked him and decided to take a walk on the Mall first rather than go directly to my office I desperately needed to sort things out.

The weather had turned nice I mean for Washington at this time of the year, low humidity in the morning followed by increasing moisture during the day broken by the occasional thunder shower. I firmly believed the founding fathers had picked the location on the Potomac for more than the stated reason of being midway between the northern and southern states. They picked it because the weather here was almost inhospitable in the summer. What better way to keep government small than by forcing it to close for four or five months a year. Washington, Adams and Jefferson and the rest of the boys knew what they were doing. At least that was the case until the use of air conditioning. I had read someplace, but I don't recall where and it was an astounding number, the amount of growth of the federal government that occurred after air conditioning had been installed in the U.S. Capital building.

Sometimes just getting out and moving around helped clear my mind. I needed to decide on how to proceed now that I knew my phone had been tapped. Was it related to my current assignment? The timing would seem to indicate that it was. Or it could be a coincidence? There wasn't much of a doubt that we were dealing with a professional; the signs pointed that way. The clues were there. They ranged from the way Mark Ruben had been killed, to the type of electronic surveillance equipment I had found at my home. This assumed, of course, all of these clues weren't coincidental; by the way, did I say that I didn't believe in coincidences?

Professional was an interesting description. To me it meant either a current or former agent either of foreign or domestic origin, not a doctor, lawyer or accountant. That left a lot of territory to cover, but it did narrow it down from every human being currently in the Washington-Baltimore Metro area to a slightly smaller number. I have been at this a while and I still don't have a lot of clues to go on. The latest one is a scrap of paper with a number on it. However for all I knew, it could have been an old dry-cleaning ticket.

By now I've made it to the Washington Monument. I look up at the monolith; it is an impressive site deserving to honor our first president. When the kids were young Mo and I would take them here. We would ride the elevator to the top where we could see all over the District including the White House, the Capital, the other monuments, the tidal basin, even Union Station.

The walk has helped but I need to get back. I know I've pressed my luck with any potential killer following me waiting for the right moment to pop off Sean besides the humidity has really started to settle in. Part of me wished I could play hooky all day. That happens to be the part that is still in denial about being the target of an assassin.

The moment I turn to head back it strikes me. Suppose for the moment the number on the slip of paper found at Mark Ruben's was a locker number. Further suppose that if it was a locker number, maybe it belongs to a storage unit in Union Station. Yes, that was a possibility. I need to see if the number sequence at Union Station agrees to one of the orphan numbers pulled from Amanda's computer. For the first time in some time, I felt or at had the beginnings of a feeling that I was moving in the right direction.

- 128 -

It was late and had been quite a day, a very productive one, yet very tiring. I had discovered the number from Mark Ruben's slip of paper matched one of the orphan numbers from Amanda's hard drive. Additionally, the numerical sequence of locker numbers found at Union Station included the number in question. Whether or not there actually was such a locker and what its condition was would have to wait until tomorrow. By the time I had figured this out, it was too late to get a warrant. I called Alan Mitchell, and he told me he would make sure one was ready the next day. He and I were scheduled to meet at Union Station at 9:00 am, he with the needed warrant and me with my great investigative skills.

The traffic was light, so my mind wandered a bit as I drove home. Whoever had planted the bug was someone with resources. Whoever it was certainly had the ability to get sophisticated eavesdropping equipment. Not only that, but the person had the ability to or could hire someone to break into my home undetected. If the equipment had worked properly, I would have never known as undoubtedly, the bug would have been removed before Christmas.

It struck me there was only one person or one type of person who could manage this. It had to be an operative, someone from an intelligence agency. The skill sets needed to work at the Bureau were not it; rather it was more like someone from the CIA or the NSA. There were two chances that it was an official investigation, slim and none. Someone had gone off the reservation. I just needed to know two things now, why and who. That's not much, right?

I knew that even if I figured out the why and who, I wasn't entirely convinced it would help my current assignment in any way, though it would be a start. More to the immediate point, I was going to have to be very careful as to what I said at home. To protect them, I needed to keep Mo and Kelly in the dark. At least for the immediate run. The Bureau was going to have to covertly, and I mean covertly, protect my wife and daughter, at least until I could sort things out.

- 129 -

I didn't really want to stop, but I needed to phone Lukas Schafer and I needed to get some prepaid disposable cell phones for me, Mo and Kelly. I pulled off the freeway an exit before my usual one. The exit went right by a busy strip center with a drug store and a Starbucks. I went into the drug store and purchased three phones, one for each of us still at home. When they asked why they were getting these new cell phones, I decided would put the blame on the Bureau, some upper management directive that would last a month or so. From there I went across the parking lot to the Starbucks where I could easily blend in with everyone else making calls or using their computers there. I walked in and ordered a cappuccino. The barista, who couldn't have been more than twenty, gave me a strange look. In the back of my mind I remembered hearing someplace that one simply didn't order cappuccino after some hour of day that I couldn't remember. I was tired, didn't care, besides I liked cappuccino. Of course, I would have liked a beer better, but that would have to wait until later.

I took my order to a far corner. As I sipped my coffee, I rummaged through my pockets until I found the paper with

Schafer's number. I dialed the number and hoped Lukas would pick up. The phone rang and rang. I silently swore, damn he wasn't there. I was about to hang up when I heard a voice answer that didn't sound like it belonged to Lukas Schafer.

I responded, "Hello, Lukas Schafer, please."

"One moment please. Who may I say is calling?"

"Tell him that Sean Murphy is returning his call." I heard what seemed to be a muffled conversation, then silence. I wondered if the next thing I would hear would be a dial tone.

"He'll be with you in a moment," with that the line went silent.

I waited. Finally Schafer came on the line, "Hello, Sean. How are you?"

"Just fine." I wasn't quite sure how to address my old parish priest. Father? Your Eminence? So as a compromise I chose the no-title type approach.

"It is good to hear your voice."

Something didn't seem right, so I kept my response bland. "Same to you. Mo said you called."

Sounding distracted, Schafer answered. "Yes." He paused, "Yes, I did."

"Is there something I can do for you?"

Schafer lowered his voice. He was becoming hard to hear. "Sean, I need to see you."

"Sure, anytime."

I could barely hear him now. "I need to see you as soon as

possible."

"Where? When?"

I can't talk right now. I'll call you. Please give me a number where I can reach you."

I gave him my cell number. "Sean, I will call." With that he hung up.

- 130 -

To say the least my call with Lukas Schafer both startled and disturbed me. I wondered what could be so pressing that it would prevent him from speaking with me? Of course he was a busy man; I'm not kidding myself about my own importance. It was most likely that he was in an important meeting and was simply indisposed. Still he was very evasive. As I pulled into my driveway, I concluded I would just have to wait to find out if something was wrong. As it turned out, it was sooner than I thought. I had just hit the garage door opener when my cell phone rang. It was Lukas Schafer. I quickly put the car in reverse and headed back down the driveway. I needed to get at least 250 yards from the house, or more precisely the bug in the house, to be out of its range.

The phone rang several times and I was afraid it would go to voicemail. I hit send and blurted out before he could say a word, "Could you please wait one moment, I need to go to a place of better reception?" I then hit the mute button. I headed away from the house and made sure I was far enough away before I began speaking. I just hoped he was still on the line.

"Lukas, Sean here."

"Sean, it is good to hear your voice. I miss hearing from my old friends. It seems so long ago, yet I know it isn't." I could still barely hear Schafer.

"Lukas, could you speak up? I can barely hear you."

"I'll try, but it isn't safe for me to speak."

I needed him to get straight to the point. I could find out the whys and wherefores later. "Okay what did you need to tell me?"

"We need to meet."

"I would like that, but I'm tied up on a current case right now. It may be a few days."

"Sean, I'm not sure there are a few days."

"Why don't you tell me what you know, and I'll be the judge?" Over the years I had learned that "civilians" would almost always over estimate the value of their information or problem.

The priest's voice dropped lower again, "You remember the recent small plane crash where several members of *The Movement* were killed?"

"Yes, of course."

"The plane was sabotaged."

"Are you sure?"

"Yes."

I was stunned. This "civilian's information just became the exception to the rule. I didn't have time to begin another investigation. And air crash incidents were the responsibility of the FAA and the NTSB. However, I was sure that Lukas Schafer would only work with me, at least initially. "When and where?"

"Tomorrow at noon at the food court of the Air and Space Museum." With that he hung up.

- 131 -

"How are you doing?" My wife called out as I walked into the house, my head swimming. Tomorrow was going to be a busy day. It was full of promise, I could feel it. The pertinent question was whether or not that promise would be fulfilled or, as in so many cases, would it turn out to be a bust?

"Earth to Sean, how are you?" Mo said to me again.

It finally registered that my wife was speaking to me. "I'm doing fine."

"Busy day? You're a little later than normal."

"Traffic was heavier than normal, no biggie." I had learned over the years to include my wife in my professional life. The trick was to tell her enough to keep her interest and curiosities satisfied, but not reveal enough to cause her concern or to put her in danger. Now I had to do that without revealing anything of value to whoever was listening in.

"Did you finally make contact with Lukas Schafer?" Mo asked.

"I will call later tonight."

"You better. You don't want him to think you are rude do you?"

"I'm never rude to the clergy, that is a sure fire ticket to hell."

"Have you had a chance to hear the news today?" Mo

288

asked thankfully changing the subject.

I thought this was an odd question. Not something my wife generally asked. "No, I was pretty busy, why?"

"There were several unconfirmed reports of sectarian violence around the country."

I was stunned. "Was anyone killed?"

"Fortunately not, but there were several rather severe injuries."

"Tell me more." I said as I picked up the remote.

"The reports are sketchy, but it seems that a number of ministers and priests were attacked."

"How many? Where did they happen?

"There were six incidents. It seems they were spread randomly around the country."

"Who attacked them? How do we know that the attacks had anything to do with religion?"

"No one knows for sure right now. All that's known is that those who were attacked were the victims of groups of three or four." Mo hadn't yet answered the most crucial question. I desperately wanted to find out, but I had learned over the years not to push my wife. She would tell me all she knew in her own fashion.

Mo continued, "The attackers were made up of both men and women. Can you imagine that?"

"Mo, times have changed for women in America and in many ways not for the better, I think. Why is there speculation that the attacks were religious in nature?"

"Apparently the words used by the attackers as well as the symbols they left behind."

As Mo said those words, a shiver ran down my spine; I remembered from those earlier briefings that certain words and symbols led the Bureau to conclude the church bombings weren't racial, but rather were religiously motivated. "I see," was all I could say.

- 132 -

As agreed, I met Alan Mitchell at 9:00 am in Union Station's management company offices. I was fifteen minutes early, a policy I tried to follow any time I was supposed to meet someone higher up the food chain than myself. Not at all surprised, I found SAC Mitchell already there and in conversation with a middle-aged man who I could reasonably assume to be the head of the management company. In the past, the government had tried running the old railroad station with limited success. Eventually, after a number of less than successful fits and starts Congress turned the daily operations over to professionals.

"Good to see you, Sean," Mitchell stuck out his hand.

I shook it and said, "thank you, sir."

"Sean, I would like to introduce you to Mr. Julius Jones. He is the executive manager of the management company that operates the station. "Morning, Sean."

"Good morning," I shook the manager's hand. "Looks like you have a big job here."

"It is. We do everything from finding retail tenants to

290

making sure the building is safe and properly maintained. And that is with over 200,000 people passing through here every day."

"Mr. Jones said he would take us to the train platform and the associated lockers," Mitchell said.

I could see the warrant stuffed into Jones' shirt pocket. It was undoubtedly the instrument of his current high level of cooperation and attention.

As we headed off to the Northeast Corridor, Jones explained that he had arranged for a maintenance technician to meet us there. Without doubt, he didn't want us tearing up his property. The walk took about five minutes, and as we moved along I briefly wondered how the janitor or maintenance man had become a "Maintenance Technician." Fortunately, we arrived at the locker before I had much time to think about it.

We rounded the final hallway, and I could see an elderly gentleman waiting for us. He seemed to be at ease. Waiting was clearly something this man had done his entire life.

Jones spoke, "Ed, these two men," he pointed in our direction, "are FBI agents." They have a warrant to open the box here." Jones pointed to the locker we were authorized to open.

"I have the master key, Mr. Jones. It won't take but a minute."

The workman walked to the locker and placed his master key into the slot. The locker easily opened. Everything was routine. What wasn't routine was the look on the man's face when he turned back to us. As he slowly moved aside, I could see why. The locker was filled with cash, lots of it, in neatly stacked piles several feet high.

- 133 -

"Holy shit!" was all Julius Jones said, while the maintenance guy simply stood there with his mouth hanging open. For myself, being the sophisticated federal agent I was, I merely stared at the cash. From the corner of my eye, I could tell Mitchell hadn't moved since the locker had been opened. Then our little bout of inactivity stopped. Jones slammed the locker shut, and Mitchell and I began quickly began looking around. Thankfully, we hadn't attracted any attention, at least not that I could tell.

"Ed, could you do me a favor?" Ed didn't immediately respond. Jones repeated himself. "Ed, Ed could you do me a favor?"

Ed finally came out of his trance. "Yes, Mr. Jones, what can I do?"

"Look, the FBI may want to move the money." I need you to go down to maintenance and get a trash can, cart, something that we can use move the money with that won't attract a lot of attention."

"Okay."

"Ed, don't tell anyone about this, all right?"

"I won't, Mr. Jones."

"I mean it, Ed, no one. Not your mom, your wife, your minister, not even God Himself."

"God already knows."

"The you won't need to tell him will you? Just keep it quiet, please," Jones sighed.

"Got it!"

Mitchell and I had been silent during this exchange. Mitchell then spoke, "Julius is there any time the station is closed, or at least this part of the building?"

"No," was all he said.

"Thank you. If you would please give us a moment, I need to talk to Agent Murphy."

Jones nodded and moved discretely away. "Sean, that looks," Mitchell tilted his head in the direction of the locker, "like one hell of a lot of money."

"I agree. Sure is a lot of cash to keep in a train station locker."

Mitchell continued talking. "Seems we have two choices: leave the money here and stake out the locker to see who comes…"

"…..or take it with us, do the stakeout and see what happens next."

"That is pretty much it. What would you do?"

"I think I would take the money. On first glance, there is simply too much here. And there appears to be euros and English pounds, as well as dollars. I think whoever has stored the money here is getting ready to make a move. Of course, once we take it, whoever is involved will know the money has been found. I'm not quite sure what that means, but we'll lose an element of surprise. Still, I would take it. The money itself may give us additional important clues."

"I'm inclined to agree. I'm going to arrange to have the place staked-out. I am sure when whoever comes to retrieve it finds it missing, he'll get mighty excited. Maybe that person will make a mistake and that'll be the break we need. Who knows?"

I shrugged as Alan pulled out his cell phone and placed a call. I assumed it was to get some undercover agents to Union Station ASAP. Personally, I doubted that whoever had planted the money would make another mistake, the first being the fact that he or she had lost all their money, but sometimes breaks were caught in the strangest ways. Time would tell.

As Mitchell finished up his conversation, Ed had returned with a janitor's style forty gallon trash can on a roller platform complete with mops and brooms.

"This was the best I could find, sir," Ed said to Jones.

"Ed, thanks, that should be just fine."

Mitchell looked at Jones and then spoke to the maintenance guy. "Ed, please bring the trash can over here," Alan waved the man over.

Ed rolled it over, "Thanks, Sean, would you please take Ed and Julius and form a little wall for me?"

So as we formed an informal little barrier, SAC Mitchell placed untold thousands of dollars of currency in a forty gallon trash can. I wondered how casual it would look as two Feds, the station manager and a maintenance guy escorted an unarmed trashcan out of Union Station.

- 134 -

SAC Mitchell and I were back at the Hoover Building before 10:00 am. That was the way it was sometimes during investigations, hours and hours of nothing and in a short few

Robert Burson

minutes a major breakthrough. I didn't know if finding the cash was a major find, but it was certainly better than a poke in the eye with a sharp stick.

We set up in a secure conference room and began arranging currency into piles by denomination. There were large stacks of dollars, euros and pounds and smaller ones of Swiss francs and Australian dollars. It was hard to say exactly how much was piled on top of the conference table, but there appeared to be well over $1,000,000 in currency.

"Why do you suppose this one stack is different?" I asked Mitchell pointing to a stack of mixed currency notes.

"Good question, sorry I don't have a good answer."

I grabbed the money and leafed through it. The notes were in random order and, as a general rule, were rather small in denomination. I put the money down and stared at it. A lot of thoughts were running through my head. Unfortunately, they were all in a jumble. While I sat there, a guy from property had come into the conference room and was officially cataloging the money.

It was amazing the way the guy was so blasé about it. One would have thought that he had seen this much currency many, many times before. He was almost done, when he reached for the orphan stack.

"Don't," I said and grabbed the money before the property man could touch it.

"What?"

"Sorry, go ahead and count the money, but please don't change anything about the way the stack is arranged."

"What are you thinking, Sean?" Mitchell asked.

"This stack," I said pointing to it, "has to mean something."

"Possibly a code of some kind?" Mitchell remarked.

"That's my guess," I responded.

"Then if that's the case, our friend here," Mitchell nodded in the direction of the property man, "shouldn't handle it at all."

"Fine with me."

"What's your plan, Sean?"

"Alan, let's send it to the NSA and let them do their number voodoo thing. Maybe their guys up there can turn something up."

"Okay, I'll have it sent over right away."

"Maybe you should contact your buddy there; maybe he can expedite things."

"Good idea. I'll call Dennis Hamilton."

"Thank you. Sorry sir, but I have to run; I have a meeting I can't miss." With that I was out the door for my meeting with Lukas Schafer.

- 135 -

It was almost noon by the time I got away, so I took a cab from the Hoover Building to the Smithsonian Air and Space Museum. I got out of the cab and headed into the museum. I flashed my credentials to the ticket taker and again to security. They waved me around the metal detector, and I headed towards the food court. As I approached it, I started looking around for Lukas Schafer. I didn't immediately see him. Then I noticed a tourist hanging around the entrance. This guy could have been the definition of tourist: loud Hawaiian shirt, D.C. baseball cap, sun glasses, camera dangling from around his neck, wrinkled shorts with a pair of Birkenstocks. He appeared to be studying a visitors' guide. What caught my attention, was the fact that it seemed a little early in the season for such attire. I continued to scan around until my mind clicked and I did a double take. It was Lukas Schafer in disguise.

We made eye contact, and he nodded for me to follow him. He headed out of the food court and went to the Main Exhibit Hall. He entered and began reading the different placards. I followed him in and shortly caught up with him.

"Father, that's quite the outfit you're sporting."

"Sean thanks for coming. I couldn't afford to be spotted. Either some press guy would have wanted a quote or worse."

"What is worse?"

"That's why we need to talk." We were walking slowly from exhibit to exhibit. Schafer paused and looked around. "Can you tell if I've been spotted?"

The question took me back. Of course, I had never been in the public spotlight either. I casually glanced around. Everything looked okay to me. "Lukas, I don't see anything suspicious."

"Thank the Lord for that." We kept walking and occasionally would point towards a plane or some other early flying machine. Finally Schafer began, "Do you know who Adrian Chalmers is?"

"Yes, rich as Croesus, owns radio stations, big donor to Catholic education." I could see that Schafer was a little surprised by how much I knew.

"And he was, and probably still is, the main benefactor of *The Movement*. He was instrumental in getting the press our group needed to get going. He bankrolled us. Without him I don't know where we would be."

"Maybe you would still be part of the Roman Catholic Church," I conjectured.

Schafer looked at me in a strange way. I wondered if I had spoken too freely, too quickly.

"Sean, you might be right," Lukas Schafer said softly. "Anyway, what is done is done. And in this case I really do believe God has worked through Adrian Chalmers."

"I didn't know this last part, but now that you've mentioned it, it does make sense."

"He hides his involvement very well."

"I agree, however you must know there are a lot of rich people who, for perfectly legitimate reasons, kept their involvement in certain organizations secret. "Tell me, Father," I really wasn't quite sure what to call Lukas Schafer these days, "why do you think the plane crash was suspicious?"

"Several reasons really, but two or three big ones, kind of an accumulation of things."

"What were they?"

"For one, the aircraft and the pilot had just been recertified by the FAA. They were given a clean bill of health absolutely no comments."

"Even planes and pilots with clean bills of health crash."

"True. The cause has yet to be determined, but has tentatively been listed as pilot error."

"The standard catch all," was all I said.

Schafer kept talking. "The weather was perfect. There was no reason for the plane to crash."

The priest was rambling, and I needed to keep him focused, "Okay, what else?"

"The flight was a last minute addition. It was suggested by Adrian Chalmers and he picked the passengers."

Playing the devil's advocate, I asked, "Didn't all of those things make sense to you at the time?"

"Yes."

"Did you approve of the entire plan?"

"Yes."

"Father, Lukas, I can see why you might be concerned, but I still don't see where the dots connect."

Schafer stopped walking. I looked him in the face, and he seemed to struggle with what he wanted to say next."

I waited. Pushing him at this point would do little good.

Schafer finally spoke. This time his voice was low and in earnest. "Do you know who Raymond Gates is?"

I had heard the name and knew I would eventually remember, but I didn't want the tempo of the conversation broken. "The name is familiar but I don't recall why."

"He is the number two man at *The Movement*. I have known him for years. In fact, we were in the seminary together. Unfortunately, while we were once good friends, over the years a strong rivalry has developed between us. I can see Raymond try to hide his true feelings from me, but he doesn't do a very good job at it, at least not to someone that has known him as long as I have."

"Now I remember, please go on."

"The men in the plane were all put in their positions by Gates, and were therefore loyal to him."

"Isn't everyone loyal to *The Movement*?" I asked.

"Yes, of course, but every organization has a political side. As a matter of fact, the Catholic Church is one of the most political organizations in the world."

"So what you are saying is that while you may have the nominal leader and public voice of *The Movement*, Gates controlled its daily operations?"

"Yes, at least up to and until the plane went down."

"Do you control the organization now?" I asked.

Schafer looked away. When he turned back to me, there were tears in his eyes. "Not operationally, no, not really. I'm not a good administrator. I know that, so when Adrian Chalmers suggested the replacements for the four dead souls, I agreed."

"Was Raymond Gates consulted?"

"Not that I'm aware."

"I see."

We both said nothing for a few moments. Then Schafer spoke. "I'm sure something isn't right. What it is has not yet been revealed, but I pray daily that I am wrong and it'll only be something for good." As the priest spoke, my head spun. I had just learned a very powerful man, Adrian Chalmers, secretly controlled

300

a new and powerful religious organization. My gut began to churn. Schafer was right; something was wrong. I needed to sort this out. I needed time to think. It was just that I didn't think there was much time left. Schafer spoke again, "Sean thanks for hearing me out. I must go now."

Before I could say anything, Lukas Schafer had spun around and left.

- 136 -

My head was spinning, in a few short hours I had found stacks of money left behind by someone, for some purpose at a locker in Union Station. My first and probably very safe assumption was that the money wasn't going to charity. Then within the last few minutes I learned that one of America's foremost media owners was potentially involved in murder, and if not murder, certainly some kind of conspiracy.

Searching my memory I realized I knew very little about Adrian Chalmers. He was from an old wealthy Washington D.C. family meaning mostly Protestant while he was a Catholic or at least a Catholic in name. In the old days that fact would have undoubtedly caused issues. His family fortunes as I vaguely remembered had been more affected by the women they married than anything else.

The pedestrian traffic was light and the day pleasant, besides I needed to think so I decided to walk back to the office. This was a nice time of the year in D.C. I drifted slowly along, thinking. I had many more questions than answers. Hopefully the odd sequence of bills would yield some answers. It had to mean something. No doubt the NSA cryptographers and their powerful computers would come up with something. Until then, I needed to concentrate on who was making all this happen. All the signs pointed to an insider, CIA or NSA. A rotten apple had to be working for/with someone, possibly Adrian Chalmers. I didn't think the reason really mattered, though it would be easier if it were simply avarice. Loyalty or belief will make people do things that greedy people won't.

I continue to walk slowly, mulling things over. Why would someone monitor my home calls and conversations? Logic would say it had to have some to do with Lukas Schafer and if so was it Chalmers' doing, Mustafa al Bevcar or one of his subordinates or someone else, totally unrelated?

I was about half way back to the office when I started to sense something. I felt like I was being followed. I'm not sure what triggered this sensation. Possibly it was seeing someone behind me in the reflection of the store window. This looked like the same person I had seen as I left the Air and Space Museum. Ever since my close encounter of the deadly kind, I had become more observant. That was the nice way of putting it. In fact, I was a bit paranoid. Before leaving for my meeting with Schafer I had even had made sure my wife and daughter were BOTH under protective surveillance. I had been assured that everything was all right. Still, safe was better than sorry.

I quickened my pace. Sure enough my shadow picked up speed. By now I had reached the corner of 7th and Pennsylvania Avenue. Normally I would have turned on Pennsylvania to return to the office. Instead, I waited until the light changed and ran across the street just ahead of the traffic and headed into the Navy Memorial. It was an open circular area. With any luck there would be some visitors, and I use them as distractions so I could double back on whoever was following me. Fortunately for me, the plaza was filled with school children obviously on a field trip. Based upon the time of day, it appeared they had been brought here by their teachers to eat lunch and have some quiet time. I circled at a full sprint to my left behind the fountains. I hid behind a statue and waited. Within seconds the man appeared. He looked wildly around. He had lost sight of me.

Now would come the tricky part, I needed to catch this guy arrest him and then interrogate him. I waited. He slowly drifted to the right and into the center of the memorial. I moved counter clockwise away from him, trying to keep the sun to my back and the groups of school kids between us. As I moved, I could see him become more frustrated, first looking quickly to his right and then to his left. He clearly had lost focus and was obviously upset. Meanwhile, I kept moving slowly to his left, staying low and making no sudden movements.

By happenstance a large group of the children had gathered near my pursuer in front of the main memorial to have their picture taken. He moved away from them and me and reached into his pocket. He took out his cell phone and appeared to be making a call. This complicated things. I had to assume that he had at least one partner. Would they meet? He turned his back away from the class and began to talk. With that I ran as quickly and as quietly as possible towards him, reaching for my service weapon as I went.

I was about three feet from him when I slowed my pace and withdrew my weapon. "Listen asshole, I don't want you to move. I have a gun and it's aimed at your spine."

The guy began to move and said, "You can't talk to me like that!"

"I god-damn can and will. Now I don't want to get all these schools kids excited, so we are going to take a nice stroll out of here. I want you to walk in the direction of Pennsylvania Avenue."

As we moved slowly away from the kids and headed towards the street, my friend spoke again. "Do you know who I am?"

"Yes, you are the fuck-up who lost his tail and then to boot let the tail capture you." The man began to slow. "Keep walking.

303

When we get to the street, you'll turn right. We are going to take a little stroll together down to the Hoover Building, where with any luck; someone other than me will get to kick the crap out of you, in the name of Homeland security."

"Fine, fine, but just to let you know, I'm FBI."

I laughed, "That's a good one. What were you? The dumbest in your class?"

"Listen, let me show my credentials. It'll save both of us a lot of embarrassment back at the office."

The guy acted like a Fed and was more compliant than a regulation bad guy, so what was lost, "Okay, show me. And you know the drill if you are Bureau."

My tail complied, handing me his credentials in the proper FBI manner. I glanced at the documents and believed him. I didn't drop my piece yet though. I guess I wasn't that trusting. "What's the deal?"

"Alan Mitchell assigned me to your protection detail."

"I didn't ask for any protection." I was getting a bit pissed.

"I know. And don't blame me. After Mitchell learned of the request you made regarding your family, he decided to add you to the list."

I really wanted to launch into a blue language tirade, but it wouldn't have done any good, including making me feel better. "Your surveillance job was one shitty piece of work."

"It was my first time."

"What the hell do you do at the Bureau?"
304

"Counterfeiting."

"Then why were you put in the field?"

"Two reasons. I want out of counterfeiting and into field work."

"And the other reason?"

"I was all that was available."

I threw his credentials back to him and holstered my weapon. His story had to be true. No one would make up such a yarn if it weren't. "Go back to counterfeiting, or at least get better training. Someone else could have killed you and been gone ten minutes before those kids would have noticed your lifeless body lying there leaking blood all over the memorial."

I didn't wait for a reply as I headed for the Hoover Building. I needed to get back to work, and I needed to have a "Dutch Uncle" talk with SAC Alan Mitchell.

- 137 -

The Alitalia 747 was on final approach into Dulles International Airport. It was due to land at approximately 1:00 pm Washington time. The giant aircraft seemed to hang in the air, not moving but it was slowly descending, a modern marvel. It seemed incredible that something so heavy and large could fly.

Alitalia, the Italian national carrier, had carried the Pope on hundreds of trips over the years. It was a source of national pride, the Italian markings on the tail and the Papal Insignia on the nose. Even though His Holiness was coming as a private citizen and not the head of state, he was still the leader of the world's largest religious organization and as such could hardly travel in a manner described as light. There was always a pool of reporters, as well as various prelates of the Church and, of course, security.

The airport grounds were large, something in the area of 11,000 acres. The airport authority had originally been happy with such a large amount of real estate. It meant that your typical expansion issues, noise abatement and pollution would not interfere with the airport's growth. However, after 911 all that changed. Now all that acreage meant security issues, lots of them. The airport's security budget had gone up five times in as many years, and still the operators knew there were holes. There was a limited staff, and it was stretched every hour of every day.

A threat had been phoned in about a half-an-hour earlier, something about an explosive device in a cargo shipment. The chief of security knew this threat like so many others would undoubtedly prove to be false, some nutcase getting his or her jollies. Still, the prudent thing to do was to send his team to investigate. Unfortunately, that meant he had to call in all his perimeter crews to supplement his terminal staff. He knew it was a choice, and a hard one, considering the Roman Catholic Pope's plane was due to land shortly.

The jumbo jet's final approach was from the south with the prevailing winds pushing in from the north. As the plane descended, the pilot was in contact with the Dulles tower. Nothing was out of the norm. It was then it happened.

The tower saw it first, the pilot's view being obscured by the plane's angle of descent. The controller saw a bright flash, followed by an object streaking skyward. Instinctively she knew a rocket had been launched in the direction of the Pope's plane. She had only seconds to react. She ordered the pilot to hit full power and at the same time to lower its nose to increase its rate of descent.

Everyone on board was thrown back into their seats as the jumbo jet powered down as four General Electric turbo fan engines pushed the plane down. Anyone looking out the window would have seen the ground rapidly approaching. Later it was reported that only few passengers screamed as they undoubtedly believed they were doomed.

The missile tore through the right wing between the two engines and continued to rise and exploded two seconds later. The controller's and the pilot's quick actions had saved the plane. They had shortened the distance between the launch and impact enough to keep the rocket from detonating when it made contact with the wing.

The hole made by the rocket tore through the primary set of wing flap avionics. Thankfully, Boeing had designed the craft's backup systems to be situated away from the primary one. The fact the plane was under full power had allowed the pilot to maintain sufficient control to stabilize the craft. The key was to get the plane on the ground. The controller ordered the plane to land immediately, as there was always a chance another missile could be fired. "Equipment" was rolled in case the landing wasn't smooth.

About the same time as all hell was breaking lose at Dulles Airport, an unmarked, executive extended range 737 touched down at Washington's Reagan Airport. It quickly taxied to the far end of the airport where a series of cars, including a limousine were waiting. This was not an uncommon event at the airport and as such, drew no special attention. However, had anyone made a special effort, he would have seen a man dressed in completely white quickly deplane and board a dark sedan which sped off in a different direction than the one taken by the limo and its entourage.

- 138 -

I made it back to the Hoover building in one piece and rode the elevator to my floor and headed back to my desk with very mixed emotions. I truly appreciated the fact that Alan Mitchell had enough concern for my safety that he would have me watched. But I felt like I was being treated like a two-year-old. From my recent experiences with the man, Mitchell did have a nasty habit of doing this. At the same time, I knew I didn't want to lose sight of what was truly important.

Speaking of which some things had finally become a little clearer. Amanda Chehwan's contact with the NSA was most likely Mark Ruben. That fact gave her access to a lot of information, the CIA, the NSA and the FBI's. Both Amanda and Ruben had the number to the locker at Union Station. I had to assume Ruben stumbled on it in the first place and then had passed it on to Chehwan; it would be unlikely that she would have passed it on to Ruben. Whether Ruben knew who the actual owner of the locker was probably irrelevant but Chehwan had to. Both were probably killed by the same person, that being the locker owner.

There were two more sets of numbers, and I needed to find what they meant. I also needed to learn more about Adrian Chalmers. I needed to find out in what way, if any, he was mixed up in this whole process. There were a lot of leads to follow. The trick was to follow the right one. At the moment all appeared promising, but some would undoubtedly turn out to be red herrings, doing more harm than good, because false leads eat time, something this investigation didn't have in abundance.

"Sean, I heard you had a little excitement at lunch." Alan Mitchell said as I passed by his office.

I could see he was trying to ease off the tension. I still wasn't sure how I felt about it. At times like this, my wife always told me to shut up, say nothing. Silence couldn't harm you. Today my Irish temper had one hell of a hard time implementing her sage advice. I just sat there for a moment, boiling.

"Sean, are you okay?"

….eight, nine and ten. I took a deep breath and turned to my boss, "Alan, thanks for your concern. Please, next time let me know, okay?" I said in a barely audible voice.

I could see Mitchell strain to hear me, which helped my attitude. "Okay."

"Oh, and by the way, get the guy you sent better training or you'll be looking for a replacement agent, soon."

Mitchell nodded and then spoke again, "Did you hear what happened to the Pope's plane?"

"No, what happened?"

Mitchell explained to me about the attempted shooting down of the Papal plane and how the air traffic controller and pilot managed to save the plane and everyone on board. "What about the Pope?"

"The general public doesn't know it but he was never was on the plane. It seems that someone in the Vatican was on the ball. He flew into National on an executive 737 about the same time."

"How come it isn't all over the news?"

"Everyone has put a brick on it. From what I've been told, the head of Homeland security has called everyone, all media sources, and told them to hold off running anything until tomorrow morning. Threatened them with anything he could think of."

"What about the people at the airport, the passengers, airport workers etc.?"

"Those working at the airport have been threatened with job loss if they say anything."

"How about the general public and especially the passengers?"

"There's nothing can be done about them."

"Alan, the story will get out."

"Yes it will. But hopefully not until tomorrow we'll get a day hopefully to maybe figure who was involved, that sort of thing."

I knew Mitchell was right about the importance of time. At least that was something. "Do you know where the Pope is now?"

He shook his head, "No one seems to know."

"Well, then who is in charge? People know the Pope is coming to America."

"From what I've heard and been briefed, the Pope still is, but to get to the Pope you have to go through the Vatican Secretary of State, a Cardinal Camperelle."

"What a story. Things are moving fast, too damn fast."

"So it would seem, Sean." Mitchell looked at his watched and silently swore under his breath. "I have to attend another GD meeting."

After Alan left, I briefly reflected on the fact that Mo had been right again; shutting up and remaining calm was the best thing to do. Hell, maybe she could help me see through all the options starring me in the face. In the meantime, I needed to start dealing with the list of bank account numbers.

- 139 -

It was late when I finally arrived home. My wife was

310

waiting for me in the kitchen. I, along with a number of junior agents, had spent all afternoon associating the bank account numbers listed in Chehwan's computer with various banks and religious organizations. At the beginning of my involvement in this investigation, Amanda had confessed to me, and I use that word charitably, that four or five U.S. banks were receiving funds from Switzerland. Of course, she never said which ones. Finding them was one of the things I had spent my afternoon doing. I wish she had been more forthcoming; it would have saved a lot of valuable time. But that's not all.

I recall asking her about the trail from the banks to the account holders. At the time she looked me right in the eye and said, *"We haven't found where the money goes next but feel we are getting close."* Now it is possible that the list of bank numbers found on her computer were discovered after I had asked about the money flows, but I wouldn't count on it. Not that it matters anymore; Amanda is dead and the NSA and the FBI have the bank account numbers. True, the NSA computer was hacked, and so there is a good chance that whoever hacked in also knows about the bank accounts, but at least I have a trail to follow, finally.

My plan for tomorrow is to have my young staff contact all the bank account owners. We needed to know the source of funds. As one can imagine, there are a lot of numbers to call. My thrown together crew was young and inexperienced; I hoped they could handle this. Personally, I planned to follow up with the largest and most promising organizations and those who refused to talk to us. I figured anyone refusing to talk deserved further investigation as the FBI brings a lot of clout to any investigation. For further encouragement I also plan to use the power of the IRS. Simply put, I plan to threaten them, first with a loss of tax exempt status and if that isn't compelling enough, I'll tell them that they will shortly read their names in the paper as being subjects of a criminal fraud task force. I have found over the years that a nice word and a gun goes much further than just a nice word when trying to find something out. Having the gold shield division of the IRS knock on your door is one of the best weapons I know of.

"Sorry I'm so late," I bent over to kiss my wife who was seated at our little alcove desk, paying bills, I might add, one of the great joys in life.

"No problem, thanks for calling. I saved some dinner for you. It's in the fridge."

I hung my coat over the back of a kitchen chair and headed for the refrigerator, peeked at what was for dinner and grabbed a beer. "Thanks." A beer or two would definitely make my reheated microwave dinner taste better.

I popped open the beer and sat down, "how was your day?"

"Nothing special at work, but you won't believe what I've heard."

I cringed a little with those words. Sometimes Mo and her scoops were fascinating and there were other times that well, you know…. "What did you hear?"

"Alice O'Brien called."

I cringed again when I heard the woman's name. In my opinion she was a complete busybody. She talked way too much and said nothing of value, or to be kind, almost nothing. She was heavily involved in the local parish and somehow managed to make herself a gatekeeper of local church information. I think she stepped into the vacuum created when Father Schafer left, and no one has had the authority or the heart to ease her back to her former role of parish pest.

"What did she have to say?"

"She says the Pope is coming to America."

"Yes, we all know that," I sighed.

"Please, let me finish," Mo snapped back.

"Sorry." I took another gulp of beer.

"Anyway, she says that she heard there are a lot of Catholics who are very unhappy with the new Pope and that someone may try to kill him when he comes to America."

Since I knew the story wouldn't be short, I and my beer had taken a place at the kitchen table. It seems that old Alice was like the blind squirrel in the forest: she had eventually found the nut. In this case, the fact that the Pope's life was in danger was more than a rumor. That is, unless of course, you consider a surface to air missile attack a normal method of greeting. "Did she say why people were unhappy enough to kill the Pope of Rome?"

"I asked her that. She said it was everything from the name he took to his, quote, liberal policies."

"How the hell would anyone know what his policies are? He just got the job. He hasn't had time to do anything but put out fires," I said.

"I know. It's just the rumor," Mo responded. "But Alice says it's all over."

"What is all over?"

"She didn't say, she just made a sweeping statement."

"People can be such twits." I wanted to change the subject. Any more discussion wouldn't help anything, and unfortunately, I think old Alice was right this time.

"Where's Kelly?"

Mo looked at her watch, and then looked back at me with a look of concern, "She's late."

"Late from what?"

"She said she had to look some things up at the public library."

"Doesn't it close at 8:00?" I asked.

Mo nodded and then said, "Maybe she stopped by one of her friend's houses."

"Isn't she supposed to tell us this stuff? Isn't that the reason we agreed to pay for a damn cell phone in the first place?" I was beginning to get more worried than annoyed.

"Yes, she probably just forgot."

Considering everything that had gone on, I wasn't about to live with that hopeful response. Then, my cell rang.

- 140 -

Night had fallen on a very frustrating day for Adrian Chalmers. Over the years, as Chalmers' power and wealth had grown, bad days had become a rarity. That was why he was even more frustrated than one would normally expect. He was simply out of practice. At least, that is what he kept telling himself; it was only a minor bump in the road, not a major disaster. Still he seethed. He had paid good money to that asshole David, and he had completely fucked up the assassination attempt. He was going to ream him out but good, and that was if he was feeling kindly. If not, only God knew.

314

Chalmers heard the slight knock on the door. Without turning around, he pushed a button and the door automatically opened. "Good evening, David. Please come in," Chalmers said in a very quiet voice.

David approached Chalmers, "Sit down, David."

Chalmers had arranged the lights in the room so that David's chair was in direct light while Chalmers remained seated in the shadows. David sat and said nothing.

In a cold voice, Chalmers spoke, "What are you going to do about your failures today?"

For years David had learned to put up with Chalmers' arrogance. His feelings of dislike had grown into hatred; still he continued to work for the man. The pay had been just too lucrative. David had always assumed he was the more ruthless of the two of them. He believed Chalmers was simply too rich, too connected, to soil his hands. David was about to speak when he saw the small .22 caliber gun Chalmers held. This turn of events took him by surprise, and it must have shown.

There was a hint of glee in Chalmers' voice when he spoke. "Well, David, please speak up. What you say will determine your immediate future."

David instinctively knew Chalmers would use the gun. The man was a snake and as mad as hell. Ice water rather than blood flowed in his veins. He had to think of something to say. Something that would buy him time. "They were lucky and we weren't."

David could see Chalmers gripping the gun, fighting hard to contain himself. In the same low, cold voice he spoke again, "Do you know that even if the plane had been brought down it wouldn't have mattered?"

"Why is that?"

"The fucking Pope wasn't even on the god-damn plane, that's why, you overpriced, egotistical piece of shit." David had never heard Chalmers yell before. "I paid you a fuck of a lot of money and you failed. I don't pay for failure, do you understand?"

"Mr. Chalmers, I screwed up. It won't happen again."

"David, those words might have just saved your life, at least temporarily. You have three days to kill the Pope. Do you think you can achieve that?"

David hated Chalmers and he hated him the most when he was sarcastic, but he had failed and he knew he had to succeed. Success, he knew would be doubly difficult. He had no other option.

"Yes."

"Good."

"When you have accomplished your task, I'll contact you in the usual way. Oh, and by the way, I don't want you to neglect the other tasks I outlined for you previously."

David stared back at his employer and wordlessly got up and left the room. He wondered if Chalmers planned to kill him whether or not he succeeded in any or all his tasks. Of course, he had his own plans for Adrian Chalmers.

- 141 -

"Murphy here."

"Agent Murphy, this is Agent Sanchez."

316

"Yes, Ms. Sanchez, what is it?"

"I'm one of the agents assigned to keep an eye on your daughter…"

I was deeply concerned. Something had to be wrong with Kelly to get a call from a field agent. "….what's wrong?"

"Did your daughter know she was being protected?"

"Yes, and she was none too happy about it either, why?"

"I followed your daughter to the local public library."

"That agrees with what my wife said."

"When it closed, she stopped at a coffee house, *McHenry's.*"

"She hangs out there sometimes with her friends. Again, what is wrong?" My level of anxiety was going off the charts.

"I'm not sure if anything is wrong at the moment. That is why I'm asking these questions."

"Okay, I'm just worried."

"I understand, Agent Murphy."

"Anyway, I waited outside, didn't need to go in as I could see clearly from the car. Anyway, it looks like she went to the restroom and hasn't returned."

"Did anyone else go to the rest room at the same time?"

"Yes, a black woman about thirty and very fit looking."

"How long ago did all this happen?"

"Longer than a normal potty stop, but less than ten or

twelve minutes. That's why I wondered if she was trying to ditch me. I have had that happen before."

"Agent Sanchez, please go in and check out the rest room. I'll wait on the line." By now I was practically shouting. I could hear the car door open and close. The next thing I heard was the FBI agent whispering into the phone.

"She is out of the bathroom but looks a little disoriented or light headed. The black lady is helping her."

"Agent Sanchez, as far as I know, Kelly doesn't have any black lady friends around thirty."

"I understand."

"Have you been spotted?"

"No, I don't think so. The black lady has been joined by a friend, white about the same age. They seem to be almost carrying your daughter."

That was it. I couldn't wait around any longer. The coffee house wasn't more than five minutes away, less the way I was planning on driving. "Don't lose sight of them, Agent Sanchez! Consider this a kidnapping situation. Stay on the line. I'll be there in about five minutes." With that I dashed for my car, cell in one hand and weapon in the other, but not putting a call into Alan Mitchell's office.

- 142 -

I was driving like a NASCAR driver, only the prize, rather

318

than cash, was my daughter's life. Thankfully, the streets were fairly deserted, so I was able to run every light and stop sign on the way. I had turned on the speaker phone feature so I could hear Agent Sanchez.

"They have escorted her out of the shop. She seems really out of it. If I were to guess, I'd assume she's been drugged. They are on the front sidewalk and seem to be moving towards a late model white Toyota Camry parked in the lot next door. Your daughter is struggling a bit now and that has slowed down their progress. Is there anything you want me to do?"

I was a minute away at the most. "I'm almost there. Do nothing unless it looks like they are going to leave. If that is the case do whatever it takes to delay them."

"Got it." I could hear Sanchez run for the car. "Okay I'm in my car and they've gotten her into the back seat. What do you want me to do?"

"Are there any cars around the Toyota?"

"No it is by itself."

"Okay good, here is the deal. We are going to do the standard pinch move. You come from the passenger side and I'll come from the driver's. Do you have any questions?"

"No!"

"Then let's do it!" I had just swung onto the street where the coffee shop was located. I could also see the parking lot. A dark sedan I assumed was Sanchez's Bucar, was heading towards a white Camry sitting by itself in the middle of the parking lot. I also could see two women getting ready to get into that Camry. I knew the timing would be close. My plan was to use our two cars as barriers to prevent them from going anywhere. They still hadn't realized we were onto them, I knew this wouldn't last much longer. Right now they were vulnerable and didn't know it.

We were coming from opposite directions; Sanchez was the first to position her car. I was right behind her, closing the gap. I slammed on the brakes, spun the wheel. We had the Camry trapped. I hopped out and drew my weapon.

I ducked behind my open door and shouted, "Put your hands in the air, this is the FBI!" I could see the surprise on the black lady's face. This was obviously totally unexpected.

"You are surrounded. Get out of the car, NOW!" I shouted. The black lady hesitated. I could see her speaking to her accomplice. Then I heard Sanchez, who had by now positioned herself so that she had a clear view into the backseat. If either woman tried to turn towards Kelly laying there for whatever reason Sanchez would have that covered.

"Listen bitch, get out of the car! Put your hands in the air. Do it now!"

Her timing was perfect. The two women now realized they couldn't get away. Their only hope now was some kind of hostage negotiation and I wasn't about to let that happen. The black woman just sat there, I think she was stunned. "Put your hands on the front dash. Do it now." I yelled.

"Listen to me. I will shoot you. This a promise and not a threat." I had brought my service piece into a firing position. "You have two choices. You'll die or you'll do time. But time is better than dead. We'll make a deal with you if you work with us."

The black woman moved to put her hands on the dash but her partner hadn't. Her hands were still hidden from view. I assumed she had a weapon and was considering using it.

"Hands on the dash now!" I yelled again.

I could see the black lady was ready to cave. Good thing. I still couldn't see what the white woman was doing though. Then I heard a shot ring out. The black woman screamed and I was ready to fire.

"Sanchez! Are you okay?"

"I am but the driver is not. It looked like she was making a move."

"Call 911."

"Got it."

I moved cautiously from around my car, weapon drawn and aimed at the passenger side of the Toyota. "Now get out of the car. Do it slowly and do it now! Keep your hands where I can see them."

The black woman swung open her door and slowly got out. "Okay down on the ground, do it now!" I yelled. She complied

As soon as she was down both Sanchez and I ran to the car. As we got there, we heard the sound of sirens approaching our direction. The paramedics had arrived.

"Check the one in the car!" Sanchez shouted, "I got the other one."

"Got it."

I was dying to check on Kelly, but the key was to secure the situation. It seemed that Sanchez had already done most of the securing as soon as I saw the driver. There was a lot of blood and she wasn't going anywhere either, unless it was to the beyond. Finally, then I turned to look at Kelly in the back seat. Thankfully, she was out of it. Whatever they had given to her had numbed her. She was totally unaware. I pulled open the back door and leaned in.

- 143 -

David seethed as he left his meeting with Adrian Chalmers. Normally, being a professional prevented such emotional feelings. They had met in high school, two outsiders seemingly thrown together more by position than personality. While Adrian Chalmers was the only Catholic at the WASPY private school they attended, he was the only orphan. Strangely they remained in touch after high school and throughout college. At first, David was unsure why this had happened. However, later as his relationship with Adrian evolved, he realized how close they were in so many ways.

His parents had met while both worked for the Department of Defense. They were employed by the precursor to the National Reconnaissance Office. Both his father and mother were crack intelligence officers. As a team they were able to read and decode aerial photographs as well as anyone in the world. That was what got them killed. In those early pre-satellite days the only way to get the necessary pictures was to over fly the target. Unfortunately for David, to determine the true target and to take a really good picture one needed to be in the plane at the time of the photograph. His parents happened to be on a highly classified mission when the plane they were aboard crashed. Why it crashed was never revealed. David always believed it had been shot down by the Soviets.

His mother's uncle, a rich but cold man who he had never met became his guardian. Strained would have been a nice description of their relationship; from the beginning the two men

322

never much cared for each other. His uncle's solution to this problem was to pack his nephew off to a series of pricey boarding schools. Money for these schools was never an issue as his uncle was very well heeled. David knew he would never see any of the money, as his uncle had children of his own. However, in the process he found how much he enjoyed wealth and all it could buy. Since his uncle had made it quite clear that once his education was complete he was on his own, David decided to join the military immediately after graduating from college. His parents' genes must have flowed strongly because he quickly ended up in military intelligence. He found he liked the work and its associated independence. But he quickly learned that the modest income and associated lack of creature comforts were not to his liking.

For the first several years after college they, David and Adrian, had had almost no contact except the occasional phone call around the holidays. During that time David knew Adrian had taken over a small radio station in Richmond, but little else. Then, out of the blue, Adrian called and arranged for a meeting. More out of curiosity than friendship, he had agreed. During their meeting Adrian had told him about some of his business problems and how he thought David could help him with some of them, for a fee, of course.

Loving his work but hating its associated income, he quickly agreed. Over the next several years Adrian's radio station grew into a media empire. During that time he had helped resolve some difficult problems, all to Charmers' satisfaction. He had been richly rewarded for his efforts. Always working in the background, he was both amused and bemused by how the public press glowingly described Chalmers' achievements as a great American success story.

Their latest venture, the most ambitious ever, was proving to be more difficult than he had originally anticipated, but the monetary reward was so much greater. To compensate for the additional risk, he had managed to squeeze an extra million from his old high school chum, who he knew hated being shaken down, but since this would be the last time they would work together, he, David, simply didn't care.

- 144 -

In a few days it would be over. Within a short period of time he would be living the life of luxury without a care in the world. Of course, the trickiest part of all was to be able to enjoy the money after the job was done. He knew his job wouldn't be a problem. He was old enough to take early retirement and most likely no one would question his doing so. He had spent the last several months laying the ground work. During that time he had morphed from being a dedicated agent into a complaining bureaucrat. No, it was Chalmers. The man had an incredibly long reach. But still, Chalmers' reach would be much shorter without his services. This thought calmed him. He had made it to his quiet place, his safe haven. This was his place where he could conduct business and where his calls, as far he could tell, were untraceable. He dialed and waited. He didn't have to wait long.

"Hello."

"David here."

"Go ahead."

"I need you to implement phase two."

"When?"

"Immediately."

"Okay." With that his contact hung up.

David smiled and pulled on his right ear lobe, an unconscious tick he did anytime he needed time to think. The conversation was just what he wanted to hear, no questions, no objections. He knew within hours the news networks would have breaking news, very disturbing news about sectarian violence occurring and then spreading across the country. First there would be the initial incidents followed by retaliation killings. Knowing the state of the country, soon others would join in, more violence and more killings, ones that he didn't have to pay for or arrange.

It would be just as he had envisioned. So Chalmers would end up with more wealth and power. Adrian could have it. All he wanted to do was to live on the beach and relax in the style he deserved. To that end, he had set aside a great deal of money. At first he thought it would be more than enough, but then he began to have his doubts. To ensure his lifestyle, he needed anonymity from the U.S. Government and from the likes of Adrian Chalmers. He needed insurance, and this kind of insurance cost money, a lot of it. Fortunately, he knew where to get the necessary funds.

Finally, he had one last task to do. He had been tempted to pass on it. But in the end he knew that wasn't an option. Because all the money in the world would do him no good if he was dead; besides there would be the ultimate satisfaction of a difficult, professional job done well. He would be an uninvited guest at the meeting between the Pope and Lukas Schafer. He still didn't know precisely when that meeting would occur, but that didn't matter. He would know where and when, when it mattered. He would be there for a final meeting between these two men of God.

He smiled again, thinking how both men would soon meet their Maker, if there was a Maker. Now it was time to go. He needed cash to finish the job.

- 145 -

It was one of the longest rides of my life. Kelly was unconscious, her breathing shallow. The paramedics told me that they thought she would be okay. That meant a lot, but I was terribly worried. I had called Mo from the ambulance, gave her the quick version of the events. Outwardly she sounded calm, too calm. From our years together, I knew that meant she was completely turned inside out.

"How is she?"

"Paramedics think she'll be fine."

"Is she awake?"

"No."

We had arrived at the hospital at almost the same time. Kelly was being wheeled into an ER room, and the doctors and nurses were drawing blood and performing other procedures. We sat down and waited and waited. We didn't say much during this time. What was there to say? We were both worried as hell and powerless to do anything. I know I prayed and I assume Mo did also.

Several hours, which felt like several weeks, passed. Finally, a doctor approached, an entirely too young a man. For my daughter I wanted an old guy with the wisdom of the ages. "Mr. and Mrs. Murphy?"

"Yes," we said at the same time.

"I'm Doctor Rand."

"Hello, doctor. What can you tell us?" I said.

"I have good news."

"Your daughter was given a relatively common anesthesia. There shouldn't be any side effects. It appears her kidnappers wanted her awake and coherent within a few hours after the abduction."

"Probably to make a call to me," I commented.

"That would seem logical," Rand agreed.

"May we see her now?" My wife asked.

"Yes, certainly."

My wife hurried off. Before I left to see Kelly, I turned back to the doctor. "You said they used a common anesthesia?"

"Yes."

"Common to where, what, doctor?"

"Medical facilities, human, not animal. These substances aren't available from veterinary sources."

"Is it easy to get?"

"Why no, not really. It is a controlled substance. One has to be licensed to get it."

"So whoever did this had access to a physician or some high pharmaceutical contacts?"

"Mr. Murphy, your conclusion is accurate."

"Thank you," I responded and hurried off to join my wife and daughter.

- 146 -

I was exhausted, but things were all right. Thankfully, Kelly was okay, but was going to be kept in the hospital overnight for observation. Mo had finally calmed down. The kidnappers had failed, by the will of God or luck, whichever you prefer. Mo had agreed to stay at the hospital. I wanted to, but she insisted I needed some rest. For that reason, I was at home trying to sleep but was wide awake. I can't tell you how many times I looked at the clock, at lot anyway. I would have to get up in a couple of hours. I needed to be sharp and being sharp meant being rested. I was failing miserably.

I eventually just gave up and laid in bed thinking about the case. Things were beginning to spin out of hand. There had been an assassination attempt against the Pope. America's tolerance towards many kinds of religious beliefs was fraying. Amanda Chehwan's prediction was certainly right-on about that one. Undoubtedly, time was running out. Whoever tried to kill the Pope would try again, of that I had no doubt. Furthermore, I doubted we would get anything from the black woman we took into custody. My guess was she was too isolated from her employer to provide anything useful.

At least there were other possibilities. They were spread out all over the place, but having something was a damn sight better than having bupkis. I believed the same person had killed both Amanda and Mark Ruben. Without a stretch, I would guess that person was also the one who bugged my house and had arranged Kelly's kidnapping. I had decided, reinforced by tonight's attempted abduction, that whoever it was had to be working or had worked for government intelligence or law enforcement. What had happened was just too sophisticated, from the phone tap equipment to the drug used on Kelly. I was enough of a chauvinist though to believe whoever the person was, he or she wasn't FBI. That left the NSA or the CIA. Earlier I had thought it was the NSA for a variety of reasons, which I am now beginning to doubt. Whoever it was, that person had to be fairly high up the food chain. Because of that, I didn't believe it was someone from the NSA, since it made no sense for a high NSA employee to hack into his or her own system. There would have been no need. Why leave any kind of trail? Unless the purpose of the break-in was to create a false trail, but that was just too complicated, movie kind of stuff, not what one found in the real world. Now I leaned towards the CIA the facts as I knew them seemed to fit the Company best.

First thing tomorrow I decided I needed to contact, rather meet, DDI Harold Hanson. We needed, or at least I needed, to talk to him in person. He had to have some answers that he didn't even know about. It was possible he was the mole, but my gut told me he wasn't. Time being short, I knew I had to make a leap. I would follow my gut and meet with Hanson, though it wouldn't be too bad of an idea to include Alan Mitchell in the loop.

The other thing I had to do was to start tracing down the money. Something had to come from that exercise. Money made the world spin for bad guys as well as good guys. I was also pretty sure the NSA would turn up something from the odd stack of currency we had found in the locker, if there was anything to turn up. Finally, there was also a chance the person who owned all the cash would return to the locker in Union Station. The locker was staked out day and night.

My mind raced around itself, examining various options and possibilities, for another forty-five minutes or so before I finally drifted off.

- 147 -

First thing in the morning, I called Deputy Director Hanson's office and made an appointment at his earliest possible convenience. At least that was how I would note it in my report, though it was possible that Mr. Hanson's secretary would have described our conversation more in terms that I had demanded to see the Deputy Director as soon as possible. Frankly, I didn't give a damn. I was tired and grumpy and needed some answers. My next call was to Alan Mitchell. I told him of my plans to meet with DDI Hanson and that I would be back in the office to follow the money trail. Again, and I'm not sure I used the kindest of words when I asked, some might have said I demanded, that Mitchell find out how the NSA was doing with its analysis of the assorted currency stack and light a fire under them if progress was lacking. He said he would, which I appreciated. I would probably pay dearly for this level of role reversal service.

I arrived at Langley and told the sentry at the gate that I had an appointment with Harold Hanson. He looked at me like I was a Martian. I showed my credentials and assured him I wasn't part of an FBI plot to discredit the Agency. Agency paranoia, it seems, flows all the way to the guard manning the entry points. I guess paranoia, like just about everything else, seeks its lowest level. Because the appointment had just been made that morning and I wasn't the President, my name wasn't on the official visitors' list. This caused a great deal of consternation. Finally, after sitting there and backing up a lot of traffic, which must have motivated the guards to keep trying, I was finally given a pass and directed where to go. From his look, I think the guard meant for me to go to another gate, but I chose the one at the front door instead.

I easily re-found the Director's office, re-introduced myself to the receptionist and sat down and waited. I was pretty sure that I would be made to wait. The reason was the unwritten rule of government waiting. Persons from within an agency had one schedule as compared to those outside the given agency. Certain agency relationships demanded a different schedule. Competing agencies such as the Army and the Marines had a longer wait quotient compared to cooperating branches. As I sat there, I realized there might not actually be any cooperating agencies considering everyone competed for the same budget buck. Nonetheless, within each agency quotient was a ranking differential schedule based upon one's government service (GS) rank or equivalent. That is, if one were an employee at GS 19 and that person had a meeting with a GS 27, it would be appropriate for the GS 19 to wait for x number of minutes. However, the wait would be less if one was a GS 25. Since I was from a competing agency and there was a rather large GS gap differential between

330

my position as a FBI Senior Agent and the Deputy Director of Intelligence of the Central Intelligence Agency, I began to chastise myself for not bringing along a lunch.

I settled in with some paperwork I had brought and waited. Eventually I was shown into the DDI office. He wasn't there, but it least it was a nicer place to wait. The door opened, but it wasn't Harold Hanson.

"Sean, I don't know if you remember me, but I'm David Brown," a rather nondescript man said as he crossed the room and extended his hand, "I'm Mr. Hanson's assistant."

"Yes David, I do recall meeting you. How are things?"

"Very hectic. Of course, it usually is."

"David, is there something I can do for you?"

He paused, looked around the office a bit, pulled on his right ear lobe and sat down. "You know the director is quite busy. I was hoping we could talk. I could get the details, and when the Director finally gets here, we could just go over the highlights, you know, the bullet points."

I had no desire to talk to anyone but the Director. There was a mole, a traitor, however one described a sellout, in the Agency, of that I was convinced. I was also pretty sure it wasn't the DDI. "David, no offense but I would rather meet only with Director Hanson on this matter."

"I understand," he said, pulling on his ear lobe again. "Well, okay," he said, rising and looking at his watch. "I was just trying to save you some time. It may be awhile before the Director can make time for you. He is tied up in some very high level meetings."

331

"Thanks again, but I think I'll wait. I brought along a lot of paperwork I've putting off," I motioned to my briefcase.

As it turned out, David Brown was right. The wait was substantial.

- 148 -

Harold Hanson finally returned to his office. "Sean, I'm terribly sorry but this was just the first time I could get away. I have meetings scheduled until, well, until I just don't even want to think about."

I started to rise, "I understand, sir."

"Sit, please stay seated." The Director waved me down.

I re-took my seat and continued speaking, "What I've got to discuss very sensitive, for your ears only. That's why I didn't go over anything with your assistant."

"You mean David Brown."

"Yes, that's him," was my reply.

"Mm… I didn't send him in to talk to you. He's very efficient, sometimes too much so."

The DDI had an odd look on his face. Something wasn't completely right. I decided I needed to know more. "How long has David Brown been your assistant?"

"Quite a while, long enough that I really can't recall," Hanson replied.

"I see. He seems to be a good chief of staff."

Hanson first looked startled and then his face went blank like he was thinking about what I had said. "I guess I never really thought of his role quite like that, but yes, I would say he has acted as my chief of staff."

"Has he always had that role?"

"Not originally, but as time has gone by and our relationship has grown, yes.

"So, Director, he basically knows everything you know and maybe more?"

"Sean, I suppose that's correct. But I thought you came to see me about something important."

I hadn't originally come to talk to the Director about his assistant, but I believed there was a mole and David Brown could be that person, though I doubted it. At all high agency levels there are substantial amounts of vetting done even before candidates are selected. "True sir."

"Well, please get on with it." Hanson was being gruff but I thought I could see just below the surface a look of some concern.

"I want to discuss agent Chehwan's special assignment." I went on to describe what I had learned, reminded him about Mark Ruben and the compromise of the NSA computers, concluding with the description of how my home had been bugged and my daughter almost kidnapped. "For these reasons sir, I believe you have a leak, a spy, a bad guy if you will, within the CIA."

I thought my arguments had been well thought out and my conclusion logical, though clearly disturbing. I waited for Hanson to digest what I had said. As I waited, I watched his expression, blank, totally blank. The man was a good agent. I had to hand him that.

"Sean, what you have described may or may not be accurate. I'll need to think about it, and of course, do a little checking myself. There is most likely a bad apple, but that bad apple could be with the NSA or even your FBI."

"Sir, that could be true, but I don't think so. I urge you not to reject the message just because of the messenger."

"I assure you I won't do that. The truth in this case, as in all cases concerning the safety of the United States, is paramount. Now I have to go, more meetings." He pointed to the door as he began to shuffle papers on his desk. No final handshake. I thought that wasn't a good sign.

"By the way, did David Brown know about Amanda?" I asked really as an afterthought as I was getting up.

"Not originally. It was just the four of us. Amanda, Alan Mitchell, Simon Stallings at the IRS and myself. I'm sure that it was only after she was assigned to the FBI task force that anyone else was aware of what was going on."

I shook the Director's hand and thanked him for his time. Hanson was silent as I left with a look I couldn't readily describe.

- 149 -

I got back to the Hoover building later than I had hoped from my meeting in Langley and immediately called my temporary staff together. I spent the better part of an hour quizzing the group as to what they had found. The first and most obvious was they had been able to track the cash flows out of the Swiss bank account to the American banks and from those financial institutions to various religious organizations around the country.

334

We were able to do this because we had gotten an extensive list of account numbers from Amanda Chehwan's computer.

Using those same numbers, we were also able to backtrack into the upstream bank accounts. This might seem redundant, but I also wanted to see if there were deposits getting into these accounts other than from the one Swiss account we knew about. Additionally, I wanted to see if there were any sub-accounts. I found it interesting that the answer to both of my questions was no. The only money coming into the American accounts was from the primary Swiss accounts, and there weren't any other accounts spider webbing out from the ones we knew about. I was glad to learn this information as it made the trail easier to follow.

As part of the exercise and allowed by our FISA warrant, I had the staff create a summary of all the cash flows. The amounts were substantial, millions of dollars. Unfortunately, the team hadn't yet finished calculating the account of money flowing through the account in Switzerland. When questioned why I wanted this, I told the group I wanted to make sure all the incoming deposits were being originated by our terrorist friend Mustafa al Bevcar.

The conversation around the conference table then turned to the various religious groups receiving contributions. I asked if the religious bodies had any common characteristics. The group hadn't been researching for a long time so the answer wasn't definitive, but they had what appeared to be a common link. The groups receiving money were all activist. It didn't matter what brand of religion it was. Money had gone to all of them whether it was Christian, Jewish, Islamic or groups associated with lesser known beliefs. Finally, I turned to a young woman who had become the task force leader in my absence.

"Susan, did you find a relationship to the sums given and the level of activism of the different organizations?"

335

"Yes it seems the more active the larger the contribution."

"That would be expected," I responded.

"What's their attitude about getting so much money? I mean, don't most charities have to scramble and beg for every dollar they get?"

"Religious groups can be a little different from your ordinary charity, particularly the militant ones. They are filled with true believers. Those kinds of people are so committed to what they believe, whether it is crazy or not, they tend to assume anyone else willing to give time or money to their church is equally committed."

"Collective amnesia?" I asked.

"No, not at all. Collective moral superiority."

I thought for a while. That made sense. "So as a group, no one really questioned the large sums of money they were getting?"

"That is correct, from what we have learned so far. Now that may change."

"Susan, I doubt it," was my response.

"Did the people you talk to mention whether or not there were any strings attached to the money or other provisos?"

"No, nothing specific; however, all were definitely given the impression that they needed to get the money out and working as soon as possible."

"So they felt the money might dry up if it wasn't spent rapidly?"

"Yes Sean, that seems to be the consensus." I looked around the room and everyone's head was nodding in agreement. "I also might add aggressively."

"Susan, aggressively?"

"Sean, maybe confrontationally would be a better adjective."

"Okay. Here is the million dollar question. Did anyone ever actually meet their benefactors?"

"No, not really. Everything was done by phone, fax, wire transfer and email. Everyone agrees the donor or at least the front person was male, probably not older than fifty and most likely college educated, but other than that he never met anyone in person. That is, except one."

"Susan, who was that?" I almost yelled.

"The one group you need to contact directly."

"Which one?"

"Lukas Schafer's *The Movement.*"

- 150 -

"Your Holiness, you simply can't go. It's too dangerous," Cardinal Francesco Camperelle could barely contain himself.

The Pope stood calmly staring out a picture window. "Isn't it beautiful here?"

Camperelle couldn't believe the response he had just heard. What was this man thinking? Not only had His Holiness been forced to sneak into the United States arriving by private executive jet. If that wasn't humiliating enough, hadn't his 747 had been practically blown out of the sky? If the plane had crashed, many good, and important to the Church, people would have perished. Yet Peter II tranquilly stood there, seemingly without a care in the world. All the effort he and his friend the late Pope had put into this man. Was he going to throw it all away? "Yes, Holiness, it is beautiful, but that is not the point."

"Oh, but that is precisely the point. We are blessed with God's beauty and we should pause to appreciate it, to thank the Lord for all his gifts, to live in the moment without fear or hate. What is this place called again?"

"Chesapeake Bay our view is to the west."

"It is nothing like my home or Rome, so much water, so many trees. It's calm and peaceful here."

Camperelle sighed and waited. Times were indeed fraught with danger. The Catholic Church was over 2,000 years old, and Camperelle feared it wouldn't see another five years at the rate it was going, let alone 1,000 more years.

The Pope was certainly no fool, but he was in Camperelle's opinion taking too many chances. Thankfully, what operated as the Holy See's intelligence network had worked, this time as he had been warned of a plot to shoot down the Papal jet. However, Camperelle knew the network wouldn't prevent, or be able to warn him of every scheme to kill the Pope. Right now the Holy Father was standing in front of a giant picture window. What a perfect target. Maybe he should paint a red bull's eye on the Pope's white cassock.

"When will the American delegation arrive?"

"Within the next couple of hours, Your Holiness. I should remind you once it gets here the press will know and then everyone will know you are staying here."

"That can't be helped."

The Cardinal knew His Holiness was right. Still, if he would just step back away from the window, he would feel better. "Is there anything else you require of me?"

"Not at the present time, though please let me know when you hear back from Bishop Schafer. If you need me, I'll be praying."

Camperelle watched as the Pope left the room. How curious he had referred to Lukas Schafer as a bishop. This was the first time he could recall the Pontiff call the leader of the schismatic *The Movement* by his official title.

- 151 -

We talked a few more minutes about what the group needed to do. "Susan let me know if you find anything else." I then excused myself and headed off to call Lukas Schafer. I first tried his cell phone with no luck. I left a message saying it was urgent he contact me. Then I tried his assistant. He wasn't available, but I was assured that Bishop Schafer would call me back shortly. I hoped and prayed he would.

All the while I was dialing through the back of my brain I was wrestling with the rogue numbers found on Amanda's computer. With one set we had gotten lucky. Mark Ruben's number had led us to a locker in Union Station. Inside of which was a rather substantial amount of currency. The other two had still eluded us. Well actually, three sets of unknown numbers.

There was still the incomplete sequence of numbers with which we had to deal.

Numbers, ideas and possibilities bounced around my brain. It was like I could almost make things out, when the fog would roll back in and I would be lost again. I was frustrated. To me all the signs were flashing red. Something bad was going to happen, and it was going to happen soon. Increasing violent sectarian incidents were cropping up all over the country. The situation could unravel very quickly. My own internal pressure for results was increasing dramatically.

Money was the mother's milk of all activity, good and evil. What if? I reached for the phone and dialed NSA headquarters and asked for Dennis Hamilton.

"Yes Mr. Murphy, Mr. Hamilton will be with you in a minute." I apparently had moved up the response food chain at the NSA.

"Sean, are you calling about that wad of currency Alan had sent over?"

"No, but now that you brought it up. How's it coming?"

"Slower than we had hoped."

I was disappointed by this news, and it must have come through in my response, "I see."

"Sean, don't be disappointed. Taking longer isn't necessarily a bad thing. We are making progress. There is just more there than we had originally guessed. So why did you call?"

I wanted you to do some of your number crunching voodoo on the last sets of numbers we got from Agent Chehwan's computer."

"How is that?"

"I wanted to see what we got if we assumed the numbers were all bank account numbers."

"Makes some sense. But there is one hell of a lot of bank accounts in the world."

"I can imagine, or maybe I really can't imagine, but anyway assume they are all Swiss bank numbers."

"Okay, that'll cut the search down. Why Swiss though?"

"If Swiss was good for some of the bank accounts as well as being good enough for Mustafa al Bevcar, why wouldn't Swiss accounts be good enough for all the accounts?"

"Good point, Sean."

I was about to hang up when another thought crossed my mind, "Dennis, one more thing. Don't tell anyone else about this. Make up some kind of false story about this search."

"Okay," I could hear a real hesitation in Hamilton's voice.

"You haven't yet gotten to the bottom of the leak over there have you?" I knew they hadn't.

"No," I could sense the frustration in his reply.

"Well, until you do, I think it is better if only the two of us know what is going on."

"What about Alan Mitchell?"

"I'll take care of letting him know."

There was a pause and then Hamilton said, "Okay Sean, fair enough. I'll let you know as soon as we turn anything up."

- 152 -

Camperelle knew the Pope had returned from prayer to the room he was using as his office, to wait for the last of the delegation to arrive. As predicted, the press had gotten wind of the meeting and was beginning to swarm outside the front gate. The Cardinal also was aware that his Eminence John Cardinal O'Connor from the Washington D.C. Archdiocese would have to run the gauntlet of reporters, technicians and their equipment. Not that he minded, there had been many times over the years Camperelle had gone to calling the man the late Cardinal O'Connor. It seemed he couldn't get anywhere close to on time. Maybe the hassle of dodging the press core would teach him to be on time, or at least only fashionably late.

The house and associated grounds they were using had been generously donated by one of the Church's great American benefactors, Adrian Chalmers. Chalmers called it his weekend retreat. As Camperelle walked the grounds, he likened it more to an English hunting lodge. The grounds had to be at least twenty acres, almost all wooded except for the beach that ran the length of the property with its share of small coves and inlets. The property fronted Chesapeake Bay and was protected by a brick wall with security cameras on the three landed sides.

Camperelle knew that even with a monitoring system, security was marginal at best. A condition the U.S. State Department had imposed upon the Pope was that he had come as a private citizen, not the head of a foreign country; as such he wasn't afforded Secret Service protection. When their benefactor, Adrian Chalmers, had learned of their problem, he had also offered to provide security as well as lodging. Camperelle had kindly thanked him but turned him down. The number two man at the Vatican, though appreciative, wanted to make his own security arrangements.

342

The facilities fit their needs well, besides the main lodge of roughly fifteen thousand square feet; there were several outbuildings. There were enough bedrooms between the guest cottages and the main building for the Pope's small entourage and the visiting prelates.

The location however made security problematic, very rural, very isolated and heavily treed. Guarding all these men under the best circumstances would have been difficult. Under the current conditions, Camperelle knew it was almost impossible. The best he could do was to try to keep the delegates inside the main lodge or in the cottages. If they decided to take a walk-about, only God would be able provide protection.

The American delegation was now seated around a large oak table in the great room waiting for the last and most senior member to arrive. The table could seat at least thirty people, many more than the current group.

As he moved around the grounds checking things he could, Camperelle's cell phone rang.

"Si."

"The Cardinal is here at last."

"Grazie, please guide him to the house."

"Yes, Your Eminence."

Francesco Camperelle closed his cell phone and walked back to the house. He needed to greet the Cardinal O'Connor, after which he would let His Holiness know that the conference could begin.

- 153 -

When the Pope entered the room, everyone rose and began moving to form a line to formally greet him. Camperelle, as custom dictated, moved to lead the small procession.

343

Prophecy

Unexpectedly, His Holiness Peter II sat down and waved to his fellow delegates to do the same. Camperelle was surprised. Never in all his years as Cardinal, had the Pontiff not had the traditional greeting ceremony. Traditions ran deep in the Church, and this particular one was to emphasize to all the primacy of the Bishop of Rome as leader of the Catholic Church. Looking around the room, Camperelle could see equal amounts of surprise and astonishment reflected on the faces of his fellow priests.

The Pope then rose and began to speak, "Thank you all for coming. These times are most trying, and I believe the decisions we make here in this room will affect the future, the very essence of the Holy Mother Church. Let us now pray for Divine Guidance." Peter II then led the group in a simple but moving prayer. He concluded uttering, "Amen." He then sat down.

"For many years I believe that Catholic Church in America has been ignored by the Vatican. It did so at its own peril, a peril we are now seeing the consequences of."

Camperelle looked around the room, waiting to see which Bishop would speak first. As best as he could determine, the delegation was about equally split between traditionalists and progressives. As a general rule, the older the man, the more traditional he was. He and John Cardinal O'Connor were the oldest ones there. Camperelle could see from their body language that some of the younger men were anxious to speak, though it looked like they were waiting for something, some protocol.

Finally Cardinal O'Connor cleared his throat and began to speak. He had a voice that if he hadn't entered the priesthood, would have stood him well in Hollywood. It was a deep baritone, and any word he uttered sounded as if God himself had spoken.

"Your Holiness, there are many things we Americans squabble about, but not the assertion you've just made. For years

344

the Vatican has basically said to the American Church, send us your money and shut up. In my opinion, the issues affecting us here in America were never addressed or adequately dealt with."

Camperelle was surprised to hear such a comment from what he considered to be the rock upon which the traditional American Church was built. Gazing about the table, he could see agreement from all those present except His Holiness, whose expression was perfectly blank.

It was obvious to those present that the Pope was not yet ready to respond to O'Connor's comment when a soft quiet voice was heard. "For those who don't know me, and probably most of you don't, my name is Russell Johnson and I'm the Bishop of Memphis. I am here because Saint Louis Cardinal Rousseau has just had by-pass surgery. I was his auxiliary before my present assignment, and he asked that I represent him." Camperelle knew Rousseau to be a progressive and assumed Johnson would also be one. "I and this must seem strange to those who know me, agree with what Cardinal O'Connor has just said."

Using only a small hand gesture, the Pope said in a quiet voice, "Please continue."

"Thank you, Holiness. Though I agree with Cardinal O'Connor's description of the past, the overriding concern is where do we go from here? We are on the threshold of a schism if not already in one. It is paramount we deal with this."

"What is your recommendation?" Camperelle asked.

"The Pope should meet with Lukas Schafer and try to convince him to return to the fold."

"That is an entirely wrong course of action," Cardinal

345

O'Connor shouted. "His followers are heretics. One doesn't make nice with heretics. They need to follow the rules here on earth, and if they don't, they will suffer in hell, burning along with their leader, the good father Schafer."

Camperelle was amazed. A few minutes ago everyone was at ease; now all of that had changed. From a quick count based upon body language, the group appeared to be about evenly split with half agreeing with the proposal and the other half wanting no part of it. Tempers were rising, and Camperelle knew nothing would be accomplished if this session got out of hand. Someone needed to calm the situation. He looked at the Holy Father who gave him the merest of hand gestures.

"Excuse me for one moment; let's not get ahead of ourselves. Whether or not the Pope decides to meet with *The Movement* is one thing, but let me pose another question." Camperelle looked directly at each prelate. "One is it safe to meet and even more importantly, whether the Holy Father meets Lukas Schafer or not, is it even safe for him to remain here in America?"

Silence followed. The mention of the Pope's safety reduced the partisan tensions in the room. Finally Johnson spoke. "Regarding meeting with Lukas Schafer, it depends on when and where."

"And what about the second part of my question?" Camperelle drove home his question.

"All of us are deeply concerned about the Holy Father's safety. However, times now are like no other. We need the Pope's presence, it is paramount to the Church here in the United States. I think as long as we are careful, it will be reasonably safe for His Holiness," Bishop Johnson concluded.

346

Camperelle looked at Cardinal O'Connor for a response. The Cardinal nodded his agreement to what Johnson had said. The conversation ensued for another forty-five minutes with each side making points during the time. From what Camperelle could determine, there was no objectively correct answer. The course of action would be a matter of opinion. He wondered what the opinion of the only man that mattered in the room happened to be.

Finally, the discussion slowed down and stopped, all the men emotionally exhausted by the process. After a few moments of silence, the Pope rose to speak. "I have listened to all you have said. Your points were all well taken, and I am deeply moved by your unanimous concern for my personal safety. However, the paramount concern is what is best for the Holy Mother Church. I am merely a man. If something were to happen to me, it would be of no consequence, providing the Church mission on earth is saved. I believe it is my duty to meet with Father Schafer and to heal the schism we see developing."

Peter II turned to Cardinal Camperelle, "I would appreciate it if you would make all the necessary arrangements."

- 154 -

It was late in what had become an increasingly frustrating day for lack of concrete accomplishments, when I heard a voice. "Excuse me, Sean, do you have a minute?"

I spun my chair around to see Susan standing there. "Sure, what do you want to talk about?"

She pulled up a chair and began, "I'm having trouble making the numbers work."

Not being on the exact same page she was, I was

perplexed. "What numbers are those?"

"Oh sorry, your mind must have a thousand things going through it."

I liked hearing that as compared to *"listen you old fart, you told us to develop some spreadsheets. Have you forgotten that already?"* Susan continued, "Remember you asked us to create a spreadsheet showing the cash inflows and outflows from the master Swiss bank account."

"Oh yes. What's the problem?"

"Well, the numbers just don't add up. I think they should, but I can't make them work."

"Why don't you show me?"

Susan gave me the computer address to access the spreadsheet her group had been working on. In a few seconds it popped up. She began going over the columns and figures. I might add she did quite a good job presenting her information. "See what I mean?"

I looked at her data and she was correct. "Let's go over this slowly." I didn't want to go down the wrong road because of some simple logical error.

"Okay."

"Susan we've backtracked and estimated the amounts of money that Mustafa Bevcar has "taxed" from his sources, correct?"

"Correct. And we have adjusted those amounts for normal bad guy operating expense such as bribes and intimidation costs."

"We have then traced the cash flows from Bevcar's Swiss

accounts to the master dispersal account."

"Correct."

"Okay. And then you have used the numbers we got from Amanda's computer to trace the amount of money flowing into the various Church bank accounts?" I asked.

"Yes sir."

"And the money coming out doesn't equal the known amount flowing in."

"In a word, yes."

I sat there for a moment, absorbing what my young staffer had discovered. There was another player or players in the game. "Anything else?"

"As a matter of fact, there is."

"Go on."

Each time the cash leaves one of Bevcar's accounts heading for the master Swiss account not all of it gets to that master account.

"How is that, Susan?"

"Looks like there are leaks."

"Leaks?" I asked.

"Yes, at least two."

"Maybe they aren't leaks. Maybe there are commissions being taken."

Susan stopped, looked up from the screen and said, "Yes, that could explain it …commissions."

"Have you had any luck tracing down either the leaks or unknown deposits?"

"No. Both the disbursements and the deposits are very well camouflaged, expertly I would say."

My frustrating day had just ended. My staff had turned up some very valuable information. The FBI was good, very good in fact, at tracking the flow of money. If we were having trouble finding out the sources whoever was involved was very, very good, a seasoned professional. This was another confirmation, it had to be someone with either CIA or NSA training; no other explanation was even close to reasonable. "Susan, you and your group did a great job. Just keep digging."

Susan brightened, "Thank you sir, I feel and I know the team will be pleased."

Susan started to leave when I stopped her. "Make the assumption that whoever is behind the unknown cash flows are either current or former NSA or CIA."

"How's that?"

"This is totally classified, but I think we have a bad apple in the barrel. Make it your first assumption criteria that it's CIA." By now I had more than a multitude of reasons to think the entire operation was being run by an agent. Not the least of which had been the two who had been recruited to kidnap my daughter. One was dead and the other one had yet to say anything, even though I knew from my discussions with Alan Mitchell, she was being interrogated with extreme vigor.

Susan said, "I'll get the team on it right away," as she hurried out.

- 155 -

David had done as instructed. He had taken a series of cabs and busses to arrive at Adrian Chalmers' Washington D.C. hotel suite. He had thought it all quite silly. No one in authority was following him. If he had a tail, it was someone Chalmers' was using to make sure he was obedient to his quirky instructions. He hadn't been concerned about his safety. David knew if Chalmers was going to kill him, it wouldn't be before he received his instructions. As usual, Chalmers was sitting in the shadows in his large overstuffed leather chair. He chose not to wait for his invitation to sit down.

"David, you know I advanced you a substantial amount of money."

"Yes, you did pay me a large amount of money."

"Let's not get into semantics. I gave you money for information that I no longer need."

"That isn't my problem."

"I thought that would be your position, David. And I really don't want to quibble."

David remained silent, waiting to hear what Chalmers wanted.

"I'm thinking this will be our last meeting. You have served me well over the years."

Testing to see what Chalmers would say, David interrupted him, "We were friends."

Calmly Chalmers continued, "Yes I suppose so. Well, however you want to define our relationship, it is time for you to do one last thing for me."

"What is that?"

"I'll tell you in a minute. It will be quite dangerous and most probably you'll need to leave the country afterwards, most likely for the rest of your life."

"Travel can be expensive."

"David, I thought you would mention that. And of course, it can be. Because of that, I'll pay you two million dollars for your last job. Half will be transferred to your Swiss bank account immediately and the other half upon the job's satisfactory completion."

David remained silent, waiting for Chalmers to complete his thought. "And by the way, I'll forget about the fact the information I purchased from you was worthless."

"Listen Adrian, the information you bought was good."

In a silky, calm voice Chalmers continued, "I suppose so, but you were such an incompetent when it came to shooting down the plane, I simply couldn't trust your information to be accurate enough for my purposes."

"God damn it, Adrian!"

"Now David, calm down. It'll work out better this way. We know exactly where the Pope will be, and with that certainty of information, you'll be able to kill him without any difficulties."

David had suspected this was going to be Chalmers' final request. He had planned for it and with this payment plus the other cash he had set aside, he knew he could live quite well under a

352

new identity, several of which he had already established in anticipation of having to leave the country in a hurry.

"Killing him won't be a problem. Just give me the plans to your place."

"You'll get the plans." With that Chalmers rose from his chair and its perpetual shadow and crossed the room to David's chair. He stuck out his hand and simply said, "Good bye," and left the room.

Up until that moment, David had thought he had played his hand well, faking anger, groveling just enough. But it was the way Chalmers said goodbye that caused David to think he would need to be very careful with this last assignment and more importantly afterwards.

- 156 -

Adrian Chalmers heard the front door close, and with it a chapter in his life. He had known David Brown longer than he had known almost anyone else. In many ways Chalmers knew David was a living, breathing anti-definition of a tragic hero. The man seemed to possess all the opposite characteristics of Aristotle's definition.

Chalmers knew David chafed at the lack of income his government job provided. The truth be told, Adrian didn't remember much about David's uncle, just that the man was rich and his old friend had gotten used to living well as his dependent. However, once he was out of school, the cash had stopped. Knowing his problem, Adrian had eventually sought him out. At first he had asked very little of him, at least in comparison to how much he had paid him. No, David would not suffer more than he deserved. He would die swiftly in a hail of bullets, the despicable killer of the Pope of Rome. Furthermore, Chalmers knew Brown hadn't been doomed from the start of his life. Brown had had choices, real options. For one, he simply could have lived within his means. For another, had he not gotten greedy, Chalmers would have kept him on his payroll for years. Yes, David Brown was responsible for his own fate. He was a man who could have controlled his avarice.

The man was greedy and self-centered. He saw the world only in terms of his pleasure and short term wants. He wasn't noble by nature, but he was perfectly self-centered. He had sold out in the pursuit of money. Brown had robbed him, taking more and more from the Swiss account. He was a man who blamed others and life for those things that had not gone well for him. He was also stupid. How could he have possibly thought he wouldn't have been caught?

Once it was all over, Adrian planned to tell the world about David Brown, to use him in death as he had used him in life. Brown's death would help him cement his goals. David Brown would be reviled as he should be. David Brown would die. His death was necessary, and as such, good would follow it as surely as day followed night.

Yes, as Chalmers clicked off in his head the anti-definition of a tragic hero, that was David Brown. There was one last element he couldn't quite place. What was it? Then Chalmers smiled. Yes, that was it. The tragic hero must see and understand his doom as well as the fact that his fate was determined by his own actions. David Brown would die too quickly for that. So quickly he would never know what had hit him.

Chalmers pulled out his secure cell phone and began to dial. It was time to put the final piece of the puzzle in place.

- 157 -

I got in early the next morning, and my day was already

354

filled with too much work. My "To Do" list had grown rather than shrunk. I think there is a direct connection between the amount of work performed and the length of the damn list. Not an inverse correlation, but a direct one. The more one worked, the longer one's list became. I looked down to see my voice mail light flashing. At least I took some cold comfort in knowing some lucky soul was having even more fun than I was. I hit the button, punched in my personal code and waited. It was Dennis Hamilton's voice, "Sean, we have made a lot of progress on that pile of money. You should come over as soon as you can. There is a lot to tell. I'll leave a pass for you at the main desk."

I immediately headed for my government issued chariot and drove out to Fort Meade, where, true to his word, Dennis Hamilton had left a pass for me. Not only was I given a pass, but I was escorted to his office and ushered into the large conference room next to it. "Hello, Sean. Glad to see you," Hamilton extended his hand.

I shook it and looked around the room. It was large, and I expected at any moment to have it filled with NSA staffers of various government levels. "It's just you and me Sean." I must have given him a look because he continued, "Just like you asked."

I took a seat and asked, "What do you have for me?" I really wanted to say I busted my balls getting over here. It better be damn good. But I was such a good team-member; I kept those thoughts to myself.

Hamilton lit up with a big shit eating grin. "We cracked the code."

"Great. What did it tell you?"

"All kinds of things."

355

"Tell me. Quit keeping me in suspense."

"Ah Sean, work with me. Sometimes it's fun to make the FBI dangle a bit." He waited for a couple of seconds before continuing. "Okay, here is the poop." Hamilton hit a button, the room darkened and a computer screen lit up, within moments, a series of names, phone numbers and addresses appeared.

"Dennis, you found all this from the pile of money we got from the locker?"

"Indeed we did. It just took us a while. The encryption was rather sophisticated, even elegant."

I knew elegant was a term of art meaning simple to use but hard to figure out, "How's that?"

"Sean, there were quite a lot of variables."

"Like what?" I asked.

Hamilton responded, "To start with we had two, the sequence of the bills themselves and the order of the countries in the package of bills." He paused before continuing. "In addition, there were the serial numbers of the bills as well as the issue date of the notes. As you can imagine, these different permutations could easily keep our supercomputers working full time for days."

"Okay."

"So before we just went into our mega number crunch mode, we did a little bit of brainstorming. We started with the assumption that whoever needed to decode the information would probably not have access to a powerful Cray computer. It was equally safe to assume the person would probably need to be able to use readily accessible information. We made one additional assumption."

"What was that?"

"That the user would probably be short on time."

"Seems reasonable."

Hamilton continued. "Using those guidelines, our first breakthrough came when we decided the country sequence was important. We wrote down the countries in order and next to each we recorded the international telephone country code."

"Go on."

Hamilton smiled, "Of course, there are a great many iterations of just these numbers. However, someone under time pressure wouldn't have hours and hours to do some form of exotic manual decoding. A tried and true encryption methodology even in today's world is the conversion of numbers into names and vice versa. So we started with the country codes running them forward and backwards. That's how we got our first names. We then fiddled around with a number drop in the same forward and backward approach and got more names. We continued on, dropping a country code in sequence both forward and backward until we had gone through the bills once. This analysis generated the rest of the names. We followed the same procedure with the bill number sequence to arrive at street and city address."

"How did you find out the countries the cities and streets were in?"

"We cheated on that. We ran our parameters through the computer. When we got the answer back, we were all a little red faced. The country was the currency."

"What about the Euros?"

"Simple. The back of those bills shows the country of issue."

Shaking my head, I thought the coding did seem ingenious, "What about the phone numbers?"

"You won't believe this; it was the serial number of the bill."

"The exact number?"

"No, no not the exact number. There were the usual skips, drops and repeats. But it was the serial number."

"I suppose you cheated on that also?"

"You bet your buns, but it did confirm what we had laid out in our brainstorming session and it did so rather quickly."

I had to agree with that assessment. Turning back to the screen and being thankful we were finally done with my computer geek decoder lesson, I continued, "So tell me what've got."

"See the highlighted phone numbers and addresses?"

"Yes."

"That is Bevcar's contact information. Whoever put the currency together was the American contact for Mustafa Bevcar. Furthermore, I assume that person and the person who rented the locker is one in the same."

"I can't say for sure, but that would be my guess also," I replied.

"You've staked out the locker, haven't you?"

"We have, but there hasn't been action yet. What's the story behind the other numbers, the non-highlighted ones?"

"We don't know for sure, but we think they are mostly likely safe house addresses."

"And the phone numbers?"

"Probably general contact information, someone that can get a gun at a moment's notice or passage out of the country, no questions asked."

That made sense. Undoubtedly the NSA would track the rest of the data down in short order.

"What is that?" I pointed to one number being displayed at the bottom of the page. "It looks like a Swiss bank account number."

"That is exactly what it is. It seems to belong to Bevcar's contact."

"Do you have a name?"

"Indeed we do."

"Who is it?"

"A gentleman by the name of Mohammed al Hasim."

"Who the hell is that?"

"Sean, you might know him better by his alias."

"And that might be?"

"Mark Ruben."

- 158 -

I made two calls as I drove back to the office, my head still spinning from what I had learned. One was to Alan Mitchell because I thought it would be a good idea to let my boss know where things stood. The second was to Susan, my staff leader. I asked her to find out all she could about Ruben's Swiss bank account and do it immediately. I knew it was a difficult task, but I needed to know as much as possible as soon as possible.

Dennis Hamilton had assured me that his Agency had been re-investigating Mark Ruben ever since they found out he was Mohammed al Hasim. No doubt heads would roll and procedures would change once this was over. Somehow a mole had worked his way into the NSA and no one knew it. He had been vetted and had been cleared. I wondered how many other undercover agents were working at the NSA. The thought of any made me shudder.

I knew the locker at Union Station didn't belong to Mark Ruben. So whoever it belonged to either worked in conjunction with Ruben in some fashion or was Ruben's enemy. Two completely different options coming from the same set of facts; this wasn't that common, but it wasn't that unusual either in my line of work. At this point I simply didn't know which it was. Hopefully, with a little more information, the answer would become apparent. What was apparent was that there was more than one leak. We had found the one at the NSA that left the CIA, probably.

The traffic going into Washington was normal. But today it seemed incredibly slow. The pace was driving me nuts. Rather than fume and waste more time, I decided to give Lukas Schafer another call. Hopefully he had something that could help me. I picked up my cell and dialed the number.

"Good morning, *The Movement.* How may I direct your call?" A way too cheery voice answered.

"Lukas Schafer please. This is Sean Murphy."

"Mr. Murphy, I'm sorry to say that Bishop Schafer is not available."

I was becoming a little perturbed and a little worried. I had tried to talk to my old parish priest a number of times and had been unable to for one reason or another.

"I see. Do you expect him in later? You see it is quite important that I talk with him. I have tried to a number of times without luck."

"Yes, I know you have, Mr. Murphy."

The tone in her voice made me wonder. I decided to take a chance. "Is everything okay?"

I could hear her breathing, but the receptionist was silent. Finally she spoke in a low voice, one I could barely hear. "We don't know where he is. He was supposed to officiate at a morning service. He never showed up."

"I see. Do you want me to come over?"

"No, not yet. Father Gates is in charge in Bishop Schafer's absence. He has strictly forbidden us to talk to the authorities."

"Okay. But if you think you need to talk to me, please do." I gave her my cell phone number. She thanked me and said she would keep my number handy. As I entered the D.C. driving maze, I wondered if Lukas Schafer was still alive.

- 159 -

"Then it is all settled, Francesco?"

Francesco Cardinal Camperelle was having a hard time

getting used to the new Pope. The two men were clearly from different generations. The familiarity the younger generation maintained was something with which he was unfamiliar. Even his old friend, the recently deceased Holy Father, would have called him Cardinal Camperelle. "Yes, Your Holiness, all the necessary arrangements have been made."

"Good. That's very good."

"I'm glad you approve, but I still have grave doubts."

"I know you do. But it is the will of God. I know it. Please, now let's review the arrangements. I want to make sure I have everything straight in my mind."

"Yes, Holy Father. Father Lukas Schafer will meet with you here tomorrow. He'll come with only one assistant. The meeting will be held here at the main lodge, for everyone's safety."

"Does our host know of this?"

"Yes, as a matter of fact, he was the one who suggested the location. Apparently there have been a number of threats both on your life and the life of Lukas Schafer."

"I see, well I hate to hear such things. I will pray for those disillusioned souls. But it is so very lovely here and knowing our host, Mr. Chalmers, approves makes me feel better."

Camperelle was not as comfortable with that fact as the Pope, but felt there was nothing gained by mentioning his reservations. "The agenda has been almost completely agreed upon. I'll greet Father Schafer and escort him into this room."

"Where is he to sit and where am I to sit?"

"We'll have the chairs arranged. Both of you will look out onto the bay."

"I see, I see, very well. It's truly a beautiful view."

"Yes it is, Holiness. Here is the agenda." Camperelle handed the Pope a piece of paper. "Please review it, and let me know if there is anything you want to change. We are about to go final with it."

"I assume Schafer has agreed to it?"

"He has."

The Pope took the paper and put it down. "I'll review it in a couple of minutes." Peter II waited a moment and looked at Camperelle. "I know you are concerned about me. You shouldn't be. All is as it is supposed to be. It's God's will. I am but his instrument. Relax. Please."

The Cardinal looked at the Pope. "I hear your words, but unfortunately I still worry. I'll worry until you've safely returned to Rome. I do believe you, but I am human and I worry. Undoubtedly I will suffer some time in Purgatory because of this weakness. Nonetheless, I do pray for your safety every day."

The Pope crossed the short space separating the two men and gave his second in command an embrace. "You will not spend any time in Purgatory, of that I'm sure."

All Camperelle could do was to smile. He loved the new Pope, and he truly feared his reign would be a short one. "I hope you are right. Purgatory never has sounded like much fun."

His Holiness smiled serenely and quietly said, "Now let's review that agenda."

- 160 -

"Susan, what do you have for me?" I always felt bad when I got right to the point without any conversational niceties. I had this deep sensation I was reverting to my alpha male Neanderthal style. I attributed part of this to the late twentieth century FBI training and the rest to natural Irish Catholic guilt.

Thankfully Susan didn't mind my matter-of-fact style. "Do you want the good news or the not so good news?"

"Give me the good news first."

"We've managed to trace money going from Mustafa Bevcar to Mohammed al Hasim."

"Excellent, Susan. Tell me more."

"It seems that each time Bevcar received his tax, a small amount, a commission if you will, would go to Mark Ruben's Swiss account."

"Makes sense I suppose."

"How's that?"

"It seems even for those who are true believers, an earthly reward is necessary," I said.

"Either way, there is cash to follow."

"Exactly, Susan." So if that was the good news, I wondered what wasn't. "Okay, what's the down stroke?"

"We found the account, but it has been cleaned out."

"I'm not surprised."

"Sean, what do you mean?"

"My guess is that whoever killed Ruben also got Ruben's cash. I don't suppose you have found where it went after it left Ruben's Swiss account."

"Not yet, but we are confident we'll turn something up soon. It may just take some time."

Without a break I wasn't so sure. However, there wasn't any point in sharing my concern with my staff. No need to have a self-fulfilling prophecy. "Okay, it'll be tricky but have at it. Let me know as soon as you have anything, I mean anything, regardless of how small it might seem to you."

Susan had jumped up and was headed out the door, her voice filled with enthusiasm. "You got it."

As I turned back to a pile of memos and files that needed reviewing, I thought about how I both loved and hated youth.

- 161 -

I had been working all afternoon reviewing different aspects of the case, trying to tie all the pieces together. It was a tedious but necessary job. Over the years I had found it was in the small details that major cases were cracked. To help clear my head, I found that periodically jumping on and off the internet would help. Today that wasn't the case. It seemed every time I checked out the news, more and more sectarian issues were surfacing. Polling had become a staple to the twenty-four/seven news cycle. All of the major surveys were saying the same thing.

The public was in general uneasy. Those with a religious persuasion felt others not of their beliefs were impinging upon their personal freedoms. Those without a religious bent felt persecuted by all those who believed in God. Those believing in God, it seemed, were growing daily in intolerance. The message of love and forgiveness was clearly being overwhelmed by fear and intolerance.

My cell rang. I was hoping it would be Mo. Over the years she seemed to have developed the uncanny ability to call when I badly needed to talk. I looked at the number, but didn't recognize it. "Murphy here."

"Sean." The voice was low, barely audible.

God, I hated getting old. Things just kept working more and more poorly. "Hello, hello."

"Sean."

"Yes, this is Sean Murphy. Who is this? I can barely hear you."

Only a little louder, "Sean, this is Lukas Schafer."

"Father, good to hear from you. Are you okay?"

"At the moment, I'm fine."

I didn't like hearing this. "Can you speak freely?"

"Yes, for the moment."

"Where are you? Do you need me to send someone?"

"No Sean. I don't think so."

"Okay Father, I need to ask you some important questions. Questions about *The Movement*."

"Sean, I have things to tell you, important things."

366

"Okay you go first," What followed was a story of confusion and concern. Schafer told me about Adrian Chalmers and his role in *The Movement.* How the man had initially been supportive and helped the organization grow. Then over the months how he had become more and more demanding. Finally how Chalmers had created a competition of compliance between Schafer and his number two man, Raymond Gates. What I couldn't tell was how much of this was real and how much was just paranoia. I needed to get some facts, so I interrupted the priest's ramblings. "Father, one moment, please!" Thankfully he paused. I spoke up immediately. I didn't want him to begin his monologue again. "Did Chalmers deal directly with you?"

"Yes, on personal matters, never when it came to money."

"Father, please explain what you mean."

"Well, when he wanted me to do something or go in a direction, we would personally meet."

"Where?" How?"

"Usually at a hotel or other rented location."

"Was it the same location each time?"

"No."

Smart, I thought. Hard to track someone who kept moving around. "Tell me about the money."

"Sean, when I say money, I also mean organizational help."

"Okay."

"That kind of help always came from an organization."

"What organization?"

"Hope for America Foundation."

I wrote the name down. I would need to do a little investigating. "Was it always the same?"

"Always."

Great. That fact would make things easier for me. "Father, I need to ask you something else."

"Okay Sean, please hurry."

I thought I could hear noises in the background, but I wasn't positive. "I need to ask you about the person who gave you all your money. I mean the person other than Adrian Chalmers."

"I only met the person once. I think it was a man, but you never know. Not today."

"You didn't get a good look at him?"

"No. He was in the shadows and he spoke in a low voice."

Classic technique, I thought. "Anything, anything at all you tell me about your conversation?"

"No, not really. He just reiterated how our benefactors wished *The Movement* would spend the money."

"Father, let me guess, quickly and on controversial type topics."

"That's it exactly. I was quite uncomfortable, but I became seduced by the money. There was a lot of it, and I'm sorry to confess I had fallen under its power."

"That is understandable, Father. Is there anything else you

can think of?"

"Well, the person had a tick."

"What do you mean?"

"Well, it seemed when he needed to think or pause, he had a habit of pulling on his ear."

Bells were beginning to go off in my head, "Any ear in particular?"

"Sorry, I really didn't notice."

I wanted to hang up and pour through some paper work I had. I wanted to be sure but, I thought I knew who the person was. However, before I hung up I needed to ask Lukas one more question. A thought had crossed my mind as we talked. "Father, you mentioned earlier that as of late Adrian Chalmers was treating you differently."

"Yes, I don't think I'm making this up."

"Please go on." There were definitely noises and they were getting louder.

"Sean, he has been dismissive, almost like he is done with me. Not unkind, more impersonal basically, like I'd become a disposable."

Schafer's comments bothered me, especially combined with my phone call to *The Movement*. The one when I had been told Raymond Gates was dictating policy. Was a coup in process and Schafer didn't quite know it yet? I remembered something I had just read on the internet. "Father, are you going to meet with the Pope?"

"Yes I am, though the public is supposed to be made aware only after the meeting. How did you know?"

"Internet rumor." And my superior investigative talents, but I didn't add that.

"Yes, it seems secrets are impossible to keep, at least at *The Movement.*"

"When?"

"In a few days. The final details are being hammered out."

"Where?"

"Adrian Chalmers' house on Maryland's eastern shore." I then heard what sounded like a door opening and the phone went dead.

- 162 -

The answer hit. It hit me like the proverbial thunderbolt or flash of light. It was David Brown. The key had been Lukas Schafer's comment about the unknown benefactor tugging at his ear. Every time I had met Brown, he would end up pulling on his ear. It wasn't something one would pick up right away, but in the accumulation of everything it was obvious. The bad guy was CIA, not only CIA but damn high up in the organization. It all made sense now, from the ability to bug my house, the kidnappers, to his relationship with Amanda Chehwan. Everything tumbled into place. Being DDI Hanson's assistant, he had to know everything that was going on. He had been ubiquitous. Every time I had tried to talk to Harold Hanson, David Brown was present. The prototypical gatekeeper was the ultimate traitor. I pulled open my drawer and fumbled around until I found what I wanted. I had two pictures from Amanda's cell. The ones she had taken the night she had been murdered. I stared at the pictures. They were now as clear as day. It simply amazed me that it had taken me this long. There staring at me, were two fuzzy, but definite, pictures of David Brown. Thankfully I had enough years of experience not to get too much down on myself for not seeing the likeness before.

The problem was to determine what to do with this information. I also had to make an airtight case. I had some evidence, but certainly not enough for court. Not for some fancy high priced lawyer to tear apart. I needed more. The more that I needed was hard evidence in the form of cash. I jumped and ran to the bullpen where my crew was working. "Susan, please come here for a minute."

"What do you have, chief?"

I smiled; I liked the way she called me chief. "Remember I told you to look for an agent."

"Yes, but even with that, we still haven't found the other end of the money trail."

"That's okay. I know this is somewhat a change of direction but I need you to look into someone."

"Who?" Susan asked.

"David Brown."

Susan looked at me, stunned. You mean the DDI's assistant?"

"One and the same," I responded. "Look, narrow your search to focus on him. See what you can find. I need preliminary data ASAP. Remember though, at the end of the day we'll need your information to be rock solid. It'll be the data the Bureau will use in court to send the bad-guy away for the rest of his life, whoever it turns out to be."

Susan spun around to relay my instructions, and I was about to leave when another thought struck me. "Susan wait!"

"What Sean?"

"I want you to split the team in two. Put half to work chasing down David Brown's information."

"What about the rest?"

"Look into the finances of the *Hope for America Foundation.*"

"What's that?"

"I suspect it's Adrian Chalmers' private charity. If not his alone, it is an organization with which he is intimately involved."

"Do you want us to take any special direction?"

"Yes, I think the unexplained cash flow is coming from it. I want you to see if you can prove me right. This is top priority. Stay as late as necessary, and call in whatever help you think you might need. Use Alan Mitchell's name if you have to."

"Got it. I'll let you know as soon as we find anything."

"Anything, no matter how small it might seem to you." With that I headed back to my office.

- 163 -

As I walked back to my office, I still had too many questions. True, I now knew David Brown had killed Amanda

Chehwan. It also appeared he had been in cahoots with Mark Ruben. I could imagine Ruben's motivation, but I was certainly unsure of Brown's. Another question: was Lukas Schafer just being paranoid or was there another play going on out there, one that I hadn't yet figured out? Was what he said true?

I was back in my chair staring into space. I needed to sort out what I had just learned. I needed to separate what I thought I knew from what I actually knew. However, before I had a chance to begin, I received another cell call.

"Murphy here."

"Agent Murphy, Agent Edwards." I knew the man, black, age anywhere from the late forties to the early sixties, a face you couldn't remember. In the right situation, meaning a fully diversified metro area like the District, a blend-in if there ever was one. He was the agent in charge of the surveillance detail at Union Station.

"Sam, what do you have for me?"

"Just thought I would let you know we got some action at the locker."

"What happened?" Things were moving quickly, I had the feeling things were coming to a conclusion, and I wasn't ready.

"About twenty minutes ago, a male, a well-disguised one, opened the locker. Whoever it was, was simply amazing."

"How's that?"

"Didn't flinch, not one bit. He acted like having an empty locker instead of one filled with money was as natural as going to the bathroom."

"Sam, what did he do?"

"Just closed it, though I would have loved to see his face, and walked away."

"I assume he's being tailed."

"As we speak, Sean, as we speak."

"Listen. I want to send you a picture. Hang on for a minute. Give me your phone number."

"Okay."

I turned to my computer and called up Amanda's pictures. Within minutes I had sent them to Sam. "Sam, are they coming through?"

"Just starting to. Okay, got them, yes they are here."

"Take a look at them. Does either of them look like our mystery guest?"

Silence. "Sam?"

"Give me a minute, Sean."

More silence. I was ready to crawl out of my skin. Waiting a minute seemed like waiting an hour. Finally he spoke. "Not conclusively, but as a lead yes."

"Sam, the pictures I sent are of David Brown, assistant to CIA DDI Hanson."

More silence. Finally, "My God!"

"I need to tell my guys they are trailing a pro."

"Sam, a pro gone bad, and very dangerous."

"You got it."

There was nothing really left to say. Both Sam and I had just learned Sam's team was in grave danger. "Thanks, Sam. Let me know when you have some progress."

"Will do."

"Please be very careful."

"We will."

With that final exchange, we hung up.

- 164 -

David Brown had taken a chance. Now he hoped it wouldn't be fatal. The locker was empty. He had to assume it had been under surveillance and that he was going to be followed. He was glad that it was dark. It would be easier that way. He would get away regardless of what it took.

He began to walk casually towards the train platforms. Commuters were still pouring through the station. This was good. Their bodies would provide the cover he needed. First, he needed to determine how many were following him. With luck, there would only be one, at least for a while. Certainly the Bureau was now calling in all the support it could muster. That help would start showing up within moments.

He stopped at a newspaper stand. He grabbed a *Post* and used it as a shield. He held it up, pretending to read it. Within a couple of minutes, he spotted his tail. Because staking out a locker was low level work, the man trailing him was young, probably a rookie. The man looked around. He apparently had lost Brown in the crowd. Brown waited and waited. Finally the man saw him. They made eye contact and the rookie turned away. Brown knew he had him.

David looked for the nearest men's room. He knew it was

too predictable, but it was as good a place as any to take care of the problem. Besides, he needed, desperately needed, to make some financial overseas calls. He saw the sign pointing to the restrooms and headed in that direction.

A number of trains had just left, and for that reason the men's room was unoccupied when he entered. He looked around, smiled and headed for a urinal at the end of the row. The setup was perfect. The urinal was one of the new kinds, one with an automatic flush mechanism. The sensor was housed behind a shiny chrome plate which acted exactly like a mirror. All he had to do was to wait. Eventually his stalker would come in. The only negative would be if others came in. David thought this unlikely as he had checked the train schedule before formulating his plan but if not it was something he would just deal with when it happened.

Several minutes passed. More than David had originally anticipated, but his pursuer finally entered the restroom. He continued to stand at the urinal. Brown could see that he was surprised to see him still standing there. David knew the man would have to do something that would not draw attention. So either he would wash his hands or pretend to go to the bathroom. The rookie chose to fake a trip to the can. Naturally, he chose the fixture at the opposite end of the row.

Brown faked a zip up and pretended to fumble around, struggling with his overcoat as he stepped back from the urinal. David slid slightly to his right as he pretended to struggle. Unnoticed by his tail, he had subtly moved closer, only a few feet away.

Then in one quick motion David Brown pulled out a knife and took one step towards the FBI agent. Before the agent could move back from his position in front of the urinal, Brown had grabbed him around the chest while stabbing him in the back below his ribs with an upward arching motion cutting into his heart. The FBI agent almost immediately lost consciousness and began to collapse. Brown held him for just a moment to make sure the blow he had inflicted was fatal. Once he was assured the man was gone, he gently allowed him to fall to the floor while he cleaned his knife on the man's coat. The killing occurred in a shockingly short time, less than fifteen seconds, and then Brown was out the restroom door. David believed there weren't any additional pursuers. There was simply not enough time, and with that knowledge he quickly vanished into the latest crowd of travelers.

- 165 -

I got the call. It came so quickly I was almost certain it would be dreadful and unfortunately I was right. Sam phoned with the news that he had lost a rookie agent. The man had been stabbed from behind, a very professional job, and had died almost instantly. Thankfully the young man didn't suffer, except of course for the fact that he was dead. Sam Edwards also had the unpleasant task of telling me that David Brown had vanished without a trace.

I sat at my desk fuming. The Bureau had lost another in the line of duty. It didn't really matter that I didn't know the young man. He was a fellow agent; that was all that mattered. Every time something like this happened, I'm reminded again how short life really is. Like many couples, Mo and I have talked about it from time to time. Discussed how we could use our time more wisely. And like many couples I'm sure, we have haven't been able to come up with a real good strategy. Over the years I've heard, especially from cancer survivors, not to sweat the small stuff. They have also told me that after cancer everything is small stuff. I have tried to incorporate that philosophy into my life. I can't say I have done a very good job at it. Situations like this, though, give me added impetus to try harder in the future.

I was very deep in thought, so much so I didn't notice

Susan standing in front of my desk. "Are you okay, Sean?"

"No, not really." I then explained what had just happened. Needing to move forward in so many ways, I asked, "Have you come up with something?"

"Good news or bad news?"

I wanted to get the bad stuff behind me, "the bad."

"We found Mark Ruben's money."

I grimaced, "And it happened," I put an emphasis on the "ed" part of the word, "to be in a Swiss bank account owned by David Brown."

"Right, Sean. The account was cleaned out within the last ten minutes."

"Damn! That S.O.B. After he killed our guy, he must have transferred the money."

"Any luck finding where it went?"

"Sorry, no. Sean, he's good. We'll eventually track it down, but it could be quite a while."

I figured as much. "Okay, what's the good news?"

"You were right about the *Hope for America Foundation*."

"Susan, talk to me."

"The missing money going into the main Swiss bank account came from Chalmers' foundation. We tore the records apart and with Alan Mitchell's help we got the IRS to confirm what we had discovered."

"Good, good." I was glad to have some good news. "Is your evidence rock solid?"

"Good as granite."

I took a deep breath. "Okay, what can you tell me about the foundation?"

"The foundation and Adrian Chalmers are one in the same." Susan waved the report she had been holding. "He started it. He's nurtured it through its early years. Now that it stands on its own financially, he continues to control it."

"Explain that to me," I said.

"He controls the board and all corporate officers. All of them are either on his payroll or in his pocket in some other way."

"Susan, thanks," I waved her report. "Let me study this."

"Chief, call me if you need anything else."

"I will, but don't stop hunting."

"Wouldn't think of it," she said and waved to me as she left.

- 166 -

I took Susan's report and scanned it quickly. I was certain, particularly after the IRS confirmed the numbers, her group had been correct. I was really looking for any additional clues that might help me. I had "the who" part of the investigation; what I really needed now was "the why" part.

Why would a man like Adrian Chalmers be interested in

stirring up the pot in America? He was rich and controlled a media empire. What more could he want? The question baffled me. I knew in the question would be the answer.

I flipped on the computer and did a search on Adrian Chalmers. The amount of data was simply amazing. I was overwhelmed. There wasn't any chance in this world I could get through it. That wasn't entirely correct; I could get through it but after it would be too late. I checked my watch as I grabbed the phone. Damn. It was getting late and I was getting tired, cursing way too much. "Susan, drop everything you are doing. I'm coming down. And," I put a great deal of emphasis on the word, "make sure no one leaves."

"Okay," was all she said.

I grabbed the report and headed for the conference room where my "staff" was holed up.

Within a few minutes, I was standing in front of a group of what I could tell were very tired people. "I'm sorry to do this but I need your help." I explained how Lukas Schafer's tip had been instrumental in breaking open the case. Because of that tip, I now needed research on Adrian Chalmers, from when he was born until today. How I needed numbers and personal stuff and that I needed it right now. I asked the group to divide itself, between those who felt more comfortable with either the financial or the psychological data. Thankfully the group was young, still with enough enthusiasm to get going. I planned to be available to direct and guide them. I didn't want anyone getting bogged down in dead ends. However, I knew it would be a while before I could provide constructive help. So in the meantime, I decided to make myself useful. First I called Mo and told her I wouldn't be home. Then I made fresh coffee and ordered pizza for my team. I figured food and fuel would help a tired brain work a little better.

- 167 -

Chalmers looked about. The setting was perfect. He had purchased Holy Trinity Abbey from a literally dying order of Dominican nuns about ten years ago. The deal he had made was that he would allow the few remaining sisters to continue living, working and praying in the abbey until the last ones were dead. That occurred about a year ago. Since then, the place had been vacant. Chalmers never quite knew why he had bought the old broken down complex until tonight. It was the perfect backdrop for the next part in his little plan.

He was seated in the front row of the small chapel waiting for his appointment. The only light was from hundreds of votive candles he had spent the last half-hour lighting. Finally he heard steps echoing off the granite slabs that made up the floor of the small church. He waited, not wanting to turn around. He needed his appointment to come to him.

The sounds grew louder as the guest came closer, louder and louder until they stopped completely. It was only then that Adrian Chalmers allowed himself to turn towards the main aisle of the chapel.

"Hello Raymond, I'm glad you could make it on such short notice. Please have seat."

Raymond Gates sat silently in the hard wooden pew next to Adrian Chalmers. "I assumed it was important because of the hour you called."

"Your assumption was and is correct." Gates waited silently for Chalmers to continue. "I have been thinking. I need a man I can count upon. Can I count upon you?"

Gates didn't immediately respond. Then in a quiet voice,

one very much appropriate for the building they were in, "Yes, I'm a man you can count upon."

"I can't tell you how much better that makes me feel. You see *The Movement* has grown so. It is much larger than one man. It needs a man that can lead an organization. Bishop Schafer, though a wonderful holy man, is not such a leader."

Gates nodded and mumbled something incomprehensible that Chalmers knew was meant as an acknowledgement of his last statement.

"I don't want to. I couldn't let *The Movement* just wither away, especially now after all our hard work if something were to happen to Lukas. These are very dangerous times. You and I both know there have been many threats against his life."

Gates nodded but remained silent. "Father, I want you to be ready in case…" Chalmers paused. He liked playing with people like Gates. Chalmers knew that Gates would kill his own mother if it would get him the power he wanted. "… in case something were to happen to Lukas."

"Adrian, you can count on me."

"Thank you, Father." Turning to the altar, he said, "Raymond, perhaps you could lead the two of us in a small prayer for Lukas and *The Movement.*

- 168 -

For a while there wouldn't be anything for me to do. "The kids," that's what I had begun to call my team, would need some unfettered time. If I helped them too soon, progress would stop. I

382

recall my first all night bullpen. It was back in the days when smoking was what real men did. You could cut the haze with a knife. My boss then was a guy about my age today, who I thought was ancient, kept coming in and asking how we were doing. Then he would go stand behind everyone and anyone and peer over their shoulders. I really hated that part. Anyway, each time he would ask, it would slow me down and each time he came over to give his special insight, my production stopped entirely. Later I learned he had affected everyone in the exact same manner. Besides, if it was something crucial, Susan would seek me out, regardless of the time or my location, including the men's room.

I don't know what time it finally was when I dozed off; some-time after 3:00 am and before 4:00 am. I can't say I was refreshed by my nap as my sleep was fitful at best. I kept repeating the same dream. I would just pick it up in a different place each time I nodded off. My daughter kept trying to tell me something. Each time I saw her, she would be waving and talking to me behind some kind of glass, like a car or picture window. In her other hand she was holding something. She kept jumping around in age; sometimes she was a young child and others she was in high school. Her clothes also kept changing. At times she wore white and others she was in red. The real spooky part was when she was in red; she seemed injured in some fashion. Finally, around 6:45 am I woke up for good to the smell of fresh coffee

"Here Chief, I thought you could use this." Susan put a cup on my desk.

"Thanks. I hope this isn't the stuff I fixed in the middle of the night."

"No way, that stuff didn't last. Not to offend, but making coffee isn't your forte."

"No offense. How's the gang doing?"

"They've pulled together some interesting information on Mr. Chalmers."

"Time for me to get down there and give them some of my pearls of wisdom?"

Susan shook her head. "No need, I think a general meeting will do it. Everyone will need about forty-five minutes to get organized."

"I'll trust you on this. Let's meet at 7:30 am."

- 169 -

When I walked into the conference room, I was filled with pride. My group, I could tell they were exhausted but still remained full of enthusiasm. I took a place at the head of the conference table and began, "I would like to thank all of you for your efforts. I and the Bureau appreciate it. As far as my approach, I want to do this in the following order, financial data and information and then psychological factors. Anyone have any problems or questions?" I looked around the room. They were all ready to go.

I looked at Susan, "Why don't you begin?"

"Sure." Susan began to go over the information the group had distilled over the last several hours. She described his media empire, its approximate earning as well as the man's other sources of wealth; it, not surprisingly, was in real estate. On our first pass there wasn't anything in particular that brought caught my attention.

Looking at Susan, I asked, "Tell me about what we know

about his charitable contributions."

"For many years he was a major contributor to the Catholic Church and its associated charities."

"You sound as if this isn't the case anymore."

"Sean, from what we have learned, it appears he changed his giving pattern about three or four years ago. It's a little hard to tell."

"Who does he give to now?"

"Appears to be almost exclusively to the *Hope for America Foundation.*"

I knew there wasn't anything unusual about wealthy people creating foundations and using these entities as a conduit for all their donations. In fact, it was quite common, probably the norm in certain economic brackets. If asked, I would have mentioned that I was surprised, based upon his wealth, that he hadn't gone the foundation route earlier. This was probably as good a time as any to transition to the psychological aspects of Mr. Adrian Chalmers.

I looked around the room, "Did anything happen three or four years ago that would have caused Chalmers to change his gifting pattern?"

A tired looking agent, about twenty-seven, with what appeared to be a two day beard growth, responded. "Chalmers got into an argument with his local bishop. It seems the disagreement grew in scope over time to include the American Catholic Bishops Council."

"Wow. That's unusual." I wondered how many lay people ever got into major tiffs with the Catholic Church hierarchy. "I gather Chalmers is a religious man?"

"Yes, it seems that religion has always been important to him."

"Important to an extreme?" I asked.

The agent responded simply, "in my opinion, yes."

"What was the disagreement over?"

"Obviously we didn't have much time, but we did manage to track down a Bishop who was on temporary assignment in Rome."

"What did he say?" I asked.

"Because of confidentiality reasons, he wouldn't say much other than it was a doctrinal issue."

"And Chalmers lost, right?"

"As would be expected."

"I'll bet that didn't set well with Chalmers," I commented. No one disagreed.

"Tell me about his personality type." I was looking for a clue something that might help me figure out what made this guy tick.

There were murmurs around the table. Finally a young Asian woman spoke up. "In a nut shell and without unnecessarily demeaning our thirty-eighth President, the guy has a Nixon-type personality."

"For my own benefit, when you say a Nixon personality type, by that you mean someone who is prone to holding grudges and wants to get even."

386

"Yes sir. Additionally, the type usually shows up in people who crave power but aren't very popular. Many spend their entire lives being frustrated because they can never attain the power and or the popularity they crave. The successful ones usually use public surrogates."

I looked at the young woman who wasn't even alive with President Nixon was in office. "Yes, Nixon was a bit of a fluke, an unpopular man being elected twice to the country's highest office. Is the type paranoid?"

"Paranoia is a characteristic in some, but not all cases. These types are highly intelligent. They think strategically and are also quite ruthless."

This young agent described a very dangerous man. Unfortunately, I didn't think she was off base, not at all.

"Thank you. Does anyone have anything else to add?"

Everyone looked at each other. Then finally Susan spoke up. "We just found out that Chalmers and David Brown attended high school together."

"Susan, were they in the same class?"

"Yes, Sean." She said in a low voice.

"Did they know each other?"

"We aren't certain and we'll find out for sure once we can start calling, but their high school year book did list them as being in the same clubs. My guess would be yes. The school was not large."

As Susan spoke, I felt all the air go out of the room. It was as if I were there alone. I couldn't believe it. My hands began to shake. I checked my watch. It was approaching 9:20 in the morning. "Please give me the phone."

Someone handed it to me, and I began to dial Mitchell.

- 170 -

When your mind is running one hundred miles an hour, everything else seems to move in slow motion. Mitchell's assistant finally picked up the phone. I told her I needed SAC and it was an emergency. As I waited, I wondered if I should have called from my cell. Less lost time and all that. Only problem would have been that I probably would have piled up my Bucar while talking. I needed all my concentration to go over my conclusion with my boss. Eventually, my current boss picked up.

"Sean, what's the emergency?"

I needed to tell Mitchell what I knew factually and succinctly. I couldn't very well tell the man that I believed the Pope was going to be assassinated today because of a dream I had earlier in the morning or that it was based upon a man who had been dead for over nine hundred years. "I believe the Pope will be assassinated today." I figured that would get the man's undivided attention.

"What?" Mitchell exclaimed.

"My team's done a great job tying down a bunch of loose ends." I went on to explain how we finally sorted out the cash flows.

"So you mean to say that Adrian Chalmers has been supplying the missing cash flow."

"Yes, through his *Hope for America Foundation.* Not only that, he has been active, very active in stirring up the pot. To boot, he has been the driving force behind Lukas Schafer's *The Movement.*

"Okay, it sounds like Chalmers is into some series stuff, but that doesn't mean he plans on killing the Pope."

I knew Mitchell would most likely respond as he had done. I then went on to explain David Brown's role, how he had killed Amanda and, in my opinion, Mark Ruben.

"Okay, Brown is a turncoat. That doesn't make him a killer."

"But he did just kill," I exclaimed. I went on to tell Mitchell about the young FBI agent who had been murdered at Union Station.

"Okay, Sean. Maybe, do you have anything else?"

"Yes, I do. Chalmers and Brown know each other."

Silence, followed by more silence. I waited and then waited some more. Finally the SAC spoke. "Sean, it's not conclusive but it is very circumstantial. "I don't suppose you have a clue to where this might happen?"

"I do. The Pope is a guest of…guess who?" I didn't wait for Mitchell to respond. "…of Adrian Chalmers. He's staying at Chalmers' Eastern shore place."

"Okay, Sean I'll buy it. Besides, if you're wrong, we'll know by this time tomorrow. Prosecution won't be an issue…"

"….And if I'm correct, saving or not saving the Pope will

prove the case."

"Sadly so, Sean."

"Alan, I need a helicopter and someone to meet me near Chalmers' place. Then I'll need all the help you can spare."

"The chopper and the ride aren't a problem. The SWAT team will take a little longer."

I figured as much, but I would have a ride and some help. "Thanks."

"Good luck, Sean." I hung up. I knew I would need a lot of luck if I was going to be able to keep the Pope from being killed.

- 171 -

I ran back to my office, grabbed my weapon and went to the armory to get a rifle. I wanted to make sure I had distance between me and David Brown. It only took a few minutes to check out what I needed. I then headed for the helipad on the roof. When I got there, I could see the pilot was Simon Sloan and the copter's blades were already turning. Mitchell pulled a lot of weight and he pulled it quickly.

I climbed in and we immediately lifted off and almost immediately banked hard away from downtown. There was no point in having Homeland Security shoot us down before we had logged three minutes of flight time because we overflew the White House or the Capital. Once we circled out of the District, we headed northeast towards Annapolis and the Chesapeake. Within a few minutes we had streaked over the Maryland capital and were out over the water.

Unfortunately, the day was beautiful and as we flew towards land, the Bay was filled with boats, both sail and power boats. If the weather had been crappy, a boat hanging around offshore would stick out like a sore thumb, but not today. I figured if Brown used a vessel, it would be a fast mother. As I grabbed some binoculars and began searching, I told the pilot to keep an eye open for a fast boat trolling along the shore line. Two sets of eyes were better than one.

We swooped low over a couple of potentially suspicious looking cabin cruisers. Unfortunately, the only thing that remotely looked like criminal activity was a group of people partying in their birthday suits. It was a nice day, but not that nice. Undoubtedly they were all being warmed by an inner glow. There was a middle-aged couple sunning themselves in the other vessel.

I kept scanning the horizon, but without finding any more likely candidates. I pulled the microphone down and spoke to the pilot. "I don't see anything. Maybe the kill will come from the land side."

"The water would be better," was his response.

"I agree, but I don't see anything right now. Let's head to the pickup point. But first let's do a fly over Chalmers' place."

"Your wish is my command."

"Very funny, very funny, let's try and keep our visit as low profile as possible."

"Okay," the pilot's voice crackled through the intercom.

We flew along the beach. Along the way there was a small strip of sand separating the Bay from the heavily wooded forests. I could barely make out many of the houses tucked along the way. If Brown came by land, he would be hard to spot. Still, I leaned to his coming by water as it was just easier to make an escape that way, at least initially.

"We need to go east and then swing back to the west," the pilot said.

With that the chopper banked hard and the g-forces really

increased. I didn't think much of it until I looked at the side window and saw trees. Ten minutes later we had swung around. I noted that we were approaching midday as the sun was slowly climbing in the sky. Then out of nowhere a large mansion appeared out of the trees.

"That's the place." I nodded. It was huge and magnificent. The pilot then pointed out where the press had set up camp. He moved south away from the press. "See down there, where the gravel road is?"

"Yes," was my response.

"You can get into the estate there without the press knowing. You can probably get in without anyone knowing."

"Thanks." Not only didn't I know what the security was like, I didn't know who had arranged it. If it was Chalmers, telling them we were coming would be very counterproductive. I had seen enough. "Let's go to the pickup point."

We went south for about five minutes when the chopper slowed and began to descend onto a grassy field.

I looked at the pilot, "County park, your ride is waiting for you."

We touched smoothly and I got out, but before I did, I asked the pilot to wait. I had a feeling I would be in need of this bird. As I ducked my head and ran toward the car, I saw a young agent waiting for me.

- 172 -

As I approached, the man waved and seemed familiar. I racked my brain and then it came to me. It was Ben Johnson, the young agent who had been with me in Rock Creek Park the night

Amanda Chehwan was killed.

"Good to see you, Sean," Johnson said, extending his hand. We shook and he motioned for me to get in the Bucar.

It seemed I had hardly closed the door when Johnson hit the accelerator, spun the tires and took off.

"Hi Ben, do you know what this is about?"

"Yes sir, SAC Mitchell filled me in."

"What's the status of the cavalry?"

"We are on our own for a while. SWAT is coming, but not for about forty-five minutes to an hour."

By now we were flying down country roads. I couldn't make out the trees we were going so fast. If a tractor of a local came out, we were toast. As a precaution, I tightened my seat belt. No point in getting killed in an auto accident before I saved the day. "Any other news?"

"Yes, it seems the Pope is having his powwow with Lukas Schafer today."

"Do you know when?"

"Best rumor…"

"You mean intelligence?"

"Yeah, intelligence is around midday."

I looked at my watch and swallowed. "Ben, step on it, we are running out of time."

- 173 -

"Your Holiness, Father Schafer and his assistant are here."

"Thank you, Francesco. Please make them comfortable; ask them if they need anything. I'll be in shortly."

Camperelle bowed slightly and left to attend to his assignment.

Peter II watched his faithful servant Cardinal Camperelle walk out the door. He could see the man was unhappy about the entire situation. So was he, but for different reasons. It was a tragedy that the Papacy and the Holy Mother Church had fallen so far. He had to save the Church from schism. If not, he feared America would slide into sectarian violence. If a country with over two hundred years of religious tolerance could convulse, then the world was in for very hard times, all in the name of God.

The Pope fell quietly to his knees and began to pray. This meeting had to work. It had to end the schism. There was simply no other option. He remained unmoving, kneeling on the stone floor imploring God. Finally after ten minutes he rose, he reached for a glass of water on the table near him and drank slowly and deliberately. He then straightened his white woolen cassock and walked to the door connecting the study to the main meeting room, paused and slowly opened it.

- 174 -

Agent Johnson cranked the car up, and we flew down the two lane road. I kept looking at my watch. Time was moving quickly. We came around a bend, and Johnson slowed the car. "We are almost to the back entrance."

Fortunately, there hadn't been any other vehicles on the road. Now looking up the road, I could see what appeared to be a convoy of vans coming in our direction. "Ben, it looks like press to me."

Johnson looked up. "Yeah, probably, must be the Schafer

meeting. Maybe those vultures are looking for another way in."

"Just fucking great, just what we need, to have the press in our way."

Johnson slammed on the brakes and made a quick right hand turn. "What are you doing?"

"Actually, there are two paths to get us to the back entrance. This is one here," He said as we hit the gravel road. "The other is much nearer to those vans."

"So what's wrong with this route?"

"It doesn't get used that much." I could see what Johnson meant. We had slowed to almost a crawl and were bouncing through a heavily rutted trail that was little more than a cow path. A real off-roader's delight if you had a four-by-four. I wanted to stop and camouflage the path's entrance, but didn't dare take the extra time.

"Just do the best you can." I continued to watch the time fly by.

- 175 -

David Brown had just finished tying up the couple. Both were in their late fifties or early sixties, good shape. Brown figured it was all those hours spent on the water. He had presented himself as a broker, and they had invited him on board. Looking down the barrel of his service piece had made everything easy after that. He didn't know them and that was good. It would make it easier when the time came. He still hadn't decided when, or for that matter, whether or not, to kill them. At least for a while, they would be useful for his alibi. He was glad he had not been hasty about their fate. When the helicopter buzzed them, they proved to be most useful.

The boat was south of Chalmers' estate. An easy sail of no more than ten or twelve minutes would put him opposite the main room. That was where the meeting was to be held, and that was where the Pope would die.

Brown checked his watch. If everything was running as scheduled, the meeting would be starting any moment. The key to success would turn on the Pope making himself a target. For that there were two possibilities. Either the Holy Father would get up and move around, exposing himself, or if that didn't occur, someone would have to direct him to the window. When he questioned Chalmers about the Pope being where he was supposed to be, he had told him everything had been arranged.

This had better be the case. Brown wanted to make the hit and then make good on his escape. The rifle he had brought was accurate up to 1,000 meters. His plan was to get within 500 to 600 meters of the shore. It was about another 50 meters to the house, a total of 550 to 650 meters to the Pope. He would have liked to have been further away, but he needed to offset the inaccuracy that would be caused by the swell of the Bay. He figured he could get four shots off before chaos broke out. That would be enough, more than enough.

He would then run five to seven minutes at full speed north. He had scouted out a small cove where he would tie up. He had left a nondescript sedan in the woods out of sight there. He planned that as he was speeding away, he would send an anonymous tip to the press corps waiting outside the mansion that the Pope had been killed. The ensuing melee would undoubtedly assure his getaway in plain sight.

- 176 -

The Pope entered the room, and as he did, the three other men present rose to greet him. Francesco Camperelle was the first

396

to greet the Pontiff. He kissed his ring. Then turning toward their guests, he said, "Your Holiness, let me introduce you to Lukas Schafer and Raymond Gates."

The Pope looked at the men and proceeded to his chair and sat down. The two guests approached and greeted the Holy Father in the traditional manner. After this the Pope spoke, "Please sit down."

Again keeping with tradition, both priests sat silently and waited for Peter II to speak. "My good friend and aide, Cardinal Camperelle, and I debated how to address you. To the Holy Mother Church you are still priests. Though your standing may be somewhat strained at this point. Additionally, I do understand that Father Schafer has been consecrated a bishop. As I pondered this issue, it occurred to me that both the Cardinal and I are also priests. More than anything else, I want this meeting to be productive and not to be one caught up in protocol. I suggest, therefore, that we treat and speak to each other as what we are, priests."

Schafer and Gates looked at each other and then back to the Pope and Cardinal. Schafer was the first to speak. "Holy Father, that is most gracious. We too want this meeting to be part of a healing and holy process."

"Very well Fathers, let us begin. Why don't you tell me about your new movement, its aim and how you see it relating to the Holy Mother Church?"

- 177 -

We finally arrived at the back gate to the estate. We parked behind a small rise, got out, popped the trunk and grabbed our duffel bags. No doubt our Bucar was going to need a serious alignment job after this day was over.

"Sean, the perimeter is protected by both ground sensors and cameras."

I figured as much. "Ben, you sound like you've scoped this out. What's our plan for getting in?"

"Since we don't have a lot of time, I thought we could shoot out the camera's motor as it swept its focal point towards the gate.

"Then what?" I had feeling I knew where this was going.

About ten yards towards the water, the brick wall makes a jog. With the cameras aimed at the gate, a blind spot is created. We go over the wall there."

"Won't that trigger the ground sensors?"

"It will, but security will see that the cameras are still working and most likely will send someone out to check it out before doing anything else."

"You hope."

"It will. Just be sure you can get your sagging middle-aged butt over the wall." With those kind words, he handed me the rope and grappling hook he had been carrying.

I moved towards the bend in the ten-foot-high brick wall and waited. Johnson took out his service piece and waited for the camera to swing in the direction of the gate. He fired. From my location I could see the unit had stopped moving. With that, I sprinted for the wall and tossed the hook and rope over and pulled hard. Fortunately, it caught.

I managed to get up and over the wall with my duffel bag without kicking Ben Johnson in the teeth.

We hit the ground running. The main house was about three hundred yards to our north. Our plan was to move west to the shoreline because we could travel faster, with less vegetation in our way and then turn north towards the lodge. However there were still plenty of weeds and plants that slowed our progress down more than I had hoped. The other advantage to our route was that we could keep an eye on the water. I still felt that was the most likely point of entry or attack.

Almost immediately we heard dogs barking in the distance. Their barks seemed disorganized and confused. That was good because we had thrown chemicals as we ran to mask our scent and consequently the direction we had taken. At least that part of the plan was working. Though it wouldn't take a rocket scientist to figure we were most likely going towards the main house. Hopefully these little delays added together would buy us the time we needed.

At last we made it to the house. It was magnificent and huge. We ducked down in the last of the undergrowth that formed a perimeter around the lawn and other manicured grounds. I needed to catch my breath. As I looked up at Ben I could tell he needed a break too. I couldn't tell you how grateful I was to see that, Ben being younger than I.

As we rested, we took the rifles out of the bags we had been carrying. We loaded them and put the sites on. I tried to steady my breathing as I pulled out my binoculars and swept the area. Ben did the same.

By now the sun was almost directly overhead, and as a result there was no glare on the windows of the lodge. I could clearly see into each room. The rooms were empty until I focused on a large central picture window. I could see four men seated in comfortable chairs. Their conversation appeared to be friendly, though quite animated.

I quickly realized I recognized two of the men. One was the Pope and the other was my old friend Lukas Schafer.

- 179 -

Brown made one last check of his watch. It was time. He headed for the wheel and fired up the twin engines. Speed was critical. The cabin cruiser leapt forward. It would be over in no more than fifteen minutes. By then he would be in his car driving away from the scene.

Everything was ready. His untraceable Israeli-made sniper rifle was loaded and in its tripod on the back of the craft. His plan was to put the stern toward his target. He would then engage the engines at just above idle. In that way he would be moving slightly away from the target and towards open water. Because of the tide, the movement away from the beach would be negligible. However, the motion would reduce the rocking and pitching of the boat. His gun platform would be as still as he could make it, completely acceptable for a marksman of his caliber.

- 180 -

I heard it before I saw it. A powerful cabin cruiser was approaching from the south. I swung my binoculars to look and see. Unfortunately, the angle of approach was such that I couldn't see anyone or anything out of the ordinary. The chances were that it was nothing, just someone curious about the magnificent beachfront home.

I pulled out my radio and toggled to the chopper. Hopefully, the pilot was still sitting on the ground waiting for my call. In a whisper I said, "Murphy to chopper 1121, over."

The response came quickly. My earpiece squawked, "10-4 Sean, what do you need?"

"Get your bird in the air and fly it to the cove in front of the main house. There is a cabin cruiser approaching from the south at high speed. It's probably nothing, but you never know."

"Will do, out."

There wasn't anything else I could do at the moment, so I swung my view back to the picture window. Once things settled down, meaning the fast approaching boat was cleared, I figured Ben and I would move into the house. Get the Pope and whoever else was there out of harm's way. All we had to do was to hold on for another half an hour or so and SWAT would take over.

I could see movement for the first time in the room.

- 181 -

Cardinal Camperelle was pleased the meeting had been going along amazingly well. Both Schafer and Gates were deferential to the Pope, as they should be. The issues discussed had been in a positive and open atmosphere. In the Cardinal's opinion, the Pope's personal magnetism was the reason. For the first time in months, the number two man in the Vatican felt hope. Maybe, just maybe, a schism could be avoided. If that was the case, there might also be hope for all the sectarian hatred now rocking America.

Camperelle was more than somewhat lost in thought, and it took him a couple of seconds to register, Raymond Gates was saying something. His Holiness was nodding, as were Fathers Schafer and Gates. Everyone was getting up.

"Excuse me. I'm embarrassed to say this. I must not have heard something. My old ears have failed me."

Lukas Schafer spoke, "Sorry Your Eminence, we just asked His Holiness if we could take a break, a couple of minutes to stretch."

Gates chimed in, "Yes, the view is so beautiful out towards the Chesapeake; I thought it would be nice to take a break and look at one of God's creations."

Camperelle smiled, "Yes, a break would be nice."

As he began to struggle to get up, Schafer moved to help and Gates walked the Pope towards the picture window, while at the same time pointing out something out on the water.

- 182 -

Brown held the binoculars to his eyes. He could see the room's occupants beginning to stir. It was time. At that moment he powered the engines, driving one engine forward and one into reverse. The stern immediately swung around and faced in the direction of the house. Brown then immediately dropped the engines to idle and waited for the craft to settle itself. Within seconds it had stopped dead in the water. Satisfied that his platform was aimed properly, David then moved the engine levels to just above standby. The boat began to move almost imperceptibly away from the beach.

Brown then ran to the stern, jumping from the upper deck. He pulled the cover off his sniper rifle and sat in the chair he had secured to the deck and began sighting his weapon.

- 183 -

I heard the engines cut back. The change made me look away from the action inside the house. To my horror, I saw someone aiming a rifle in the direction of the house. I brought up my field glasses and saw it was David Brown.

"Ben, the boat, can you hit him?"

"What?"

"Brown is on the cabin cruiser and he's got a sniper rifle sitting on a tripod," I shouted.

I then screamed into my microphone, "Simon, David Brown's on the cabin cruiser. What's your ETA?"

"Three minutes."

Too much time, we didn't have three minutes, we didn't have a minute. "Ben, take your best shot. I'm going to the house."

"Okay," was all I believe I heard Johnson say.

I began running towards the house, screaming and waving my arms. My only hope would be to distract someone, the shooters, the victims, someone.

As I ran across the lawn, I could see a man in white turn in my direction. I began to motion for him to get down. Then it happened. I heard three shots in succession, followed by two, much closer ones, and then one again from a distance.

Later I would be told that it had taken only a few seconds, but to me time had stood still. The first shot destroyed the picture window. It also hit someone in the room. I couldn't tell who, but I knew it wasn't the Pope. The Pontiff wasn't as lucky with the second bullet. The sniper found his mark, and I saw blood begin to stain his white cassock as the man toppled over. From my direction I couldn't tell what had become of the third round.

Ben Johnson had returned fire with the next two rounds. Instinctively, I knew they hadn't hit their mark. As I approached the shattered front window, I tripped on the uneven brick patio and fell. The final bullet buried itself in the wood window frame just above my head. God it seems takes care of fools and Irishmen.

I rolled across the patio and into the house. As I scrambled to get up, I heard the cruiser's engine roar to full power. Almost immediately the chopper's distinct whoop-whoop echoed off Chalmers' summer house.

I knew the assassin was trying to make his escape. Hopefully, the copter could tail him long enough for the SWAT team or the state police to catch him. By now I was up and jumping through the opening where the picture window had been seconds before.

What I saw was probably the most horrifying thing I had ever encountered. Three men lay motionless on the floor; all had been hit. The only person uninjured was an elderly Cardinal who I assumed was the Vatican Secretary of State, Francesco Camperelle. He was hovering over the Pope holding the Pontiff's head in his lap. The Cardinal was crying.

Epilogue

I attempted to console myself. There was nothing I could really have done. It was meant to be. An old Irish priest, Malachy, had predicted what would happen 1,000 years ago. My daughter and my wife told me the same thing. It helped, but not much. The Pope had died instantly. Fathers Schafer and Gates lingered a little while longer, enough to receive the last rites from Cardinal Camperelle, but not long enough for the paramedics to arrive.

America was shocked and embarrassed, rightly so I might add. The successor to the long line of Popes had been brutally murdered in a country that had until a few months ago considered itself the paragon of tolerance when it came to all matters religious. Without Schafer and Gates, the popularity of *The Movement* receded almost as fast as it rose. I suspect that Chalmers hadn't intended to kill Schafer and Gates as well as the Pope. One died by chance, which one, we will never know. There was no schism between the Vatican and the American Catholic Church.

That's not to say things remained as before, quite the

contrary. Francesco Camperelle was elected Pope. His first act was to issue an encyclical revising the standard of authority and power of the Papacy. Even though the Church was a spiritual institution its structure had mirrored that of society in general; as a result the Papacy had grown more imperious over the centuries. However, when the world moved toward collaboration and democracy the Vatican remained unchanged. Because of this the Pope would issue decrees that were often ignored by the Church's rank file, secularism followed. Francesco Camperelle, now Pope John the Twenty-Fourth, proclaimed that he was only the first of equals. He pledged to regularly consult with his College of Cardinals. The authority of the local bishops was restored to a level that had not been seen since the early days of the Church.

The new Pope called for the leaders of all religions to meet with him in Rome to discuss ways of reconciling their various beliefs. In the shock and reaction to the murder of Pope Peter II, all leaders readily agreed. It didn't seem to matter that the location was the Vatican and thus home to the Catholic Church.

The Archbishop of Canterbury and the Patriarch of Constantinople took the rapprochement one step further. They offered to meet with the Pope to discuss reunification of their religions. John XXIV readily accepted, agreeing to have round robin discussions in Rome, Istanbul and London.

Here at home, I figured Alan Mitchell would have my tail for having failed to save the Pope. To my surprise, that wasn't the case. Instead he had me promoted to be his deputy SAC.

David Brown was found dead in the cabin cruiser, one bullet execution style to the back of his brain. After a little debriefing, both Simon Sloan the helicopter pilot and I realized that we had seen the boat as we first crossed the Chesapeake. At the time, we saw what we thought was a slightly older than middle aged couple sunning themselves and waving to us. We hadn't yet proved it and probably never would, but my guess was that the couple had been hired by Chalmers to kill Brown. It all made sense. Several days later we found an abandoned rental car with Brown's fingerprints and those of two other people. We hadn't yet matched the other prints. My guess was we would never match them.

So David Brown ended up joining his once, and now future, partner Mohammed al Hasim, aka Mark Ruben, wherever scumbags go when they die. Seems Hasim had outlived his usefulness, so Brown killed him and ended up laying enough clues for us to find his locker. Unfortunately for Brown, he didn't know all the contents of the locker. If we hadn't been able to crack the code left by Ruben, we would have never found out about Brown. It seems there is some poetic justice in the world that Mr. CIA traitor ended up essentially killing himself.

I also learned what had become of Andy Young's family. After twisting enough arms I had learned where they had moved and managed to get a phone number. I learned that Andy hadn't been cured. In fact he had been given only a short while to live. How he managed to keep this information from the Bureau I'll never know. Anyway he had never been able to save much money and his government pension would have been inadequate to support his family once he was gone.

It is a testament to the perversity of our system that he found the only way he could take care of his family after he died was to be divorced and to die while on active duty. Sadly, he managed both. His wife had gone on to tell me that neither of them liked the idea but it was their only option. She moved away saying that if she hadn't they would never have been able to pull the charade off. You see they still loved each other deeply and she was beside herself not being able to attend his funeral. I still miss him.

I spend most of my time these days enjoying my family, realizing all the more how precious life can be. Thankfully, my daughter recovered from her near abduction and drugging with no apparent ill effects. I had my fifteen minutes of fame and I hated each and every second. At work I am building my case against Adrian Chalmers. The man is powerful and has covered his tracks well, but I've vowed to bring him to justice in this lifetime, before God has a chance to do so in the next.

Made in the USA
Charleston, SC
22 September 2013